KNITWITCH

Knit on!

Oxx

CHRISTEN ROBERTS COMER

CMRComer

KNITWITCH

A *Stitch is Cast* Novel

"From far, from eve and morning
And yon twelve-winded sky,
The stuff of life to knit me
Blew hither: here am I."
A. E. Housman

PROLOGUE

Deidre was helping Elva in the shop. She had been organizing the yarn at the window – bargain bins are always such a mess – when she saw Addison in the square. The dark-haired girl sat on a bench holding a coffee cup, her face lifted to the sun. She was waiting.

Deidre had never seen the girl before, but she could feel that Addison was something special. It wasn't just the feeling of a girl in town who needed a place to rest, who needed a home and stability, who came long distances, all of which Deidre understood with just a glance. As a witch, Deidre knew it was more. Addison was one of them; Deidre just didn't know *what kind* of one of them.

She tried to think nothing of it; the last thing she needed to worry about was a new witch in town when Elva was already worried sick about Katrina. But a few moments later, she went back to the shop window and watched Addison walk by, then stop outside the shop windows. Realizing she was staring, Deidre picked up some yarn and debated. Finally, unable to harness her curiosity, she reached out.

It was a small spell through the glass to heighten whatever feelings this young girl had. As Deidre's finger twirled, concealed under the ball of yarn in her hand, she felt a tendril from the girl reach back. Her spell grasped it firmly. The tendril grew longer and crept inside Deidre. She felt it radiate up her arms and shoulders until suddenly she knew.

A knitwitch. In Brookwick!

Deidre dropped the yarn and ran to tell Elva that the apartment upstairs needed cleaning; she was going to get a new tenant that afternoon. As she faced Elva, excitement bubbled in her throat. She was trying to tell Elva what the girl was, but the word "knitwitch" refused to come out. She stomped her foot, and as it landed heavily on the hard floor of the back room, a bolt of energy sparked behind her eyes. It hurled itself into her with explosive power. Her eyes had seen the girl outside for less than a minute and already, she had become important. A sickening fear breathed through the hair on Deidre's arms.

If Deidre and Elva did not help her, Addison Thompson – the only knitwitch Deidre had ever known to exist – was going to die.

CHAPTER ONE

Addison fumbled for the discman player that fell from the passenger seat. Driving at seventy miles an hour on the thruway and reaching for a discman was not a noble way to die. She could only imagine the skepticism of the paramedics come to scrape her carcass from the pavement: "What is that?" says Paramedic Guy Number One.

"I've never seen anything like it before," says Paramedic Guy Number Two.

Paramedic Gentleman Number Three, a mature man in his early hundreds, rounds the corner to see what they are talking about. "Oh," he says, a smile on his face. "It's been years since I've seen one of these!" He leans over to pick up the battered discman. "This here plays music. Yeah. You put compact discs in it and it plays music."

They all are mystified.

"I got to get it together," she mumbled to herself, sitting back and leaving the discman on the floor. She tried to ignore it, but she kept seeing it out of the corner of her eye. She pulled the tape deck adapter from the tape deck and tossed it beside the offending player. "Be happy together," she muttered, and started fumbling with her other ancient modes of entertainment, tapes. She threw in the first mix she found, "Cherry Broken Glory Horses," a mix she put together last year, following her high school graduation.

What a debacle that was. Nobody thought she was going to finally make it, but she persevered, and Addison knew she only did it out of spite. From her foster parents to her guidance counselors, she could not stand to hear one of them say anything at all that sounded like "I told you so." Two days after graduation, she turned eighteen and she left, *vamoose*, just like that, no questions asked. She decided to do whatever the hell she wanted. Graduation was on a Saturday. By Wednesday, she was in her red-gone-pink 1991 Toyota Corolla with faulty volume button that only played tapes, heading for a highway with no place in mind. She's been on the road ever since. In fact, in just two more months, she will be nineteen years old.

Addison couldn't get the discman out of her mind. She checked her odometer and saw it had been two hundred miles since her last stop. Tapping her fingers on the wheel, she looked at where she was. Big surprise, a long stretch of highway. With one more desperate reach, she grabbed the tape-adapter cord close enough to the discman that a gentle pull allowed her to sit upright again and see the huge green interstate sign she was about to hit. She swerved to the left as her foot instinctively tapped the brake and sharply turned the car back in the lane. "Holy shit!" she hissed. "Discman! Argh!"

She stroked the steering wheel. "Shh…" she soothed. "Great job, Marlowe. Great job. It's why I picked ya!"

The day Addison test drove the Toyota with a whopping 129,000 miles on it, she accidentally went down a one-way street the wrong way. Another car approached, and in a panic, Addison yanked the wheel. The car obeyed without a hiccup, smoothly taking the sharp u-turn on a one-way street. It was then, before she'd gone five hundred feet from the seller's house, that she knew the car was hers, bought with every cent she ever saved. She had been working summers since she was thirteen years old, and during school years on weekends since she was sixteen. Her foster parents let her keep every dime, as long as she kept ninety percent of it in a bank account. She fought them about it tooth and nail, insisting her money was her money and they couldn't tell her what to do with it. It was only in senior year, when everything was falling apart, that she realized they had made a good plan. If it weren't for them, she would never have been able to buy the car and have money left over for traveling until she knew where she wanted to stop. If she ever decided she would stop.

It was harder to leave the Reids than she expected. She had been with them only the last year and a half before graduation. Being her eighteenth foster home, she settled in to her routine: get through this day, read a book, stare out windows when in cars and on buses, and soon, something will change. But they often tried to get her to look up and at them. She resisted. From "Did you hear what I said?" about picking her up after school, to "Can you look at me when we're talking?" Addison had become quickly irritated with them. Her eye rolls had never been higher and her sighs never quite as contemplative and heavy. They didn't seem to notice, despite all that she tried.

NEXT EXIT, 1 MILE. GAS, LODGING, FOOD.

Addison felt her stomach vibrate. There were remnants of fear still evident in her chest from the near crash on the thruway, and she had already gone two hundred fifteen miles. "I need a coffee," she whispered. "And I really have to stop talking to myself." She looked at the discman again. "You're a real tool, you know that?" The discman said nothing.

Addison stared at the gas station, miles from the exit despite the sign clearly saying "one mile." It turns out that one mile was just to get her to the road that the gas station was on. Not wanting to drive the fifteen minutes back to the thruway and risking who knows how long before finally having sustenance, she tossed the discman on her seat and strode in.

The gas station had a short counter with a short woman sitting behind it. Three gallon-jugs of windshield washer fluid sat on the floor, and five quarts of oil sat on the counter. Beside her was a large Plexiglas shelving unit stuffed full of air fresheners, pens with rose decals, and several key rings with a plastic tag that said, "Found me!" in bright neon colors. Behind the woman, hanging from hooks suction-cupped to the open window, were several more open air fresheners, bouncing lazily against the glass. Aside from the cash register, there was nothing else in the closet-sized interior of the gas station. How can a gas station in the middle of nowhere not have snacks?

"Excuse me," asked Addison, "but do you have a restroom I could use? I've been traveling a long time."

Bored, the woman scanned Addison's body and shoved the corner of her lips into her right cheek. "I'm sorry, darlin', but there isn't one here."

Addison got annoyed with a lot of gas station attendants who told her there were no restrooms. She knew they didn't want the added hassle of cleaning up after grubby travelers and risk litter and germs and whiny kids with horrible diapers – she got it. She understood. Really. But she was a pretty clean looking person, even if she didn't always smell it (traveling could be stressful and the Corolla had old-fashioned air conditioning – you know, roll down the windows and enjoy the natural breeze sprayed delicately with road fuel). She had gotten into more than one argument with attendants who insisted she drive elsewhere, despite her best attempts to be polite, coy, and even down right flirtatious.

"Do you have any snacks I could purchase?"

This time the woman's lips smashed together and disappeared inside her mouth. "Sorry," she said, her chin tucking slightly under. Addison couldn't help admitting to herself that the woman did look genuinely sorry.

"Can I maybe use the employee's bathroom? I really need to go…"

The woman's lip did the cheek thing again. She looked behind her shoulder on the ground. Addison leaned forward to see what she was looking at. The bathroom key, maybe? No. Not the bathroom key at all.

Trying not to gag, Addison backed away and smiled as politely as she could. "Thank you anyway. Thirty dollars on pump one, please?"

Addison headed north on the same road. Just as Addison was prepared to inhale a deep circle of fresh air, the woman told her that the town eleven miles away had plenty of food and toilets, including some cute stores. If she hurried, she could get there in eight minutes. "But watch out! The police like to nab you about a mile outside of the village." Addison only nodded before stumbling from the station closet.

She was singing loudly to the radio. With her right index finger holding in the volume button – since it was the only way to get both speakers to work – her other hand drummed the wheel. Addison watched for signs for the village, mindful of the speed limit, and replayed over and over in her head the visit to the gas station. She wished she had someone she could tell that story to! She considered picking someone randomly from her yearbook, sending them a postcard with no signature. McCartney Adams was a great choice. The quintessential high school barbie doll who pined for prom crowns and varsity players, she'd probably barf in her silk-lined trash can reading the story. Addison grinned at the image, but had to admit she liked McCartney's bitchy sense of humor and quick-witted retorts. As much fun as it was to imagine being so snarky, she would get no pleasure from it, so she nixed the idea. Maybe later.

When she next looked in her rear view mirror, she saw blue lights.

One speeding ticket later, Addison kept her eye firmly on the speedometer. She took a right where the officer had directed her and drove another mile before seeing the "Welcome to Brookwick" sign. "Enjoy your stay!"

The town square was adorable. Four streets lined the center park where well-manicured lawns were pleasantly intersected by cement paths running from the surrounding sidewalk and converging at the white gazebo in the center. Staring at the park benches placed around the square, flowers poking from cast iron pots set up at the corners, and a flag that waved in the breeze, Addison nearly ran into a woman crossing the street. Addison was traveling at a crawl, but that didn't stop her from reacting with horror. She slammed on her brakes and held her arms out. "I'm so sorry!" she said, though not loud enough that the woman with her palms on the hood could hear her. The woman stood straight and looked Addison in the eye. Addison was ready to open the car door with all the remorse she could muster (she did feel awful), when the woman smiled, nodded, and mouthed "It's okay." Addison put her hand to her heart to calm the beating and watched, dumbstruck, as the woman finished crossing the street. Addison was stunned. Okay? It was okay? She watched the woman walk across the green of the town square. Despite nearly committing vehicular manslaughter, Addison still recognized how striking the woman was. She was wearing a great wrap around her shoulders, one that you would expect old grandmothers in rocking chairs to wear, and zebra striped heels. Her short black hair highlighted the bright blue eyes that Addison could still feel in her horror-stricken heart.

The woman never turned around, deciding things were not okay. This surprised Addison, but she wasn't going to question it. "What a great lady," she said. "We lucked out with that one, Marlowe."

At the opposite end of the square, she spotted a brightly painted sign that said "Diner," and headed that way. Once parked around the back side of the building (the side streets were just as great looking as the square), Addison locked all her doors and headed for food.

After a great meal consisting of the best chickpea salad she had ever eaten, followed by a generous fruit salad, Addison decided to take a walk around the square to stretch her legs before heading back to the highway. She still hadn't decided where she was going to stop next, but she wanted to be sure she got at least three hundred miles every day. There were some days that she'd decide to bunk down for a spell, like if there were a practically-free hotel with a pool, or a really great camping site with privacy and a comfy ground. For the most part, though, she wanted to drive. Her music was starting to get old, though, so maybe good ol' Brookwick had a music store.

Addison soon found that Brookwick had a lot of good stuff to get into. A bookstore opposite the diner offered a huge selection of both new and used books in categories

Addison didn't even know existed. She always went for straight up literary fiction, but also loved to read mysteries. Lately, she recognized a slow, romantic burn for young adult dystopian novels. Sadly, driving provided little time for that and the bookstore had some books on compact disc but they were far out of her price range, or if they were used, she understood why. After spending several moments reading the middle of a novel about a family of women in Newfoundland, Addison tore herself away and continued on. She found a consignment shop that actually sold gently used clothing for half the price of the consignment store back in Toule, where she finished high school. She might be able to get a new album, but she had to stop there. Her funds were getting low and gas wasn't cheap. She didn't know where she'd end up.

The thought suddenly panicked her. She looked in the consignment shop's mirror, holding a short jacket up to her chest and watched her face go pale. Next to her dark hair, she looked ghostly. She was running out of money and it was only in this moment that she realized exactly how fast she was running out. She recalculated things in her head, including the food at the diner and the gas at the closet down the road. She wouldn't last another two weeks with what she had left. She was going to have to settle soon, maybe find a shelter she could stay in or a library and search the internet for people who are offering couches for travelers. But this was it.

She stopped at the coffeehouse in the square and though she had only just survived a not-too-fatal fainting spell at the realization she was destitute, she bought herself a hot chocolate. So what, it was May, on the cusp of summer. She wasn't going to let it stop her. She loved hot chocolate with soy milk and why, yes, please do add that delicious whipped cream. The boy behind the counter raised his eyebrows –

but only a little — when he took her order. As he wrote the specifics on her cup, he looked at her from under his dark lashes. "I haven't seen you before. You go to the school?" Addison stared at him a moment, trying to translate what he was saying. It was rare someone started a conversation with her and she felt incredibly out of practice. Gas station attendants only ask "Anything else?"

"Me? School?" Addison laughed a little. "I wish," she muttered. She dug in her pocket for money trying to focus on the change she'd need rather than the pain she suddenly felt in her chest. School. She always wanted to go to a college, live in the dorms, carry a sketch book around campus and draw random leaves or students on benches, but she had resigned herself to accepting that college was never going to be an option for her. With what she had saved up, she could have afforded maybe a year, but then what? Working nights at the grocery store, and weekends in a storage locker depot? Of course it was possible. She knew that; the Reids promised to help her if she wanted to go, but she firmly denied them the opportunity. Another way for them to control her? Another thing to hold over her head? Another stab during dinner or a weekly phone call, another way to insist that she would be nothing if it weren't for them? "No thanks," Addison muttered under her breath.

"I'm sorry," said the barista. "You don't want whipped cream?"

Addison's head snapped up. "Sorry! Yes! Whipped cream! Lost in thought." She hoped her smile was reassuring and gave a thumbs up just to be sure. *I must look like an idiot,* she thought, her thumb still propped on her fist. Hastily shoving her hand back in her pocket, she grabbed the carefully folded bills and struggled to grab some ones from the few twenties and fives she still had left. *Shit,* she thought for the hundredth time since leaving the consignment store. Putting the rest back in her front pocket, she couldn't help it. *Shit*, she thought again.

"Here you go," the barista said, handing her the hot chocolate and lid. "I didn't put the lid on in case you wanted to eat that whipped cream now. That's how I do it, so...you know." He smiled and lightly shrugged his shoulders as if to say, "Just thought I'd be a cool guy and be thoughtful and swell and all that." Addison smiled.

"It's perfect. Thanks."

"Spoons are over there." He pointed behind her.

Addison nodded, and said thanks again. As she backed out of the coffeehouse, she stole a glance at the counter. The barista waved and gave her a thumbs up.

Shit.

She carried the hot cup across the grass and sat at one of the park benches, looking around.

Addison forced herself to think about how *great* things were. First, the whipped cream. It was real, honest to goodness thick whipped cream. It tasted more like a custard than something filled with air and she savored every bite. And yeah, the gas station was gross, but the sky was a beautiful blue. It was so rich in blue that it looked indigo. Fantasy-land clouds strolled on by and the grass sang praises for all its lush green. She closed her eyes and sipped her hot chocolate, listening to the cars pass slowly by, shoppers chatting to each other as they came and went from shop to shop. She heard a bell ring as a door opened, or closed. She heard laughter. She heard the steamer whir in the coffeehouse where she got her hot chocolate. Quickly ignoring the thumbs-up fiasco, she focused on listening to the lights change from red to green and then to yellow. For the first time in months, Addison began to feel *quiet*. It didn't happen often. She hardly ever let it.

Despite her rush to escape Toule, she was a paranoid person, always afraid somebody was hiding in a bush, poised for attack. When she started out in foster homes, she was in a city with streetlights and lenient curfews. People were always on the streets, passing by, sometimes looking at you and sometimes not. Crime was high but as a kid, she hardly noticed. She just paid attention to where the cars were when she crossed a street and who walking by was wearing a watch so she could ask what time it was. If it was close to getting home time, she started back that way. If it was closer, she ran, thinking of shortcuts on the way. The constant noise and traffic became a safety net she never knew about. But then she moved to Toule when she was thirteen. Houses were far apart and there were no street lights. There wasn't any crime, but that didn't mean that she wouldn't be the first victim in a series of attacks that gripped the town! All Addison knew was that she couldn't see anything past the dark right in front of her and so she refused to take the trash to the dumpster at the end of the driveway, shared by the six other houses on their side road. It was odd, really. Sitting on the back deck of the house in the sunshine, hearing nothing but tree branches whispering and creaking, animals singing and even the creek several hundred yards away bubbling, she loved Toule more than any other place she could remember; it also terrified her. Sure, on the deck was one thing. The door to the house – the door with the lock on it – was only a few feet away. She wanted to go on walks in the woods at the end of the road, or the woods across the street. Or the woods right beside the deck. Fear didn't let her. So she read on the deck and enjoyed it as often as she could.

"Beautiful day, isn't it?"

"It is," said Addison, slowly opening her eyes to the bright blue of the day. Had she fallen asleep? She was then aware that at some point, a man had sat down next to her.

"I like summer, but hopefully it doesn't get too hot too soon. The flowers will burn," he tilted his head toward the cast iron pot — more like a cauldron — that sat next to the bench they were sitting on. He was an older man, maybe forty-five or so, with cropped black curls brushed lightly with gray. A tanned face with wrinkles around his eyes that deepened as he smiled brought out the green of his eyes. He wore a brown tweed suit with a maroon argyle vest underneath. In one hand he held a newspaper, and in the other, a cup from the same coffeehouse.

Addison looked at the flowers.

"Pretty, huh? They come out every year. Beautiful, really. And then when the season for them is over, new ones come up." He took a sip of his drink then drew his breath sharply. "Hot." Addison smiled. "I haven't seen you before. Are you from around here?"

Addison looked over at him. This must be a small town; the barista asked her the same thing. This man looked nice enough, but is a town really so small that you would say *that* to a complete stranger? She couldn't put her finger on it, but it sounded just a tad bit creepy.

"No, I'm just stopping through for a rest." What she thought at first would be a safe answer, because it made clear she was leaving and he couldn't follow her, suddenly felt naïve. Now he knew nobody here knew her; now he knew she was alone and traveling. Now he knew he could kidnap her and nobody would know. She quickly added, "As soon as my boyfriend is done, we'll be on our way."

The man nodded. "Rest well. You picked a good spot. It's my favorite because you can almost see the lake." He stretched his long arm a little to the right, pointing down an alleyway next to a row of shops. Addison looked, curious about the lake, but saw nothing resembling a lake, just trees and what looked like an apartment building of some sort.

"Drive safe, dear. Thanks for chatting." As quickly as it seemed he had appeared, he was on his feet, smiling down at her.

Addison smiled at him, squinting against the sun and sat up straighter. She gave a little wave. "See you later. Thank you." She suddenly felt guilty for accusing him of serial murder. He was really just a nice guy.

After failing to get back in the peaceful meditation she was in before, she stood up and stretched, then looked around the square. A sign caught her eye: perpendicular to the building hung a smooth piece of wood and painted on it was a large cauldron overflowing with colorful balls. The cauldron was identical to the ones around the square. Curious, she walked over.

The sign looked aged but clean. It was indeed a cauldron but it was filled with balls of yarn, the loose ends overflowing. The door to the shop read "A Stitch is Cast."

"Cute," said Addison. She moved over to a window and peered inside. A color explosion met her eyes. Yarn everywhere. "Holy crow!" She had never seen so much yarn in one place in all her life. "Why in the world would someone have a store with only *yarn* in it? Who needs all that? Who shops for freakin' yarn?" A woman in a yellow t-shirt stepped in her view and rubbed a fuzzy blue ball on her face. Addison was sure she was spying on some strange fetish shop. Thinking there were probably men with leather whatevers on their way, she backed up. She thought maybe it was time to hit the road. Turning toward her car, she was hit with a wave of vertigo and put her hand on the window for support. She closed her eyes and dropped, resting on her heels.

"Are you okay?"

Addison wasn't able to lift her head to look a helpful stranger in the face, so she hoped her voice sounded stronger than she felt. "I'm totally fine. Really." The words trembled and registered just above a whisper. The woman placed a hand on Addison's shoulder and rubbed lightly. Addison felt a sob creep up her throat. Lifting her head, she looked first down the road, past the end of the square, at the stretch before her. It was a long road. After letting her eyes close slowly and breathing deep through her nose, she opened her eyes again.

She was fine. Whatever had overtaken her only a few minutes before had left.

"Thank you," Addison said, happy to hear the tremble had gone. Accepting the outstretched hand, Addison stood up and turned to thank the woman properly. It was the same woman she had almost hit with her car. "Oh!"

"You're sure you're okay?" Her eyes were so striking, Addison wanted to stare and figure them out. Was she a model? She wanted to tell the woman how beautiful her eyes were and apologize in person for nearly hitting her but she could only nod. The woman smiled, patted Addison's hand and then walked into the Stitch is Cast shop.

A little shaky in the legs, but absolutely fine in the head, Addison walked back to her car and took in more of the sights. One last run into the diner, just to be sure she doesn't have to beg a gas station attendant to use her chamber pot, and she was back in her car.

She had made it almost to the highway when she remembered something.

That yarn store with all the color had a sign on the door. She thought nothing of it at the time because she was too busy coming up with cracks about a store full of cat toys, but as she pulled the wheel around and headed back to

Brookwick, she slapped her forehead for being a dope. Maybe she'll be okay this time around.

In block letters with yarn balls for o's, someone had written: "Help Wanted. Accommodations provided. Terms Negotiable."

"I might not look good in leather, but I can smile at crazy people all day long!"

CHAPTER TWO

Deirdre and Elva sat on the couch and looked at the three black garbage bags sitting by the door. The apartment was clean again, just as if a distracted, eighteen year old woman had never lived there. The chips had been swept from under the coffee table; the various mugs with dried tea bags had been collected, the tea bags thrown in the trash and the mugs clean in the dish rack; sweaters, t-shirts and shoes had been lifted from the backs of chairs, tops of tables and retrieved from the corners of the couch; lotion bottles, perfumes, make up and jewelry were carefully packaged and wrapped before going into the bags.

The women had worked slowly and methodically, Elva hoping Katrina would burst in at any moment, breathless and red-faced, apologizing for the worry she had caused, bursting with the news that she had fallen in love, or been inspired to travel and paint, or had simply had a fall and was unconscious in a hospital. Deidre went slow to ease Elva's pain.

Elva's sigh ended in a small rattle, catching in her throat. Deidre reached for Elva. "I'm worried sick," Elva whispered.

"I know." Deidre's arm closed softly around her friend's shoulders.

"Something is wrong with her. She's so unhappy. She's scared."

"I know." Deidre could feel everything Elva said. It made her hands ache and her heart shiver.

Elva looked around the room. "I'll keep her things in my bedroom closet. No, the hall closet. There's more room there." Deidre removed her arm. Elva was moving on for a minute and Deidre wanted to help her. "The ladies will be over tomorrow around seven, and we can tell them then. We can work out a plan. We'll…" Elva looked over at Deidre. "Maybe we should call."

Deidre nodded. "Best not to wait," she said quietly, so as not to admit saying it. Elva's eyes widened slightly, showing the hope she had that it wouldn't be necessary.

"Is she close?" whispered Elva.

"Yes."

"Well, we better go then. Wouldn't want to scare the poor girl, with all this stuff lying about." The women stood. Elva opened the door as Deidre's raised index fingers led the three bags ahead of her. They were raised less than an inch off the floor so nobody would notice if they walked by and Deidre had to drop them.

"Now, Deidre! Must you be a show off? All three? Someone will notice."

Deidre giggled. "I don't look strong enough?"

"You look about one arm short." Elva smiled and raised her chin. "Leave me the small one."

After locking up, Elva turned to her own bag and with a twirl of her finger, lifted it.

"Move fast," Deidre said, "She's parking the car!"

CHAPTER THREE

The brass bell rang softly when Addison pushed the door closed behind her. Stepping in slowly, she craned her neck and pulled it back, like a chicken walking around a coop. Her hands were jittery. She kept holding them to each other, then stretching them out beside her. The tips of her fingers felt like ice. With one hand, she swept a section of her dark brown hair behind her ears, a nervous habit she was hoping to break, but a habit she remembered she was trying to break only after she did it.

A voice called out. "Let me know if you need any help!"

Addison looked ahead of her. A long case of shelving, cubes stuffed to the gills, greeted her. A chaotic mess of color and snarls exploded from the cubes, the strands of string writhing around each other, slippery arms curling madly like a bowl of earthworms. Addison couldn't believe her eyes. Squinting, she leaned forward and thought she heard the yarn humming. The color saturated, grew stronger, brighter, and pain ripped through the back of her head, a javelin of white heat pricking from the base of her neck through to the top of her skull. Addison had to turn away with her eyes squeezed shut, one hand cradling her neck, the other lying heavily on the top. The pain diminished almost immediately and she turned her head back to the shelving,. The yarn was just yarn, sitting perfectly still and though the colors were abrupt in some cases, much of it was soft and quite beautiful. A delicious cream with a background of soft pink shined bright.

A woman carrying a toddler on her back in a carrier said "Excuse me," as she shuffled by and stopped in front of some large twists of a very fuzzy yarn. The child stretched, anxiety and frustration turning his face red, trying to grab the fuzzy yarn from his mother's hands. Addison could not imagine what it was used for, and wasn't sure the little kid should be anywhere near it. From what she could see, by the way his mouth twisted around the strap as he paused to smile at her, that kid still liked to put things in his mouth. Addison grinned and twiddled her fingers in a wave. She shuffled to the side and looked at the yarn. Well, she pretended to look at the yarn.

For the short drive back to Brookwick, Addison rehearsed her various statements of introduction. She managed to go from cool to polite, tough to prude, nervous to confident. She wasn't sure which one she wanted to go with, if any at all.

"Hi!" Cheerful. "I saw your sign in the window and since I'm broke and have nowhere to live, thought I'd stop in and let you know I'd love to work here and live somewhere too! Bonus!" and then there was, "How negotiable we talkin' here?" Naturally she went for funny. Or what she thought would be funny. "Hello! I'm Addison and I'm hopeless. The sign said you could help!" Typically, she wouldn't be this nervous. But this was a different circumstance. She was broke. Really broke. And she needed a place to stay pronto. On top of that, she lacked one very important thing to get a job in a yarn store: she didn't know the first thing about yarn shopping or anything you do with it. She had a foster mother into rug hooking once, but she didn't live there long, and as far as she could tell, it didn't require a yarn shop. Her mother would come home from the store with a big box, a white sheet full of holes, and bags of short snips of yarn of varying colors. Her foster mother would sit and watch reruns of America's Most Wanted, hooking rugs and mumbling to herself, occasionally announcing, "I swear I've seen that woman somewhere before." Then she'd pause to write down the woman's name and a short description of her crime.

Addison thought she might want to run away as soon as she walked in, but the longer she stood there, the better she felt. *That's right. Pull yourself together. It isn't like you're applying for college or anything.* Not that she knew what that was like.

She moved down the row and turned the corner, amazed that even the walls were lined with more shelves of yarn that reached far above her head. *What do people do with all this yarn?!* She stumbled back, not watching where she was going – caught in the beams of a tower of yarn. Once landed, she got a look behind her.

"Whoa," she breathed.

"Pretty amazing, huh? She fits a lot of great stuff in this little shop," said a man wearing a hideous yellow cardigan.

It didn't seem possible from the door of the shop, but behind the first rows of shelves was what looked like an enormous warehouse of yarn. It wasn't, of course, but it looked like it. Shelves reached all the way to the cathedral ceiling. From each shelving unit hung a booklet tied to a string that showed photographs of the yarn too high to touch, price included. In the center was a rectangular coffee table surrounded by six vintage chairs, all different colors, all bright and inviting. One was white with lime polka dots while another was orange with pink stars. A paisley chair seemed slightly out of place until you spotted the purple pillow with different colored geometric shapes. A woman with short gray hair sat in a simple black chair, the shape making it reminiscent of the fifties. She wore a blue, button-down short-sleeved shirt and black jeans. Her head was bent intently over the smallest knitting needles Addison had ever seen (not that she'd seen much), cascading from it was a very fine thread. The rest of what she was working on, attached to the needles, looked like not-much. A big mess of yarn, really, just piled up. Addison watched as the woman moved her needles over the yarn. Addison was mesmerized watching the woman's fingers slide in and out of each other. But... Addison walked over and leaned over, watching intently. The woman wasn't knitting at all. It looked like she was taking it apart, stitch by stitch. Surely that's not right? Addison leaned closer. "You're going backwards!" she blurted.

The woman raised her eyes and looked at Addison, who was nearly cheek to cheek. With a tilted head, she grinned. "Wouldn't be the case if I were paying attention when I was blasting ahead, no care at all for a little thing called 'a pattern.'" She shook her head and looked down. "I should know better with lace. I should really know better by now! 'Use a lifeline,' they all said, but nope. Elva will do what Elva wants to do and she'll stick her tail between her legs later." She clicked her tongue as she continued on. Addison watched, in awe, her head so close she could almost feel Elva's breath. She had no idea what this woman just said, but apparently, she was fine with going backwards and unraveling everything she had already done.

"You here for the sign?" the woman asked. Addison looked up, expecting the woman to be talking to someone else, maybe the man in the ridiculous sunshine coat. "The help wanted sign? People who come in here are usually looking at the yarn, but you're not, so I figured…"

"Oh! Oh. Sorry. You mean me," Addison stammered. Suddenly she stood up straight and clasped her hands behind her back.

Elva put her knitting on the table and stood to face Addison.

"Elva Moring," she said, reaching her arm out. Addison looked down at it before grasping it, concentrating on giving a firm shake but not too firm, and looking Elva in the eye, some tips she learned in the seminars held by her high school guidance counselor. *Interviewing Tips for the Graduating Students.* The tips were meant to be used during college interviews, but she figured she could use them universally without much reprimand.

"Addison Thompson." Elva smiled. Addison laughed a little under her breath. Elva continued to look at her, a pleasant smile on her face, while Addison's hands, again behind her, twisted one around the other. She walked around the table so she was opposite Elva.

Addison heard the man behind her give a little cough then mumbled an "Excuse me," as he placed a hand gently on her lower back and nudged her forward a little so he could get by. Addison hunched her shoulders forward and all but tripped over the coffee table trying to give the man room – turns out she gave him almost a mile. "Sorry!" Addison called out, not knowing if she was talking to him or to Elva, who continued to give her the same welcoming smile. Addison liked her immediately and suddenly wanted Elva to like her too.

Yes!

"Yes," she said, "yes. I did see the sign and I was, um…" She held on, hoping Elva would continue to lead the conversation. All her introductions were for naught, and without her starter, Addison felt lost (though she admits that would have been the case either way).

"Well, the position is still open, Addison," Elva said, as she sat back down in her chair and waved her hand over the red one beside her, inviting Addison to join her. Addison maneuvered her way around the table, knocking her shin in the process. She hoped she did a good job of concealing the absolutely crazy pain that resulted, but one can never be too sure how sneaky a gasp of pain and grimace of torture was without looking directly into a mirror, or viewing some hidden camera footage. Elva took it all in stride and didn't let on that she noticed the grimace or the gasp, but she did say, "Careful there. This table can sneak up on you. Would you like a drink? We have water, coffee, tea."

Addison sat down and smiled. The chair was far more comfortable than she would have thought. She leaned back and beamed. "Tea would be great. Decaf if you have it. Herbal."

Elva stood and walked into another room. Addison was horrified she just talked to her (hopefully) future boss and landlady like a waitress. Bossy, much? But Elva was saying "I'd like that myself," as she walked away, so hopefully she wouldn't be fired before she was hired.

"Keep it together," she hissed to herself, then looked around and crossed her fingers. While she waited, she chanted, *please say yes, please say yes, please say yes.*

They had agreed on terms. Elva seemed apologetic, so Addison did her best to seem grateful, as if saying "I understand and I really am okay with this less-than-expected offer." Inside? Addison wanted to fall on her knees, grab Elva by her gray pant legs and kiss her feet for giving her the most amazing offer. Addison would work at the shop every day that it is open. She will open, close, go to the grocery store for food supplies, the office supply store when needed, and do all the cleaning in the shop. Elva would teach her how to inventory everything from cups to yarn to notions (whatever those are, Addison thought at the time). Addison would also learn how to do sales with Elva's assistance, who would provide reading materials and hands on one-on-one yarn lectures.

"Now comes the most important thing," said Elva. "You have to learn to knit." As Elva said it, Addison reached over to Elva's project. It was a pile of deep indigo, a soft dizziness surrounding it like a halo. Elva had stored her wooden knitting needle in the knitted fabric, creating a combination of color and texture that Addison found irresistible. When Elva said "you have to learn to knit," Addison wanted to start immediately. She reached over and was about to grasp the needle when Elva called out and swatted her hand. Addison's hand froze in the air, her fingers nearly grazing the needle. Elva wrapped her fingers around Addison's wrist and pushed her hand back into her chair. When they looked at each other, Elva looked shocked and embarrassed. Addison knew she should be a little offended with such a motherly – not to mention rude – gesture. Instead, she felt calm and unsurprised. "Please don't touch the needles," Elva said, her voice scraped on the back of her throat. "Not yet. I want to be able to teach you, we just can't right now. Not here." Addison nodded, an apology on her lips unable to move because she really wasn't sure if that's what she should do. "We'll do it in the classroom in the back." Addison nodded and looked at the pile of yarn. The itch was still on her fingers, and her mouth filled with water. She heard a hum in her head, like the white noise that overtook her just as she was about to fall asleep, only she didn't realize it was there unless something else distracted her and woke her mind back up. After waking up, that's when she would realize the noise was there before. Waking up only offered a lack of noise, and the silence kept her awake.

"So is it a thing to not touch other people's yarn stuff?"

Elva's laughter was like a bark. She shook her head as she continued to laugh. "Oh my, girl. Absolutely not! You can't have more than one knitter in a room before someone's yarn is petted." She smiled as she gazed on Addison. "You'll see." Her smile was warm. Her closed lips had a pleasant arch, a slight pout perched at the top as if ready to speak. Addison liked her. "Deidre and I will teach you to knit, and you can sit in on the classes after you get the other work done."

The deal excited Addison. What did she get in return? A furnished apartment directly above the shop, that she had yet to see, and enough cash per week to pay for food, and maybe some gas for her car. Music may have to wait, or perhaps Addison could find something else to do on the Sunday and Mondays she had off, as well as fill up some evenings. It's not like she had much of a social life to attend to, so she could certainly spend it earning more cash. And she was going to get free knitting lessons? Addison could hardly believe her luck.

Welcome to Brookwick, she thought. She was tickled pink.

CHAPTER FOUR

Elva didn't ask Addison any questions. She had been meeting girls who loved working in her shop long enough to know that questions asked before a line was cast into the information pool was asking to get bitten. She already knew she liked Addison – she stood up straight, she smiled when she was looking at you and even better, she smiled when she looked away. Her eyes were cautious, even in a yarn shop. Despite carrying on a conversation the entire time, Addison's eyes roamed the shoppers, lingering long enough for Elva to know she was cataloging, saving details, remembering. Perhaps she was just having internal commentary. Despite that, Addison's conversation seemed relaxed, inviting and interested.

Before meeting Deidre at the upstairs apartment, Elva had spent the morning talking to Sheriff Emory. Once again, he tried to assure Elva that Katrina just thought it was time to go.

"Jim," she said, gravel creeping into her voice. "You know as well as I do that I am perfectly capable of recognizing when a situation warrants further looking into." She stumbled on the last words, frustration starting to get the best of her. "Something is wrong here!"

"First of all, Elva, give me some respect here for this badge I worked hard to get and call me 'Sheriff.'" Elva rolled her eyes. She clenched her fists before folding her arms in front of her and looking at the ground, fighting to let him continue speaking. "I know you have concerns, and

I understand where that's coming from. Four girls in four years just up and leaving does seem strange—"

She flung her arms out. "Yes! Yes, it is! So why aren't you doing something?"

Sheriff Emory held his arms out and pressed them down, not waiting for Elva to stop, "But these girls also came into town just as quick. They showed up one day, didn't give you much to go on regarding where they're from, and then they left. That shouldn't surprise you, Elva. They came from somewhere, maybe they went back. Are you sure they never mentioned—"

"No, Jim!" He tilted his head and looked at her with pursed lips. "Sheriff." She let loose a big sigh, just to show him how ridiculous he was. "We've been over this. I wasn't going to press those girls and make them tell me things they didn't want to share with me. And yes, they came right in, and yes it was sudden, but I got to know these girls. And they all, Katrina especially—" here she pointed a rather long finger at Sheriff Emory, "she *loved* it here. She just loved it! The ladies were all over her, and she told jokes and came to all the classes and she laughed, and she just… she seemed so happy."

Elva's voice trailed off. She twisted the ring on her finger as she looked Sheriff Emory in the eye. He looked back with soft eyes as tears filled Elva's.

"Oh, auntie," he said, reaching his arms out and enclosing her in a hug. At six-foot and four-inches tall, Sheriff Emory was a blanket of comfort to his five-foot four-inch aunt. Elva snuffled in his chest.

"I just know something is wrong." She pushed him away. "Your badge hurts," she said, her voice tight again. "What are you going to do about this?"

Sheriff Emory shifted his weight. His aunt was tough. She had been on him since the first girl left four years earlier. She ran to his house at eight thirty in the evening, breathless, banging on his bedroom window. He was supposed to get up at four that morning and prepare for a class he was teaching his deputies about interrogation techniques. It seemed his boys were watching just a little too much television. Even then, less than two hours after she realized the young woman was missing, Elva thought something was wrong. When it happened again, and again, her agitation got worse. But she waited longer and longer before going to him, behaving cautiously, just as he had told her to. It had been over a week this time and the panic was deep in his aunt. He could see it racing behind her eyes and her jittery hands. Even her feet seemed on fire, the way she picked them up and put them down again without ever seeming to move.

Sheriff Emory sighed. "I'll tell you what, Elva," they were back to stiff talking terms. Business talk. Elva leaned forward. "I'll look into it."

"Oh, thank the woolly heavens! Thank you, thank you!" She ran into him, her arms encapsulating him in a huge bear hug, and he swore she just might lift him off the ground.

"But, Elva!" he gasped, "You have to make me a few promises."

He was abruptly let go, cool air hitting him. He felt like he had landed flat on his arse. Confused, he looked at his aunt and got ready.

"Now you listen here, Jim Emory. You just listen here! You took an oath!" He had heard this speech before. He took an oath to protect and to serve and this is the part where he started serving and in doing so, protected. He said he would look into it, and come hell or high water, she was going to make sure that Sheriff Emory of Brookwick did exactly that, no ifs, ands or buts about it. Did he understand?

He just nodded through the entire thing. From parking tickets to stolen bikes and graffiti on the door of the shop, Elva had given Sheriff Jim Emory the same speech at least twenty times, rushing into the station, up in arms, red throat blazing from her sweater of the day, because Elva wore a sweater nearly every day.

"Good, then," she said, hands on her hips now. She was suddenly calm, as if her outburst had never happened. She looked around the station. Several deputies turned their heads, hiding their amusement, though not very well. They were all familiar with Aunt Elva and the way she insisted her nephew help her. She had gotten better about it over the years, barging in as if she owned the place, dropping buzzwords like "clues" and "gumshoe." But their laughs, once condescending and usually reserved for old ladies intent on being Miss Marple, were now more out of love than anything else. Elva had been in and out of the station regularly the last five years. When she wasn't coming in with a list of complaints for the sheriff, she was hauling cookies, pies, cupcakes or knitted items, like hats or fingerless mittens for the whole office, "This way you can keep warm and still use your walkie talkies!" One year she came in with fortune cookies made out of wool. Each cookie had a fortune inside with gems like "Today you'll leave work at 5:00pm and get a nice hot cup of tea!" They grew to adore her, and slowly got to know her as Aunt Elva, not just "that crazy lady always yelling at the sheriff."

Over time, she got to know them pretty well. It was because of Elva that Larissa and Desmond got married; in fact. Larissa had been working at the station just as long as Desmond had, yet they never found time to talk to each other. Elva, however, spent a good deal of time talking to everybody. Over the course of a few months, she couldn't shake the feeling that Desmond and Larissa just had to start

31

talking to each other. A few cunning moves later (Elva was quite pleased with herself), and Larissa and Desmond were having lunch together. Less than a year after their first lunch, they were married and a little over a year after that, they were parents. Elva was excited to see them happy and obviously in love with each other, though they were exceptional at maintaining a professional (albeit cute) relationship at work.

Elva's eyes swept the floor. "Janice has to get in here and do a good job vacuuming tonight. The floor is a mess."

Sheriff Emory raised his eyebrows. "Are you done now, Elva?"

Elva wiped her eyes with the back of her hand. She let out a big sigh. "I suppose I am," she said. She looked up. Her eyes were still red, as were her cheeks. She was a feisty lady. "Please find her, Jim. Please." Sheriff Emory nodded.

Elva turned on her heel, all fire again, and marched to the door. There, she turned to face the office and pointed her finger at Sheriff Emory. "I mean it! You do your duty!" Before Sheriff Emory could react, she was gone.

CHAPTER FIVE

Deidre and Elva met later that evening. Deidre wanted to know everything about Addison, but Elva made her wait while she made tea and got her knitting together. Deidre pretended to look through a book of patterns while she was seething inside for information.

"Tell me about the girl," Deidre demanded.

"I will not," said Elva. "You'll have to wait because while she's safe and sound upstairs, probably desperate for more money, Katrina is lost out there somewhere in the wildness of the world." Her eyes stared off over the coffee maker, presumably looking into the wilderness.

Twenty years ago, Deidre would have rolled her eyes at Elva's display of hyperbole, but she has learned over the years that it was Elva's hyperbole that gave her calm and expressed more than clever word games. Elva was scared, and she often used language as a way to allay her fears. If she said it with lightness, or even exaggerated heaviness, she felt it couldn't be as true as simply saying it the way it was. Deidre understood this sentiment to be an expression of sadness.

Elva set the tea cups down on the table in the middle of the shop. She had already closed up and the store was ready for the next day. She told Henry earlier that afternoon that she would be meeting with Deidre for some knitting. He was content to have the television all to himself after he did a few errands, and told her to be safe on her way home.

Once Elva was settled in her seat with knitting in her lap, she touched Deidre's arm. Deidre hadn't moved. She wanted tea, but she wanted information more and was too distracted. "Dee," whispered Elva. "Did you hear anything today?"

Deidre shook her head. "Nothing new. Just...the same." The same fear, the same confusion, the same anger she had known Katrina was feeling the whole of the week she's been gone.

Elva let out a sigh. "I suppose that's a good sign," she whispered.

"We'll have to hope so." Deidre waited a minute for Elva to gather herself again before she asked, "How was it, meeting the new girl?"

Elva blinked. "Deidre Wylie! You just sit there and be patient and let me tell you my day the way I see fit! No rushing, please."

After a few tentative sips of her tea, which was still too hot, Elva picked up her needles and recounted the discussion she had with Sheriff Emory. Deidre nodded and watched as Elva knit. She listened to every detail and understood perfectly what Elva was saying, but she still heard nothing. What Elva was sharing with her about Katrina was nothing Deidre didn't already know or expect. After all, Sheriff Jim Emory was Elva's nephew. He was decent and he was smart. And he was a huge pushover. With Elva poking fingers and gesticulating wildly, it was only a matter of time before he would relent and offer to look into it for his aunt. Deidre doubted he would get far, considering how little information they had. Despite the love she had for Katrina and all the concerns she had for her safety, she was learning nothing new from Elva at this moment.

Elva finished her tale, her cheeks red and her breath ragged recalling the excitement of yelling. She repeated, word for word, the speech she had given her nephew at least a dozen times since he became sheriff of Brookwick. The entire reenactment was probably not the best way to relax. Once finished, she realized she had done a straight row of knit stitches in her lace shawl, and whimpered when she realized all the stitches she'd have to remove. It was tedious work, but it had to be done. She bent her head and started tinking, lifting one stitch off at a time, undoing all the work.

Deidre cleared her throat. "And the new girl?"

"Oh," said Elva, distracted. "She's nice. You'll like her."

Deidre was going to lose it. She reigned in her feelings and took a deep breath. She looked at Elva, bent intently now over her beautiful indigo shawl. "Elva," she said, a deepness in her voice that was not there before. Elva continued to tink her work. Deidre had had enough. She reached over to her tea cup and took one small sip. Then she sat back in her chair, gazed intently on Elva's moving hands, and pursed her lips. Her eyes squinted so tightly they were nearly shut. Her forehead pulled down, and with a sharp intake of breath, she shot her spell at Elva's needles.

Elva shrieked. "Ah! I can't move! I can't move!" Fear made the lids of her eyes completely white as she gazed up at Deidre. The smug look on Deidre's face gave it all away. "You...you!" Elva struggled through the anger. "You absolute little *witch!*" she yelled.

"I need you to tell me about Addison."

"Tell you about--!" Splotches appeared on Elva's cheeks and neck.

"Yes. It's rather important. I am quite anxious to hear about her and I have asked you several times to talk to me about her, and here you are tinking away giving me nary a thought!"

"And you think that gives you the right to use your magic on me, does it? I have news for you, missy!" Elva let go of her needles, which remained upright in the air, stuck in her knitting. "I have news for you!" Elva stood up.

"Now, now, Elva. Let's not get all up in arms. You were very distraught after telling me about Sheriff Emory — as you should be. It was a great ordeal and I understand that — but please understand. I have been waiting all afternoon for word on this girl and you have made me wait and wait. I admit, I got impatient and I was rude. I apologize." She looked up at Elva. Deidre gave her a small smile. "I am sorry. I should not have done that."

Elva sat down. "It's just that I did a whole row of knit stitches and this pattern has been a pain in my arse all day. Do you know how many rows I frogged earlier today?" Deidre looked at her blankly.

"Okay, okay," said her friend. Elva then told her about Addison. When she had finished her retelling, which included details that were far and beyond, as far as Elva was concerned, Deidre sat back in her chair. She still hadn't had her tea, nor had she taken out her knitting. Deidre lifted a finger to her lips and started chewing on her nails. Elva screwed her eyes up and looked closely at Deidre.

"What's going on, Dee? Why all the fuss about this girl?"

When Deidre had first talked to her about a new girl coming to town to work at the shop, Elva had assumed her interest in the girl was simply that the position seemed to hold some risk, what with Katrina having disappeared only a week earlier. But as Elva recalled seeing Addison for the first time in the shop, Deidre's questions were not making sense. "Did she touch any of the yarn?" she asked.

"No, no. I saw her walk in and couldn't be sure that she wouldn't grab some, but like I said: she looked at one case of yarn for a good five minutes and her face was turning green and then yellow. I was scared for her, but I did as you said. As long as she wasn't touching the yarn, I let her be.

How did you know she'd look so…" Elva searched for the word. "Out of sorts?"

Deidre ignored her question. "Did she touch any needles?"

Elva shook her head again. "No. She did reach for my work," Deidre let out a small gasp. Elva rushed ahead, "but I slapped her hand away, and I felt so terrible doing it! What a rude thing to do to a woman I don't even know!"

"Don't worry about that now. That was good. Good." Deidre continue to chew her nails. "And you told her she'd learn to knit?"

"Her face lit up like a jukebox. It was so incredibly cute. I can't wait to see her holding some needles!"

Deidre was shaking her head.

"Well… why not? Why are you shaking your head?"

"Not yet. It's too soon. She obviously doesn't know."

"Doesn't know what? What aren't you telling me, Deidre? What's going on? She starts working the day after tomorrow. How can she work in this shop if she doesn't learn to knit?"

"She'll learn! She'll learn! She just— We just— We just have to take our time. She's special, Elva. She's really special." Deidre grabbed Elva's hands and made sure Elva was looking directly at her. "Can you trust me right now? I have to think this through more and then I promise, I will tell you everything."

Elva trusted Deidre dearly. She had never let Elva down, and she always knew more than Elva would wish on a normal person. The pressure it came with would crush Elva.

"Drink your tea, Deidre. It's cold and we have knitting to do. Henry will raise eyebrows if I come home with nothing to show for this." She glanced at her indigo yarn. "This thing has given me so many problems!"

She reached for the work again, but the needles still wouldn't move. "Um, Deidre? Could you?"

With a snap of her tongue against the roof of her mouth, the needles unglued.

"Thanks."

CHAPTER SIX

Katrina listened as his feet walked across the floor above him and the squeaks of what she thought was a couch or chair. It took a lot of concentrating, but slowly she was learning the layout of the house, and she was positive it was a house. He came home at different times of the day, sometimes it was dark, sometimes he didn't leave at all. It had been pretty easy so far to keep track of the days, and all she's learned from it is that if he's leaving for a job, it's not a nine to five.

Soon she heard the television turn on. Law & Order. Again.

Katrina leaned against the wall and watched the ceiling. What was she going to do?

CHAPTER SEVEN

Addison wasn't sleeping as well as she had hoped. Every time she thought she was relaxed enough and crawled back into the bed, she heard new noises she couldn't explain. Sleeping in a new place was tough. She had spent plenty of nights in the passenger seat of her Corolla, with the seat at its greatest recline, snoring her head off in rest areas on the highway (and always in the day time. It freaked her out too much to risk doing that at night), but a real bed in an apartment *that was hers?* It really should be easier than this.

After meeting with Elva at the shop, Elva handed her the key and gave her directions to the door of the apartment. Elva was going to meet her later that afternoon to show her things, but she never showed up. She probably figured the apartment was pretty self-explanatory. The door opened up to a small living room with a kitchen on one side and a bedroom on the other. The bathroom was just between the living room and bedroom. It was the perfect size for Addison, who would have been overwhelmed with anything larger. The kitchen was cute, with a counter running the whole length of the end wall. The short section of flooring had black and white checkered linoleum. Over the sink was a large window that overlooked the square. The view was amazing. Addison knew that this apartment in any other place would cost more than she could afford. It had access to everything that mattered. The only strange part about it was getting to the door. She had to go down to the end of the block and make a right turn once, then twice, until she went down a small alley into a parking lot.

There was a door to a steep and dark stairwell. At the top, a long hallway, and then finally, the door to the apartment. Addison did not enjoy walking down that hallway. It was dark and there were no other doors. She couldn't quite figure out what was beneath her, or what took up the space on the other side of the walls. She would try to remember to ask Elva when she started work in a couple of days.

The bedroom had a queen-sized bed and one dresser, as well as a pretty good sized closet. All of Addison's things fit in two dresser drawers. As soon as she saw the bed, she leapt on it and stared at the ceiling, wondering if she should pinch herself or say something corny and expected like, "I can't believe my luck!" She knew it was all true. She really *couldn't* believe her luck. A place to live, a job, furniture, her car… all because she needed to use a real toilet? Add to that that the job she got is in a yarn shop – something with which she has zero experience? She couldn't help it.

"Pinch me now!" she called out and giggled. Whispering, she said, "I can't believe my luck."

After reveling in the joy of the space for a minute, she got up and unpacked her things. A couple pairs of jeans, four short sleeved t-shirts, four long-sleeved shirts, two hoodies and a sweater all fit well in the two drawers. Beside her shirts she shoved her underthings and socks. She considered further dividing her clothes just to use up the extra space, but changed her mind when she imagined opening all the different drawers to get dressed in the morning. On the top of the dresser was a cute watercolor print of sheep knitting at a table, green hills surrounding them. One was wearing a kilt. Another picture frame held a small cross stitch sample that said, "One Stitch at a Time." Addison loved them. A small bowl decorated with hand-painted flowers sat on the back edge of the dresser. It was empty. Addison took off her stud earrings and put them in the bowl. She looked at them sitting there and felt pleased. She felt *immensely* pleased. She had a place to live. "Is this home?" she whispered. She couldn't take her eyes away from the bowl when it suddenly flew off the table.

"Holy shit!" she screamed, and fell back on the bed. She crawled up, poised to run and looked around. A furry, black animal leapt to the end of the bed and Addison was about to kick it when she saw it was a cat. A very furry, very big cat. It was adorable. It sat calmly on the edge and watched Addison, as if asking "You gonna put that foot down?" Elva hadn't mentioned a cat. It seemed likely that were Addison to take care of a cat as part of their agreement, Elva would have mentioned it.

The cat stood on its legs and took a step closer to Addison, then sat once again. Again, it looked at Addison, head tilted. Addison looked back. The cat stood up and took another step. Again, it sat back on its haunches. Addison was beginning to like this cat. She wanted to say something to it. Something like "here, kitty," but she couldn't. Her urge to speak kept dying as soon as she thought to open her mouth. In fact, as soon as she thought what she might say, she immediately felt it would be an insult. The cat stood once again, stepped forward, and sat. This time it did not tilt its head to the side. Instead, it stretched its head forward. Addison lifted her hand and reached out. The cat's head pushed her hand. It looked at Addison, walked forward again, and wrapped its paw around her wrist, pulling her wrist toward it. Once close enough, it tucked its head and fit it firmly and gently in Addison's palm. It began to purr. Addison smiled.

"I don't usually like cats, you know," she said. The cat turned its head, rubbing it in her palm.

Addison had never had pets. Her foster homes did, but they somehow never felt like hers. They never jumped on her bed, never sat in her lap. The homes with dogs were annoying. They stayed away from her and she was just fine with that. Friends at school would sometimes cry about a lost dog or a cat who had died and Addison could tell they were sad – she really felt for her friends. But she could just never understand why people had pets to begin with. It made her ache to imagine loving a pet as much as these people did, only to have them die. She imagined going to a pet store to pick one up, painstakingly looking each of them in the eye until she found the one that she would love, only to live with it until it died. She couldn't get past that part. Some homes were different than others. The ones with cats did intrigue her. Cats walked around with this sense of ownership and self-reliance. They didn't seem to need anything. They leapt on top of television sets or window sills and quietly watched the world. It was admirable. She liked hearing them purr and watching them as they rolled onto their backs in a patch of sunlight shining on the kitchen floor. They didn't come near her, and she was okay with that, but she did sometimes wonder why.

An article she had read in high school suggested animals had good senses about people. It suggested they had the ability to sense danger before it came, or if a person was good, bad or angry or sad. One article she read told the story of a fat cat in a nursing home who could tell when someone was about to die. It would go to a person's room, and if it lay on that person's bed and slept, it was a sign to the nursing home staff that that person was about to pass away. The staff believed in the cat's ability so much, they would contact family to let them know it was time. Addison believed these stories. She believed that animals, even dogs despite their bad breath and "I'm going to lick your face and you're going to like it" attitude, were able to understand things in nature that humans simply could not.

Addison did a lot of thinking about this as she drove from one state to another. She believed it had something to do with a person's ability to be quiet. The way she saw it, humans were always entertained or surrounded by noise. They heard engines and electrical wires, music and television, talking and tapping. They were always on their way to communicate, whether it was sleeping before going to work or driving to talk to a cashier or eating to watch a television show. Animals, however, even these domestic ones, were quiet. They were surrounded by the same noise, sure – but they weren't a part of it. Animals observed. Addison wanted to observe. She enjoyed sitting down at rest stops, in the grease-filled air, watching travelers racing in to the restrooms. Women holding children, sometimes dragging more behind her, faces flushed, while dads look immediately to the side walls for available food options. Men in business suits who stood in the middle of the food plazas, hands in their pockets, flapping wildly, playing with keys and change, swinging it back and forth. If she could hear the change in the pockets, she felt proud, believing she was getting somewhere. She wanted to hear. She wanted to *really hear*. In her backpack, she carried a composition journal and wrote about where she had come from and where she was. In it, she'd write down the sounds she heard, hoping to hear snippets of conversation she could copy in her book and maybe turn into a poem later. It was difficult for her to decipher other people's conversations and it disappointed her.

The cat purred loudly and Addison leaned forward to listen. "You look like a nice cat," she said to it. The cat crawled forward and sat in her lap. Addison put her hand on its back and with her other hand, scratched between its ears. "I hope you don't have fleas," she said. She lay back on the pillows.

44

Addison was surprised to wake up the next morning with the black cat sitting on her chest, as if expecting her to wake up. The last thing she remembered was the white noise. When she lifted her head from the pillow it was still there. That wasn't usually the case. Confused, she strained her ears. There was a definite difference between the white noise made by an object and that noise she heard just before sleep – as if she were listening to the blood move in her veins. This noise was just like that blood-in-the-veins noise, except she heard it *constantly*. Hearing it out of context of falling asleep was disconcerting and she didn't know how to move around it. She was both tired, feeling on the verge of sleep, and yet completely aware and awake, her body restless and begging for sleep. It was the most exhausting sleep she had ever had.

Addison found cat food in a stand-alone cabinet in the kitchen as well as a water bowl and food dish. The dishes had a light layer of dust, but the bag's expiration date was still far enough away. Addison ripped the bag open and filled the bowl. As soon as she set them both down on the floor, the cat plowed in, enjoying his meal. Addison wondered how long it had been since the poor thing had last eaten, and wondered again why Elva didn't tell her about the cat. What if she was allergic to it?

In the bedroom, Addison retrieved the decorative bowl from under the bed but could not find her earrings. They were not important to her, not really, but they were her only pair of earrings. Despite having her lobes pierced since she was about seven years old, she still held onto this fear that her ears would close up if she didn't continually stick metal in them. It was a ridiculous thought, but one she couldn't shake.

45

After another quick sweep with her eyes of the bedroom and the bathroom, Addison sat back in the well-worn couch and looked at the television. The light from the kitchen window reflected off yet another thin layer of dust. Between her and it was a red coffee table, made of wooden slats and painted in the rich strawberry color it now was. Addison liked it. At the corners and in the middle of the top panel were places where the paint had worn. The couch was a pretty pale yellow with several throw pillows with various scenes on them. One was of cowgirls on horses and holding lassos above their heads. Another was of birds embroidered in bright but rich earth tones, the cream background made the colors stand out. Addison had to hand it to Elva – she knew how to decorate. She loved everything in the apartment. Beside the coffee table and kiddy corner to the couch was a chair, not as soft as the couch but not as stiff as it could have otherwise been. There was no dining area, and Addison was okay with that. She's done her fair share of eating in front of a television, but found lately, when she stopped somewhere to stay that she preferred the quiet. It wasn't a conscious choice, it just didn't happen. She was so happy to find herself curled up on actual furniture that her need for entertainment paled in comparison.

Only this time, she wasn't on furniture for just a night or two, or even two weeks. She was staying *for a while*. It was a strange feeling not knowing how long and not really understanding why. Yes, she was out of money and in some sense she thought there was an urge to simply think, "Get some more money and get back on the road," but a quieter part of her liked this place. The apartment, her new boss, the square outside the window, the cat crunching its food loudly, learning about *yarn*… she really did love it all. One day down. How many more to go?

"A day or one hundred days, I'm going to need some food." The cat bumped into her leg. Addison knelt to pet it on the head. "Yeah... food would be good." She grabbed her new apartment keys and went out to see Brookwick.

CHAPTER EIGHT

It was good to get out of the house and away from the screaming girl in the basement. He thought she'd be so much *nicer*, kinder, happier to be with him, but all she did was whine. It was getting on his nerves. He had set up a nice room. Gave her a picture of himself, one he posed for over a hundred times in the back yard by the big blue flowers. That took a lot of work! For all her smiles, all her flirts, all the times she practically begged him to take her out – this is how she reacts when he finally does it?

Work was boring. Tedious. He had to get away, so he came out in the sun to read more of his book.

There she was. The new girl who he talked to the other day. She was nice. Spectacular smile. Should have asked her her name...

CHAPTER NINE

At the end of the square and around the corner, Addison found a small natural foods store where she was able to stock up on various beans, nuts and greens to make a real meal. She missed food! Traveling had its enjoyable moments: oil-streaked cheeks, loud music, speed traps. But when it came to food, she was downright tired. There were only so many bruised bananas and bags of corn chips that she could take before she started feeling sick and run down. She caved a time or two and picked up typical fast food that cramped her up and made her woozy. It filled her, though, and reinforced for her, once again, that being weird when she ate was just going to have to do. The Reids came back to her, "Don't know what your problem is. What — our food isn't good enough for you? Little Miss Uppity?"

Now she just wanted to scarf on real food. Oatmeal, black beans, chick peas, collard greens, kale, carrots, potatoes, lentils, peanut butter and bread, along with several varieties of fruit, filled her basket. When was the last time she could shop for herself this way? Beyond snack food? It's been too long! On the road, a banana might cost her almost a dollar, but at a real store where she could buy several and bring them home, she was saving money.

Struggling with her bags back to the apartment, she cursed under her breath for forgetting that she had to carry all those bags back and up the stairs, down the long hallway. Cans banged on the sides of her legs and her arms quivered under the strain. She imagined chasing the cans down the square because a bag ripped and losing half her food in the process. At the bench she reached in the square, she dropped her bags gently in the grass and sat with a dramatic sigh.

"Ugh!" she yelled out.

It was nearing evening but there was enough light to see across the square and into the gazebo. The man who sat next to her earlier that day was sitting inside the gazebo with a stainless steel travel mug in his hand that glinted in the shadows and a book. He looked over at her and nodded his head. She considered acting like she didn't see him. He was far enough away to not see her eyes — perhaps she wasn't really looking in the gazebo at all, but she didn't want to be rude to the first person in Brookwick to say hello to her. Without lifting her arms off the back of the bench, she lifted her hand in a wave and smiled big.

Struggling again across the street, the inevitable happened when she reached the sidewalk just before the alleyway to the apartment door — a bag ripped and two cans started rolling. Addison gasped in horror. "No no no no no…" she repeated as she hunched over like a caveman, stumbling after her two cans of beans while behind her, her pile of bags tilted and items spilled out onto the sidewalk. After crashing into one pair of jean-clad legs and hitting her head on a shop door, she retrieved the cans and stood up. With her head down, too embarrassed to look around her, she walked back to her bags where someone was piling her food back into them.

He was gorgeous. Sandy brown hair, dark brown eyes, long eyelashes. Tall, too! He towered over her, but not in a militant sort of way. He wasn't intimidating in his height, just *very* easy on the eyes. Wearing a short sleeved maroon t-shirt and dark blue jeans with red tennis shoes, he looked like a mix of band member, artist and frat boy. Addison couldn't decide. She bent over for a bag and tried to casually drop her cans into it, but one fell to the ground and started rolling again. She moved to go after it but in two strides her helper grabbed them up and put them in one of the bags he was carrying. Three more were still on the ground. She reached for those first, then turned to him for the rest.

He laughed. "It really does look like you could use some help with these."

Addison weighed her options. Small staircase and long dark hallway to small apartment with tall sexy boy, or bruised legs, three trips and crushed vegetables doing it alone? Normally, she'd throw a quick visualization of murder-by-cute-boy, but didn't have the heart. His voice was easy, the way it melted over to her, calm and serene, *calming* even. "Well." She looked down. She really could use the help, but she also knew she was blushing like crazy and she didn't want him to think anything too girly about her. She hated that – she really despised being typical.

With a heavy sigh, she had to admit that she needed help, so they headed down the alley to her back door apartment. Addison wanted to look at him, take in what he actually looked like, but she could only manage quick peeks, too terrified a peek would turn into a stare and a stare would turn into drool. Maybe she was exaggerating and he wasn't that good looking at all? One good look – that's all she needed.

"Do you live in Elva's place?" he asked.

Surprised, Addison turned toward him. "Small town, huh?" Nope. Not exaggerating.

He laughed. "Elva has been here a long time. Everybody knows her. She's good friends with my mom and so Elva comes over a lot." He laughed again. "With cookies. She makes really good cookies." He seemed almost wistful, like a little kid dreaming about an overflowing Halloween basket.

Addison couldn't stop smiling. Shoving her key in the door, she shook her head slightly. Charming little guy, this one. "Oy," she whispered. She didn't need this. Honestly she didn't. Why couldn't it have been some awesome girl who admired her beans and said, "Hey! You want to watch a movie with me?" A lot less blushing then.

Nick turned out to be a funny guy. Addison was surprised how relaxed she felt around him despite how cute he was. After he helped her into the apartment and they figured out where to put the groceries (it turns out she had to store her canned beans in a low cabinet in the living room), he just started talking. He didn't ask her many questions, but left enough open space for her to talk. When he did ask questions, it was more about her interests rather than the usual ones, like where are you from and where are your parents and what brought you here? Instead, he wanted to know what she thought of the town, if she'd been to the coffeehouse, what music she liked to listen to, and of course, if she was a knitter.

"I've never knit anything in my life," she admitted. "To be honest? When I saw all that yarn walking in, I thought I was going to pass out. I felt sick. It sort of gave me the creeps!"

Nick looked horrified.

"I'm sorry," blurted Addison. "I don't meant to--" she tried to think of the right word. "--offend you? I just honestly, really, truly felt sick. I wasn't having a good day, really."

Nick's face relaxed. "Well, good thing it wasn't yarn. You should see my mother's craft room. It's ridiculous. Her stash is practically a store in itself, yet she goes to the shop almost every other day to look at more."

"Her stash? What, does your mom smoke or something?" Nick looked confused and watched Addison cook some beans and greens on the stove. Finally, it dawned on him what she was talking about and he looked very amused. "Ha!" He laughed. "Oh, man!" He bowled over laughing. Addison flinched. Not the laugh she was expecting from a hunky guy. Full of snorts, it definitely fit a drunk frat mold than a suave country boy she was going for. "My mother? Pot? No way!" He laughed some more. Addison laughed too, though she wasn't sure why, and stirred the beans, throwing in some salt and pepper, and whatever other spices she could find in the wooden spice rack hanging beside the stove. She forgot to get some herself.

Nick sat on the couch in the living room, but it was so close to the stove, they were really in the same room. "A stash," he continued, "is what knitter's call their collection of yarn, for projects. You'll find out when you start working there. Knitting is this whole other world with its own language."

He stood up and walked over to the stove, peering into the pan. "That actually smells really good. What is that?"

"It's kale," she said. "Really good kale. That store is awesome. I'm so glad it's not that far away and their prices are good too. Do you like kale?"

Nick squinted his eyes a bit. "I'm not sure, but if it tastes anything like it smells, then yeah." He looked hopefully at Addison and she laughed again. She really must stop doing that.

"No problem, dude. I'll share with you."

Addison was having a great time. It had been a while since she shared a meal with somebody. Her bones felt relaxed and she was happy to hear herself talking again —

and not to herself, for once. But she did wish she'd stop grinning like a middle schooler. It was getting embarrassing.

Nick stayed over for two more hours, talking about food, music, traveling, and television (Addison had missed a lot of what was going on in the world). He asked her if she was nervous about working in the shop.

"I don't know," she said. They were both drinking some tea she had found stored in the cupboards. Coffee would have been nice, but she didn't want to mess up her sleep since tomorrow would be her first day working. She made an internal note to start a new shopping list for the comfort things she might want later. "I don't know anything about yarn and I guess I am a little terrified somebody will get upset by that. Like, what am I doing there if I can't help them, you know?" Nick was nodding. "Elva will teach me everything. I'm sure of that. People always make me nervous though, especially if they expect me to be able to help them. I really like people though, and talking, so I don't think I'll be bad at it." Addison sipped her tea. She was convinced that made no sense. Nick was nodding though. Maybe he was just being nice.

"I can tell," Nick said. "That you like people. You're fun to talk to and most knitters I know love to talk."

"Honestly, I'm sort of worried I'll get bored there."

"Why?"

Addison shrugged. She wanted to phrase her words carefully, afraid she'll insult her one and only friend. Hopefully-friend. "It's a yarn shop. How busy could it get? I don't know how to knit and I don't think Elva will like me reading on the job, and how much yarn could I possibly organize?"

Nick shook his head. "You are really in for it, you know that?"

Addison tried to smile but it was obvious to Nick that she really didn't.

Nick put his tea cup down on the red coffee table. "This place is chock full of knitters." Addison looked at him. "I can see you don't quite understand. Have you ever known a knitter?" Addison shook her head. "That explains a lot. Knitters are typically really passionate about what they do. It's this huge underground social group that is made up of literally millions of people."

Raised eyebrows was Addison's specialty. "Come on!" she laughed. "Aren't you exaggerating here just a little because your mom knits?" Just the right head cock, and surely he could see for himself how ridiculous he was being.

"Absolutely not." The seriousness of his voice made Addison listen. "They are everywhere. And they are all ages and types. Old women, middle aged men, teenage boys," he said, raising his eyebrows significantly.

"No way!" She nearly jumped in her seat, the tea sloshing in her mug. "You knit? Really?"

Nick was nodding. "I couldn't escape it! My mom has been doing it for years, way before I was born. Ever since I can remember, when my mother sat down to do anything but eat, she was knitting. Isn't it only natural that I get interested in what my mom is constantly doing?"

She couldn't believe it and it was apparent on her face. What did that mean if a man knit? Was Nick gay? Is this how he was telling her? No wonder why he was so cute. Addison tried to relax with this new information. "So what do your friends think of you knitting?"

Nick looked confused. "Who cares? I'm not as into it as my mom, or Elva, but I do really like to do it. It's relaxing and there's something mathematical about it that really appeals to me. Do you know some of the most formidable knitters were fishermen?"

"You said 'formidable.'"

"So?"

"Just saying," Addison was trying to be funny. She felt tense now that she suspected Nick was gay. Because he knit. That was ridiculous. So Addison just had at it.

"Are you gay?"

"What?!"

Addison shrunk into the couch. Aw, man.

"What makes you think I'm gay?" He looked down at himself as if he forgot he was wearing his "Ask Me If I'm Gay" t-shirt.

"I'm sorry," Addison said. Then she started laughing. He looked at her like she was crazy before deciding he was just going to laugh too. Soon, tears were falling down Addison's face and she was trying hard to stop. She could feel her face screw up and her eyes close tight – she knew she looked maniacal and there was nothing she could do about it. But it felt so good to laugh without worrying how she looked, and this was too big a moment to stop it and be cute.

"Aw, man," she whispered. She sat up straight and wiped her eyes. She was relieved to see Nick was wiping his eyes too. "I'm sorry. Really." A giggle choked her on its way out.

Nick shook his head. "No," he said simply.

Addison waited but he didn't say anything else. "No, what? No, I'm not sorry?"

"No I'm not gay," he said, stressing the gay. "Why did you ask that?"

Surprised, she said, "Because you knit!"

Nick burst out laughing again. "That's *ridiculous*!" He was probably right, but Addison didn't know that. She has only ever heard about knitting and from what she's heard, only old ladies did it while watching Wheel of Fortune and The Price is Right on television. She felt a little stupid, and suddenly wasn't sure Nick was as nice as all that... she probably also insulted him. Making friends was hard!

"Listen, you're going to love working at the store. Elva and her friends can be a little weird though." His look seemed meaningful, as if she should be picking up what he was laying down, only she didn't get it and she told him so. "Well, my mom thinks something is up with some of them sometimes. Like, they have these other knitting groups they go to and when my mom wanted to go once, Elva shut her down immediately. It was pretty rude, actually, and my mom's feelings were hurt. She stopped going to the store for a couple of weeks until Elva came over to the house with some cookies and apologized. She never told my mom why she couldn't go to the meeting, but my mom was still a little freaked out by it. Ever since, she comes home from the store and just says over and over again, 'There's something going on over there with Elva and those other women and I don't know what it is, but I don't like it.' Just like that, almost every time she comes home."

The news made Addison curious. "You think it's okay to work there though?" Jeez. What if Elva was some weird worshiper, or the leader of a cult or something?

Nick nodded his head while sipping some more of his tea. He swallowed. "Totally. I swear. She's awesome. I think my mom just gets bored with Brookwick being so ... *tame*." He rolled his eyes. "I love my mom, but she can get a little paranoid about things sometimes." Addison could relate and was relieved she didn't mention the cult thing out loud.

The cat slinked from the bedroom and jumped onto Nick's lap. "Ha! Hey there, sport!"

"You know that cat?"

"Of course! This cat has been here forever! He used to be in the shop but for one reason or another, Elva had to take him out. I think some customers complained about cat hair in the yarn and how some people might be allergic or something," his voice trailed off as the cat nuzzled his neck and started purring loudly. Nick laughed. "Wow, he must have missed me!"

"I didn't even know about the cat," Addison said, "He totally scared me when I was in the room earlier."

"He's a sweetie. You'll see."

"Do you know his name?"

"Derwin." Stifling the urge to wrinkle her nose, Addison leaned forward and stretched her arm out to Derwin.

"Okay. Derwin." The cat lifted his head and looked at Addison who couldn't help but smile at him. Derwin slid off of Nick's lap and lay his head on Addison's instead.

"Well, then!" said Nick. "I'll take that as my cue."

In a few short moments, Nick led himself out with promises to stop by the store and say hello.

CHAPTER TEN

Addison was knee-deep in yarn and didn't know what in the world she was doing. Reading labels and checking off inventory sheets while learning what fiber was wool, bamboo, acrylic, cotton and what all else left her with her head spinning. Several times, she wanted to cry out to Elva to just stop because her head was absolutely spinning, but she was too afraid she'd lose her job. Elva was obviously a nice person, and it was just too easy for Addison to picture her saying, "If this is too much for you, sweetie, maybe this isn't going to work out." Addison was close to tears more than once, but she kept refocusing.

The problem was the noise. The humming she had heard the first two nights was louder now and it made her sleepy. Her head was pounding and every time she looked at the yarn, she had a strong instinct to squeeze it tight and turn her head away. The feeling was close to anger, but it also felt like intense love. She thought she was going just a little crazy.

"Elva," she said quietly, "I'm really sorry, but I think I need a break. I'm really thirsty and a little bit hungry. Would you mind?"

Elva looked at her watch. "Oh my goodness! I'm so sorry, Addison! How could I keep you doing this without giving you a break. It's been four hours!" Elva stood up faster than Addison thought was possible and ran over to the door of the break-slash-class room. When she returned, she was holding two glasses of water.

"Of course you can leave the store and walk around or go home or what have you to eat some lunch and rest a while, but I thought you might not want to wait. Plus I feel awful making you work so hard without a break." Elva must have seen the defeat in Addison's slumped shoulders. She added, "You're doing great. I'm really happy to have you here." Her smile was nearly as wide as her shoulders. Addison felt relieved. She drank her water and looked at the boxes surrounding her.

"Elva," she asked, "do you hear a noise?"

"What noise?" Elva tilted her head as if listening, then shook it. "I hear Sally Hamstead out there talking about her wretched afghan — *that thing is sort of ugly* — but no. I don't hear anything else." Elva looked at her over her glass.

She liked that Elva was honest this way. She was always kind about it, but she also had this little streak in her that said "fire" whenever Addison recognized it.

Addison didn't want to say anything more about the noise, afraid she'll discover she's insane, but it was making her crazy and wouldn't let up. "It's just that I keep hearing this humming like noise, and I hear it especially in here. I think it's making my head hurt."

Elva put her water down on a step stool and took the clipboard from Addison. "Do you think maybe today was a little too overwhelming? I did go a little fast this morning."

"I can handle it!" Addison rushed. Oh no. This is not what she wanted to happen. "I can! I think I'm just getting used to a new environment, really. I feel okay. I promise." She beamed brightly just to prove it and started leaning down to another box.

Elva smiled and put her hands out. "Stop that right now," she said. "Why don't you go and take a break for an hour and we'll start something new. I can get this done with Deidre's help."

Addison hadn't met Deidre yet, but she seemed to be an important part of A Stitch Is Cast yarn shop. It was evident in the way Elva talked about her that they were good friends and perhaps even good business partners, though Elva didn't disclose as much. "Are you sure? I really can keep going. I just--" Addison's eyes filled with tears.

Elva shook her head, almost madly. "Now, now! You stop that right now. I was very distracted and never meant for us to work this long. I get caught up in my own shirt! You just go out, right now, and take a break. You never mind; have no worries, dear heart. You're a great help and this job is for you, I just know it. Today was just crazy! Now go!"

Addison nearly fell flat on her face when Elva pushed her out the door.

Nick was right to laugh when she suggested she might get bored at a yarn shop. This store had been busy all morning long. Addison was beginning to wonder if knitters had jobs or perhaps knitting *was* their job. She was thunderstruck by the number of women (and men, she was embarrassed to admit), who came into the store. Some went straight to cubby holes and snagged up what they needed and then left. Others physically put their hands beside their heads as if making blinders when they walked to the counter to pick up an order. Others languished, shopping for what felt like hours. No amount of "Can I help yous?" made any difference. Elva seemed to have the hang of recognizing which people may need help and which did not. She knew nearly everyone and Addison suspected this had more to do with it than actual salesmanship, but she was surprised when Elva would randomly walk over to somebody and say something about the yarn, like how it was spun and what it would look like in a cable, and the person holding it would say, "That is *exactly* what I needed to know. Thank you!" Addison was impressed.

Addison decided that sitting down in a dark place would be perfect for her first break. She didn't want to go to her apartment though because she was sure she'd be spending plenty of time there. Instead, she walked across the green lawns and by the gazebo to the coffeehouse. When she went inside, it was exactly what she was hoping. The air was cool and just enough darkness to soothe her eyes. The same guy who was at the register her first day in Brookwick was there again. Addison smiled as best she could. Her headache was still there though it hurt her a lot less. Her smile must have come out like a grimace though.

"Bad day?"

Addison grinned. "I'm sorry. I'm trying to smile, but my head hurts so much!"

The barista bent down behind the counter and she heard some rummaging. When he came up he was holding two bottles of pain relief. "Name your poison. Red or blue?"

Addison couldn't believe she hadn't thought of that.

"Thank you so much!" She reached for the blue and he quickly handed her some water as well. Addison wasted no time swallowing the magic pills. "Thanks again. Really."

He nodded his head, looking happy to be of help. Addison read his name tag.

"Brian. Thanks, Brian." Brian smiled, bright white teeth gleaming in the dark of the coffeehouse.

"Wow! You have great teeth." Brian smiled more.

"Thanks! I brush them."

They both laughed.

"So would you like something to drink?"

Addison put in an order for a hot chocolate with whipped cream and a cranberry muffin. It was a splurge to be at the coffeehouse, but knowing she had a job made her feel better about it. Plus, she convinced herself that a treat is just what she needed after such a busy morning in the yarn shop.

While Brian made her drink, Addison looked around for something she could look at while she sat with her hot chocolate. An old architecture magazine was next to some soft couches. She picked it up and chose a table against the wall, away from the windows. Brian came around with her drink and handed it to her. "I'll leave you to rest. Enjoy!"

Addison sat back, grateful for the cozy space so close to work and to home. She closed her eyes and tried to relax the tension she felt on her scalp. The humming noise was gone now and she couldn't have been happier. Her shoulders were cramped and she felt knots punching away in her back. What a horrible first day at a job she was so excited to have. She exhaled slowly.

Two young boys came into the coffeehouse. They were probably only fourteen years old. It made Addison wonder what time it was. Aren't kids in school around this time? She watched them walk up to the counter. Brian's smiled disappeared and he suddenly looked more stern. "Shouldn't you be somewhere else?" he asked. Addison was surprised by his voice. All kindness and smiles when she got her drink, it was now dripping with adult authority. She was amused by it, really, until one of the other kids responded.

"Oh, shut up, zit face."

Addison gasped.

"What do you want?" Brian asked, his voice not as stern as before, but definitely not as nice. Addison put her head down and focused on her drink and magazine. If these boys harassed Brian, she didn't want to make it worse by watching. Hoping she looked oblivious to what was going on at the counter, she strained to hear.

"Just give us coffees, dummy."

She listened as the boys cackled and Brian squirted coffee into cups. The register dinged and the boys continued to fling insults at Brian. Addison was getting angry.

The boys made their way over to a table just behind Addison. Not exactly what she wanted. She listened to them talk about Brian in the way only high schoolers can. "Did you smell that guy? He smells like farts." Finally, Addison lifted her head and looked over at Brian. He seemed to have let it all roll off his shoulders, but she didn't care.

"Hey, Brian!" she called out in her sweetest voice. She was suddenly happy she was wearing a corduroy skirt that she found hanging in the bedroom closet. She didn't think Elva would mind since it obviously didn't belong to her. She was also wearing tights and her converse sneakers, and a short sleeved t-shirt. Mascara and a bracelet completed the feminine look she was hoping she had. Brian lifted his head. He didn't smile, but he didn't look mad either. He just looked interested. "This is really good!" She lifted her cup. It felt weak, and she wanted to let it hit home, so she said, "When do you get off?"

The boys behind her had shut up.

Brian tilted his head, looking a little confused. His eyes looked behind her at the boys but quickly turned back to her. He swung his head in a way that said "Come here." Addison got up.

"Those boys are infantile. Really. Don't worry about it." Addison ducked her head down a little.

"Did I make it worse?" she asked.

Brian grinned. "Not one bit. Why wouldn't I want a pretty girl to ask me out?" Addison laughed. It wasn't exactly asking him out, but she knew what he meant.

"They do that a lot?"

Brian looked down at some form he was filling out. "Nah."

Addison wished she could do something. Brian was really nice and kind, and she could see it. "Well, we should hang out some time anyway. I don't have any friends here. What are you doing Sunday? I'd like to see the school you told me about and have no tour guide."

Brian looked up.

"Not as a date or anything!" she stammered, suddenly realizing he could have a girlfriend or assume she wanted the position. "I just..."

"Feel bad?"

Addison's heart sank. There was nothing worse than pointing out that irritating twits make you feel bad, and becoming one of them in an attempt to make you feel better.

"No. Really. I am interested in seeing the school and it's totally fine if you don't want to go. I'm just looking for some friends, and you've been really nice to me."

Brian looked at her. He had dark brown eyes that matched his nearly black hair and long lashes that nearly covered his eyelids.

"That would be great. I don't mean to make you feel bad. But I do have to work on Sunday. We're short-staffed, so until we get someone else, I have to fill in the shifts. But I'll keep it in mind, okay? Really, I will. It will be fun." His smile wasn't enthusiastic, but it was better. It wasn't sad either.

Addison nodded. "My name is Addison, by the way." She held out her hand. Brian shook it and she saw his shoulders visibly relax.

CHAPTER ELEVEN

"Do you feel better?" Elva asked when Addison returned from her break.

Addison nodded. "Much better. Thank you!" She was actually smiling. When she left, she didn't know if she would be able to come back. Her head was worse than she'd ever felt. It dumbfounded her. She never really got headaches or migraines and that was more than she thought she could bear.

"I want you to meet Deidre." A woman stepped around Elva. She was about the same age as Elva, with dark shoulder-length hair swept through with gray. Addison was starstruck. *Deidre was beautiful.* She was an older woman, but her skin looked flawless despite having wrinkles. It just looked so smooth and elastic, as if she were already airbrushed. High cheekbones framed her eyes, dark beads set a little back with a small nose. Her red lips were smiling and everything about her felt elegant and *regal.* Regal was exactly it and the moment the word came to Addison, she couldn't let it go. Deidre was definitely regal. When she said hello to Addison, her voice was deep and somehow younger. Addison could not look Deidre in the eye as she shook the older woman's hand. Instead of trying to smile big and impress the woman with her friendliness, she wanted to admit that she knew nothing about yarn or if she could work at a store that seemed to make her crazy. She wanted to crawl into Deidre's chest and cry and tell her about how hard it is to be so stressed and worried that she'd lose a really good situation: the job, the apartment, and already one friend, maybe two if Brian liked her enough. The cat was a bonus! And the thought of losing it all because the yarn seemed to be yelling at her all the time was eating at her. No matter how ridiculous it all sounded – especially that yarn part – she wanted desperately to tell Deidre. Addison had become lost in her thoughts and was horrified when she felt tears in her eyes.

"Oh, dear girl," Deidre whispered. She stepped up to Addison and wrapped her arms around her. "You're doing great. You are going to be just fine here, don't you worry." Addison nodded her head and accepted the hug. Deidre's neck covered her head in an embrace. Never in a million years would she have hugged some older woman she just met *in a yarn store* but it felt absolutely right to do it. "I think I can help you a bit. It will probably help if you learn to knit."

Elva clapped her hands, excited and giddy. "Yes!" she said.

Elva's excitement convinced Addison to draw back and stand up straight. "Oh, yes," she said, wiping her tears. "That would be great."

Deidre had prepared a project bag for Addison to keep. In it was two balls of a cream colored wool yarn (it seemed exactly the same shade as the ball she spotted when she first walked into the shop), a set of circular knitting needles and book that promised to answer all her knitting questions. Deidre had suggested they do the lesson outside in the sunshine where they could enjoy the fresh air and not worry so much about other people peeking in. "Knitters can be so nosy and helpful. It's beautiful and irritating all at once! You'll grow to love it and to *be* it. Trust me," she said. Addison loved the conspiratorial tone Deidre used. She did not mention how grateful she was to do it outside. It had only been about fifteen minutes, but the humming had already started again and more people were filing in.

The temperature outside was perfect. The wind cooled her when she felt the sun was too hot, and then the sun warmed her when she felt too cold. The sun was perfectly shaded by clouds so it was still bright but didn't hurt her eyes. Addison couldn't help but look around for Nick remembering his promise to stop by and see her, but there was no sign of him. She was hoping he'd stop by the shop while simultaneously hoping he wouldn't because it was her first day and she didn't want to make a bad impression. Friends visiting so soon? *Not cool, Addison, not cool at all.*

Deidre led them to the same bench Addison rested on after her grocery trip the day before. She pulled out her own project bag filled with more yarn and needles than Addison thought one person could possibly need all at once. Did knitters carry their "stashes" with them? Addison didn't touch anything until Deidre said to.

"When you're in the store, around all that yarn, what do you think of it?"

Addison was startled by the question. Nick had mentioned the night before that knitters can feel pretty spiritual about knitting. He said it can put them in a meditative state, as if they were really sitting with legs crossed and saying "Om." Addison giggled at it, but her eyes were wide and interested too. Nick assured her it was true. He said that some knitters excelled in college simply because they kept their hands so busy – it quieted their minds enough to absorb and learn the information. He was picked on in high school for trying it himself per his mother's suggestion when he was studying for the SATs senior year. "I went to those preparation classes and some days, you didn't have to take notes. So just in case, I brought a tape recorder and I knit while the instructor gave his tips.

I did it during a college course I took that year too, for extra credit. The college kids were a bit cooler about the knitting. But it totally helped. When I forgot to bring my stuff to the class, I felt a little out of control. Taking notes was hard and I kept getting lost in the lecture." Was Deidre trying to tap into this "Zen" thing about knitting so soon? Addison was nervous. Just last night she thought if men knit it meant they were gay – and already she was supposed to feel at one with the yarn?

"Um," Addison grasped. Deidre was smiling. "I don't know. I guess, to be honest," she looked at Deidre, who was nodding now. Suddenly, Addison felt completely relaxed and knew Deidre wouldn't hold it against her. "I feel weird around it. It makes me nervous and anxious, and sometimes it seems really loud and crazy. I mean really crazy! I'll look it and I just want to almost pass out. It's horrible." She was nearly whispering after realizing how frantic she sounded.

Deidre put a bracelet clad hand on Addison's arm.

Addison decided to spill it all. "The first time I walked in there, I thought the yarn was attacking me. It looked like it was moving."

Deidre didn't question her. She just picked up her needles and yarn, told Addison to get hers and said, "We're about to make that go away. This will help. Trust me." Addison believed her.

They sat on the bench for over three hours and Addison didn't mind one bit. She could see why Nick enjoyed knitting. She had about three inches of stockinette stitch and she just knew she loved it. When Deidre suggested Addison continue on her own, Addison felt her stomach lurch. But Deidre reminded her, "I'm not saying you have to stop, Addison! Don't you worry. But I have to go to a very important meeting and can't be late. Elva is closing the shop, so you can go on home and keep on knitting." She took Addison's swatch from her hands and looked at it carefully through her reading glasses, which were stylish in a leopard print. "How did you feel doing this?"

Addison beamed. "I felt great!"

"Great!" Deidre looked at her. "This looks well done. Your stitches are even, there's no weird tension, no dropped stitches. If you want to fool around with new stitches later on, you can look through the book, but promise me that as soon as you feel tense or tired — especially if you feel grouchy - put this down." She took her glasses off and leaned close to Addison. "You hear me? You feel one iota of tension and I want you to put this down and take a rest, yes?"

Addison nodded. Deidre was still looking Addison in the eyes, searching them. For what? Addison thought. "Knitting is a tool for the mind. It is flexible, but it can break. Relax, and it does your bidding. Tense up, get stressed, angry or grouchy, and chaos follows. Do you understand?"

Addison nodded. "Of course." It was another whisper.

She didn't know where it was coming from, but she respected Deidre and since it seemed important to Deidre, Addison filed the thought away and promised she'd pay attention and stay relaxed. *They really take this knitting meditation thing seriously!* she thought.

CHAPTER TWELVE

This was the most critical part, Deidre thought. She was nervous leaving Addison in the square with her first piece of knitting. She knew she shouldn't have been so stern at the end, but she couldn't help it. Fear made her do it more than anything. Usually, women have some sense of their pasts and could be made to understand. History could be explained, reasons offered to why and should we? Any sane person would hear them and say "Okay, I'll make sure I don't do that, but what do I do otherwise?" and tips could be given. This was sensitive. One wrong word too soon to Addison and all hell could break loose, or worse! And now she had the knitting bug. There was no going back. Addison was going to have to know soon, but hopefully, Deidre and Elva could ease her into it.

Deidre hurried across the street and into the empty shop where Elva was waiting for her with her bags. Elva looked at her watch. "Great! We have a good twenty minutes to get there. I have cookies for the ladies. How did it go?"

"Let's talk about it when we get there. I'm sure they're all anxious." Elva nodded and they headed out the door. Deidre flicked her finger at the lock and tapped her teeth together. The lock slid with a thunk. The action made Deidre pause. What will Addison say when she finds out?

"Oh, Elva. I hope this goes well." Elva looked at Deidre. Deidre still hadn't told Elva everything, and Elva was trying to be patient.

"You always know what's best, Deidre. Whatever it is you have to tell us, we'll take it in stride and we'll work on it together. We always do."

Deidre looked at her good friend and smiled in an attempt to reassure herself and feel as good about it as Elva seemed to.

As Addison was packing her bags, she watched Deidre and Elva rush to Elva's car at the end of the block. She swept her eyes over the square one more time and spotted the man from her first day here coming down the path in front of her.

"Well, hello, there!"

"Hi," said Addison, smiling. Knitting made her feel good, she realized.

"So you guys are still here, huh? Good old Brookwick caught you in her grasp?"

Addison was confused by his reference to "you guys" before she remembered that she told him she was there with her boyfriend.

"Oh! He went on ahead of me. I actually, um…" she felt horrible. Did she really have to admit that she lied? "I actually live here now," she said. She stood back and put her hands on her hips.

The man raised his eyebrows and stuck out his hand. "Welcome to Brookwick, where the sun always shines and happiness comes with the morning!" Addison laughed and shook his hand.

"I'm Addison. It's nice to meet you. I work over at the yarn shop."

The man turned his head to look at the cauldron sign swinging now in a light breeze.

"That's a real cute shop," he said. "I'm Michael. Michael Fernlee. I teach history at the college."

"I heard there was a college here!" Addison wondered about the school. She hadn't noticed any signs, and there didn't seem to be a large group of students hanging at the square, which is where she would want to hang if she were in college.

"Oh yes!" he said. "It's about five miles from the square. It is almost an exact replica of the square, except what are storefronts here are department houses and dorms there. It's rather small, but we have a great selection of serious students, all very creative, all very smart. More would probably come here if Brookwick had a bus system, but it doesn't. And the campus provides everything they need, really. Food, shelter, coffee." He grinned. "No yarn shop, that's true."

He was quite charming when he smiled and talked about school. Addison felt bad about not trusting him before. "So you knit then, huh?"

Addison beamed. "I do now!" she said. Without thinking, she reached into her bag and pulled out her three inch by five inch swatch of cream colored yarn. "Deidre just showed me today."

"Deidre!" he almost shouted. "Deidre Wylie?"

Addison shrugged. "I don't know her last name, but she's really good at knitting. She taught me to do this in only three hours!" Addison couldn't pull her eyes away from the creation hanging from her needles.

"You didn't learn how to knit until today?" Michael asked. His head cocked to the side and he looked worried. Addison looked at him. Why did he sound so shocked? Why did he look so worried? It's not like talking or potty-training; it's not something everybody does. Maybe he was concerned about her job? People sure were nice in this town. "You mean, nobody showed you before this?"

Addison would have thought he was afraid if it wasn't so ludicrous an idea. His mouth was hanging open and his eyes were wide as he looked at her, waiting for an answer. Addison found it difficult to keep the cheer in her voice. "Why? It's not like everybody learns to knit when they're kids…"

"No, but—" he cut himself off. Addison shoved her swatch back in the bag with an angry thrust. She couldn't explain it, but she felt offended and hurt and mad.

Michael shook his head, as if realizing he was being a complete nut job. "Look, I'm really sorry. I am. I just expected you to be an expert knitter, working at the shop and all!" he raised his voice and said it in an almost sing-songy tone of voice, trying to cover up for his obvious blunder. "I really didn't mean anything by it. Don't be mad." Addison started to walk away when he reached out and touched her arm. Even as she did it, she knew it was rude and inexplicable. Why was she so offended? So what? Somebody was surprised she couldn't knit – big deal! Why was she being so mad at this perfectly nice stranger? His hand was warm and comforting, and when Addison looked down at it, she came to her sense. She suddenly felt washed in calm, like when she first met Deidre. She stopped and looked at him. "I'm sorry," he repeated. "For what it's worth, your swatch is beautiful."

Addison smiled a little, but only a little. She mumbled a thanks.

"Did Deidre tell you…" he trailed off and looked away toward the gazebo and then back at the shop. "Did she tell you to only knit when you're relaxed? If you get tense or angry, you stop. She tell you that?"

Addison was going to kill Nick for not telling her how crazy the zen knitting thing was.

"Yeah, she told me that. What is up with that? Some knitting Zen rule or something?"

Michael chuckled. "Something like that."

"Well, I'm going to go home and practice some more."

"Sure, sure!" he said. "Hey, listen! You know what cheers up my day? Music. Music and tea. When you get home, relax to some music and tea. Knit with the music. It's relaxing. Really."

"Um, okay."

Addison turned and walked away, waving back at Michael who said he hoped to see her again soon. He stood there for a while. She could tell. When she got upstairs to the kitchen, she looked out the window and saw that Michael was sitting down on the bench where she cast her first stitch. He was just sitting there, still as can be. She looked around the square one more time for Nick, then put water in the tea kettle and sat at the couch. Derwin came in and purred on her lap. Addison pet him. "Hey there, little guy. How are you doing today? Do you have food?"

With tea in hand and a Claude Debussy CD playing in the DVD player, Addison couldn't help it. She pulled out her swatch and admired it in the soft light of the end table lamp. Her first bit of knitting. It took three hours to make a square patch of yarn. String turned into yarn. She couldn't believe she had done it only two days after thinking it was a fetish shop, but she was so proud. Picking up one end of the cable needle in her right hand, she pushed the stitches onto the left hand needle. Remembering Deidre's instructions, she dropped the left needle and wrapped the yarn around her fingers. Picking it up again, she took a deep breath, rolled her shoulders, closed her eyes and exhaled.

Derwin purred beside her, his warm body snug on the side of her leg. She opened her eyes and began to knit.

CHAPTER THIRTEEN

The drive to Sara's was uneventful so far. Deidre had to hand it to Elva; she was being quiet, concentrating on the winding roads in the dark and giving Deidre the peace she needed to work out what she was going to say. Her speech had amounted to piffle. *I believe that a knitwitch has come to Brookwick. No, she doesn't know she's a knitwitch. She doesn't even know she's a witch. In fact, I'm quite sure she thinks we don't exist.*

Deidre imagined the women's faces, the questions, and all the answers she could not give because she simply did not have them.

They knew nothing about knitwitches. To play with the information before they knew the facts could wreak havoc. Could she trust them to hold onto it? She didn't know. But it was too big an announcement to merely *sit* with. Deidre had been having a horrible time trying to keep it to herself. And these women weren't just witches; they were also *knitters*. Yes, they have superior patience, despite the expletives often called out in a typical knitting circle, but put them in a room with something unique and special like a cashmere blend yarn and a beautiful pattern and it would take toothless gums and limb amputation to keep them from the loot. A knitwitch? It's even better. They might hold the knowledge close to their chests for a day, but they would all steal to the shop and hang around watching Addison. They would all approach her, ask her questions, test her skill by forcing her to hold yarn and needles. Addison could not do that. The bombardment would make her suspicious and then she'd be anxious and then she will knit with that anxiety and the effects will spread to any person who touches or sees her work. At least, that's what Deidre *assumes* will happen. There haven't been many knitwitches, so she couldn't really find out. She felt terrible thinking so little of her friends' impulse control, but she had to be safe.

She was in a pickle.

As a knitwitch, as an *untrained and unskilled knitwitch*, Addison had no experience quieting what her body compelled from her. Most witches discovered the truth of their ability when they hit puberty. It is suggested that this accounts for why witches are unaware of their 'witchiness.' When so much is happening at once, how do you point out the weird tingles and the vibrant colors and determine "This isn't puberty"? You couldn't. The heritage was in the blood. It may skip several generations – maybe as many as fifty – but if you were a witch it is because someone before you was one. Deidre's own parents were both witches. Elva's mother was a witch. Sara, who was hosting tonight's meeting and possibly the only person Deidre knew who would hold the information close to her heart, came from a family of witches, including her siblings and several aunts and uncles. Her power was very little, and perhaps this is because the magic had spread too thin between them all, but it was still there.

Deidre knew right away that Addison came from powerful people. She felt it coming from her as soon as Addison walked into the shop. It must have been a frightening experience for Addison. A knitwitch, with no inclination of her talent, walking into a store filled with triggers.

Yarn triggered a knitwitch's power. It yearned to be in her hands. Elva heard the hum when Addison walked in, but she did not associate it with Addison; she thought perhaps it was lingering on the yarn from her earlier inventory, using her own magic to unbox and shelve (it makes her job easier, but it doesn't negate her need for an assistant). Too much of this sort of stimulation, and who knows what could happen to Addison. The day Deidre went to the shop to teach Addison to knit, she too felt new life in the yarn. It was as if the yarn yearned to be with Addison, but Deidre was sure it was actually the opposite: a part of Addison was reaching out for the yarn and made it sing. It was the starved part of her, the witch part of her, begging to be nourished.

Deidre may have very little knowledge about craft witches, and more specifically knitwitches, but she knew that approaching triggers like yarn when unaware of her ability could cause undue harm. On one hand, an explanation may calm Addison, who already expressed concern about the yarn and a humming noise she had heard all night from her apartment; on the other hand, touching yarn that has already been handled by witches of various strength just because they were curious could cause more severe damage. What if the knitwitch magic, once it touches yarn handled by another witch, counteracted? The possibilities, the questions – the horrible reality of how many unanswered questions – forced Deidre to admit that she could not announce her suspicions to the group.

Yes, a yarn shop was bound to inundate Addison with requests to touch yarn, but it would be unsoiled by gossiping witches. At least Deidre hoped so. No matter what, she had to accept that there were some things she couldn't control. Addison had to stay at the shop. One step at a time.

Oh dear, concluded Deidre. Elva was going to be so mad at her.

Elva shot itching spells at Deidre all evening. Deidre did her best to ignore them, pretend she didn't even feel them (which was near impossible; Elva was a very skilled witch and her prowess to irritate as a human only strengthened that same ability in her spells). Elva even dared to go so far as to announce that Deidre had an announcement to make. Deidre shot Elva a glare, stunned by her sweet-tempered friend's gall. She managed to turn the tables and talk about a find in a bag of yarn at a thrift store in which she found some Qiviut yarn – ten balls of it, in fact.

Elva was horrified that Deidre had kept her in suspense this long and still wasn't going to tell her what was going on, but she also couldn't help but be completely distracted by the find at the thrift store. From there, it was easy to keep the ladies talking about knitting.

They loved to meet, these witches who loved to knit. They could let their needles knit at frantic speeds without fear of strangers asking questions. They could freely discuss how being a witch affects their day to day lives. And like most people, they liked to gossip about what they learned of the people in Brookwick with their witchy powers.

Sara, for instance, was like Deidre. She could empathize with a touch. She knew when somebody was lying, fearful, happy, sad, anxious. Her intuitive understanding of people's feelings made her especially gifted with her magic; rather than simply feel love or sadness, jealously or admiration, she could sense from their skin something to which those feelings related.

"Young Brian is interested in somebody," she said absentmindedly as she worked on the sleeve of her sweater. Unlike many of the other ladies, she knit with her hands at a typical human speed. Her magic touched her mind more than her hands and she was fine with that. She just truly enjoyed knitting.

The other women in the room hummed their acknowledgment and continued on.

Sara had been thinking about it all week. She stopped knitting.

"Something about it bothers me," she announced, using the voice she used to let them know they should be paying attention. The words were surrounded in the echo of a bell as she spoke them.

It was important when something bothered Sara.

"I acknowledge that since this whole thing between Tom and I started, some of my feelings may be... drifting over when I pick up on others, but this is *not* that." A few of the women lowered their eyes when she mentioned Tom. Being married to a witch had been hard for him. He denied vehemently that witches existed despite Sara's attempts to convince him otherwise. He now called her crazy and the words hurt Sara deeply despite knowing they came from confusion. "Something is very fishy about this. It is *frenzied*, the way he feels. Like he's out of control." Sara frowned.

"This is the boy at the coffeehouse? Brian Gross?"

"Grosse," Sara said, "Like 'posse.'"

"Ah," said Deidre. "You've mentioned him before, haven't you?"

"Yes," said Sara with a heavy sigh. "He had so many problems in high school. He's the youngest of six kids, all so much older than him that they left home before he was in junior high. He was always alone, walking with slumped shoulders while other kids called him names and threw rocks at him." Sara's eyes filled with tears remembering the pain she felt holding a coffee he had made her. Her spine wanted to fold over inside her; her guts wanted to implode and disappear while her chest swelled with an explosion of anger. It was the most horrible thing she had ever felt. She didn't go the coffeehouse as frequently as she once did, but she was happy he was not as paralyzed with sadness as that first day. But it was still there – a deep blackness she did not want to welcome.

"What is it about this? Still sad, yes? Wouldn't interest in somebody be a good thing?" Deidre looked at her friend with concern. Like Sara, Deidre could empathize, but unlike Sara, she could also give back a new feeling. When people were anxious or scared, a soft touch by Deidre would calm them. It is, Deidre believes, the only reason she is a completely patient person — she makes other people wait for her without them ever realizing it. She did not use this on Sara, however, who believed it affected her own abilities.

"You think it would, yes. But this is mixed with something else." Sara shook her head. "It confuses me. On the one hand, it has the joy, that soulful happiness that one would expect in feeling love; on the other hand, it is that blackness — but not attached to being sad or lonely or angry. It's something else. It's..." Sara bit her lower lip as she searched her mind for the feeling, trying to shy away from it while feeling around its edges. "It is like hate; a hate I don't want to feel." She looked at Deidre to see if she could feel it from Sara.

"I can't," Deidre said, shaking her head. "We have had this conversation so many times, Sara, and I know it's hard to do but we must separate ourselves and realize that we cannot solve it all for them. They must come to us, as humans, as people, and want our help, and we can help them *as humans*. But just because we—"

Sara was nodding her head vigorously and tears had come back to her eyes.

"I know, Dee. I do. I understand. Just because we have this power does not mean we must hold the burdens we pass, but Deidre — this is more than just a burden. I can feel that this is something more."

Deidre understood what Sara was asking of them; of *her*.

"You want me to go see him?"

Sara inhaled deeply, waiting.

Deidre looked around the room. Fourteen women in all. Many were weak witches. Sara herself was a weak witch, but compared to the others, she was strong. Elva and Deidre were the strongest of the lot, but it was no secret that Deidre was the most powerful, the most in control. Growing up with parents who were witches was helpful in that way. She understood how to harness it, practice it, leave it and rest it. She did not fear her magic anymore like many of the women here. They liked the small tricks, but the matters of the heart — of other people's hearts — the responsibility of understanding other souls so completely; those things terrified them all. She already knew the answer but she asked it anyway. "I suppose you all think I should do this for Sara, yes?"

They slowly nodded; Elva actually smiled at her.

Deidre looked at Sara. "Alright. I will stop by for a latte one day and get back to you."

Sara let out her breath in a rush. "Thank you, Dee. Really. Thank you."

Deidre nodded.

"It's not all bad news though!" said Sara. "I also met a lovely girl. Twice in one day! First, she almost hit me with her car. She was so adorable; completely apologetic, sweet as can be. And then I saw the poor thing having a dizzy spell on the sidewalk. She was right outside your shop, Elva!"

Deidre looked over at Elva. If she mentioned Addison, could Deidre pretend she was normal and did not matter?

Then a thought struck Deidre. Did Sara feel the knitwitch in her, as Deidre had felt it when Addison was a few miles out of the town's limits? That is how strong it rang with Addison; if Deidre felt it from miles away, then it was quite possible Sara felt it standing right next to the girl!

Unable to control the sudden panic she felt in her chest, Deidre looked at Sara; her gaze was met with Sara's round eyes, white along the edges.

Oh, Deidre, you are a fool, she thought to herself. Sara had not suspected anything – and Deidre had just given it all away.

CHAPTER FOURTEEN

Addison burst into the shop the next morning, her fist already curled around the knitting in her bag. "Elva!" she called out. Elva appeared from the back room with the coffee pot in her hand.

"You like coffee, right?"

"Yes!" Addison was yelling, but she couldn't help it. "Look what I did, Elva!"

Elva gasped at Addison's excitement as the girl pulled the cream pile from her bag. When Addison looked up, Elva was smiling. "Look!"

The cream swatch had grown to nearly fifteen inches. Every stitch was carefully wrapped in the stitch above it, all accounted for. "My, my, Addison," whispered Elva in obvious admiration. "That looks beautiful. I don't think I have ever seen a beginner knitter take to it so wonderfully. Look at that…" Elva took up the knitting and held it in her hands. As she did, her eyes opened slightly and her body unfolded from its natural curve.

"Not one dropped stitch. And every row has the same tension. Look how neat and orderly the stitches are." Elva looked at Addison. Addison noticed that Elva looked more awake today than she did yesterday; her skin was glowing and her cheeks were perfectly rosy. She looked fresh and happy. More so, even, than she did a minute ago. When she burst through the doors, Elva looked ready to dump the whole coffee pot over her head just to wake up. Now she looked energized and focused.

85

"You look very pretty today, Elva!" said Addison. Boy, did she like knitting! "And I love those shoes!" Elva was wearing some sparkly red ballet slip ons.

"You know," said Elva, holding the yarn still in her hands. "I think I have to tackle some things on my to-do list that have been languishing today. Business stuff that I just feel too tired to do usually. But I feel pretty good today. So, would you like to help me?"

Addison was still looking at her growing swatch, reveling in the joy she felt knowing she had created it.

"You know what," Elva continued, "I think I'll actually tackle that on my own." Elva was rubbing the yarn between her fingers. She looked down on it again. "Really impressive work, Addison. Will you continue on this or do you think you'll start something new?"

For a brief second, Addison thought she saw a look of horror pass Elva's face, as if she had said something she shouldn't have. She let it pass since she could think of nothing that Elva would have regretted saying.

"Actually, I'm going to wait for Deidre on that one. She wanted me to just practice for now. She assured me that though I'd feel anxious to start something new, it really pays off to stick to what you have in your hands. She said knitters have a problem sticking to one thing sometimes."

Elva grinned. "That Deidre knows what she's talking about! And I must say, she is exactly right. You should stick to this. I don't know what I was thinking."

Addison loved that Elva was still holding the yarn, as if she couldn't quite let go of what was so marvelously done by her. From the tips of her toes to her chest and head, Addison just felt so much *pride*. She couldn't remember ever feeling quite so happy about a project – one that wasn't even finished. Not only that, but it didn't even have a real purpose beyond practicing! She supposed it could be a scarf, if she really wanted it to be one. She had considered its possibilities the night before, as she stayed awake until after midnight, knitting stitch into stitch, enjoying the swiftness with which her fingers moved, the tip of one needle gently scraping against the backside of the other tip, saying hello and clapping, creating. "This is what they mean," she had thought, thinking of Nick and Deidre. "This is the part that makes people keep going. This feeling." She was talking about the joy of creating, but an hour later, she thought again, "No! This is it! *This!*" And it was the focus – not the focus on the knitting, the clicking and the movement, but the focus on the creating. She was calm, at ease, thinking of nothing at all but simply feeling what her hands and wrists were doing. Chuckling, she had whispered to Derwin, "Is this Zen, Derwin? Am I meditating?" Derwin purred. Claude Debussy continued on through the television's speakers.

Since she had started knitting, Derwin relaxed entirely into her. He was not sleeping, but seemed as entranced by the moving yarn and resulting fabric as she was. At one point, she noticed her armpits were sweating and she raised her arms briefly, took a deep breath, and continued on. She could barely remember when or why she decided it was time for bed, but when she shuffled into the room and pulled off her skirt and tights, she fell on top of the covers and fell quickly into sleep, which was filled with dreams.

In her dreams, she wandered from house to house in Brookwick, marveling at the different styles of each. One house was decorated in art deco while another was all modern pop art. Another seemed ready to migrate to the high mountains of Colorado with Native American design in the rugs and throw pillows; huge tusks from cows hung on the wall above a fireplace. She walked through A Stitch Is Cast, all the yarns caught in a film of nighttime blue, wavering before her like a mirage in a cartoon. All the furniture and decorations were exactly the same, except there were cauldrons scattered throughout holding balls of yarn, wound up like in cartoons – the ball carefully wound into a perfect ball so a cat could roll it and unwind it and kick it around. These balls of yarn were shifting and moving, rolling around each other as if boiling in the giant black pot. Addison wasn't alarmed by it; she simply noticed it.

Out in the square, people sat on the benches, knitting. As she watched their hands, they grew before her, as if she watched them through binoculars. She watched as their needle tips dove into one stitch, caught the yarn, and swam it back out. She watched as each old stitch stretched its back and folded, giving the new yarn a place to stand. Every hand grew in size before her, her gaze zooming in on their process. All moved the same… and after a while, going from person to person, including Elva, the professor, Brian, Deidre and Nick, she heard a noise. She stopped looking and turned her head, straining to understand the hum. Just as she thought she understood, Derwin was butting her head with his own.

Stitch in one makes it two. Blessed me, this spell's for you.

"I'm going to go tackle that stuff."

Addison was startled by Elva's voice. The words from her dream had started in her head along with that hum she felt the day before. She was relieved to notice that it was much quieter though. "Why don't you just check today's shipments against our invoices and prepare them for shelving. Then you can mind the counter."

She put the knitting back in Addison's hands, who balled it up greedily as Elva sped to the back room to the makeshift desk.

Elva had been working steadily for nearly four hours when Deidre came into the back room. "Elva! Have you been working this entire time? Addison wasn't even sure you were still back here!"

Elva lifted her head and looked at Deidre, and suddenly, she was *exhausted.* "Oh," said Elva, in a sort of surprised whisper. "What time is it?"

"It's nearly one-thirty!"

"Is it?" Elva looked around her. She had managed to complete four months-worth of paper work in only four hours. It was incredible! "I do not know what came over me, Deidre! I was just so tired this morning, and then suddenly, I was ready. I just had to get this done. And look at that!" she gave Deidre a beaming smile, though she felt the effort. "Done! All done! Invoices entered, account balanced, bills organized and new contact information saved... I can't believe it. I have had all this junk waiting for ages..." Elva yawned. Her head began to ache and her eyes burned. That wonderful energy was completely gone; she suddenly felt like death was knocking on her door. And her mouth was dry.

"I'm so thirsty," she whispered.

Deidre got Elva a glass of water. When she returned she watched her friend drink and noted the red rings under her eyes. "Well you look like you've been running yourself ragged. You must feel horrible!"

It was true. She did feel horrible. But she *had* felt incredibly energized in the morning; the momentum carried her until the task was done. She didn't stop to wonder at the attention to detail, the ability to see it all so clearly, divvying up the tasks accordingly in quick fashion, never once complaining or feeling that it was going to be too much. She simply did it.

"Well," said Elva, fighting back another yawn and failing. "I don't know what to say. I felt great up until you entered the room." Elva smiled a tired smile, the skin around her eyes turning blue.

Deidre's eyes closed slightly as she studied Elva, who seemed content to keep sitting and was now letting her head tilt to the side. "Elva," she said sharply. "Perhaps you should take a break?"

Elva left the shop with her purse, intent on running home for a quick twenty-minute nap. Deidre assured her she would stay with Addison in case a customer came in and Addison needed help.

"You are doing very well." She noted that Addison's knitting went along swiftly, but carefully. Each stitch had purpose. Deidre was happy to see this. She eyed the needles crossing one behind the other and the care Addison took to ensure each fell off the needle cleanly, smoothly. It was the most hypnotic knitting that Deidre had ever seen. Teaching knitting classes for twenty years gave her the authority to decide such things.

Quite often, knitting can be erratic. The needles will click rhythmically, but only in the way that knitting can. There wasn't a steady stream of click, click, click, like a ticker used for learning the piano. It was more like a click, click, click then a slight pause when the next stitch would be knit. It was the sound of *humanness*. The sound that said, "I am a person controlling these sticks and I have my own energy inside of me." The needles moved because the human chose for them to move and the stilted clicking accounted for it. But Addison did not knit this way. Addison knit like the second hand of a watch – each click just as steady and firmly spaced apart as the previous.

Deidre watched and listened as Addison's concentration never broke, the stitches looking each to be their own, unconnected from the one next to it, but landing beside the previous knit stitch and recognizing only then that it is part of a great whole. It was truly mesmerizing. Deidre reached out tentatively, wanting to touch the fabric. Her suspicions about Addison kept her from doing what she has done countless times to every knitter she has ever met. She still has not told Elva her suspicions, not knowing what they should do about it. Deidre was thorough, and to not have a plan or a method was frightening to her. It made her feel unfinished, as it if wasn't fair that she even leave the house, like her hair was undone and her pants were only half on. She felt vulnerable and exposed. She drew her hand back and continued to watch, waiting for something to happen, but nothing did. Addison just kept knitting.

Addison had taken to the art quickly. Many people could, if given good instruction by another person; there were even many who taught themselves simply by reading books and looking at pictures, over and over again, like Deidre had when she was just twelve years old. But not many mastered the fluidity with which Addison now knit. There was no pausing to push newly knit stitches down her needle; she just managed to do it somehow without Deidre even noticing the 'how.' The speed, the evenness, the quiet concentration and the resulting, perfect fabric all convinced Deidre of what she had before suspected but until now could not wholly believe for the fear it planted inside her. A real knitwitch. Sitting right beside her.

"How do you feel when you knit, Addison?"

"I know you guys have this total zen thing about knitting and I totally get it. I do, but I have to tell you, if I can be really honest?" Addison beamed at Deidre. "I feel totally jazzed!"

Deidre was just about to confirm her suspicion that Elva had held Addison's project when the bell sounded on the door. Addison's hands kept moving as she looked up and proudly called out, "Look, Nick! I'm knitting!"

CHAPTER FIFTEEN

Sheriff Emory was waiting for Elva at her house when she ran home for a quick nap. "Oh, Jim!" she called out, pleased to see him even though it took more effort to say his name than she cared to admit.

In response to the wary look on his face, she guffawed. "Come on, now! You certainly don't expect me to call you 'Sheriff' while you're standing on the very porch where you learned to walk, do you?" His smile and shake of the head was enough in answer.

He held Elva's shoulder and leaned down to look at her face full on. "You look tired, Aunt Elva." She felt his concern and appreciated it.

"I am tired," she said, in nearly a whimper. "I really need a nap."

"Well, I'll be quick," he said. It was almost perfect. He didn't want to rile her up, and so he could just get the information he needed and be off without much of a fuss.

"Come on in. Help yourself to some tea or something if you'd like." It took all of Elva's willpower not to ignore him completely and land on her couch. She was frightened just driving the two miles home from the shop and several times had considered pulling over and sleeping in her car instead.

"I'm ready to start looking into that thing we discussed," he said. Elva looked around her, wondering what she could do to distract herself from the sleep, and decided filling the teapot was a good first start.

"Uh-huh," she said, nodding.

"And when I went to start doing it, I realized I didn't have any information about her."

"Uh-huh," she said again, nodding, reaching into her cupboards for the chamomile tea then quickly changing her mind for the Earl Grey. Chamomile would knock her out just by smell, at this point.

"Elva, are you okay?"

"Uh-huh," she said again, ripping open the foil around her tea bag.

"Elva!" Jim snapped. He stood up and let the bar stool scrape against the tile; as it started falling, his hand automatically reached back to catch it, an action practiced and now habit over the years. He reached her just as her head nearly cracked on the counter top.

"I'm so sorry, Jim. But I worked myself like a horse this morning at the shop and I think I'm just too tired to do anything right now." Her words were slurring. Jim looked at her carefully, trying to determine if he should call an ambulance.

"Should I call an ambulance?" he asked her quietly.

"No, no. I assure you I'm just tired. I feel fine. I just worked myself much too hard. Can you come back later and I can help you then?"

"Are you *sure* I shouldn't call a doctor or something?"

"Yes. I assure you. I am positive. I am just incredibly tired." Kindness had left her voice and it was dripping with irritation instead.

Jim took her word for it. Elva was always a careful and mindful person despite her quirky character, laughing loudly and speaking in blunt terms around near perfect strangers. But she was, he admitted to himself again, always careful. She would have told him to call somebody if there was the slightest concern.

She went off to her bed and by the time he had placed her teacup on the night table, Elva was sleeping – shoes still on, face smashed securely in her flowered pillows.

Deidre pulled down the few books she had about witches and what little was known of craft witches. What she found served her no real practical purpose. The convoluted and short history told her what legend already had, but nothing about how to train one.

It was obvious, almost from the start, that craft witches were different. They didn't lift things with their fingers or click their teeth to do the dishes; they did not have simple premonitions that gripped them at odd moments or extreme empathy when they rubbed shoulders with strangers. Outcasts from the start, they were laughed at and often doubted to be witches at all.

The more craft witches were ridiculed, the more catastrophes befell the towns from which they came. Tornadoes, plagues, hurricanes, massacres, widespread starvation, heartache, suicide – each town or village that had at least one craft witch soon fell victim. It became evident that they did exist and they had to be controlled, quickly. The spells they cast were sent out into the world without guidance or end, killing, injuring and harming their communities. These witches hung hand-knit garlands on the trees in town, nailed hand-crafted bird houses to neighbor's fences, gave neighbors baby bonnets as gifts of congratulations and surely they were all given in kindness, perhaps as a way to reconcile their oddity with the town. But anybody who walked by, touched or tried to remove the items were affected by them. The trees died; the birds starved; the babies cried interminably. Widespread panic and anxiety followed. If a birdhouse were left in a tree and a new traveler passed it one hundred years later, that traveler would feel and be affected by the same anxiety and panic that stilled the hearts of so many a century before. Deidre understood the spells: the witches who made those items were panicked and full of anxiety themselves as they created. It was their panic and anxiety that caused the chaos.

Craft witch spells did use empathy – and even premonition – but it was the exceptional ability to control one's thoughts and emotions that made them successful. There could be no background mind chatter: the music one may find themselves humming, or the quiet conversations and imaginings, the to-do lists, the running commentary of a person's actions, daydreaming – it all had to be silenced and controlled or the spell would go awry. How incredible then that these witches learned to do it all on their own, believing in themselves when nobody else would. Further, craft witches needed to maintain that control for the length of time it took to complete the project into which they were putting the spell. No wonder why it was so hard to believe in them. Who could maintain that sort of concentration? How could craft witches possibly be real when it was so impossible to imagine doing?

The doubt about craft witches soon turned into fear. They were methodically eradicated, burned at stakes and thrown in holes forty feet deep where nary a tool could be found with which to cast a spell. Legend became fact; fact perished and became, once again, legend.

Yet here was Addison. The knitting she had completed in her first day was amazing. It was clear Elva's manic energy was caused by handling Addison's yarn. Deidre wasn't sure if the spell worked by proximity, but as she didn't feel it, she was sure the result of the witch's work had to be held in order to be cast.

She had given little thought to the premonition she had the day Addison arrived in Brookwick. As she had nothing else to go on except the emptiness of death that lived in Addison's future, she began where she thought made the most sense: Addison would die at the hands of her own untapped and uncontrolled ability as a knitwitch.

Deidre stayed up late reading and re-reading her history books. They told her nothing that she did not already know, but she started again, trying to find something. Anything. She had no idea how to train a craft witch, but she knew there were dangers, especially if the craft witch did not know what she was capable of. One bad mood, one excited thought, one *projection*. The images of bodies flung over fences after a freak tornado filled Deidre with dread. It was well within that realm. Would Addison really cause her own death simply by *not knowing what she was*?

So far, Deidre has gone with common sense. Teach her to knit, because she had to. She couldn't get around it. The woman was drawn to Brookwick, and that meant she was drawn to the shop and quite possibly the women from the shop who met outside of it – other witches. It was not uncommon. It is exactly how so many witches came to be together in Brookwick – they were drawn to it.

Elva had an apartment that was available and had been made so only a week earlier, as if it had been determined already that Addison would arrive. If Deidre did not teach her to knit then someone else would. Quite frankly, Deidre didn't trust anybody else. Worse still, if Deidre did not teach her to knit, then it was inevitable Addison would buy her own yarn and needles and tackle the task on her own. Doing that was guaranteed disaster. The tension and stress and frustration of just trying to figure out a cast on would be catastrophic for the town and possibly Addison herself.

But after that, what does Deidre teach her? She again thanked the heavens Addison had never tried before now.

All references in her book were simple, mentioned on the periphery as if even history denied craft witches a place in it. It was as if not even history could comprehend its complexity. Or was history laughing at the notion, but still unsure, mentioned it just in case?

Deidre was once that person, laughing at the thought of a craft witch, until Michael Fernlee mentioned it at a group meeting several years ago. He had met some, he said, many years before, when he was barely in his 20's, traveling Europe, seeking other witches who could help him figure out where he belonged.

She knew Michael would most likely have the books she needed to teach a craft witch. If not the books, he had information. He was the only person she had ever known to have met real craft witches. She sat upright, startled to realize that Michael may know how to train a craft witch. At the very least, he may know who to contact, seeing as how he met two of them, a married couple, on his travels. But contacting Michael was the last thing she wanted to do.

Stubbornness in tow, she went to the computer and started again. As usual, it turned up nothing except references to the mythical witches, or the other witches – Wiccans. Beyond the magic factor, real witches were neither. Nearly every website that popped up from search terms including "craft" or even the more specific "knitwitch" had nothing to do with craft witches. She became increasingly more frustrated and decided to make another pot of tea. She had reached the end. She knew she had reached the end. She needed help.

Less than a minute later, the phone rang. Deidre looked at it with ambivalence. Addison was going to die and

Deidre had the power to keep it from happening; but she couldn't without help. She lifted the receiver.

"Took you long enough," she said as a greeting.

"I just needed to wait," said a man's voice, a grin coming through the receiver. "Any sooner and you were more likely to throw the phone in the toilet."

Deidre smiled. As always, Michael Fernlee was right.

CHAPTER SIXTEEN

The sheriff was still shaking his head at his Aunt Elva an hour after she came to the station.

He had called her the night before to check in on her. She assured him, still sounding sleepy, that she was fine. Deidre had checked on her, made sure she was cozy and left. If Deidre believed her to be healthy, why couldn't he? Sheriff Emory had to admit she had a point. Deidre loved Elva with a ferocity that was tough to match. Also, Uncle Henry didn't seem fazed at all. But when she walked in the next morning, he couldn't help checking in with her one more time.

"It was really all because you were tired?" he asked, a stern concern hanging on every word, as if saying "Tell me the truth, or else." He leaned forward with his elbows on his desk. It was kept meticulously clean, something Elva was proud of. As a child, he had been very messy and disorganized; most children were, of course.

For what felt like the hundredth time, Elva assured him it was. This time, her own tone was dripping with annoyance. "Let's get over this, Jim. Nothing is wrong with me. I do not have cancer. I do not have *chronic fatigue syndrome* and I most certainly am not drinking heavily or doing drugs! Now quit it! I appreciate your concern, but I am not talking about this one more bit."

When Elva did not return to the shop after an hour, Deidre went to her, leaving Addison to mind the store with Nick, who had more than his fair share of experience. Elva slept heavily for about three more hours before Deidre could rouse her enough to drink tea and eat some toast and apples. Henry had strict orders to keep an eye on Elva and call Deidre immediately if anything seemed out of the ordinary. But Henry had known Elva a long time; if she said she was fine, he believed her.

When Deidre was satisfied that Elva was in good hands, and when Elva felt comfortable with the idea of someone else closing up her shop, Deidre left, mumbling about research and wasting time. Elva did her best not to take it personally. She knew the research Deidre was off to do had something to do with Addison, but she could not figure out what. Her own experience with Addison was all good; the girl had proven to be sweet and excited, if only a little nervous about losing her job. Elva could only assume she desperately needed what little money Elva could offer her as an employer. If only Deidre would open up and let her help! It was clear that Deidre was frenzied, trying madly to solve some sort of problem. Admittedly, it wasn't out of the ordinary though. Deidre was always guarded, waiting until she was positive about every angle before sharing any news.

Elva did not like being out of the loop. She probably would have spent more time with the problem, guessing, pondering, assuming, imagining – but with a muddled mind from too much work and too much sleep, she simply couldn't deal with it. She ate more toast, made more tea, and decided to watch television and knit a simple cowl for one of the ladies at the sheriff's station. Henry suggested some Miss Marple, which was fine with Elva. She better not tell Jim that though! The last thing she needed was to be compared to an amateur – yet successful! – small town sleuth.

"Okay, okay," Jim said, laughing. "I believe you now. I swear I do. So let's get started then." He leaned back and turned slightly in his swivel chair. With his hands on his belly, he stared off at a spot high on the wall. Elva has seen this look before. It was his "let's think this through" stare. "I need you to tell me everything you know about Katrina, starting with her last name."

Elva stuttered. She knew this was not going to go well. "Well, I don't really know much."

He sat up and faced his aunt. "You must know something," he said. "She worked for you. Did you bring the papers I asked you to?"

Elva pulled the few papers she had from her enormous tote bag, just big enough for a few projects, some needles, scissors, a yarn scale (because you never do know, do you?), extra yarn, and her wallet. The print out of the pay stubs paid to Katrina and the paperwork Katrina filled out before starting the job were wrinkled with one corner accordion-folded over, but they were still readable. Jim flattened the pages with the palm of his hand. He raised his eyebrow at Elva as he put his shoulders into the work. Elva rolled her eyes. With a grin, he shuffled through the meager pile, inspecting each with care. "This is all you have?"

Elva nodded.

"Elva," he said. She could feel frustration bubbling in his fingers. "The social security line is blank." He looked at her.

Elva shrugged. What else could she do? "She said she'd get that to me when she found her card. She couldn't remember it."

"Couldn't remember it?"

She could tell pretending it wasn't important was not going to work. She should feel foolish admitting that she didn't gather all the proper paperwork before hiring Katrina – and worse before paying her, but he didn't know Katrina well.

"She was nineteen years old, Jim! She probably never had to use it in her life, relying on her parents for that sort of thing."

Katrina had come to the store looking frazzled and desperate, such a tired face for a young girl. But her smile was infectious and she was so bubbly. She walked around the shelves of yarn as she spoke to Elva, interrupting herself to rub some on her cheek and ask what that particular yarn was used for. She used words like "delicious" and "lovely" and said "I could just eat it, I swear." Elva knew she would work so well in the shop. Would Elva's inability to push the girl for more information be the one thing that made her impossible to find?

Jim tried to hide his irritation. He did a poor job of it. "So you know the girl's last name, how much she made in April, and that's it? Nothing else?" He left the pages on the desk in disgust and sat back again. Elva could tell he wanted to raise his arms up in surrender.

"March is there too," she said quietly, her head down.

"Elva!"

Elva snapped her head up. "You have to find her, Jim. I'm sorry I don't have more." Elva could feel she was going to be hysterical again. It was the last thing she wanted right now. Jim was a sweet boy and he loved his job; she could feel he was being sincere in his efforts. But she knows Katrina is in trouble; she *knows it*. She couldn't waste time feeling guilty about what she could not change. "I didn't get her number. I'm sorry. It was a terrible mistake. But I liked the girl, Sheriff." Elva appealed to his authority. "She's in trouble. You have to find her, okay? You just have to!"

"This isn't much to go on, Auntie." He leaned forward again, lifting the small pile of papers with meager information. Elva held back a smile. His use of 'auntie' was a sign he felt for her. "Surely you can see that?"

Elva met his eyes and nodded. Her cheeks burned and her eyes started to fill with tears.

"Oh, Auntie. Please don't."

"I can't help it, Jim. What else can we do? There must be something else we can do. Please. Her name is there. Just look it up, right? The DMV maybe, or missing persons reports?"

"She could have picked any name she wanted, Auntie. Without a social security number..." Jim looked down at the scraps of paper and his nearly empty report. It wasn't one of Elva's usual requests, and by 'usual' he meant 'unreasonable'. It wasn't a request to boot a car. It wasn't a request to ask the grocery store to stay open later. It wasn't a request for a longer red light outside her shop. The look in her eyes was the same he'd seen when he was a kid, wanting to rush out just before a storm to practice riding on his bike. She was afraid. And she was sincere. He knew very well that she was not asking to ease curiosity, but she was asking because she believed something was terribly wrong.

"Do you have any photos of her? Maybe something in her apartment that could give me more info? A photocopy of her ID, maybe?"

Elva shook her head slowly as she slumped back in her chair. Jim tried to hide his frustration. But then she sat up and her face brightened. "Yes! I have bags of clothes and the things she left at the apartment!"

"She left things?" This surprised the sheriff. He always assumed Katrina left of her own will, ready to escape a small town. That she left behind anything could change his assumption; Elva *could* be right. "What kinds of things?"

"Everything! A whole slew of clothes, hairbrush, jewelry, toothbrush!" she said, with added emphasis. "Can you use her toothbrush? To get DNA or something?"

"Technically, yes, but our department can't afford that just yet, Elva. We have to start smaller. Did she leave any papers behind, or photos? Maybe a journal? A receipt with a credit card number on it?"

"I'll have to look through the bags," she said. She already sounded defeated. Elva didn't remember coming across anything like that when she cleaned out the apartment. Almost everything she shoved into bags was wearable or used for grooming.

"You take a look. If you're not sure if an item will help, bring it in and we'll figure it out. Ask everybody if they have any information about her at all – a photo from a party or ... I don't know. Anything. Okay?"

Elva nodded, already scanning her memory for something that may help. Did any knitters take photos of finished objects, or classes that Katrina attended?

"Get some rest, Elva. Try to relax."

CHAPTER SEVENTEEN

Katrina stopped crying; she stopped yelling; she stopped listening to the creaks in the floorboards above her head. She was tired. She was hungry. He was getting more stingy with his meals. At first, he offered her steaks with vegetables and glasses of wine. Her trays had small vases with flowers on them. She was hesitant to eat the food, but she could find no other alternative. She dumped the wine. Thirsty was one thing, but wine would only prove to make her more thirsty. Drugs were also more likely in the wine than the food – or so she thought.

Every time he came down the stairs and opened the door and slid the tray in through a small window in the fence separating them, she was dumbfounded. All the times she had seen him, talked to him, laughed at his charm and kindness – all those times, he was calculating. The first time he told her he loved her, as she sat cold and scared and hungry on his basement floor, she vomited on the food tray. He was disgusted, grabbing the tray hastily, calling her ungrateful, expressing his own dismay that she wasn't at all what he thought she was. Katrina said nothing.

"I really thought you were the one," he said.

She watched as he walked back up the stairs and cried when he threw a roll of paper towels at the fence. After he had gone, she reached through and stretched her fingers. They cramped up as she tried to pull a towel through the holes in the fence. She had to pull slowly or they would roll away from her. She was afraid one sheet would pull from the roll and she'd have nothing. Over the next hour, she

106

slowly pulled the entire roll inside her cage. Once inside, she began folding each sheet at the perforation.

He had left a little while ago, when the sun had already come up but wasn't yet at its hottest. Her throat was sore. Her stomach was empty. The bread he tossed down with a bottle of water did nothing for what she was sure was starvation. She ate it slowly, taking small sips of water, saving both for later in case he decided today was her last day with food.

She looked down at the pile of paper towels and she prayed for help, again. Then she picked up a sheet and unfolded sheet after sheet until it stretched across the small space she had: fifteen paper towels. And then she carefully folded the sheets lengthwise at one inch intervals. Taking her time, careful so as not to rip the paper unevenly, she tore the paper towels along the folds she had created. She also tore apart the cardboard roll and made two short sticks as sturdy as she could. Using those, and working loosely, carefully, laboriously, she wrapped the paper towel yarn she had created around her fingers. With one cardboard stick, she cast on some stitches.

It gave her something to do.

CHAPTER EIGHTEEN

The second class of the *Learn to Knit* series had just ended at A Stitch Is Cast. As usual, several students remained to share with more detail the work they had done since the last class. Some were asking questions about technique, but most just wanted to talk. It seemed to be a common theme with every class Deidre and Elva taught at the shop. Learning to knit, or learning a new technique, seemed to act as a cover for the real joy of the class: talking to like-minded people. Most knitters, especially those at yarn shops, were not just in it for the hobby or distraction from everyday life. They weren't there for the skill set gained. 'Look! I made a scarf for you. I knit it myself.' They were there because it was more than a hobby; it was a lifestyle. It encompassed more than just the tools used and the knowing how to use those tools.

Melinda, for instance, already knew how to knit, but she loved meeting people who were just starting out. She confessed to Deidre that she got a thrill out of the transformation. "That fierce concentration suddenly turns into a big *aha!* I just love that."

Melinda decided to knit because, she said, "I had no hope for the future." She explained that she never looked further ahead than the next sale. "My goals were short ones, and really only present if I was already mired in the process. Like school, for instance. I knew I had a goal of graduating college because I was already *in* college. High school too. But after college? No goals." Shortly before her graduation ceremony, she and her family attended her initiation into an academic fraternity. While they mingled afterward, an important woman of the fraternity – Melinda knew she was important because, she said, "She wore a suit, heavy lipstick, and I saw her sitting on the stage up front," – came up to Melinda and her mother and asked, "What are you going to be doing next?" Melinda immediately told her about the lunch they had planned at a local Mediterranean restaurant, and admitted they hadn't thought much beyond that. The woman had smirked at Melinda. Her mother, however, laughed and said, "I think she means *after college.*"

"I probably looked rude, and she probably wondered how in the world I was ever invited to the fraternity, when I said, 'Oh. I don't know,' and left it at that."

She eventually realized that living this way was much harder outside of school. She often felt lost, as if she were wandering. Every day was short, and every morning she felt exhausted. "I had no idea what I was doing," she said. So, she decided to learn to knit. She had been trying to learn for about seven years by reading books. She quickly grew impatient and threw her needles down, stuffing them back under her bed. When she realized that she had no goals, however, and that she had to start learning to take one day at a time toward *something*, she thought there was no better way than to learn the one thing that had bested her for years: patience.

"It took about a year," she said, "but finally, I could knit. And it's not a real goal, *per se*, but it had taught me something."

New students are usually a little confused by now. How did knitting teach somebody a valuable life lesson?

Melinda always laughs. "It just taught me to hold on, keep going, do it right, take your time… you know. All that stuff the Buddhists say. I start a project and I don't know when it will be finished, but I have that to look forward to.

And I work on it, every day, little by little, until lo and behold, I have something that I worked on, slowly, over time. And it's beautiful!" After a slight pause, she says, "Unless we're talking about my first sock, in which case, scratch that last part."

She was fun to have in the classes, feeding off the vibe of social gathering and knitting all in one space. Elva appreciated the time she took to help other students, but when offered class discounts for all that she did, Melinda refused. She didn't want to feel at all like an employee. She wanted to be sure it was one hundred percent joy that kept her there. Elva appreciated that.

Melinda was still chatting to Addison when the last of the students filed out with all their new yarn purchases. "I am still so totally shocked," she said to Addison again. "This is awesome. Maybe you were, like, a knitting expert in your previous life." They both laughed at the idea, a glow of pride evident on Addison's face. It made Elva happy that Addison was fitting in well with the women of the shop and thought that she and Melinda would get along quite well.

Deidre told Elva she had a lot to discuss with her. They were waiting patiently for Melinda to leave, but finally Elva had to lay down the law – gently – and Addison dragged Melinda away. Addison was laughing. "I think we really have to go!" she said. Deidre was happy to hear the laugh. She didn't want Addison to feel at all stressed, scared or otherwise *not calm* if she chose to knit once she was home.

The two women sat at the table with their tea. Because it was on Elva's mind, Deidre asked her first about her morning meeting with Jim, and then Deidre took a big breath.

"So what happened the other night?" Elva asked, unexpectedly.

Deidre's mouth was hanging open, still undecided as to how she should start the conversation about Addison. She closed her mouth and eyed Elva curiously. "What do you mean?"

"At the meeting," said Elva, almost absentmindedly, but clearly she was curious. Elva could not hide her true intentions. "You got me all worked up, telling me that you had to talk to the group about something important. Then we got there, and it was just another meeting." Elva shrugged, as if this meant nothing to her... she was just curious, after all.

That first lesson had gone well with Addison, and in the course of it, Deidre was startled to realize how much she liked her. She wasn't at all like Katrina, although they were both generally complacent and happy. Where Katrina was loud and somewhat unrestrained – on the surface anyway (after some time getting to know her, Deidre discovered her flamboyant behavior was just a way to get over her shyness and underlying serious personality), Addison was more in touch with her seriousness and drizzled it with bouncy cheer. It was refreshing and intriguing. Deidre found herself wanting to know more about Addison, but was also just content to sit with her and ask absolutely nothing. That is how big her personality is, Deidre reflected later. Just being in her company felt like *enough*.

Elva snapped her fingers before Deidre's glassy eyes.

"I just decided it wasn't a good time. I hadn't considered some things and I want to be sure that... that I'm sure." She bent her head to sip some tea. "But I want to tell you now. And only you. But we may have to visit Sara again at some point." Elva raised her eyes. "And Michael."

Elva's tea dribbled down her shirt after she nearly choked on it. Michael?

Nick was waiting on the small landing behind the yarn shop, leaning against the door to Addison's apartment. She gave Melinda a quick hug and thanked her for the short car ride. It was completely unnecessary because of how close Addison lived to the shop – she was practically in the shop, actually – but she really liked Melinda and didn't mind the few extra minutes she spent talking with her.

"I feel like I've been here forever!" grinned Nick.

"Sorry. Knitting class, and I met Melinda and we were talking and blah, blah, blah."

"No worries." He picked up his bag and stood out of the way so Addison could unlock the door. She had trouble getting the key into the lock and was beginning to get embarrassed.

"I haven't had this much trouble before." The whole five or six times she's actually gone into her new apartment. She leaned down in the dim light to look more directly at the lock. She held the key up to it and tried again but the key would only go in a few millimeters.

"Want me to try?"

Addison handed her keys over and stepped back. She imagined he'd pull out a lock-pick set and amaze her with his stealth, fitting the image of secret spy she had quietly imagined to herself this morning while getting breakfast. *Why not?* She looked down at her outfit. Boring, as usual. Jeans, a plain blue t-shirt and some Keds. Not exactly Heidi Klum. She stood up straight and threw her bag over her shoulder. If she couldn't dress herself in style, she could *pretend* that she did. She was pretty sure that she read that somewhere: stand tall, be confident, and that's what people see.

"I'm not entirely sure, but it sort of looks like that part where the key goes is a bit twisted, or bent or something."

He was still trying it. Addison looked at his outfit. Jeans and maroon t-shirt. Nice jeans, really. Some black chucks on his feet. She looked at his jeans again as he shifted weight on his heels.

Addison cleared her throat. Get over yourself, she thought. He's a friend. You need friends right now, not hunky spies for boyfriends. "Should I call Elva?"

"Nah. Hold on a second." He reached into his pocket and pulled out his own key chain. Dangling from it was a small Swiss Army knife. He leaned over the key hole again.

Addison looked around the parking lot, content to let him figure it out. She liked Nick, but was having trouble determining if she like-liked Nick or just wanted to be friends with him. She felt compelled to determine that before anything else. Both sides of the matter were great starts. As a potential boyfriend, hope sprung eternal. Tall, blonde, sweet, funny, creative, relaxing. She could go on. But as a friend, there was little chance of her hopes being dashed or the relationship coming to a screaming halt because one day insisting he try the lock became a suggestion he invite himself in. All the time. Especially at night. Her cheeks burned and she knew she was blushing.

There was a small lot behind the house with enough space for some shoppers to park. Nick mentioned they get tourists sometimes, either parents who came with their kids to look at the college or people who just liked the feel of the square and the small but special shops that surrounded it. The fall drew the most tourists with the trees changing color. Nick mentioned there were also several apple orchards and pumpkin patches in surrounding towns and the nearby lake provided idyllic rides in canoes for a fair price. Addison still couldn't see the lake, even from her back porch, and she was sure Professor Fernlee said it was this way.

The lot was mostly empty right now. Nick's car was the closest to the apartments and one other was in the farthest spot, diagonal from Nick's. Behind that car was the alleyway leading down another side street. Addison craned her neck forward and peered closely. Someone was sitting in the dark colored car. The streetlights were too dim to tell for sure, but she thought for sure someone was there. She took a step forward and squinted her eyes, trying to get a better look. The car jumped to life, lights on, the engine starting up as if out of gas, then with a screech it was off. She jumped at the suddenness of it and didn't realize she called out until Nick mocked her.

"Holy cow?" he said. "That's your expletive of choice when something scares you? 'Holy cow'?"

He swung the door inward and folded his knife back together.

"Whoa, whoa, whoa!" he called out, and bent over quickly to grab at a black streak halfway down the stairs of the landing. With a wail, he caught Derwin's tail and gently scooped him up. "How'd you get out, little buddy?" He looked at Addison. "Did you leave your door open by accident?"

"No!" Addison said, concerned. "Is he an outdoor cat? Maybe there's a cat door somewhere?" It seemed unlikely, but hardly important. "And um, 'whoa'? You dis my 'holy cow' and counter it with a 'whoa'?"

"I wasn't scared," he said. "I was calling attention to the escaping cat." He cocked his head as if to say "obviously."

"Sure," said Addison, chuckling. She wrapped her arms around Derwin and held him close to her chest. His loud purr hummed comfortingly on her neck. "Let's go knit!"

Oddly enough, Addison's apartment door had a similar problem which led both she and Nick to suspect that her key was somehow damaged since the same key was used for both doors. She made a mental note to bring it up with Elva and maybe get a new key.

All day Addison had been looking forward to hanging out with Nick. He was impressed with her knitting and decided she was ready for some social knitting. They agreed to hang out, listen to music, maybe watch a TV show, since Addison was feeling starved for pop culture, and eat food. As soon as they got in the house, Addison dropped her bag on the sofa and went to the kitchen. Walking in somewhere and dropping her bag on a sofa felt surreal. A *home*. She still had trouble believing it.

Addison poured some water in her kettle and started pulling from the shelves ingredients that could be thrown together and resemble a snack toward the end. While she did that, Nick pulled yarn from his own bag – a huge wad of gray.

"So what did you bring to work on?" Addison asked, already bitten by the pattern bug. When she wasn't knitting at the shop, she perused patterns in the magazines they sold. She was stymied by all that she could do with her newfound skill. Sweaters, mittens, scarves, some things she never thought she would ever want to wear suddenly looked amazing. She wasn't sure if it was the pattern she liked, or just that she knew she could make it if she wanted to. It seemed everything was a potential fashion statement, and she wasn't afraid to do it as long as she got to knit it.

"A shawl for my mom," he said. Addison tried not to do what she immediately wanted to do, which was collapse at the knees in a dramatic representation of swooning. How sweet is that? How sweet? *Way sweet*, she thought.

"How do I ask this without offending you…?" she asked aloud, her words trailing as she considered the next few words. Nick didn't need her help though; he was already ahead of her.

"Do people still wear shawls?" he asked.

"Yes! I'm sorry! But aren't they for really old ladies who can't – I don't know – lift their arms up for sweaters?" She shuffled through the ingredients in front of her as she spoke.

Nick laughed, shaking his head, his blond hair changing colors in the light from the lamps. "Good one."

Addison chuckled. Nick continued. "Naw. You'll see soon enough, now that you're more aware of hand knits, that tons of women wear shawls. Men too, but they'll typically wear them as scarves. Like this," he said, reaching up to the burgundy scarf around his neck. He untwisted it, pulled it, then shook it out. Addison hadn't noticed the scarf – er, shawl – earlier.

"Wow!" she walked over to him, cinnamon jar in hand, and reached out to touch the shawl. The shawl was triangular, each side perfectly mirroring the other. The pattern reminded Addison of the clouds she saw over the ocean in Florida when she visited with a foster family in junior high school. In it, she saw the waves move and the clouds chase them out. She wouldn't have chosen burgundy, but she could understand the switch from her own imagined indigo color, because the burgundy suited Nick. It said frat boy and style vixen, but also "hey, I'm just cold here." When her fingers touched the fabric, she felt a jolt of giddiness and a laugh escaped her lips. Her lips widened into a grin and with it, a huge sigh. Nick let go of the shawl and let her hold it. As she did, she looked more closely at the pattern and again, that same vacation came to her.

She had been with the Brooks family only seven months total, but in that time had done more than she ever had before. Twelve years old and in the seventh grade, the Brooks were her eighth foster home. The sting of moving had begun to die down somewhat. At least, that is, the sting didn't last as long. She learned to adjust, to start talking to the people she lived with, asking them questions, and assuring herself that she could get them to like her. It was easy with the Brooks family. They really did like her. She was included in every activity and felt, for the first time, like a real person – respected and cared for. They asked her what foods she liked to eat, what chores she might enjoy doing, what books she wanted to read, and if she needed any new clothes for school. Their interested questions made her feel looked after. She rode a horse for the first time while she was with them, having mentioned that it was something she always wanted to do. Her birthday was a month after she arrived and a horse riding lesson was her present.

Two other kids lived at the house. A seven year old named Devin and another teenage girl named Jody, three years older at fifteen. Amazingly, they all got along together. They enjoyed playing card games like Uno and Gin Rummy (though Devin got frustrated so often, Jody and Addison never kept score when he played), and got a kick out of tether ball.

Three months after moving in, they all went on a family vacation to Florida, getting special permission for all three children. That part was stressful for all of them. The Brooks home was Devin's first foster home. He had been there a year already and called them "Mom" and "Dad." Jody had been there six months longer than Addison. It was also her first foster home. Her mother, she said, was too sick and she had nobody else who could take her. The need for permission from the people who placed them pointed out their "different-ness." It was like going on a field trip with the school and getting permission from your parents at home, only this way it was your parents getting permission from some strangers who barely knew you. When it was granted, they were all mostly excited. Addison, however, tried to keep her excitement at bay. It had happened before: someone calls at the last minute, and suddenly she would no longer be allowed to go to that dance, or join them for that vacation, and will have to be "temporarily placed" in the meantime. But that call didn't come, and they all got on a plane and flew to Florida.

Addison loved it, struck dumb by the flat expanse of sand, the blinding light and the tall grass, the way the water changed colors as she stepped in it, and the breadth of the ocean. She was afraid to step into it at first, but Jody made it impossible to stay away. Her yells and laughter were infectious. With a deep breath, Addison launched her body toward the water and ran quickly. She already knew it was going to be cold, but she was unprepared when she dove. The ocean was shallow. Who knew?

She laughed out loud at the memory. Jody's laughter, the sand in her mouth and down her bathing suit, the long trek into the ocean just to get it thigh-high. It was so simple a memory, and yet it was more.

"How long did it take you to make this?" she asked Nick, still smiling at the vacation memories.

"I didn't make this one. A friend did." Addison could tell by his tone of voice and hesitation over the word 'friend' that it was made by a girlfriend.

"Old boyfriend?" She winked. Nick shoved her a little and took back his shawl-slash-scarf.

"What are you making us? I'm starving." He tossed the shawl on the bag, unknowing that when he next wrapped it around his neck he would smell salt water, have the urge to laugh, and behind it all, feel a twang of unexplained melancholy.

Elva was still staring wide-eyed at Deidre, unbelieving. It was expected, and Deidre allowed her the time as she made another cup of tea for them both. She then started flipping through a magazine as Elva continued to process the information. After another ten minutes, Deidre pulled out her knitting. It was a pair of socks, simply made, with a picot cuff. After every round, she looked over at Elva. Deidre couldn't blame Elva for remaining quiet so long. It was a lot to take in. In fact, her reaction only cemented Deidre's expectation that Addison would all but disappear before their very eyes once she was told.

Deidre had decided to tell Elva because she needed support and another witch's experience to help her wade through the mire of history that was already scarce. She needed Elva to know because Deidre couldn't keep the secret much longer. Also, Elva worked with Addison daily, so could watch her and quietly guide her until they both determined how training should begin. If she tried to get to the truth of her reasons, however, despite how practical the other reasons were, she had to admit that she was just scared and needed her friend.

"Well then." Elva let out a long breath, as if she had held that same breath since Deidre made her announcement. *Addison is a knitwitch.* Elva was nodding her head. Despite all of Deidre's warnings when Addison arrived – don't let her touch your works in progress; limit her exposure to the customer's projects; don't let her try to teach herself to knit on the first day – she never suspected *knitwitch*. She thought that perhaps Deidre just felt something special in Addison and wanted to teach her herself, create a bond. Perhaps, she had wondered, Deidre was afraid Elva would become attached too soon after Katrina's disappearance, and in that Elva thought maybe she was right. But knitwitch?

119

"I've searched through everything I have, Elva. I even giggled it."

"Google."

"What?"

"You Googled it."

"Right."

In the moments Deidre left Elva to think things through, half the time was spent repeating *Addison is a knitwitch*. The other half was putting it all together, what Deidre knew, what Addison didn't know, what the ladies at the meeting didn't know – about Addison and craft witches. The side with information was flimsy.

"Deidre--"

"Don't say it," she pleaded and hung her head, looking at her hands folded tightly around her mug. "I thought the same thing. I just tried and tried to think of other options. But finally, I just knew I had to and of course!" Here she stole a glance at her best friend seeking a reaction. She was disappointed to see just a sideways half smile. "He called." She paused, remembering how her heart raced when she heard his voice. "Yeah. Laugh all you want, missy miss. But it was horrible."

Elva waited, knowing Deidre would spill it all. She didn't have to wait long.

"His voice! That horrible, awful, vile, ragged, manly, arrogant, deep, self-involved--" Her face grew a deeper shade of red. With a loud breath through her closed lips, she shut her haunted eyes and sat up straight. "I don't know if I can do this," she whispered.

Deidre's best friend leaned over and placed her hand on her arm. Deidre could feel the angst in her chest ebb just a little. It was part of Elva's gift, spreading warmth. She knew not to use it completely on Deidre, who becomes offended and angry when others use their magic to manipulate her, whether it be for good or not. It was just enough to offer solace; to make her able to speak. Elva convinced herself it was only slightly more than what her company and support was already doing. Deidre lay her hand over Elva's and squeezed it tenderly. "Thank you, Elva."

"You don't need me to tell you anything, do you?"

"No. No, I don't," agreed Deidre. "We're meeting at my house in about an hour."

CHAPTER NINETEEN

He was almost caught today. He knew he only made it worse by racing away in his car like he did, causing more of a scene with the screeching tires than simply taking a casual route out of the parking lot, but she had looked at him. Did she see his face? Did she know who he was? Mixed feelings stirred him – did he really want her to know who he was, or was anonymity the better choice? He must have messed up with the lock on the door. It's tricky to practice, and he didn't want to do it, but necessity dictated.

The boy she was with looked familiar. Boyfriend? So soon? He consulted his notebook and wrote down some notes. "Relax," he spelled out slowly, speaking the word under his breath. "Relax…"

CHAPTER TWENTY

After a long night knitting with Nick, laughing at the stories he told about people at the yarn shop, his mother's knitting groups and her predictably poor choice of knitted gifts (apparently, she was particularly desperate one Christmas – and usually desperate every Christmas - when she decided to knit everybody from cousins to hair stylists cosies for their apples!), Addison was more than ready to fall asleep. She didn't have to work at the shop the next day and looked forward to a lazy day, sleeping in, knitting, reading and wandering around Brookwick.

She wandered around the apartment, as small as it was. In the bathroom, she put the lid of the toilet down and sat to look around. The small tiles, in varying straight-edged shapes, were lifting from the floor. With her bare toe, she pulled up a loose tile and watched as the one beside it shifted as well. The loose tiles took up about a six-inch square of space. The faucet on the sink to her left had a small brown ring of grime around its base. Addison leaned over to look under the cabinet and saw a small cup of old toothbrushes in the back. She grabbed one, along with the small box of baking soda. It looked damp and old, but it didn't really matter. She dug the toothbrush in and lifted out a small scoop with the head of the brush. Carefully, she turned the faucet on and let small driblets of water fall on the brush. She smeared it the mixture around the base of the faucet. She scrubbed lightly, and then hard, and was pleased to see the grime spreading, diluting and disappearing. Pleased, she rinsed the brush and searched for a sponge or wash cloth under the sink. Sure enough, she found an old red rag.

Addison made her way through the bathroom with her toothbrush, baking soda and red rag. The tub needed serious work; her toothbrush grabbed grime around the faucet and grout while her rag scrubbed the invisible film she could feel beneath it in the basin of the tub. Sweat turned her hairline damp and she trickles of sweat slivered down her back. There were no windows in the bathroom so she took off her t-shirt. Wearing her bra and jeans, she scrubbed some more.

As she worked, Addison thought about Brookwick. She thought she might love it, and wast terrified. She had never lived anywhere that didn't come with an intended departure time. Foster homes were always temporary. Driving the car was always temporary. Brookwick – was Brookwick temporary too? The realization that she had the choice threatened to overwhelm her. How does a person choose to make a place her home? Leaving in her car was the first choice she was ever able to make about her future – she didn't need permission; she wasn't pulled there by social services; she wasn't pulled, prodded, treated as stuff that needed storage. Packing her car and pulling out of the Reids's driveway was the first time she decided where she was going next. It was clear to her now, though, as she scrubbed the tub of her own apartment, that leaving Toule was not a choice to go somewhere else – it was simply a choice to leave. Is choosing to stay the next step?

Addison paused. The next step to what? To home? The word gave Addison a chill. She wasn't sure she even knew what 'home' was.

The toothbrush, rag and baking soda went back under the bathroom sink. In the mirror, she looked at her flushed face. Looked in her eyes. How strange, she thought, that she couldn't *really* look into her own eyes, not the way she could look into someone else's. Was that the same for everyone? "I'll have to ask Nick," she said. "Or Elva. Or Brian. Or Deidre." She chuckled. Not only was she talking to herself, but she was talking to herself about *friends*.

After a relieving shower and a cup of tea, Addison sat in bed and knit a few rows. She thought about what she would do the next day on her first day off from the shop. The college campus sounded intriguing. Brian said he would have to work, but maybe he didn't have to work the whole day, because surely it wouldn't take that long to look around? She was hesitant to hang around with Nick *too much* – she didn't want to give the impression that she like-liked him, but she also wanted to be sure she made more friends. Friends were important. After a year of being alone, she realized more and more that alone is not what she always wanted to be. Melinda was very nice, but Addison failed to get her contact information. At the next class or if she's in the shop, Addison decided she was just going to hurdle the awkwardness and ask Melinda if she wanted to hang out. No sense surrounding herself with guys all the time.

Derwin hopped up on the bed and snuggled in the crook of her foot and ankle, bent outward as she relaxed on the bed.

Addison was watching herself. She was about two years old and she was sitting on the floor in front a blue recliner. The seat was faded in the middle and the arm rests too. A foot pushed the red train around. Addison laughed and chased it, saying, "Again, Mom! Again!" in toddler tones, some of the sharpness missing. A laugh came and Addison watched the woman with long dark hair keep her gaze focused on the baby Addison as she laughed, kept her balance by holding the recliner and continued to maneuver the train around

Addison. Baby Addison was so cute, with dark brown eyes and blonde hair, wispy and honeyed, grazing her neck and ears. She wore a blue dress with a white collar, white socks with lacy ruffles on the edges, and white, patent-leather shoes. Baby Addison clapped her hands and grabbed at the train. "I got it!" she yelled. Big Addison smiled to herself. She looked at the woman – her mother? - and was startled to find the woman looking back at her.

"This never happened," the woman said. "I wanted it to. I desperately wanted it to…"

Addison felt herself leaving, being pulled backwards, and then fell into another room. This room had orange shag carpet and dark wood paneling on the walls. The same woman sat in a high-backed, Victorian chair at a window. Her dark hair smooshed against the pink fabric of the chair, and she grasped it all in her hand, pulled it from her neck and from behind her back, then draped it over her shoulder. Addison watched in fascination as the woman sat taller, pulled her shirt more securely around her waist and smoothed it in the back. She was pregnant. Very pregnant. With Addison? She sat back and pulled onto her lap some cream wool and two long knitting needles made of bone. The woman rolled the yarn in her hands, smelled it, rubbed it on her cheek. Then she kissed it and laid it back in her lap. Each hand now held a needle and she flattened her palms, allowing them to roll from one edge of her palm to the other. Her grasp closed suddenly and the woman began to cry. It was quiet crying at first, silent but for the tears and the loud splash Addison heard as they fell onto her belly. But soon she was moaning, her hands tightly holding the knitting needles as her arms crossed over her belly. Her shoulders shook and Addison wanted to hold her, to say something to her, to assure her that whatever it was that made her this sad, she was going to be okay. The woman started whispering. "Nein, nein, nein…" But Addison was being pulled again, and her heart broke as she watched the woman get further and further away, her loneliness made more apparent by the silhouette of her shaking body against the window aching for more.

Addison was at a park. She saw herself, at about four, running in a playground with a group of children. Her hair had gotten darker, almost brown but still more blonde. She was laughing. At the edge of the park, behind the fence, was a man. He had dark glasses with tinted lenses and a mustache. His Scottish-style hat was pulled low over his face, but she could see his curly brown hair and tanned skin. He looked familiar, but she didn't know how or why. When she craned her neck forward in the hopes she could see his face better, he lifted his face and nodded at her. His face was too blurry. Addison stepped back. His lips began to move and seconds later, she heard his voice in her ear as if he had been standing beside her. "I have something for you," it said. Addison turned and began to run.

She came to the shop. The boiling pots of yarn were everywhere. Elva and Deidre sat at a table in the back, cackling. They were wearing black robes with tall black witch's caps. Elva's had a broad purple stripe; Deidre's was green. "Abracadabra!" shrilled Elva. Her fingers were splayed over a cauldron, yarny tendrils rising up to meet them. Steam thick like fog poured over the edges of the cauldron. Deidre laughed crudely, her palm hitting the table, hysterically amused.

"Open sesame!" Deidre bellowed back, and Elva let out a long hoo-wee of a laugh, tipping her chair back as her arms crossed her belly, as if it ached from all their jokes.

Deidre turned her head and looked at Addison. All signs of laughter had left her face. Her eyes were sad, her mouth drawn. When she tilted her head to the side, she looked like she was pitying Addison. Elva stopped laughing and looked at Addison as well. With a voice so sad and heavy that Addison felt a sob grow in her throat when she heard it, Deidre said "So much you'll never know."

"So much," Elva nodded. "It's true!" She was still giddy, but her face was grave.

"And it was so nice to meet you," they said in unison. The women nodded their heads together.

Addison backed out of the store. The bell sounded as the door slammed behind her. When she turned, the square was filled with men *and women sitting on the benches, in the gazebo, on the curb surrounding the square, on blankets and chairs, crowding the lawns. Children were perched in the cauldrons of flowers, crushing them. One by one, they looked up from the knitting in their laps and stared at her. Like a wave in a sporting arena, the loud rumble of their chatting and knitting turned to silence. Just as quickly, they began whispering. Addison moved off the curb and into the street. She heard the voice of the woman in the blue dress who pushed the toy train – her mother; Addison was almost sure of it now. "This never happened," she said. It was followed quickly by the man's. "I have something for you."*

"Abracadabra," whispered Elva.

"So much you'll never know…"

And then the square. The people. Together, their whisper was like a microphone turned all the way up, sitting between her ears. Addison wanted to disappear – it was too much!

"Stitch in one makes it two. Blessed be, this spell's for you."

Addison woke with her legs tangled in the sheets. Her t-shirt clung to her neck, damp with sweat, and her tongue felt swollen. Red and white lines stretched across her knuckles, the covers still balled up in her hands, and her legs were sore, as if she had spent the night running. She tried stilling her ragged breath only to hear her heart hammering in her ears.

"Derwin?" she whispered. She longed for company, even if the cat was all that would be available to her. "Derwin?" She felt a light thud at the bottom of the bed and breathed a sigh of relief. "Hey, guy. Come sit with me?" Derwin sat on her pillow and purred. Addison breathed a sigh of relief. He stretched forward and rested his head on her shoulder, his purr radiating through her body. She smiled. "You're a good roomie, you know. Did you know that?" The sound of her own voice filled the darkness, and the comforting purr of Derwin made her feel a little better. But the longer she lay there, the more she tried to convince herself that she just wasn't going to fall back asleep. That dream was freaky, and she was afraid she would fall right back into it. She didn't want that. She wanted to forget it entirely.

With a tender rub to Derwin's head, Addison got up and pulled on the jeans she left crumpled by the bed. After a visit to the bathroom – now sparkling clean and reeking of satisfaction – Addison went to the kitchen for some tea. Settled on the couch, Addison grabbed her knitting and placed it in her lap. Derwin sat beside her. She was still antsy, and watched the apartment door handle, wary that someone from her dream would suddenly appear in the living room. The problem is that she was so tired, her stare made the door handle waver until it looked like it was moving.

"Stop freaking out," she said. Derwin raised his head. "Me, I mean," she assured him. She gripped her needles and threaded the yarn between the fingers of her left hand.

"This will help, Derwin." He put his head back in her lap and she took that as a sign of agreement. She heard Elva's voice again. *Abracadabra.* It seemed ridiculous and out of context but the more she remembered it, the more malevolent it became. Addison shook her head. She started singing *Mary Had a Little Lamb* quietly, a trick she learned when she was seven-years-old. It was a way to forget things that bothered her. Sometimes, she found she could still obsess over what was bothering her even when the words she was singing remained unchanged, so she taught herself to really focus on the words, sometimes changing them around, out of order, to keep her focus. She counted the syllables at the same time, or she simply counted in general, keeping track of how many times she sang it. The more wrenches she threw into the practice, the less likely she was to think about what had been bothering her.

The needles felt awkward in her cold hands.

This never happened.

Addison bent her neck further into the knitting, concentrating on the song and the knitting without letting part of her dream in. The process was frustrating. And then she messed up. Since the day Deidre taught her to knit, sitting on the bench in the park in the great sun, Addison hadn't made one mistake in her knitting. She had no idea what she was supposed to do to fix it.

Tears threatened to take control and the last thing Addison wanted to do was cry over a knitting mistake. Her breath was ragged as she forced it in her lungs and held it for a moment. Slowly, she let it out. Shaky. She looked at the stitches on her right hand needle and couldn't quite figure out what the yarn was doing. It looked as if she somehow *added* stitches, except she didn't know how to do that yet. *Mary Had a Little Lamb* was still running in her mind as she remembered Deidre's book. She leaned over the arm of the couch to get it from the bag she left on the floor.

"Son of a bitch," she said angrily. "Just go away!" Remnants of her dream clung to her memory. Without realizing it, the words to *Mary Had a Little Lamb* had morphed into a childlike version of *Stitch in one makes it two, blessed be this spell's for you.*

After many mistakes and many consultations with the book Deidre gave her, Addison finally decided she was tired enough to go to bed again. But she never made it to bed. She and Derwin slept comfortably on the couch well into the following day, curled into each other, dreaming about absolutely nothing.

CHAPTER TWENTY-ONE

Her muffins tasted terrible. Deidre was not the best of bakers, and she was sure she confused salt for baking soda or baking powder for salt or *something*. Really it didn't matter. She had succeeded with these muffins once before, with Elva's help, and so thought they would be a safe choice. They were quick, easy, and edible – the last time, when Elva helped her.

Michael had called to say he'd be late, so she spent the extra time making a snack they could share. Why? Because she was hungry, that's why. She threw the muffins in the trash and covered them up with various other bits of debris in a silly attempt to cover her failure should he need to throw something away later (*like my heart*, she couldn't help adding – melodramatically, she also noted).

Back when Michael and Deidre lived together they shared several laughs about Deidre's kitchen mishaps. But laughter turned to guilt whenever Michael described yet another wonderful dish he had during his many travels or from his childhood. Half of them she had never heard of, but the home cooked meals he mentioned were typical: lasagna, meatloaf, mashed potatoes. So many families made these foods. She had convinced herself, despite never having made a successful pot of pasta, that she could as well. Love was involved this time and love was, she believed, the only skill she needed. She purchased new pots at thrift stores and wandered through grocery stores looking for ingredients that spoke to her, that sparked a thought about Michael and his intestinal memory. She was so doe-eyed, hypnotized by his lavish attentions but most especially by his *choice* to be with her that she felt she had to keep her lack of skill in the kitchen a secret lest he want to leave her. More than anything, she yearned for a recipe he would crave – like the goulash he wanted from Hungary.

Her first lasagna was a disaster. Deciding that love accounted for everything she needed, including practice, a cookbook, and the ability to boil water, she decided to wing it. She put tomato paste in the bottom of the pan, not recognizing there was a difference between that and its brother, tomato sauce. She broke the lasagna into pieces so it could fit in the pan then added more sauce and slices of American cheese. Using her bare hands and a grimace, she pulled hunks of meat from the pound of ground beef, and lay the raw pieces artistically on top of it all, then repeated the process until the pan was full. She put the pan in the oven, set the heat to three-hundred degrees and put her kitchen timer on thirty minutes.

Whenever she became furious with Michael, she remembered his laugh when he saw the lasagna and her fury turned to angst, a resentment that sat deep in her heart. While tears spilled down her face, the lasagna steamed on the kitchen table looking more like a child's preschool project than a meal. He hugged her tightly and assured her that he loved what she tried to do, that it was okay, that it was no reason to cry so much. All of that was true, she knew. But all she really heard was his laugh. To others, she knew it sounded joyous, loving, endearing, like laughing at a child who is trying to help and only makes a bigger mess. But to her, it sounded like ridicule because she wanted so much to please him. She didn't understand where this came from, why she reacted so aggressively to what seemed like a loving response – but she always followed her gut, and her gut told her that he found her *insufficient*. She accepted his hugs and assurances but she did not believe in them.

And then there was the cake. Deidre threw it in the trash in disgust and they drove to Dairy Queen. It was the least she could do for his birthday.

"Stop it." She sat down at the kitchen table and laid her hands on the top of the wood grain. Focusing on her palms, she reached down into her stomach with her mind and asked it to rest. She moved the thought to her chest – desperate for a deep breath – then her tense shoulders, tight neck and back, and her chin, which had started to quiver when she first tasted the muffins. She focused also on her cheeks, eyes and forehead, and then she sent those thoughts to her hands. She stayed that way for several more moments, reassuring herself that she was calm. "He is just a man. He is coming here not for you, but for Addison. You don't want him here for you. That is over." She stuck her chin out and clamped her teeth tight together.

Deidre was born into the witchy way of life. She had been cleaning her room with spells since she was twelve-years-old, when her powers became strong enough to lift more than socks. She used empathic spells on friends when they became angry because she also thought that boy was cute. She used her magic to wash off two different counters and do dishes at the same time while she filed her nails. Her mother scolded her for cheating on her chores, but changed her mind when Deidre pointed out that her chores were being completed with the skills she possessed; why is that wrong? It was an argument her mother remembered making as well.

But as fun as it was to play *Bewitched*, Deidre was frustrated she didn't know other witches her own age and she could not show her non-witchy friends what she was. The witch friends her parents had did not have children who inherited the witchy genes. Knowing how children can talk, they chose to keep their secret from their children. This was easy to understand. Deidre knew the cruelty of children, especially adolescents when it concerned "different."

Against her parents' warnings, she once broached the topic with her best friend in high school, Annie Dreyfuss. Annie was an easy friend for Deidre. Though Annie often became angry because she believed Deidre held harsh feelings against her, a quick apology and empathic spell smoothed the waters. Deidre didn't feel bad about using the spells because she knew Annie was wrong; Deidre loved having Annie as a friend and didn't think a bad word about her, ever. Annie never asked questions; she just wanted to be around somebody else and this suited Deidre as well. Her short, red hair highlighted the spread of freckles over her cheeks and nose. She was pretty, but like most things that were different, she got her fair share of torment over her freckles and thick, bushy hair. It was too short for a pony tail, but Annie didn't seem to mind the remarks. Deidre knew otherwise; her empathic spells often returned contempt and hatred for those who picked on her.

Several times, Deidre caught Annie with her hands combing the thick mass of hair. Annie said she liked it; the way it felt heavy and soft at the same time. Deidre agreed with her when she was granted permission to play with it. It did feel nice. She also felt that Annie wanted to shave the heads of every girl who passed her in the hall with thin, straight hair. She was relieved she wasn't included on that list, her own being curly and long. And though Deidre envied the way Annie's cool, thick hair enveloped her fingers as if embracing them, she did not envy the remarks the silky bounty got Annie in the school hallways. Deidre was sorry her friend had to hear it.

The witch conversation started off simple enough, talking about movies, books, music, and nail polish. It felt loud to Deidre when she finally asked, though she tried to get the movie and book conversation to work in her favor, even the nail polish conversation because didn't purple nail polish relate?

"What do you know about witches?" Deidre remembered the disgust she felt at her own lack of creativity.

Annie's responses mimicked the ridiculous caricatures of movies and cartoons: flying brooms, bats for friends, long noses and lizard guts in soup concoctions. Deidre was shocked, but she laughed along with her friend. "What if you found out I was a witch?"

Annie's bark was sharp and Deidre jumped a little off the floor.

"Don't be ridiculous! You're too pretty to be a witch. Besides, witches are evil and mean. *Real* witches don't even exist. Magic is just a bunch of tricks. What's up with the witch stuff?"

"But if I was a witch?"

Annie gave Deidre a pointed stare. "Then I'd ask you to make me a love potion to slip to Jason and we can spy on him using your broom." She giggled, her stern look melting away.

Deidre giggled as well, but she was hurt. First of all, love potions didn't exist. At least, that's what her parents kept telling her (she had to ask). But mostly, how could her friend, a friend she chose and liked and with whom she wanted to share her wedding day, be so close-minded? Deidre's questions came up repeatedly as time went on, and Annie's responses became more and more cruel until Annie decided that Deidre was just a freak with an obsession. "Go home and pet your cats then, witch."

Deidre didn't know what had happened, how her greatest friend had turned unkind, but it happened. Deidre no longer wanted to use her magic to make Annie accept her. Perhaps it was too much to expect a normal human to accept that the cackling, green-nosed, wart-riddled caricatures of Halloween were real and once played with her hair. Perhaps Annie was tired of the ridicule she got at school; perhaps she wanted Deidre to get along as she always had, without questions. Whatever the reason, Deidre cried her tears and hugged her pillows and passed Annie in the hallways without a glance. Her parents assured her there was nothing Deidre could do to help her friend and avoid the torment; there was nothing she could do to make her kindness return to Deidre without being dishonest. "Being a witch is wonderful, but we are also still human." Their words and hugs were of little comfort.

She chose, then, to keep her witchiness close and never broach the topic again. It was hard for her. She craved friendship – true friendship; one without secrets. She wanted camaraderie, the kind she saw in her parents when they invited friends over for barbecue and sat around the fire, talking, using their fingers to toast marshmallows because it was faster than searching for sticks. Those evenings and weekends spent away in the woods were refreshing and rejuvenating. Being around other witches was like drinking a vat of caffeine – the high she felt for days and even weeks after made her skin glow. Her mind was sharp, her body was relaxed, her life was imbued with a blue glow that enveloped her every thought. It was being around other witches that made her so secure. After high school, she knew she had to find her own circle of friends; her own witches to be with. Her parents suggested Brookwick. The college was inexpensive, the town had enough witch history that even if no witches were around she would feel the same charge because their lives had lived on the soil. It sounded great to Deidre, so she did. It was in college that she had met first Elva, then Michael.

One month after moving to Brookwick, Deidre met her first witch, Elva. They were drawn to each other at the end of a Western Civilization class. Each class, Deidre could feel Elva watching her; she sent out a tendril of a spell to the small woman with sandy brown hair to see if she could get something, anything. She was wary of making friends and had used her magic several times as a way of communicating because she still longed for contact. When her spell crept to Elva, Deidre was startled to feel it whip back at her. It actually stung her arm. Confused, she avoided doing it again. Elva still stared at her though so Deidre simply decided that the girl was curious about her – or "simple," as they said in those days. But quick glances over her shoulder, ears straining to hear her if she spoke, seeking her out at the beginning of each class and noting the girl's clothing and posture – Deidre couldn't escape the urges. Elva was a strange name; and a girl with a strange name staring at her from the back of the room felt... strange. Deidre couldn't ignore it but could think of nothing else to do.

Finally, after one full month of classes, Elva stood at Deidre's desk and looked down at her. Deidre was piling her notebooks and pencils, ready to put them away. Elva's fingers rested on the edge of the desk, the sterling silver ring on her index finger glinting in the light from the window. On the ring was a sheep, a garnet as its body. Deidre could hear her breath, soft and hot from Elva's small parted lips.

Deidre had recognized that normal humans looked away when Deidre looked them in the eye; but when she looked up to see the subject of her greatest curiosity, Elva returned her pointed look. Deidre's body filled with a cool liquid that settled into her skin and exhaled from her pores. She felt it spread through her veins and begin to warm the muscles. Everything inside her awakened and she felt a kindness unlike any other for the young woman who stood before her. Deidre didn't think she had ever smiled so big in all her life; she stood up and hugged Elva, who didn't seem at all surprised, matching Deidre's strength in her return embrace.

They went for coffee, walked through the woods, studied together, used their magic to pick bouquets of flowers and sharpen their pencils. It was Elva who told her Brookwick's history; the history of its witches and about safe places to practice magic. And it was Elva who took her to her first meeting – a meeting just for witches.

It was a week before Elva told Deidre about the meetings.

"Don't be alarmed. A lot of people freak out a little when they find out how many witches are here."

Deidre couldn't imagine being freaked out by it; she had been dying to be around witches since she lifted her first Barbie doll with a twirl of her finger.

"My parents told me there were witches here."

"There are," Elva bit the crusty end off a chunk of baguette. She held her pinky finger over her lips as she chewed, the baguette in her fist dropping crumbs down her blue cotton shirt with large pink roses spattered all over it. Deidre thought she was going to say more, but Elva drank some wine after she finished her bread and suggested they go to a bookstore. Deidre didn't push it. She just wanted to go to the meeting.

Meeting Michael had been a breath of fresh air. When she stepped into the room with Elva, she felt him right away. It was wind in New England coming off a lake, dust from fallen leaves swirling around her neck as it kissed her lightly, her hand lost in a soft sea of marbles, her face covered in kisses from a butterfly. She searched the room, intent on locating its source, and when she found him his eyes were already pressing into her, reading her. All she saw was his face: days old shave around a square jaw, white teeth that spread out in a smile, a crooked front tooth, short curls tight against his head, dark skin everywhere. She noted the dip beneath his Adam's apple, a well to hold sweat, charms, his pulse. She knew he had felt it too. She knew it as soon as she found his eyes. They said *hello* to her, and *how are you*, and quieter but clear, over and over and over again: *I love you*.

They didn't do what normal people do. They didn't date, get to know each other, or even introduce themselves. They did what she imagined all witches do when they meet their soul mates. He stood and walked over to her, held out his hand, and they left the meeting to walk around the streets of Brookwick. There were no words; no interviewing questions; no attempts to impress or share a story. She truly felt she already knew everything. And what she knew was enough. She wanted Michael, almost as badly as he wanted her.

It was hours before she returned to her dorm room and days before she told Elva.

"That's how it happens with witches," Elva said, the smile on her face coming through her voice on the telephone. "I've never seen it, but everybody did that night!" Elva told her how Maggie was disappointed because she'd had her eye on Michael for over six months; Jocelyn clucked her tongue and giggled; little Sara, who would later host the meetings herself, was content to draw pictures in her notebook on the floor at her mother's feet and noticed nothing – except her mother, Cassandra, revealed at the next meeting that she had drawn an hour glass, constantly spinning – a witch sign for Forever.

In two short months, Deidre's life had changed completely from the witch girl with no friends to the college girl in a community of witches with a soul mate she could not imagine life without.

Her palms were beginning to hurt as she pressed them into her kitchen table. The smoke from the muffins still stung her nostrils. Tears fell down her face as she remembered. She had felt an empty space inside most of her body since she left him, but her pride was too wounded to go back. She had been in the same room with him since, the monthly meetings making it necessary. But he stopped attending them over ten years ago, letting the group know that he found them too painful. No other explanation was necessary. They all knew. She found them painful too, and the scorn she chided him with – in her own mind, because she could never do it aloud – did nothing to soothe her. She was relieved and pained simultaneously. Her heart ached to be so close to the man that filled her, but just one meeting a month gave her rejuvenation. It was his soul, she knew. She always felt a little more awake for a couple of days after being around him. When he left, her relief was for giving up the pain; but sadness took its place because nothing could refute what they were. The energy that enveloped them was proof of that.

Sarcasm, cynicism, bitchiness – these things saved her whenever she thought of him. Self-help buzzwords and exercises separated her from the reality of his presence. If she got lost in thoughts about their relationship, she hissed judgments and criticisms to ease the pain. "Arrogant!" she'd spat. "Melodramatic fool!" she'd whisper. "Cheater," she sobbed.

Their bond was lessening, yes, but these other exercises were all band-aids. That's all they were.

She wiped the tears from her eyes. "Relax," she repeated, and started again.

Michael waited by the front gate. His heart beat rapidly. He had parked several houses down so that Deidre would not become more anxious when she heard his car. Michael expected Deidre to be a bit of a mess tonight, and he wanted to help her as much as possible. Little did he expect that he would become a wreck as well. Walking up to her house, he noted the low fog in the darkness, the wooden fence he knew she always wanted surrounding whatever home she ended up with, a plethora of brightly colored wildflowers flourishing between the rails. Her mailbox, simple and wooden, standing guard like a doorbell at the gate's door, waist high. He could hear himself wanting to "perform" and crack a joke about her home being like a Thomas Kincaid painting, but he didn't really feel it. It was quite beautiful. A light post stood just inside the fence, its dim light a homing beacon in the fog. He saw a comforting light shining deep within the bay window.

And he felt her. He felt her sadness, her anger, her confusion… with a swell of excitement and anxiety, he felt her love. It was reluctant love, pulled in two directions. The hollow cave it left behind as it pulled out and in again made his chest ache. It hurt him that Deidre had to feel it. Can he really do this? Can he walk in there, talk about a young girl who may be dangerous to herself and others, dangerous to the world, and walk back out? Can he look at Deidre without melting at her feet?

He took his hat off his head, a pompous afterthought as he left his apartment at the college. He felt ridiculous with it now, trying to look young and wise in the ways of fashion, like he did when he met Deidre. He crumpled the brim in his fists, rolling it around. He heard her remembering and he felt all of it. The memories made his knees shake. He thought he was waiting by her gate so she would have time to recover, to pull herself together, to relax and *be ready*. "Don't be an ass," he mumbled. "You're waiting for *you* to be ready."

He took a deep breath. He ran his hand over his shaved cheeks and chin. He sent his voice to his shaking knees, chest, shoulders and arms. He stilled his cheeks and eyes, and looked down at his hands, knuckles growing pink in relaxation. Calm came from the house. Calm came from him.

He walked to the porch and reached the first step just as Deidre opened the door.

CHAPTER TWENTY-TWO

Deidre tried to feel ashamed. She knew she should feel ashamed but it was hard.

"Just stop trying, Dee," Michael whispered, using the name she heard only from him. He pressed his forehead gently into hers.

"But Addison…"

"We'll get to that. Just—"

"—one more minute," she finished.

Their clothes were strewn all over the Persian rug in Deidre's living room. They lay on the floor, beside the couch, its pillows under their heads. Michael's hands kept a constant connection with her skin. It smoothed the ridges on his fingertips as they remembered and recognized his soul mate. "Your skin is softer," he whispered.

"Wrinkles add that special something," she giggled. By the end of their relationship, his touching after lovemaking annoyed her. Now, in the glow of the candles that she foolishly lit before his arrival, she couldn't understand why. As the fingers glided, she felt light where they had touched, and when they left, soft and slow only to quickly land on a new spot, the newborn energy ached for the moment it took to reconnect with him again.

She felt an urge to talk, babble, ask questions, to turn her head into the warmth of his neck and breathe him in. The familiarity of his smell brought tears to her eyes. She remembered their apartment above the coffeehouse, the hut they rented on the outskirts of the college, the picnic in the park – her first and only foray into lovemaking in public. The tweed jackets he wore, all nearly identical, but each telling her something about his mood that day. The pillows they shared. The light on the kitchen table as it came through the windows that faced the square, splitting the glass of the salt shakers, sending flares of color over the floor. Her nostrils flared.

"Where have I been?" she asked quietly.

"*We*," he stressed, "have been lost."

His breath was warm on her head.

Yesterday's Deidre would have said, "So dramatic," teasing him for the honesty that they both deserved. But now she smiled, kissed his neck, and said, "Let's not get lost ever again."

Agreement came by way of a kiss.

The Sheriff's car and a deputy's car were parked in front of A Stitch Is Cast when Elva walked around the corner to go into the shop. Panicked, Elva rushed forward. "Jim!" she yelled, thinking immediately of Katrina and what Jim must have found out about the blonde girl who shared part of her days with the shop owner. "Jim!"

Sheriff Emory stepped out of the antique shop that had shared the building with Elva for almost ten years. Business there was always quiet. The items sold by the shop owner, Ed Morrison, were beautiful pieces found mostly in places like Vermont and the Adirondack Mountains. Several of her customers burst through her doors after visiting the shop to share their excitement over the purchase of a spinning wheel, some from as far back as 1850. Elva tried not to think too much about how much such an item must have cost her customers, but they ordered roving by the bushel-full and she was only too happy to accommodate. One customer used maple sap buckets as yarn holders, the yarn to be knit coursing its way through the long narrow spouts, sitting pretty on the floor by a couch or chair.

No customers were around this morning, however; the antique shop's windows were bright with the red and blue reflections of the deputy's emergency lights.

"It's okay, Aunt Elva. It's okay."

"Katrina?" her heart was pounding in her chest.

"No. Nothing like that." Jim stepped aside and Elva looked again at the antique shop. The lights were covering it before, but she could now see that the front window and door had large cracks in the glass, from top to bottom.

"Oh, my."

"Yes. The inside is much worse. Everything is a wreck."

"Is Ed okay?"

"Ed's fine. Just a little irritated. Well, that's putting it lightly." Jim closed his eyes and turned his head slightly toward Ed and Deputy Lynley, who was patiently listening to Ed rant and rave. By the comfortable position of the deputy's shoulders and back, plus a touch of magic, Elva could all but hear her thinking, "I've raised four kids and a husband while earning a degree, a badge and cooking dinner. I can handle you."

Elva watched the scene unfold for a few minutes longer before opening her shop. Quickly she stepped inside, relieved to shut the door against the increasingly angry voice of Ed Morrison. Deputy Lynley's quiet patience is probably what drove him to yell louder and louder as she continued to answer him back with soft spoken questions and assurances that she heard every word he said.

When Elva turned to face her shop, she was stunned. Yarn was everywhere. The shelves were virtually empty. The floor was covered in every fiber imaginable. Some yarn had simply fallen from the shelves but some was also mangled, tied up into each other, hopelessly lost. It filled the room like a ball pond for kids at children's amusement-slash-pizza joints. The smell of burning hair hung lightly in the air and she raised her eyes. Stepping in, she saw that most of her yarn stock hung suspended, floating in the air only inches from the ceiling. This was the source of the smell, indicating that it had been hanging in suspension for hours.

Quickly she dropped her bags and faced the wall she shared with Ed. With both hands raised, palms facing the wall, she relaxed her shoulders and elbows, then tilted her hands slowly forward, bending at the wrist. As she did, her index fingers bent forward as well, and she let out a long breath through pursed lips. Because she was listening closely, she heard one soft thud and several small thuds that sounded like foot falls. Running to the door, she stuck her head out. Keeping the door close to her body she craned her neck to see if the movement had caused any ruckus in the antique shop, but nothing looked amiss. Nobody came running out, screaming of ghosts or magic or "the witch next door cast a spell!" Ducking her head back in, crossing her fingers and hoping nobody noticed her, she picked up her bags, set them down on the counter top next to the register, and faced the enormous mess in front of her. She didn't want to know yet what the storage room looked like. "I'll get there when I get there," she muttered.

The bell at the door began to jingle as someone turned the knob to the shop's door. With a sharp jerk of her head, the door slammed shut and the bolt landed home. "We're closed today!" she yelled. She had no time for manners.

A woman's sharp complaint was muffled and Elva eyed the shadow as she walked away.

She sighed. "It is a damn good thing I came here for that dratted shawl!"

Rolling up her sleeves, she closed her eyes and took a deep breath. She would be tired after this, she knew, but the new old-fashioned way just wasn't going to cut it; she needed the *real* old-fashioned way. Muttering chants under her breath and flicking her arm out in various directions, she started to clean her shop.

Floating skeins of yarn was a good idea, so she first piled them all in the middle of the room, in the air, so she could then account for the other damage. Baskets, needles, notions and yarn samples were strewn about the floor. With a net of magic holding the yarn in the air, her fingers flicked and twirled until shawls, sweater samples and mittens were once again hung back in what she hoped were the correct spaces.

The shop normally had a floor plan with yarns categorized and shelved according to their weight – sock yarns with sock yarns, worsted weights with worsted weights – but she was already losing steam just holding the yarn in the air. She wasn't sure she would get it right, so decided to make a new floor plan. Customers might question it, and the more impatient ones would become angry and no doubt file complaints, but she had priorities. Stopping a knitwitch from blowing up the town seemed to be more important than shutting up the mouths of a few feisty customers.

After all the baskets were righted, the notions on their carts and hooks, and the yarns that were tangled wound back into beautiful new balls of yarny loveliness, she decided to break for iced tea. The yarn she held against the ceiling spread across the entire room and into the break room as well. If she wasn't so exhausted, irritated and in a *mood,* she would probably stop to reflect on how pretty it looked – like an impressionist painting with brighter colors and better inspiration. And while she normally praised her shop for its large yarn selection, she saw no end to cursing it. With the floor now cleared, she lowered it slowly; when the continent of fiber hovered a few inches above the floor, she let go. The thud was enormous; the notions and needles she had just put on the rack banged the carts and swung from their hooks.

Within seconds, Jim was banging on the door.

"I'm fine! Doing yoga in the shop is a bad idea, Jim!" She tried to laugh to make it sound convincing. "Whoo!"

"Open the door, Aunt Elva."

"Sorry! No can do!" She bit her lip. She could see the silhouette of Jim's body still standing by the door. "Downward dog makes me have to go to the bathroom and I can't wait!" This time, she didn't have to try to make the laugh sound real.

Jim didn't either. She saw his head shaking from side to side as he finally stepped away.

She sat at the table in the backroom with her head resting in her fist, elbow propped on the table. Sweat poured from her forehead. As she sipped the tea, she considered calling Deidre for help. Would Deidre panic? It was possible. With a start, she remembered Deidre was meeting with Michael last night. Elva smiled. "Can't interrupt that!"

But she had to admit that of the two women, Elva was more likely to panic and she was doing a fine job handling the situation by herself. Granted, she had no idea how far Addison's magic had spread, but still... a start was a start.

She gritted her teeth. Fear was playing a big role here. What if something worse had happened? Nobody really knew much about knitwitch spells, but if a mess was the only concern, it was easily fixable. It may remain a mystery to the regular people, but a lot of things were (she couldn't help but laugh out loud at this thought). But what if this were just the small end of the spell, the "tip of the knitting needle?" What if something worse had happened? She rushed to the front of the shop and looked out the window to see if anything else was out of place. The shops across the street all looked fine. The sidewalk was still there, cars were upright and in one piece.

But then she moaned with sadness. The park was a mess: the pots that were normally filled with petunias were all upside down on the park benches, the flowers crushed beneath them; and inexplicably, the gazebo looked *backwards*. She shimmied outside the door and stood against the shop windows. She looked carefully up and down the street. Fortunately, it was still early in the morning and a Sunday – serendipitous? Jim and his deputy were still busy trying to calm Ed, but Elva couldn't wait.

The strain of cleaning the shop, which still wasn't done, threatened to make her useless for the rest of the day but somebody was bound to notice the gazebo and raise a stink.

Oh, what I wouldn't give for some of Addison's scarf energy today! She briefly considered sneaking into Addison's apartment for the scarf but immediately decided against it. Not only would she feel awful and wrong to invade the poor girl's personal space without permission, but she had to admit that Deidre was right: they had no idea how Addison's magic worked. If the scarf gave her energy one day, it did not mean it would the next. Deidre said it was possible that the spell wasn't officially cast until the project was done, but she also said it obviously reached out before it was done too. *And what would it do to me now?* After the chaos of her shop and Ed's next door? No. That wouldn't help at all.

Closing her eyes, she pressed her back further into the shop window as she concentrated on the gazebo. Reaching into her memory, she pictured how the gazebo should look. Her left foot tapped frantically as she used her fingers and quiet chant, which took less energy than quiet concentration alone. Without opening her eyes, afraid it would make her realize exactly how tired she was, she then pictured the pots and flowers.

The whole thing took her about three minutes, but she felt like she had been lifting weights for at least three hours. Her body left a wet streak on the windows as she turned to go back into the shop.

"Darn all that is wooly!" she muttered. The door was locked. She left her bags and keys inside, too shocked by the mess she walked into to put keys around her neck like she usually did. Her shoulders slumped in frustration. Would this morning present her with anything easy? With a deep breath, she gripped the door handle and cast one more spell to unlock the door. Once inside, she slid to the floor and closed her eyes. Looking at the yarn was too tempting an invitation – she just might decide to sleep on it all.

As soon as she could see her floor, be assured Jim wouldn't ask her any questions about her own shop, and rested off what this amount of magic has already done to her, she'll tackle the hardest part of her day: Addison. But first...

Elva's snores filled the shop.

CHAPTER TWENTY-THREE

Clothes on and breakfast eaten, Michael and Deidre sat at the kitchen table to finally discuss Addison and what they could do to help her. The stress and anxiety Deidre had been feeling about the young girl had disappeared. She was not yet sure how to train Addison, nor how to break the news to her that she was a mythical figure — and worse, a mythical figure in that myth — but she was sure that she *could* do it. She knew it had to be done, and the pressure to do it herself, with Elva at her side to support her, had changed. She no longer felt like a leader upon whom every witch in Brookwick relied. Instead, she felt like one witch who knew something more than the others and she needed to gather materials to share it with them.

When she looked at Michael across the table, his close cropped hair disheveled, bits of his curl flipping in the opposite direction of the rest, she saw a partner who shared the knowledge and accepted that they must work on it together. In fact, she knew it wasn't "accepted," it simply *was*.

"I don't have much here. Just a few history books with spotty information. Do you have others we could look through?"

She knew he would want to look through what she already had and though she trusted her own research she welcomed his second set of eyes. Perhaps he would find something related that she did not know was related.

When he arrived at the house the previous night and she had calmed her nerves enough to stand, she opened the door and looked into Michael's eyes. Her body filled with him. Without saying hello, they were partners again. It was as if opening that door happened both literally and figuratively. When it rushed in, she wondered why she was ever so stubborn.

In two steps, he enveloped her in his arms. Before saying hello, they kissed through tears. *So few experience this*, she knew. The memories she had of *before* seemed tarnished, manipulated, played with.

Michael suggested they talk more about themselves after they attend to Addison. Deidre agreed.

"I saw you talking to her the first day she came to Brookwick," Deidre began.

Michael was nodding. "I didn't know it at the time, but I knew there was something about her." It was Deidre's turn to nod. She had felt the same thing.

Michael continued. "She's guarded. I don't know if it will be easy to convince her. Then again, showing her some magic... that usually does the trick, huh?" He looked at the napkin holder at the center of the oak table and made the napkins inside stand angle to angle in the air, then spin in circles, like a team of synchronized swimmers. Once they rested again in their proper place between them, his smile faltered. "So that part will be easy."

The sarcasm was not lost on Deidre.

"I've taught her to knit already. She's quite good." Deidre leaned back in her chair with her arms folded over her stomach, as if the butterflies were about to burst from her at any moment. "It's obvious she was born with the skill and had just never applied it. I just don't know what to do next."

She felt like she was pleading, but she knew he understood. "What if somebody else notices?" She tried to sound casual. She should know better than to try that with him.

Michael looked at her quizzically. "What do you mean, Dee? What's wrong?"

Deidre didn't want to meet his eyes. The blue silver of his eyes were just as she remembered them. She used to call them 'liquid mercury.' *Just as captivating; just as dangerous.*

"What do you know?" His voice was kind but insistent.

Deidre looked down at her hands, fiddling with the hem of her skirt. It suited her tastes, the dark florals against a pale background. She owned about five others just like it, as well as dresses, all in varying shades with different size prints, but all exactly the same.

She unfolded her legs and let them touch the floor, preparing her body for the flood of stress she knew would come. What a fool she's been, waiting so long to get help from Michael, for keeping all she knew to herself, for waiting and waiting and acting like she was sure when she knew absolutely nothing – except the most important thing. A fool!

"Dee?" Michael stood and walked around the table. He sat in a chair next to her. He could simply reach out and touch her and know everything – as her soul mate, it was fast, easy and complete. But it was also personal, an invasion they promised not to use with each other; there was nothing he could do about *feeling* her, however. That was beyond his control; beyond magic. The anxiety and fear that flew toward him, with embarrassment and shame circling the bottom, worried him. He put his hand on her shoulder and squeezed. "Tell me now."

Sheriff Emory held his lips firmly together.

"Laura said she checked her voicemail at six o'clock. She remembers because she was mad at Jimmy for being late. Again. But the time thinger on her phone told her the call was left at four-thirty-seven."

Deputy Lynley looked through her notes again, as if she hadn't already been over them with Sheriff Emory multiple times in the last hour. "The phone number was a blocked number, that's why she didn't listen to it, thinking it was maybe some telemarketer. But then Jimmy called her and she needed to hear the message." She sighed loudly. "She hardly even knows the girl, she said. Says she only saw her a few times walking around the square, but recognized her name because she always notices people who are new to Brookwick."

Deputy Lynley tossed her notebook on the Sheriff's desk. She was sick of repeating herself.

Sheriff Emory rubbed his hand over his forehead and leaned on his elbows, placing folded hands in front of his mouth. Laura's cell phone sat between them.

He sat up straight and cleared his throat. *Don't look defeated; don't look cowed; look like a Sheriff; a man with answers.*

"Do not tell my aunt about this," he warned. "She'll fall over with worry, and she's worried enough as it is."

Deputy Lynley hardly needed him to tell her – again.

He snatched the phone up and flipped it open. Pressing all the familiar keys, he put the phone to his ear and listened again, closing his eyes, hoping to hear more.

"Help me! Please, please help me!" She was whispering loudly. Her voice was thin; the words sounded almost hollow. "This is Katrina Isaac. I was taken from my apartment. Elva's--" There were blank spots, like the call was made from a place with spotty service. "I'm not sure how long ago it was anymore. Please help me! He took me--" silence, then "--shop! It's him! Katrina Isaac!" More blank spots. "--me. He doesn't know--"

All he heard were sobs and some shuffling with the phone before the call ended. He only hoped she ended it herself and was not caught by whomever had taken her.

Sheriff Emory played the message again and pressed the phone closer to his ear. He plugged his other ear with his finger and listened carefully.

Katrina Issac definitely did not run off, sick of Brookwick. She was in danger, and she needed help.

He wanted to kick himself, but knew it was too late and too useless to beat himself up. There had been no reason to believe that Aunt Elva was right, he convinced himself. But as he heard the girl's voice, the desperation and fatigue that it contained, the hoarseness – from crying? Lack of water? – his confidence wavered. He had to find her. And he would not tell Elva she was right. Not yet.

Elva knocked before she finally unlocked the apartment door. Her key did not work on either door, so she used her magic to get it open, trying to remember to get the locks checked as she did so. Holding the door handle in her hand, she let her fingers wave through the mechanism until it clicked, and then she turned the knob.

Addison was curled up soundly on the couch with Derwin lying beside her. Elva was not proud of herself for checking in on her like this, but after the disaster she found in the store and the information Deidre gave her last night – not to mention the women who have come and gone (Katrina weighing most on her mind) – Elva felt better being impolite and potentially offensive than risking the alternative. She quickly stepped back into the hallway and closed the door, locking it again as she did so.

At the back landing, she met the postal service woman who was filling out a slip for a package. "Oh, Elva! How rare to find you here! I was just writing a note to your new tenant--" she looked down at the package tucked in her arm, "—Addison Thompson. I was going to put this in your shop until she could get it. Should I carry it over for you? Or…?"

Elva took the package and told Jane to leave her note. She'd be happy to hold it for Addison. The package was heavy, and Elva almost regretted taking it, but then felt it was impolite to hand it back. She had already been impolite enough today. The women walked away, chatting about their husbands and poor Ed Morrison, the owner of the antique shop. His insurance wouldn't cover the windows and door.

CHAPTER TWENTY-FOUR

Sara enjoyed feeling the sun on her face as she lifted it up with eyes closed. It was perfect outside. The sun was shining with enough clouds in the sky to lessen the blow. A steady breeze kept the air cool around her skin before it lifted the leaves on the trees in the nearby square. Brookwick always did have beautiful weather. Sara believed it was due entirely to the community of witches, both present and past. Their magic, uplifting and spiritual, allowed joy to remain in the earth. In return, the relaxed earth made life comfortable for Brookwick's residents. Gardens always thrived, lawns were always green. Warm days were comfortably so, same as winter. While it was never described as mild, it truly was; residents just preferred to note the beauty that lay in it. Hot enough for a swim in the lake; cold enough for a walk around the square with mittens, scarves and hats; beautiful enough not to stay inside, no matter which one was preferred.

Sara and Tom used to walk around the square, sit in the gazebo – he with his newspaper and she with her knitting. They would pack up, pick up iced teas, walk the five miles to the college. Sometimes they would talk, other times they would simply enjoy the sound of the other's shoes as they scuffed gravel on the side of the road. If she saw a particularly stunning flower, she would point it out; Tom would nod in agreement. If he saw a bird of particular interest, he would point, speak its name, and she would nod, appreciating his knowledge and the sharing of it.

Her heart shuddered. There would be no more walks for her and Tom. The walks were over. The last walk was not quiet; they talked for all five miles to the college, the three miles to walk around its grounds, the five miles back and then the fifty more as they lay in bed beside each other, not touching, faces damp and bodies exhausted in grief. She reached for his hand just as the sun was coming up, and as if he too hadn't slept at all, he squeezed it tightly, brought it to his lips, and left his last kiss.

Her hand still lay on her chest, hours later, after the doors had closed, the car had started its engine, the tires ground the gravel, and she could no longer hear him – though she tried. She did not move her hand, afraid his kiss would be lost in the air. *This is what it feels like to be empty*, she thought. Exactly as it is called. A box made of skin held up by the bones placed inside it – but nothing more. Her heart had expanded beyond her breast and now pushed on her skin, longing to explode out in the air around her – run away from the ache that slowly twisted it, from one small end up to the other. Like a tube of toothpaste.

The shadows on her ceiling reminded her the day was still moving without her. Tom was still driving without her. Tom was still breathing and thinking and *being*... without her. She forced herself to get out of bed. She was surprised to realize she still had her shoes on. "That's good," she thought. "It's good to notice it. That's something..."

Without stopping for water, the bathroom, or her wallet, she left the house and walked.

She walked to the square and sat in the gazebo. For several moments, she wondered what she was doing there and then decided to not think about it, but go. At the coffeehouse, she was embarrassed that she did not have money to pay for her iced tea. Brian assured her it was okay and she could pay the next time, and gave her the drink anyway. Her weak smile felt mean and insulting. *I should be nicer,* she thought. *I should be more pleasant, say thank you again, smile bigger, show him appreciation.*

Instead, she took the drink from his hand, noted the wet and how it trickled between the folds of skin on her palm. "Good," she thought. "It's good to notice the wet." And she left.

Now she sat at a park bench across from the coffeehouse, deciding she could walk no more, and closed her eyes to feel the sun, hoping it would dry her out.

It was their last talk. Their last walk. Her last attempt to remind him that they loved each other.

Sometimes she hated being a witch; not because that is why he said he was leaving her, but because she knew, despite her tears and begging and heaving chest, that his *feelings* were true – he no longer loved her. He cared for her, he wished her the best, but he wanted something else. Even their walks had become boring. He no longer cared for their conversation. He felt for her the way one would a roommate. A passing curiosity in their day and opinions, but lacking investment, belief, *love*. It did not matter to him if her day was good or bad; to hear about it was simply courteous and polite. He began to feel that he had no responsibility for her feelings and if she had a bad day, she would sort it out some how. It had nothing to do with *him*. That is not how it was between them. They were, at one time, part of each other. His feelings were hers, though she could never own them; to feel them, before the witch part of her felt them, was to love him. And vice-versa, she thought.

Sara knew she did not even like this new Tom, so why was she so heartbroken to lose him? Because there was no hope of ever having *her* Tom. He was gone.... evaporated.

"Would you like me to get you more ice?"

Sara opened her eyes. Everything was washed in blue. Brian stood over her, smiling, though it took Sara several moments to focus on him. Her iced tea had become warm though she had barely taken a sip. He took the cup from her hands.

Sara flinched.

Yearning. Anger. Sadness. Excitement. Secrets. Desire.

"I'll be right back."

She could feel vomit crawl up her esophagus. Sara bent over and put her head between her knees and swallowed.

"Don't pass out, don't pass out, *don'tpassout...*" she whispered, her words loud in her ears after so long in silence. The world tilted between her legs and she could not feel if she was still upside down or lying on her side.

"Hey, are you okay? Do you need help?"

Sara felt a hand on her back. It poured with concern, kindness, surety. The strength of it pulled on Sara's kneecaps. *A witch.* She let it pour through her for a moment, relishing its freshness. *A new witch; a* strong *witch.*

As she sat up, she took a deep breath in. The hand left her.

"Oh! No! Please don't move your hand!" The hand was back, rubbing up and down. Sara kept her eyes closed as she felt the warmth. It was glory. It was a *spine*, sitting her up. The grief that stretched her skin flew from it; her heart returned to her breast; her breath returned to her chest; her rage, hurt, sadness sunk from her forehead and spread to her limbs until it seeped from her fingertips and toes. Her sigh of relief made her shudder. She inhaled; she smelled the strong florals of the petunias in the pot beside her. Slowly, she let her breath out and raised her head, once again, toward the sun.

"Oh," she whispered. Joy. She felt it tickle her cheeks and tongue. Real joy! "Oh, thank you."

"You helped me once. It's the least I could do."

Sara opened her eyes and looked at the young girl she had become so curious about. "Ah! Addison!"

Addison was excited to see the woman she almost hit with her car the first day she arrived in Brookwick. She was handing a drink to Brian, and Addison watched the color in the woman's face completely disappear when he turned away back to the coffeehouse. Convinced the woman was about to pass out and possibly fall from her seat, Addison ran over to her. She was relieved to find her breathing, but was still concerned.

"Do you feel better?" Addison was starting to feel weird rubbing the woman's back. She was happy to do it if it was helping, but it also felt a bit ... personal.

The woman nodded then held out her hand. Her eyes were just as striking as Addison remembered, despite having just gone through ... whatever it was she went through.

Addison was relieved to take the woman's hand. Hoping the movement wouldn't be too noticeable, she shook with one hand while removing the other from her back.

"I'm Sara Giles, a friend of Deidre's."

Addison introduced herself. She was relieved to hear that Sara knew Deidre; not that Sara gave her any heebie-jeebies by knowing her name, it just eased her curiosity so she didn't have to ask.

Nervously, Addison asked, "Do you remember me?"

"Oh, yes! You were outside the shop." She laughed. "Funny we meet this way, isn't it?"

Addison laughed, relieved that Sara didn't bring up the car incident first.

"I don't know what was wrong with me that day," she shook her head, looking embarrassed.

Sara nodded her head and bit the corner of her lip. "We all just have those days, I guess." She looked over at the shop.

"I work there now," Addison said, "At the shop. Elva hired me. It's really fun. And Deidre taught me to knit."

Her smile was big. She could feel how big it was. Sara smiled in return, but something about it was beginning to make Addison feel unwelcome.

"Well, I guess I'll go--"

"Here you are!"

Brian had returned with a fresh iced tea for Sara, who took it with both hands. "Thank you so much, Brian. That was really thoughtful of you." She put the drink on the bench between she and Addison. "I will stop by first thing tomorrow to pay you for this. I swear! You're so kind."

Brian smiled. "Hi, Addison!"

"Hey, Brian, how are you?"

"Great! Great!"

Sara sipped from her tea.

"I was actually on my way over for a hot chocolate."

"Oh yeah? Great! I'll go get it for you!"

Before Addison could tell him to stop, that she'd be happy to go over with him, he was running across the street back into the shop.

"Guess he really likes his job, huh?" Addison turned to Sara. Her bright, royal blue eyes were staring hard at Addison.

"Be careful, honey," Sara whispered. Her smile was gone and Addison felt a chill run up her spine. "You be careful."

Before Addison could respond, Sara stood up and walked quickly away. In fact, Addison wasn't sure walking was the right word. She practically *flew*.

CHAPTER TWENTY-FIVE

Brian was just putting whipped cream on her hot chocolate when Addison walked into the coffeehouse.

"Oh, hey!" As he smiled at her, his aim was redirected and whipped cream spattered across the counter. Addison pointed.

"Oh shit," he said. Calmly, Addison thought. As he cleaned up the mess, Addison reached over the small barrier of the counter and grabbed her drink. She also helped herself to a spoon and walked to a table. No need standing there watching him clean up a mess, feeling as useful as a wet tissue.

Addison wondered about Sara's warning. Is that what it was? A warning? And if so, a warning against what? People said 'be careful' all the time. It used to drive her foster father mad when her foster mother told him to be safe on the road. He exhausted his fair share of "Always am!" If Sara wanted Addison to be careful, she could have at least given Addison some sort of clue as to what she should be careful of. Maybe she just found the fact that they both had 'episodes' more than coincidental and wanted to be sure Addison wouldn't pass out while crossing the street... or something.

"So how have things been today?" Her voice sounded a little too loud in the quiet coffeehouse. No wonder why Brian was walking drinks out to Sara and Addison. He probably got bored there; how many table tops could one person clean? Though Addison would use the time to read books, or now that she knew how, knit.

163

"Quiet." Brian came from around the counter and asked if he could sit at her table. Addison nodded. "It can get pretty boring in here sometimes. Thankfully, the owner never comes in or else he'd fire me just for looking as bored as I am." He pulled a book out of his pocket and waved it around before Addison could see the title. It was small, though, perfect for hiding. He shoved it in his back pocket.

Addison smiled. She remembered thinking she'd be bored at the shop, but it turns out that wasn't the case at all. Every day this week, she had been worked to the bone. Her back ached from all the bending over and stretching to put things away – proving that driving hours a day did nothing for her back or her backside. Customers had questions she couldn't answer, but she learned a smile went a long way. By the third day, she had memorized Elva's phone number for the days Elva ran errands or went home for lunch, as well as Nick's, who has proven to be quite knowledgeable about looking up yarny information. She thought it was cute how he defended his lack of knowledge and admitted to using the internet for most of the information. For the bazillionth time that week, Addison thanked her lucky stars she got a job and a place to live. She even thanked the cramp in her butt.

"So are you the manager or something?"

Brian nodded. "Yeah. But really I do everything, even write the checks for the rent. The owner is always traveling somewhere. Apparently, he owns like fifteen coffee places or something." He looked around at the dark, empty tables, his head still nodding up and down, pursing his lips. When he looked back at Addison, she smiled.

"That sounds cool," she said.

"So have you seen the college yet?"

164

Addison took a sip of her hot chocolate, which was still too hot to be sipping. She tried to hide the pain. *There goes tasting the drink for the next hour.*

"No! But I am really curious. Someone told me before that there's a lake around here too?"

"Oh, yeah. It's called Broom Lake. I used to go there a lot when I was a kid. We all would go swimming in it. You know, before we minded the algae on our feet and stuff," he laughed. "That's funny. I used to actually love that stuff. I'd pull it up and use it on my sand castles, but now I think it's kind of gross."

Addison laughed. She could relate. Clean water was always way better.

"Now we just go canoeing on it. It's small enough that there aren't many waves or anything, and you feel surrounded by mountains. The campus is really pretty too, so you feel a bit old-world."

"Old world?"

"Right! You haven't seen the campus. It looks sort of medieval like. You really should see it."

"I don't even know how to get there."

Brian laughed. "There's this new thing going on around here. It's called Asking for Directions. It's sort of high-tech though."

Addison rolled her eyes. "Ha. Ha."

A twinkle shone in Brian's brown eyes. He was kind of cute. Addison didn't know why those kids were picking on him earlier in the week. Remembering it made her feel bad all over again. And then she remembered the date she had arranged.

"I totally forgot! Hey!"

Brian raised his eyebrows. "Forgot you could ask someone for directions?"

"No, silly. That you said you'd go with me to the college. Let's plan it! I need a tour guide. You know where it is. Why don't we do that?"

Brian smiled. He had broad white teeth and Addison hadn't noticed before how nicely pink his lips were. *Uh oh*, she thought. *Isn't finding one guy hot one-hot-guy too many? Stop now!*

"Well, if you're really up for it, I'd love to show you around. The college, that is."

Addison nodded and took another searing sip of her hot chocolate. "Let's do it. When are you free?"

"Well," Brian looked down at the wide watch on his wrist. "I close up in a half hour and all the cleaning stuff is done. I just have to count out the register and then I could leave. So that'd be at about--" he tilted his head side to side as he continued looking at the watch. "--about 6:15? Sound good to you?"

Addison smiled. She hoped it hid what she was really thinking. Finding Brian cute immediately before he offered himself up for something a little close to a date made her suddenly nervous. But she did have to make friends; and she did want to see the college campus; and she did think Brian was a nice guy. So why shouldn't she? *I am Addison; hear me roar.*

When Elva returned to the store with the package, Deidre and Michael were waiting inside in the back room. Elva grinned from ear to ear when she saw them standing together, their faces both ruddy with freshness.

"This is so wonderful!" she called out to them. She dropped off Addison's package at the counter with the register and rushed over to them. In one giant motion, she squeezed them both, unable to contain her squeals. "Oh! Oh!"

Michael and Deidre both gasped and grinned as Elva squeezed them, her hair tickling their faces and her shaking laugh vibrating against them. "Okay, okay!" laughed Michael. "Okay. Yes."

"Elva," Deidre said, the laugh coming out of her voice. "We have to talk."

Elva stopped immediately. She stood back and looked at her two friends. How she has missed Michael and his sense of humor! Their faces now showed nothing of humor, however, and Elva was not looking forward to their news. Then she remembered the shop next door and the mess she walked into that morning as well.

"Well I have news," she said, determined to stave off their obviously ruinous information. "Addison is definitely a knitwitch." She recounted the events of the morning, going into great detail about the balls of yarn swimming all over the floor of her shop. They rolled their eyes as she insisted on naming the fiber content of several brands, exclaiming about the monetary value and what would have happened if she didn't open the shop that morning.

Michael and Deidre were both nodding.

"Addison is in trouble," Deidre said.

"She hardly can be held accountable, Deidre—"

"No," Michael interjected. "She is in real trouble. Dee has had signs."

Silence filled the space that had only moments before been filled with bubbling babbling from Elva. A chill coursed down Elva's spine. She started shaking her head.

They sat at the table as Deidre filled Elva in on the feelings she had been having since Addison arrived. Elva was horrified. Did she put Addison in danger? How could this happen? "We need you to keep an eye on her, Elva."

"Of course!" she exclaimed. "Of course I will!"

It was suggested that Nick be invited to work at the shop as well, so Elva could keep up appearances and still tend to the shop. Deidre assured her that should she feel the presence of danger, she will let Elva know immediately. It was agreed that Addison would not leave the shop without one of them, or Nick, accompanying her. Nick did not need to know anything. "He likes the girl," Elva gasped, "that's obvious." It was agreed Addison would be safe in her apartment; besides, there was no real way to suggest someone move in with her without making Addison suspicious. Elva kept trying to come up with new ways, including a spell to make Addison believe Elva's own house had caught fire, but there was no way to cover the fact that she had a husband who would accompany her (and a husband who was not a witch, and also not much into lying), and there was also no way to be sure the spell would last.

"Okay." Elva's nerves were getting the best of her today. She was still exhausted by the cleaning and huge amount of magic she had used, but the added excitement Michael and Deidre brought made her feel simply drunk with exhaustion. "So there's only one thing left to do."

Deidre and Michael looked at her with confused expressions, Deidre's eyes squinted, worried about her friend's ideas.

"Well isn't it obvious," Elva declared. "We have to tell Addison she's a knitwitch."

"Oh, no," Michael insisted, nearly rising from his seat. "That's the last thing we should do right now."

Addison decided not to change her clothes. She wasn't proud of the old jeans that threatened to split at the knee with one more fast-walk, or the holes she found in the thin cotton of her long-sleeved black tee-shirt, but changing her clothes would only draw on her excitement. The last thing she wanted was for Brian to see that she was excited. And what about Nick? Addison's heartbeat drowned out the sounds of traffic as she thought about Nick and what he would think of her plans for the evening. Something like guilt sat just below her excitement. But guilt over what? Nick was just her friend, and it isn't like they've been friends for a long time. She's only been in Brookwick for a week! Still, she has talked to Nick everyday since she first moved here. He has helped her at the shop, laughed at her jokes, drank tea, eaten kale and whistled at her knitting. She couldn't help being attracted to him. Throw in good looks and a nice easy fashion sense, how could she resist?

Brian was just going to be showing her around the college. That was it. And though she's run into Brian a few times at the coffee shop, she hasn't spoken to him nearly as much as Nick. She barely knows Brian. It's just a way to make more friends. Is it her fault that Brian works at the coffee shop rather than a *Brianna*? No. But the health food store, the yarn shop and the coffee shop are the only places she goes to each day – so her friend options were limited.

Satisfied with this explanation and free pass from guilt, Addison looked in the mirror, wondering if there were any improvements she could make that wouldn't be obvious to Brian. Her hair was still in a pony tail; it would probably stand out too much if she put it down and brushed it out. Besides, she would only end up putting it back up. She moved to her face. Her eyes could probably use some mascara and her lips could probably use some gloss, but she was going to have to let that go; nothing said "date" like makeup.

There was still an hour to go before she went out with Brian. Deciding not to overthink it, Addison made some food and grabbed a coffee. Derwin waited for her on the couch, resting beside her knitting. The knit session the previous night had not gone all that well. She was so angry in her thoughts, her dreams coming back to haunt her. *"Stitch in one makes it two, blessed be this spell's for you."* The image of her mother swam before her eyes as she sat next to the yarn. What Addison wouldn't give to see her mother again. Did she really look like that? Most times, dreams left people in vague, alien-like shape, their faces and clothes blurry. But her mother's face was clear, succinct, detailed. Addison felt, without a doubt, that it was her mother, but she couldn't help forcing herself to doubt it as well. Why? Was she afraid she was wrong? And does it matter? She's never known her mother. She's never seen a picture or heard a description, and she never thought that someday she may — so what harm could it do to believe she had finally seen her? Was it because it was in a dream? Would people find her crazy? Would she be afraid of being crazy? And who would she tell? Nobody. Addison would tell nobody of her strange dreams and the woman who lived in them, her eyes full of sorrow and love, kindness and fear.

The fear stopped Addison. Food in her mouth, she had to force herself to swallow. Her mother was scared. Her *dream* mother was scared. It made Addison scared as well. What happened? What did her mother know was going to happen? Because that is how it felt. She felt sure that her mother knew something was going to happen and it would break her heart, and she knew her mother felt forced.

"I have something for you."

The man's voice that whispered in Addison's ear was deep and quiet. Addison jumped off the couch just as Derwin *meowed*. Nobody was behind her. It was impossible for anybody to be behind her on the couch, which was against the wall. And Addison knew nobody was in the attic of the shop next door, which lay on the other side. Derwin stood on the coffee table, his back arched and his lips pulled back, teeth bared. A long hiss came from him. Addison didn't dare touch Derwin, or try to soothe him with her voice. She had never seen him so *animal.* It scared her more.

Derwin heard the voice too.

Addison watched the spot on the couch. Her eyes scanned the wall. Her skin felt cold as she waited, not knowing what she was waiting for. She focused so hard, the wall started to move and she could see shapes she knew weren't there. Lamps and waving fabric; smoke, the paint swirling before her like the tendrils from a fire. She closed her eyes slowly, afraid something would happen, but she had to shake her head free of the strangeness. When she opened them, the walls were still.

Derwin's hiss soon got quiet. He sat back on his haunches, but his eyes never left the wall. After waiting a few more minutes, Addison sat down on the chair beside the coffee table and faced the wall. Her dinner still sat on the coffee table next to Derwin. Addison realized she was holding her breath. When she let it out slowly, Derwin finally looked around the room. He stood and made a tight circle, his eyes on the walls and down the hallway. He looked into the kitchen area and then again at the couch. Just as Addison was about to reach out and pet him, he looked at her. Addison held her hand out while Derwin looked directly into her eyes. It was different. It wasn't just a cat looking at her. Addison got goosebumps on her arm. She was about to ask Derwin a question when he hopped over to the couch. He walked back and forth, then settled beside her yarn once again, as if nothing had happened.

The question still in her throat, Addison said, "You heard that too, Derwin?" but the words sounded strange, as if they didn't belong. As soon as she said them, she wondered why she said them.

Addison grabbed her plate of food and dug in. Derwin purred on the couch next to her yarn, his head lying on the soft ball of cream yarn, looking blissful, as cats usually do. As she sat and chewed, she looked at the yarn. Knitting was soothing and comforting. And she had to be calm and relaxed when she knit, both Deidre and Michael said it was important.

Addison took the last bite of her dinner and moved over next to Derwin. Picking up her yarn, she started to knit more on the swatch that had turned more scarf-like. As she knit, stitch after beautiful stitch, she couldn't shake the feeling that she was forgetting something.

Brian waited outside the coffee shop, trying not to pace back and forth. He did that the last ten minutes and it struck him he would look too impatient, too wanting, too ready for a date with the new girl in town. He wanted to look bored, like he didn't care. The last thing he was going to let happen was his emotions to get in a ball because some girl stood him up.

"It's not a date," he muttered to himself for the hundredth time. "It's just a tour; for a tourist." He tried to laugh at himself, but he couldn't. He looked up at the window he knew was Addison's, and waited for the light to turn out, a sign she was leaving and on her way. But after another ten minutes, it was still on. Should he go to her place? No. She didn't tell him where she lived, and it would be way too creepy if he admitted he knew. She wouldn't like that.

He pulled his book from his back pocket and tried to relax. Maybe she thought he said seven.

Addison's scarf had reached three feet. It still wasn't long enough to fit around her neck and she was getting impatient, but she was proud all the same. Three feet of stitch after stitch, creating a fluffy, creamy scarf all her own. She held it up and admired it. She went into the bathroom and put the scarf up to her neck and peered in the mirror. Her hair was down. She put the scarf down on the top of the toilet and reached for an elastic band and brush. After she had a ponytail and yanked it tight, she gasped. Looking at herself in the mirror, she yelled, "Oh, shit!"

It was dark outside the coffee shop and nobody was there. "What did I expect?"

Addison looked up and down the street, as if anybody would be fool enough to wait three hours on an airhead. Addison bit her lip and shoved her hands in her pockets. "What a jerk," she said, kicking her foot at a stray napkin that flew from across the street. Lifting her shoulders high, she let them slump – a sigh fit for a hurricane escaping her lips.

"How in the world could I forget? How in the *freakin'* world?"

CHAPTER TWENTY-SIX

Unfortunately, Michael could offer no insight into how to train a knitwitch, but he did relate the story of meeting two. It was such a rare thing to meet one that meeting two made him an authority, information about training aside.

"I had just spent a confusing week in Berlin, navigating my way around witches I never knew existed." Elva raised her eyebrows but Deidre gave her a glowering look. Elva didn't need the look, but she understood that her reactions could slow down Michael's storytelling, and it was important they learned what they could fast. "I decided to borrow a bike, and just started riding it, hoping for the best. Several nights were spent in the ditches, sleeping. I was quite warm and comfortable, I assure you," he added softly, looking at Deidre.

Michael spent a month meeting nobody of the witch-y sort. He thought he would never meet another witch again. But then he traveled down to the historic town of Erfurt, known to witches as Hexehaus. It was where Martin Luther was educated, and it was home to the first printing presses, which still stood. Littered with bath houses, it was a crossroads for all European travelers, the intersection of the two "Main Streets" of Europe, one carving a trail north and south, the other crossing from west to east. Twelve-hundred years ago, the town was rich with life. Marketers and printers, artists and authors, vagabonds and tax men, rich sultans and princes, they all collected in Erfurt. Some traveled with tea while others traveled with sand and harems. Murder and darkness was all around them, but it was smothered by religious history and historic architecture, especially churches. By the time Michael had made it there, of course, the bath houses were closed and the printing press was merely a museum.

The road was not just a cross roads for trade, but it was a national convention before such things existed. Witches who were lucky enough to survive exile and persecution from their home towns traveled the road in search of a new community, one that would provide acceptance and shelter. That town became Hexehaus. For centuries, surrounding towns were kept in the dark, and when religion found its way to Erfurt, the witch community attempted to live in an "open concealment" fashion, working together to cast a spell over the town that provided safety and anonymity. The more populated the town became, however, the harder it was to not only keep the powerful spell cast, but to also prevent witches from being witches. While living amongst the non-magical, it was instinctual to hide their powers; but now surrounded by a large community of witches, they soon let down their guard, using spells to hang laundry, turn on lights, carry home heavy baskets. Non-magical citizens started to notice.

Witches were far more powerful then than they are now, so newcomers' attempts to disenfranchise the natives was a tricky business. After a day of harassing witches, some woke to find they had only their robes around them and nothing else, their homes disappearing in the night. Some were blinded and forgot they lived in Erfurt, only to wander out of the town and never return. And some died, for no matter how well-respected and well-behaved a civilization wishes to be, being forced to hide breeds anger and violence. The witches were being invaded.

The diocese moved in and with it came thousands who believed more in an unseen magic than that which existed under their noses. The witches could not keep up. Their tricks and spells were too few and the new settlers too many. With each new generation of witches, their powers were becoming weaker. The sphere of anonymity and safety they had cast over the city was weakening. A new Erfurt was built.

In shifts, witches gathered to protect their intentions. At least fifty witches met in the fields far outside of Erfurt and concentrated their skill to create an illusion. While salesmen, tradesmen, travelers, and settlers went about their daily shopping, whipping, persecuting and disgusting lives, the witches were building a new city beneath their feet. The power of the witch was dying; their strength was weakening with each new birth, and the strength it took to conceal their building now would not last for the future. Underground was best. Underground, they would not have to rely solely on magical means for safety; they could rely on stupidity and arrogance instead. It was always easier to rely on that. "While they walk above, with angels and gods, we walk below – the earth moving them where we need them."

Taverns were carved into the rock beneath the Erfurt that had become a site for tourists, and home to those Germans who stole the history of a place. Shops, houses, a village, roadways – they all existed underneath. Lamps were filled with light and sunshine was cast on the roof of the underground town, shining as brightly as that which existed above. In Erfurt Michael felt there were no witches. But they were there, beneath the city, where the original Hexehaus still thrived.

"I didn't believe the history when it was told me by a simple witch in a pub," said Michael. He sipped his water and sighed, wiping the back of his hand across his mouth. He stared down into the clear liquid. Deidre could smell guilt coming from his skin. "I doubted the boy. He looked so out of it; so not-there; goofy."

Michael looked at Deidre and Elva; they both could see the shame Michael felt – making judgments and realizing the error of your judgment was not an easy thing to accept at any age.

"By the end of my year at Hexehaus, that poor boy was dead. He told me about the underground city and I cursed him for telling tall tales about magical creatures, completely denying him his own birthright, even as I sat with a pocketbook full of spells, even as I searched for someone like me in a place full of strangers. Even—" He sighed. Elva reached out her hand and touched the back of Michael's.

"Just some random bullies," he continued. "Clobbered him with a rock; called him a simpleton. Had they done it that night, I probably would have said 'good riddance,' my opinion of him was so low."

"What made you think he was so simple? So wrong?" Deidre tried to hide her surprise. She was always taken aback by Michael's perfect charm. It irritated her despite the connection they could not deny. He was too... perfect. It itched under her skin and made it crawl with suspicion. It was a flaw she could not look past, and she often laughed at the thought, wondering if she was being just too picky. She was sure it would come out. And it did. His eye wandered despite the tether on his heart. She would take strolls with him around the college campus and watch as the soft skin under his jaw turned red whenever he saw a young coed walk by with short skirts or red hair. Deidre was even disgusted by his stereotypical attractions and longed for something a little different. If her true love was going to be an ogler, at least ogle at something *different*. She couldn't take much of it, and he denied his long glances and tell-tale blush even existed. She could do nothing about that.

"What was it?" He repeated the question, stalling with his answer. He lifted his shoulders and let them fall again with another sigh. "Who knows. Honestly, I don't know. Maybe I was arrogant. Maybe I just feel bad that the guy died and the stories he told me were true and I didn't believe him. Maybe he was a simpleton. Maybe I just—"

He downed the rest of his water as if he wished it were scotch. Elva stood up and refilled it at the sink.

"Maybe," Elva said, "it's exactly what he wanted you to think."

Michael looked at her for a long moment. "You mean a spell?"

She lifted her shoulders as if to say "You tell me."

"I'm pretty good at picking up on spells, Elva."

"Were you as good at it then as you are now? How long ago was this?"

He blew air out from between his lips and sat back, "It was thirty years ago. I was new, but I was still pretty good at detecting spells – even if I couldn't always cast them."

Elva rolled her eyes. "Okay, Houdini. But you were also in a strange place, seeing new things, wandering without a witch around for how long? Not to mention still *a new witch.*"

Michael's eyes tightened. "Exactly. You just said it. I had been without witches around me for at least a year. So I certainly would have picked up on a spell if it was being cast on me. Any new witch would, I don't care who you ask."

Deidre thought of the spell she cast to Addison through the yarn shop window the first day Addison came to Brookwick. Addison *did* feel it; she was sure of it. She saw the girl lean against the glass only seconds after that small tendril of a spell grazed her. Yet it was unlikely she was suspicious of it enough to questions its origin.

Elva shook her head at Michael. "You're forgetting something."

Michael looked at Deidre. He looked agitated, his eyes raised. Elva did always get under Michael's skin. Her blabbering joyfulness, he said, sometimes made his toes itch. Deidre thinks Elva did that on purpose. Toe-itching was the first spell Elva learned when she was five-years-old.

Deidre smiled at him. "His stories were true," she said. "The boy in the pub. The 'simpleton.' And from the moment you entered Erfurt, a spell was cast on you, just like it was on every person who went to Erfurt."

"Concealing the city underneath," added Elva.

"But they had finished construction by then," Michael said.

"Doesn't mean they didn't still need spells to hide it. Entry ways? Coming and going? Sink holes, noise? With vehicles now, and cable television and underground wiring and that interweb thing? And I'm willing to bet it was a careful spell. They had been doing it for centuries, you said, right? It was probably perfected. They didn't need new witches coming in, right?" Elva put the glass of water down in front of Michael. "New witches would only make it more difficult to do. It's more witches to protect so takes more energy and power from other things."

"Well, shit," he said. He lifted the glass. Again, he looked at the glass as if it would be the one to tip him over the edge, and remembering it was only water took a small sip. "So you think he could have cast a spell to make him look like someone who couldn't be believed because he really just wanted to tell secrets – but not really risk the consequences if somebody found out."

It wasn't a question, but Elva nodded and said yes anyway. Deidre knew she just loved accepting credit for the solution – especially credit given by Michael, no matter how indirect.

"Did the city still exist in all that new shiny glory? Did you see it?"

Michael nodded. "Oh, yes. It wasn't really as grand as he had described, I have to admit. But now I'm wondering if that wasn't part of some spell as well. Maybe the longer you stay and commit to the town, maybe it's a cast that diminishes, welcomes you slowly?"

"Those are the best spells," Deidre whispered. They all nodded.

"Very clever," said Michael. He looked at Elva. "Very clever."

"So what was it like?" Elva leaned forward, ready to learn more.

Small cobblestone walkways still existed in the cool rock, winding their way under avenues of shopping. Some niches in the wall sold wares for the wary witch: talismans of protection, spell bags full of historic spells that probably did not work anymore, cast into stones long before Michael was born. Despite the high cost, Michael admitted he found it too intriguing to pass up. The underground city, Michael was told by those he met, had welcomed few non-witches. Martin Luther is said to have traveled through them, speaking to the other travelers – the magical people – who shied from the peering eyes and curious questions of economy-makers and travelers.

Some vagabonds, a faction of the old Erfurt that surely would never die off, had found their way to the Taverns, what the underground city was referred to. Entrance was through the beautiful cathedral that filled the center of the city, surrounded by rides and circus tents every year for the

Bridge Festival, or *Krämerbrückenfest.* Jokers and performers wandered the city above, making their way among merchants selling their wares and the history of Erfurt to student tourists and fellow countrymen. Tours of Martin Luther's rooms took place several times a day, and groups of students leered at the bath houses, some of which had working water wheels still, imagining the rich sultans of older times cavorting with women who were not their wives. Where aboveground these homeless people were barely seen and kicked out of their homes, underground they were docents, leading the confused to those who could answer their questions and informing the practiced about what had happened since they last visited. They were well paid for the services rendered to travelers: what they did not get from the uninitiated was more than made up for by the witches who wished their presence remain secret. Secrets were costly, and there were few who wanted their presence in Hexehaus known who would not pay a great price.

Despite the welcome mat that Erfurt once was, it had become the opposite by the time Michael went. There were too many witches, and many could not be trusted. When all witches were persecuted and being a witch was a reality rather than a myth, the witches banded together as one unit, a team against the world. But as time wore on, they all learned they were no better than regular people: some were good and some were not. They could no longer trust each other, and began to feel persecuted from each other. Thus the secrecy. Thus the big fistfuls of money given to vagabonds who showed them how to maneuver around the Taverns, who asked them what they needed and led them to the right place. The vagabonds were trustworthy because they all looked the same and one could never be tracked down; but forget to pay, and a vagabond could sing on the steps of the church about a witch named Michael who came looking for a spell to make a girl fall in love with him.

"It's just an example," he said to Deidre, grinning.

Michael learned that when the original town of Hexehaus was constructed, Germany had a large witch population. As a crossroads for trade, it was perfect as a meeting location and, it turned out, a training ground. All those who had been banished from their home villages and countries came with their families, some of whom would grow to be witches as well. They would need proper training because a witch without training is like a gun with an automatic trigger set off by a fly. Saint Mary's Cathedral held in its lower levels a church that was built for Bishop Boniface in the year 742. Bishop Boniface relied on a witch named Paul to assist him in nearly everything, without ever knowing he was a witch. Paul was the crux of the plan to build an underground city suitable for witches to convene. The entrance was preserved as the opulent Saint Mary's Cathedral was built on top of the Bishop's church.

Over time, Hexehause was called Erfurt, except among the witches, and it grew: more roads were built around it, surrounding towns flourished and their reliance on Erfurt became less. The Market Crossroads that forged its name on maps all over the world became less important – to humans.

Below had electricity that was weakening over time, old magic that kept it bright a hundred years earlier finally losing its power. It didn't matter. That magic and that light, imbued with protection to avoid being noticed by Erfurt's ignorant populace, became unnecessary – witches could produce light for themselves, individually, as they wandered the Tavern. Plumbing was still a problem, but taken care for and updated when it was unlikely to be noticed by non-magical people, usually during any of the several annual festivals celebrating Erfurt's human history.

All of this was told to him by the simpleton he had met in a pub aboveground. Even months later, Michael still did not believe the stories and had forgotten them, writing the young man off as a loon.

Instead, he enjoyed the scenery, the comings and goings in the church, and the bounty of people who still toured the town. Something about Erfurt made him feel settled. He couldn't explain it. The tourists were largely rude or unobservant, bumping into him without so much as an *"Entschuldigen."* The food was expensive – even when it wasn't very good. There wasn't a hostel for him to stay in, and the villagers were not the type to offer board despite the luck he had found with that in the rest of the country. But still, Erfurt felt better than any other town he had traveled in. He just wanted to stay.

"Of course, I later realized it was because of the history of the place – it just called to witches."

Michael had gone into Saint Mary's Cathedral to admire the beauty of it. And, he admitted rather shyly to Elva and Deidre, to sleep on its benches. He had become weary and discouraged. He was a young witch, fresh out of his parents' home, longing for companionship amongst his own kind. He itched to use his magic, but had become tired of it backfiring, affected by the stress he was experiencing as he bedded down each night in another empty field or leaning against a stranger's home, gleaning from the heated walls what warmth he could. At the church, he felt almost human. He admired the art work and of course the bobbles and finery on its walls and pews, awed by the several rooms inside. He recalled a woman with tight, blond curls, walking to the podium in one room, the pipes of a massive organ rising in the air, gracing the feet of angels. She turned, the pipes coming from her back like wings, and opened her mouth to sing.

The sound that came from her chest and lungs, ricocheting off the walls of the cathedral, were unlike anything he had ever heard. His ears rang and his heart ached as each note glided from her mouth and spun itself in the room like a gossamer web attached to a breeze seeking escape. He sat on the floor before her, his head falling backward, his jaw dropping – he knew he looked ridiculous. A young man – barely out of boyhood – with a hollow face etched in fatigue, enamored by the voice of a woman he had never met. He watched her carefully, her plump cheeks shaking, her long black skirt barely skimming the tips of her brown, canvas shoes. Her ringlets bounced as her shoulders shook, her arms raised out to either side, and as she sang the last long verse of what was surely an opera, he felt his chest heave. And then he saw something new – he saw the pipes of the organ *lean*. He watched them vibrate, and when he sat forward, saw small sparks – barely noticeable – spring from the tips of her shoes, striking the floor. The room became silent. The woman looked ahead. He sat back on his legs and watched as she turned again to the organ pipes. She bowed her head as if in either prayer or thanks, and walked away.

He had seen another witch. He was sure of it. He scrambled to his feet and followed her. He didn't care if she thought he was mad; he had to know.

It was she who led him to the Taverns, and it was a vagabond who told him where he was: a home to witches.

He spent three days sleeping by an old entrance to the Taverns, shivering in the cold. But when he got a spell right, warming a vagabond's hands, the vagabond led him to a niche made cozy with fire, blankets and food. Michael had to work extra hard to make new spells work that he could then use for barter with the vagabonds. When the spells did not work, the vagabonds left with the wood and blankets; they were a bit heartless, really. So in the daylight, aboveground, he practiced in tight alleys as often as he could. Without proper training, it took him far longer than he had hoped, but by the third week after discovering the Taverns, Michael learned enough to live comfortably – compared to the benches and cold ditches that had offered shelter before. If Michael could not provide something the vagabonds requested, he cast a mirage on a coin with instructions to spend it. The vagabond would, and receive three times its worth as change.

"That's an amazing spell," said Deidre.

"A thief taught it to me – my father. Was the first one he ever taught me."

For four straight days, Michael's spells had all worked. He was feeling well-rested and hopeful. He set out to explore the underground city in Erfurt, without the assistance of the vagabonds. He would ignore their warnings, their shooing, and their emphatic insistence to mind his own business. It was on this day, in this rebellious spirit, that he met the two knitwitches.

"They were married," he said, looking carefully at Deidre. "They were very young. They looked younger than even me. But they were more in love than I had ever believed possible… at the time." Deidre bowed her head and grasped his hand.

He could not remember their names. He could not remember what they spoke of. But he remembered that they had been in Erfurt for several months and were planning to leave.

"We watched you," said the woman.

They liked Michael. She had knit an extra section onto a blanket she paid a vagabond to give him. It was the blanket that made him ignore the vagabond's warnings. It was the blanket that told Michael where he needed to go to find them. They could see in him, they said, a future they were relying on. They hoped to see him again. They left. Shortly after, so did Michael.

"I remember nothing else. Absolutely nothing else about them or my meeting with them."

"That doesn't help us at all!" yelled Elva, whose anticipation and patience were colliding.

"I have to agree, Michael," said Deidre, stress splitting her words into ragged tendrils. "All of that is very interesting, but then you get to the part where you actually met knitwitches and you tell us nothing. It's frustrating."

"Now hold on," Michael insisted. "I haven't finished. I saw them again, years later."

Elva sat back. Deidre looked at him curiously. "How?"

"It was a few years after I came to Brookwick." He turned to Deidre. "Before us."

He didn't know why, as he doesn't recall it being planned, but he was studying a piece about Eastern European History at the library on campus. Without preamble, he stood up, grabbed his jacket and wallet, and got on a plane to Germany, abandoning his books at the library. He immediately made his way to the Taverns and found the two knitwitches. They sat together for nearly a week. When the week was done, he felt rejuvenated as a witch. He recognized that he was stronger.

"And," he added, "smarter. I knew more. I knew more than I had ever thought possible. Only there was a problem – I also knew none of it."

"How can that be?" Deidre was obviously confused.

"It was as if I had amnesia, except I was aware of it."

"You were struck," said Elva. "They struck you with a spell."

Deidre gasped and Michael nodded. "Yes," he said calmly. "So what you are two going to do to get me unstruck?"

CHAPTER TWENTY-SEVEN

Sheriff Emory hated being wrong, but worse than that was knowing a young girl was suffering because of his pride. He couldn't help but listen to the voice in his head that longed to blame Elva, the woman who reported parking meters and wobbly lines in parking lots, but deep down he only felt disappointment at himself. Ever since he first heard Katrina's voice in that voicemail message, he couldn't look any of his officers in the eye. He was ashamed of himself. Only Detective Lynley knew not to say anything; the other deputies tried to make him feel better, seeing how upset it made him.

"Sheriff, anybody would have thought like you did. Who knew, right?"

"Your aunt has a lot of theories, Sheriff. We can't chase every one."

He appreciated the thoughts, but he didn't appreciate hearing them out loud. At the end of the day, it fell on his shoulders and he knew it.

Detective Lynley and Deputy Desmond Lafayette sat with him in his office, preparing for the long day ahead of them. Desmond felt a particular fondness for this case because Elva is the one who set him up with Larissa. Though he and Larissa both chuckled with everybody else when Elva came in, her loud voice attracting the attention of every person in the station, they loved her tremendously and felt for her. The day Elva entered the station to talk to her nephew about Katrina Isaac, Larissa and Desmond prayed together that night for the young girl. Desmond wouldn't tell his sheriff that Larissa had bad feelings about the case from the beginning, or that he had no idea how the sheriff would ever be able to bear the guilt if something worse – God forbid – were to happen to the young girl.

"We need to know more about this girl." The sheriff's voice was raw but deep, and it demanded attention. It was important that everybody take the case far more seriously than he had intended. He worried he had weakened the resolve of his deputies with the offhanded way he tossed aside Elva's concerns. The burning in his chest intensified at the thought.

He looked again at the thin file folder that sat on his desk with Katrina's name and physical description written on the front. It wasn't enough. He knew nothing about her. Where she worked gave him no clues as to who may have taken her. Elva brought the bags of things she had left behind; he and his deputies found nothing helpful. No scraps of paper. Just a bunch of clothes and toiletries. The toiletries had given him an idea, though, and as little hope as it promised, he owed it to her to try.

"We need to do a canvas. We know she worked at the yarn store, so it's very likely she frequented businesses in the square." His gaze rested on the folder and he tapped the eraser of a pencil on the desk as he avoided the studious stares of his officers. "For breaks and such."

"Sure, sure," said Detective Lynley, her strong voice shooting through the air like an air gun at a track and field event. "That makes sense. Record stores, grocery store, coffee house. We can see if anybody saw her with another person. Maybe make some phone calls using their phones or—"

"Or her favorite singer. Maybe we can find out who her favorite singer was and we can have one of her favorite drinks while listening to her favorite singer and eat her favorite food and then maybe we can channel some poor teenage girl who has been missing for two weeks and is calling for help!"

Sheriff Emory's face was red from the strain. Deputy Lafayette slid his chair back and looked up at the sheriff.

"Anything could help, sir. Anything."

Sheriff Emory's face was still frozen, his eyes wide with the whites surrounding his pupils like the whites of an egg.

"Sir, it's what we have to do. You never know, sir." Deputy Lynley reached out her hand and placed it on the back of the sheriff's. It was a calculated move. There was nothing romantic in the gesture, and she had to be sure to quell any curiosity the act may have stirred in the deputy. But she and the sheriff have gone back decades, friends since childhood. He moved ahead because she just wanted to be an officer – nothing more. She loved her job. It didn't stop him from going to her for her opinion.

The movement worked, and the sheriff lifted his sweaty palms from the desk, moist palm prints drying in the air. He sat back down and his officers watched as he took in a deep breath.

"I haven't told my aunt yet," he whispered.

The officers looked at each other but offered no advice to the sheriff. They simply understood.

Deputy Lynley stood first and punched Lafayette in the shoulder when he didn't stand also. Once they were side by side, Deputy Lynley said, "We're on it, sir. I think it should be left to just Lafayette and myself, sir. Fewer people will take notice, I think."

The sheriff nodded and the deputies left.

Jim stared at the phone. He still couldn't do it. Not yet.

Katrina is sick of crying. She barely noticed his stomping when he got home. Her eyes were stuck on the fence that blocked her way out and the wall was starting to melt before her eyes. First it was gray, then it melted to green, then it melted to blue and then it melted to purple. She watched it as the grooves in the walls where the mortar was placed waved up and down. She flipped them in her mind so they were vertical and watched as they danced side by side like hula dances in a Scooby Doo cartoon. Blue, green, yellow, purple, pink – now there's an idea. Pink is nice. But making the transition from purple to pink made her eyes hurt so she closed them, looked at the wall again, the cement bricks, the gray. She let her eyes sit on them until they again began to melt. Gray, then yellow, then blue, then green, then purple, then white.

Oh, yes. White was much better.

Desmond knew Lynley's loyalty to the sheriff was strong. Everybody told him about their friendship; some mistakenly called them brother and sister. But he wanted to talk to someone about the case without all the false hope and unsaid screw-ups that had already happened. He just didn't know how to start the conversation.

"Just ask," she said.

They were in the square. Lynley suggested they take a coffee and sit in the park to take stock of their most likely targets. She felt it would waste time to start at a corner and go around into every building. Instead, they'd take what they did know – no matter how little – and use it to their advantage. Desmond felt there should have been more urgency, but he understood the idea. It didn't matter how fast you asked people questions and got started asking them if you didn't know what or whom to ask. But every scalding sip of his coffee made him feel like they were only bunking the case up even more.

"I know you want to ask some questions. Probably sick of not talking about the obvious. So just out with it already." She continued looking at the store fronts of the shops in the square as she said her piece.

Desmond looked down into his lap. It was like she was reading his mind.

"I can't read minds," she said. She turned her head and smirked at him. "It's just that I'm probably thinking the same thing."

"What if we never find her? Or what if we find her and she's dead?"

"You mean, if we never find her or if we do and she's dead, what will happen to the sheriff?"

Desmond took a sip of his coffee and looked toward the gazebo.

Lynley did the same. "I expect the sheriff will find a way to cope and move on, but he'll never forget it. And for a while, maybe forever, we'll be tracking down every strange car that ever comes into Brookwick, or checking out the neighbor's fences for Elva, who swears she saw a cat burglar lurking in the junipers."

Desmond chuckled. He immediately felt bad for it. "It's not funny," he said out loud.

"No, it's not," she confirmed. "It's just the truth. He'll never forgive himself for checking into everything now that he knows something may come from something else that seems completely harmless."

"That's just it. What was so harmless about it? She just disappeared, just like that. Shouldn't he have looked into it right away?"

Lynley took a long sip of her coffee and swallowed slowly. She looked down at her cup and poured it out on the sidewalk. The movement made Desmond feel like he had crossed a line.

"Look, I'm sorry. I shouldn't have—"

"You're right, Lafayette. At least, you're right *today*. But a week ago, what was harmless about it was a lady in a sweater who reports every dratted thing in this town as if they are all emergencies. And he's known her his whole life. I have too. She has a flair. So last week, you would have been wrong. Maybe. Who knows. But today, yes. Today, you're right. And he knows it."

"The boy who cried wolf," whispered Desmond.

"Exactly."

They both felt bad for Elva. They both loved her; they both knew she had good intentions, they just couldn't understand why someone so sensible in everything else, so wonderful in every other way (except for her fierce temper, and fortunately, neither of them have tread on that very much) could seem so inept at detecting real crime. Was she out searching for excitement like those women on late night television ads who wear *Whisper 2000s* so they can eavesdrop on the neighbors? That didn't make sense. It just wasn't like her. That's what was so horrible about the whole thing.

Desmond thought it was something else though. He thinks they all fell for her charm. Her kooky old lady routine. She strides into the police station, sometimes with muffins and sometimes with crazy sweaters and sometimes with a loud "Hellooooo, everybody!" and charmed the pants off of you. She lived up to the kooky old lady image and everybody loved it, believing her to be part entertainer as the grandmother you always wished you had, and the character in a sitcom who always was a thorn in the sheriff's backside. And it worked for everybody. They could all chuckle, seemingly at her expense knowing full well that she actually loved it, and get cookies, hats, mittens – or in Desmond's case, a wife – in return! But nobody had ever got caught in the cross hairs. Some people were annoyed that they had to go out and investigate silly claims, but others saw them as social moments with their peers. A chance to say, "Out on an Elva run; isn't it a little early for a break?"

Larissa said it best. "We like Elva too much to be panicked when she walks in the door and files a report. Our immediate instinct is to smile at her in this *'aren't you cute?'* sort of way instead of recognizing her as a person – not a stereotype."

Desmond had to agree. And in that regard, Lynley was right. Last week, he would have been wrong; but today, he was right. They should have looked into it right away.

Lynley had suggested they try the health food store first. Elva said all the food that was left behind came from the health food store, identified by the price labels on the packaging. While Lynley sought out a manager, Desmond hit up the more bored looking of the three cashiers who stood at the front of the store. The other two were helping people and the third was looking at his cell phone, texting someone. When Desmond approached, he saw the kid was actually playing a skateboarding game on his phone.

"Excuse me. I'd like to ask you a few questions. You have a minute?"

The kid looked up and shoved his phone in his pants. He looked around, startled.

"I don't see your manager around, if that's what you're worried about. But you might want to leave that temptation in the back or something. Less stressful and all that."

The kid looked at Desmond. He didn't even crack a smile. *Okay. This should be fun.*

"We are looking for a girl who may have shopped here. She's been missing for two weeks and we really need to find her. Her name is Katrina. Katrina Isaac."

The kid continued to look at Desmond and showed no signs of comprehending.

"Hello?"

"Yeah?"

"Well?"

"Well what, dude? You're lookin' for some chick, okay."

"Yes. Do you have any information?"

"Well, you didn't exactly ask me that, did you? I don't know no chick named Katrina, dude."

"Do not call me 'dude,' son. You can call me Deputy Lafayette."

The kid didn't respond. Desmond tried to suppress a sigh, but it was tough.

"She was about your height; had long blonde hair and blue eyes. Very pretty? Not too hard to miss?"

"Doesn't sound like my type, man."

I really hope Lynley is doing better than I am, thought Desmond.

"That was the most frustrating thing I have ever done in all my years as a deputy."

Lynley chuckled. "I should have warned you. That was Peterson's son, the guy who owns the hardware store on Shirley. He's been a punk since he could open a door and either run through other people's lawns or steal their cars. But his uncle is a lawyer and a real hard ass. That kid never gets put to task."

"Put to task to finish a sentence, you mean. It was like pulling teeth from a turtle."

"How did the other kids do?"

"A little better. They blinked when I asked them questions and used manners, but they had nothing helpful to add. I'm assuming the manager couldn't help?"

Lynley shook her head. "Hard to do this without a photo. She has no real identifying features – like a weird mole or piercings or tattoos – so this is going to be challenging."

"Wait," said Desmond. It had just occurred to him. "Weren't a lot of her t-shirts band shirts? Some not-on-the-radio bands, too, right? I think I remember a *Bauhaus* t-shirt and a *Joy Division* shirt. Those bands have loyal followings, I think, right? But most of these stores are manned by people who might appreciate that. Maybe we should use the clothes she wore as an identifier."

"Worth a shot."

Desmond felt better. He ran back into the health food store and approached the kid, mentioning the different shirts and what kind of clothes she may have been wearing. Though one of them had a few comments about the bands and even asked if they were going to throw the shirts away if they didn't find her, they had nothing to contribute in the search for Katrina.

"Don't say it," said Lynley.

Desmond shook his head. They walked to the next storefront on their list. *Sometimes I hate this job*, he thought.

The colors on the wall kept melting into brown and Katrina was getting frustrated. She closed her eyes and watched the red of her lids pulse before her. *At least there's that*, she thought. *Proof that I'm alive*. She watched the red pulse in and out, faster, slow. She tried to focus on it, but could feel her eyes cross beneath her lids and they ached almost immediately. The stomping upstairs had gotten worse, and she heard crashing, as if he were throwing things across the room. She was positive she heard breaking glass, and shuddered to think what he would do if he came down the stairs that angry. Part of her tried to cling to sarcasm, something she had always been good at *before*, but she also felt too tired. He had forgotten to get her something to eat that day. Usually, he left the house in the morning, came back in the afternoon and gave her food. But that day he only ran in, she heard the pipes going for water, and he was gone again. When he got back, the stomping and crashing began. It didn't let up.

She tilted her head and aimed her right ear at the ceiling. It was quiet. When was it that she heard the crashing? A few minutes ago? Hours? A day? She wondered when was the last time she slept. She looked up at the ceiling, at the pipes and boards she could not reach. What would she do if she could reach them? Hang herself, or swing like a wild animal?

She wondered if there was really any difference.

She wondered who she was.

CHAPTER TWENTY-EIGHT

Addison was dumbfounded. Nick was laughing on the other end of the phone. "Wow!" he said. "My company must have really tuckered you out, huh?"

Addison laughed. *I wish,* she thought whimsically, then gave herself an imaginary kick for thinking that way about her only friend in town. *Especially since I stood Brian up last night and what did I end up doing? Hang with Nick until two in the morning. Swell.* "I had some weird dreams," she said quietly. "Really, really weird dreams."

"Bad ones?" he asked, concerned.

Addison smiled. "Nah. They weren't too bad, just strange is all."

Nick offered several times to pick her up for some coffee later, but Addison wanted to meet him at the diner instead so she wouldn't feel awkward. She could already picture herself fidgeting, wondering if he thought she looked nice or put on too much lip balm, or something else equally ridiculous. She was hoping she would not be trying to go out of her way to look any different than if she got dressed for work, but she couldn't really be sure either. This all felt way too familiar, way too fast. For the one millionth time, she wondered how she managed to forget her date with Brian the night before.

With a little persuading, Nick agreed to meet her at the diner on the condition that she let him buy her coffee. Coffee at five in the afternoon didn't feel like the best idea in the world, but she wasn't going to refuse the offer. Nick was nice and she wanted some company. She hadn't decided yet if she was going to tell him about her failed plans with Brian, but if he wanted to be her friend, maybe it would be a good test?

"Oh my god," she said to herself in the mirror. "*Do not* be a test. Do not be one of those girls." She snorted. "Ew," she said.

Early evening wasn't that far off, but she still had to eat something for "breakfast." And Derwin's head-butting and meowing were signs that he was pretty hungry too. Addison rolled off the couch and tripped on her knitting. Remembering the disaster of the evening, she gathered it up and held it out in front of her, the sun shining through the stitches. She had managed to fix her mistakes from the previous night, but she could tell that some stitches done last night were uneven. Should she reknit them? The book Deidre had given her with tips and tricks for fixing knitting mistakes lay on the floor, still open to the page about yarn overs and accidental extra stitches. Derwin meowed, and pushed on the back of her legs. "The dangers of knitting with boys. Hey, Derwin, that'd be a good band name, yeah? *Knitting with Boys*?"

Derwin shoved his head into her legs, hard, and she nearly tripped over him.

"All right, Derwin!" she yelled. "I'll get your food!"

As Derwin ate his breakfast, Addison stood at the sink drinking a glass of water and looked out the window at the square. It was quiet outside. Two people were sitting at different benches in the square and one man was walking down the sidewalk. Addison looked over at the coffee house, half hoping it was open so she could run over and apologize to Brian. It was silly not to get a phone number for him. Isn't that what people do when they make plans together? But the shop looked completely locked up and closed down, despite that it was Monday. The yarn shop was closed. Oh well. It would have to wait. Being that she dreaded the encounter, she didn't mind too much — that only added to the guilt.

Elva was at home, sitting with some tea and a dish cloth she decided to knit when the shawl proved too difficult a project. She needed all her concentration to finish work on that shawl but her brain was too occupied with thoughts of Addison, Michael, Michael and Deidre, and Katrina. How did her life get so complicated? What ever happened to opening the shop, talking about yarn, getting some knitting done, and curling up in front of the television with her Henry? She looked over at Henry, who was deep into a book of maps drawn during the second World War. He bent over the book studiously, his magnifying glass casting bright spots of light over the pages. Every now and then he emitted a small "huh" as he flipped the page, as if informing the book that he did not know what he had just seen, and the book had therefore fulfilled its purpose. Elva always loved her husband and the solitude he wrapped around himself, even when surrounded by friends and family. She used to acknowledge his murmurs and mumbles as he looked through books or fixed a sink or cooked a meal. But he was so lost in his own mind he had no idea he said anything aloud; he also didn't seem to mind if she never acknowledged the noises. It was hard for Elva to stop; she realized how much she longed to please people and let them know she was listening to them. In some ways, when she learned to let go of that need around Henry, she felt more at peace at home with him. She relaxed into her life and her own quiet time.

But today, quiet wasn't working. She was stressed and anxious and desperately needed to talk about it. She had promised Michael and Deidre that she would not talk about Addison with any other people, just in case it was overheard. Brookwick was a small place, but it was still a town of witches. No matter how confident they felt that they knew every witch in the town, it was quite possible they didn't. It's not as if there were a registry (and the idea was brought up at a meeting, but immediately shut down. It was agreed that that is how wars are started. Nobody wanted to start a war in Brookwick amongst witches). She didn't know how to talk to Henry about any of her fears of late. Addison was to be kept a secret, even from her husband, just in case ears were around. She didn't feel she was being dishonest with Henry by mentioning it. She knew he would know all soon enough because a moment will come up when it will all be shared. Elva wasn't sure how she knew this, but that's how it always worked with she and Henry.

Elva would wish she could tell him something if he was at the grocery store. Without telling him anything, he returned with what she wanted. It was frequently the case that someone at the grocery store would mention to Henry how much they missed Elva's soup, cookies, or some other thing, and how that one ingredient really made it for them and maybe he could mention it to Elva when he got home. Henry would say he would, then he'd buy the ingredient in case Elva wanted to get started and didn't have any at home, and since she made it enough, surely having extra did nobody any harm? It was always the ingredient or item she was hoping for. And it always worked out that way: Elva wished she could tell Henry something, and soon enough, that very same day, Henry would find it out.

She suspected it had to do with her magic. She didn't know how it worked, because unlike all other spells, it was not cast. When she first met Henry when she was thirty-five and working at another yarn shop that had since closed down, he came in with his sister, a woman Elva had seen in various classes at the shop. She wanted to make her brother Henry a sweater, but since she had never made on before she wasn't sure how much yarn to get. Rather than take measurements she just brought him in. The first time Elva looked into his eyes, she thought nothing of him. He looked bored and mildly irritated. He didn't say hello or respond when she asked how he was doing. She thought maybe he was dumb or had a hearing problem, but eventually she just blamed a lack of manners. She helped his sister and they left the shop. But before he went through the door out onto the sidewalk, he looked back and caught Elva's eye. He winked at her. That was it. Just a wink. Elva's heart fluttered and she instantly liked him.

When his sister next came in the store, it was two months later. Elva had almost forgotten about Henry, but asked after him and the sweater she was making. Henry's sister seemed disappointed; she said she hadn't gotten very far because the button bands confused her. Elva offered to give her some tips if she brought the sweater in. As the sister left, Elva muttered under her breath, "Especially if you bring in your brother."

A week later, the sister came in with Henry, who was wearing the sweater. Apparently, she had figured out the button bands and every other part of the sweater. Aside from the tight shoulders, the sweater fit nicely. Elva liked the green that was on his face. This time, he spoke to Elva.

"My sister was going to bring the sweater in for some help, but I took a look at things and figured it out. I like puzzles and math and whatnot and it worked out great. And then I told some buddies at work about the sweater and one of them has a cousin who knits, this fisherman out in Newfoundland. I thought that sounded good, so when he told me his cousin makes these amazing sweaters that keep him warm up in the north winds, I thought I should try it. So I came in with my sister to get some yarn and maybe a book or video about how to knit."

He said it all very slowly, never tripping over a word, holding his gaze steady with Elva's. Elva smiled when she heard how he showed up at the shop. She led him to some yarn that was sturdy and warm and could stand up to rewinding just in case the first few attempts failed. The best instructional video was sold out, so she offered to order him a copy.

"Or maybe you could just teach me," he said. It wasn't a question. Elva nodded. They made plans to meet that Saturday.

Whenever she had a thought about what she wanted from Henry or for Henry, it just appeared. She was convinced this meant they were made for each other, that the universe was giving her exactly what she wanted because she wasn't using magic to get it. But after the butterflies rested in her stomach and the joy settled in her heart, and she still felt love without being blinded by giddiness, she realized something else was at work. These weren't coincidences and they were too frequent to be signs from the universe. It was magic of some kind, she just didn't know what.

It was like her reports to Jim, the ones that the office always chuckled about. She reported a dog tied to a parking meter. She thought the dog had been there a long time, so Jim humored her and checked it out. There was no dog, but he bumped into a masked man running out of the convenient store with a bag full of money from the register. Or the time Elva thought she saw an enormous snake in Mrs. Peterson's front yard. Jim and two other deputies went out to the house with nets and hooks, but instead of finding a snake they found that Mrs. Peterson had collapsed in her kitchen due to a gas leak and transported her to the hospital.

Of all Elva's complaints, as silly as they were, the sheriff's office ran into some other trouble that desperately needed help. Elva believed it was the same magic that got her what she needed when she wanted to speak to Henry, only with a twist. Because she *did* believe she saw an enormous python in Mrs. Peterson's yard, and she *did* believe that dog had been tied to that pole for ages. Was it a coincidence, or did magic create a dog and snake because there was another danger lurking nearby and Elva had the means to get help to those areas at the right time? Whatever it was, Elva would keep answering it. It didn't do any harm.

Her worry about Katrina was different. It was a real feeling of fear and danger that she couldn't shake. It wasn't a shimmer of a snake or an illogical fear akin to freeing a cat from a tree; she truly believed something was happening to Katrina and she could do nothing to help her. Then there were Elva's nightmares. Katrina was leaning against a wall, confetti falling on her shoulders, her hands on either side of her, swimming in cans of paint. Tears stained her face, thin white rivers matted against gray clammy skin. Elva sobbed in the night, watching as her arms scrambled before her eyes, trying to claw their way to Katrina.

Why could magic show up when she didn't ask it to, but do nothing to help when she desperately needed it?

"So," said Henry. His voice startled her, as did the loud thud of his book as he closed it. It was a big book, thick with heavy pages and glossy maps that folded out, nearly as wide as their coffee table.

"So," said Elva.

It was what they did.

He smiled at her. "Whatchya knittin' there?"

"A dish cloth."

"Mmm," he said. He watched as her hands continued on, simple knit stitches, back and forth.

Henry looked out the window. "Nice day."

"Mmm," said Elva. The sun was shining and it looked warm and beautiful. Terribly inappropriate for her mood.

"Would you like to take a walk?"

Elva stopped knitting. "Take a walk?"

Henry looked at her, his elbows on his knees, waiting for a reply. "And where did you want to walk to?" she asked him.

"Well," he leaned back and turned to the window again. His lips pursed as he thought it over. Elva had a feeling he already had an idea, but he liked to consider it again before putting the offer on the table. She liked to think of it as his own version of checks and balances. Really, he wanted to know if it was an idea she'd really like and therefore, was worth the effort of suggesting it more than once should she refuse the first time. Elva had a habit for saying no the first time, especially when there was knitting in her hands. Time at home was time for a crime show and some knitting and she wasn't afraid to admit it. "I was thinking we could walk over to the college. See how Broom Lake is doing right now. It's a beautiful day."

He tried not to be angry. He went to the house his mother had left him when she died four years earlier, held in trust until he turned eighteen. He sat on the threadbare couch, bleached pink from the sun that used to shine brightly through the windows, but the sun hurt his eyes and cast glare on the television so he put duct tape on them to be sure it didn't peek through. He could still see speckles of sun through the strands of tape and though it annoyed him for a while, he decided he liked it. Gave the place some ambiance. But it annoyed him today, so much that he decided to leave the house, but not before he lifted the cheap coffee table he built last summer with two-by-fours, and threw it against the wall.

Nothing went his way. Nothing.

He walked into the kitchen and saw empty bottles sitting beside the kitchen sink. He forgot to put them in the recycling bin and recycling was picked up that morning. It was her fault. It was her fault he forgot. Grabbing both bottles in one red fist, he launched them at the door leading to the garage. The glass reflected in the light coming from the window in the door and when it sliced across his eye, he roared.

"I gotta leave this shit hole!" he yelled.

He threw open the door and walked into the garage. In his rush, he tripped over the recycling bin and when bottles rolled under the car and rattled on the concrete floor, he lifted the bucket above his head and used all his strength to throw it in the kitchen.

It took him only seven minutes to get to where he needed to be. He needed to think, to relax, to figure out what he was going to do. It was ridiculous to continue to be used like this. Nobody is allowed to take advantage of him and his feelings. That's bullshit. "Bullshit!" he yelled. His voice bounced back, the waves of Broom Lake sending it back like a confirmation.

CHAPTER TWENTY-NINE

Sara remembered reading once that washing dishes didn't have to be thought of as a chore. If one wanted to truly embrace life, every action could be a testament to the quality of life you wanted to leave. Washing dishes could then transform from an everyday chore necessary to avoid germs, bugs and a bad smell, to an act of washing away ones worries with each plate – a meditation of peace and moving forward. It was no coincidence that she now had several mugs and a pile of small plates too high for a woman who has spent the last few days alone.

She missed Tom. She didn't want to miss him. She wanted to accept her new life for what it was and carry on. She wanted to clean the house, work on some knitting, bake some bread, go for a walk, do some shopping. Never before had she realized what a quiet partner added to a home. Even when Tom was reading on the porch or outside in the garden, his *presence* added purpose to the home. On her own, she didn't know what she should be doing. Should she smile? Should she talk to herself? Should she cook dinner and what if she isn't hungry and how do you cook for one? Should she knit or will she have to go out later? These questions never occurred to her when Tom was there, so she couldn't understand why they came up now. They frustrated her. Living shouldn't require so much thought, so many questions. She was tempted to call Deidre and ask her how she did it, but she was too nervous to call Deidre.

Since Tom left, Sara has kept to herself. It had only been a few days – a few days that felt like years. Part of her hung to the hope that he'd come back, loping up the driveway with a bundle of daisies in his hand, ready to come home and tell her he didn't know what he was thinking. A stronger part of her knew better and shook its head in sympathy and pity, watching her struggle, understanding it was a disappointment she had to learn to muster through.

She had just put the last small dish in the strainer, wondering if she remembered to wash away her worries, when a small, unfamiliar yellow car pulled up her driveway. The driver took each bump carelessly as it sped toward her house. Sara wiped her hands on her pajama pants and went to the side door, which walked out into the driveway. She stood at the door and locked it, keeping an eye on the car.

Running upstairs, she shot glances out of every window she passed, threw off her pajama pants and struggled into a pair of crumpled jeans from her dirty-clothes pile. She looked in the mirror, and realizing she had little time to put a bra on, threw an old university hoodie over her t-shirt. Grabbing a light winter hat from the basket beside her dresser, she threw it on as casually as possible as she ran down the stairs, stuffing beneath the brim short hairs that curled up and poked out. She felt like she screamed "I'm a depressed single woman whose husband left her because he's afraid of witches."

The car had come to a stop, and she heard a door close. By the time she was back in the kitchen, looking over the kitchen sink and out the window at the parked car, someone was rapping on the side door.

Sara had always been slightly nervous and hyper aware, but she also walked straighter and with more strength when she realized her nerves may be unwarranted. It didn't mean she threw a door open when she was alone in the house. She missed Tom; when he was around, walking straighter and feeling stronger wasn't necessary. If he were still here, she'd go to him and ask him to answer the door. She would warn him that she didn't recognize the car. She would probably still be in her pajamas — despite the fact that if he hadn't left she probably wouldn't have worn them three days in a row. He would walk to the door with curiosity but smile at her, call her silly, and say "Relax." It was even possible, she thought, that the smirk and the sentiment would irritate her, and she'd snap at him and tell him she had every right to be nervous when a strange person drives up to their house with the long driveway. "It's not like they probably took a wrong turn or were just checking out the neighborhood," she'd say. And he'd ignore her, wave his hand in a dismissive way and she'd stomp upstairs, pissed, but listen at the top of the stairs trying to hear voices and figure out who it was — all fears that it was an ax murderer gone because being angry at Tom trumped fear of serial killers when it came to her emotions.

Remembering the way Tom sometimes spoke to her as if she were paranoid, weak or silly, irritated her enough that when she got to the door, she threw it open before she even saw who it was.

"Sara! Hi! I'm sorry to drop in like this, but I was making some beer bread today and I thought maybe you'd want some and we could knit but I lost your number and so I figured I'd do it the old-fashioned way and here I am! Do you mind?"

Sara smiled, relieved Melinda wasn't a serial killer.

"Not at all, Melinda. Come on in."

Melinda pulled from her bag a sleeve she was knitting. She set it on her lap and reached forward for the water Sara had gotten them both.

"I'm sorry I don't have anything better to offer. I haven't gone shopping since Tom left for his brother's."

"You said he went to help his brother with fences?"

"No, no. His brother is building a new house and is doing the electric and bathroom tiling, or something like that. Tom's been wanting to help his brother out and when they found out how much it would cost to have an electrician do it, Tom offered to go down instead."

"Is Tom an electrician? If he needs work or something, Ed Morrison had his store broken into and maybe something happened to the electricity. He said he keeps hearing funny noises in the attic or something." Melinda waved her hand above her head as if she were standing in the shop with Ed.

Sara smiled. Melinda knew Tom wasn't an electrician, but Sara knew what Melinda was hoping to achieve asking all the questions. Melinda was a gossip. She was well-meaning, but she was also easily entertained. Part of her charm was being sociable and kind, asking questions, and giving people an opportunity to talk about themselves. She was especially charming to knitters because despite this flaw, she was extremely passionate about knitting. The problem is that she often extracted information from people by talking about other people. She had a knack for drawing out personal tidbits and it seemed she didn't realize she did it with gossip. Wasn't it obvious to everybody that whatever they told her would be used in this same way with someone else? Sara had seen Melinda in action. Though she liked Melinda, and even found it endearing the way Melinda seemed to mindlessly manipulate her friends in this way, she watched where she tread in conversation. She didn't want anybody to know that Tom had left her.

What she said about Tom's brother was true, but he had found a guy from work who offered to help him out with it.

Tom was actually grateful because he didn't want to drive the ten hours it would take to get there only to hear his brother whine about how expensive the house was getting. He and his brother weren't always buddy-buddy. His brother had borrowed money one too many times, and Tom held it against him every time he asked for another favor.

It occurred to Sara, at that moment, that each time she remembered something about Tom, she was left feeling annoyed with him.

"He knows how to do the work. So what are you making?"

Melinda stayed for two hours. Sara had to try very hard to keep the conversation on knitting. She longed to tell someone about her pain, about Tom, about the huge change her life was about to take, and Melinda really *was* a great listener, and incredibly sweet – but Sara wasn't ready to let go of all hope. She didn't want anybody to know about Tom. What if he came back? Melinda did catch her sometimes zoning out of the conversation and drew her back whenever it happened.

"Is something distracting you? Were you busy before I came? I'm sorry I just dropped in like this, without any warning."

"No, no. It's really great you came by. I like this. It's nice when people do it the way our parents used to do it, before cell phones and email." Sara leaned over and squeezed Melinda's arm. "Seriously. Thank you. It's great."

Melinda smiled and continued working on her sleeve.

"You meet the new girl at the shop?"

Sara smiled. "I did! She seems very nice! I walked all the way to the square a few days ago. It took a lot of out me, but I didn't realize how much until I sat down. I got all dizzy. She came right over to make sure I was okay. Really nice girl."

"She is! Do you know she lived in her car the last two years?"

"What?" Sara was intrigued. Melinda was not a witch, and as far as Sara knew, Melinda knew nothing of them or their huge popularity in Brookwick, so she wasn't about to mention it. However, she wanted to know why a witch, one who seemed incredibly powerful, lived in her car for two years.

"It's true! Apparently she drives this old Toyota, and when she graduated high school, the first thing she did – within *days* of graduating – was hop in her car and just start driving. Sounds crazy, right?"

Sara stopped working on her project to take in what Melinda was saying.

"I only got to talk to her for a little while – she was at a class last week – but she sounds just amazing. Imagine being her age and just taking off like that?"

"Did she mention why she did it?" She felt mildly ashamed for launching into gossip. Only at the monthly meetings with Deidre and the girls did she talk about people in town. Of course it was gossip then just as it is with Melinda, but the fact that she was sharing the empathic feelings she got from people – something she couldn't help as a witch – and was sharing *that* information with the other witches, well … surely that was okay? Yes, it was. Sara had few friends with whom she could casually speak about the emotions she picked up on a daily basis. Just going grocery shopping can be stressful because the cashier could have broken up with a girlfriend, or the woman who last touched the cantaloupe she just picked up was diagnosed with cancer. Every venture out of the house was like expecting you'd get bitten by an invisible animal at some point during the day, you just didn't know by what animal or when. Sometimes, the animal tickled. A man may have gotten a promotion or the cashier may have just fallen in love. Those feelings *sound* like they'd be great to experience secondhand, but the truth is that they aren't. Because they weren't *her* feelings; they belonged entirely to someone else. She had no memory to attach to them, no images or smells, and experience was everything when Sara felt something.

It was her first year in college when she thought her ability had surfaced, but once she understood it and how it worked, she realized it began far sooner. The confusion lay in the fact that being empathic can be easily confused with intuition. She had always believed, as did her friends and even her parents, that she was a great judge of character and people, often recognizing when someone felt down and so encouraging her family to bake a batch of cookies for them; or seeing when someone was happy and approaching them to ask how their day was so she and her family or friends could congratulate them. Everybody, including herself, believed that just looking at the person gave away enough information to move her to the next stage. When she felt joy, she believed she saw it in their eyes or the way they bounced when they walked. If she felt sadness, she believed she saw it in the slump of their shoulders or the pale color of their skin. But it was always magic; her knack for asking questions, offering hugs and recognizing emotions in others began a few months before her first period.

In college, however, it became magnified. Perhaps it was because she was suddenly surrounded by hundreds of bodies; perhaps it was because she was in Brookwick, choosing to come to an obscure college her parents had never heard of instead of attending Boston University as they'd wished. Perhaps it was the cycle of people who had been there before her – because it was an object that had triggered an empathic response and it terrified her.

A sweater for Brookwick College was hanging in the closet. She was the first to arrive to the dorm room, the other bed still unclaimed and no other baggage in the room, so she was sure it was left behind by a former student. It was dark blue with a hood and red embroidery spelled out the name of her new home. The colors reminded her of the Boston Red Sox and she wondered briefly if it was a sign that she had made the wrong decision. When she reached up to grab it, wondering if she should throw it away or try it on, she was filled with anguish. Her soul was shivering. She slumped against the door of the closet and her fist closed tight around the sweater as her body slid down the door jamb. Her fingers would not let go and the plastic hanger that held the sweatshirt snapped in two. Pieces of it flew around her, but she barely noticed through her tears, now drowning her face and bubbling at her lips while she sobbed heavily.

She had never felt such grief in all her life. She wanted to fold inside herself, climb in the closet and shut the door and fade away – quickly and without warning. But she couldn't. She was stuck here and she didn't have the courage to change it. The sweatshirt sat in her lap, soaking up her tears. It suddenly made her angry and she flung the sweater across the room in a fury. As soon as it left her hands, before it landed on her still naked bed, the grief left her. That is, it left her entire body despite her body still recovering from the shock. A sob still had to leave her throat; a tear still had to fall from her eye; a knot still had to melt from her stomach – but it was gone. The grief had done more than dissipate; it *disappeared*. Entirely. Completely gone.

Sara looked at her hands as if they had something to do with it. She wiped her eyes dry and held onto the walls for support as she lifted herself, her body shaking the last vestiges of despondency like a dog shakes the ocean off his fur. After taking a few gulps of air and trying to blow them out slowly, she walked over to her bed and sat down wondering what the hell had just happened to her. Nothing had ever felt that horrible to her. The closest she ever came to feeling like that was when Stacy Martin lost her dog and Sara hugged her in the hallway in eighth grade, both of them sobbing even though Sara had never met the dog. "You're just a sensitive soul," said Mrs. O'Malley when she dried their tears in the nurse's office. Sara took it as a compliment. Stacy became her best friend and got a new dog a few months later. But this grief was nothing like that. This was a hundred times worse. A thousand times worse!

Too frightened to think about it any further, Sara prepared to make her bed and start putting clothes into the closet and dresser. She didn't want to look too put away when her roommate came, but she couldn't stand not doing anything. A lot of new students were in the hallways, parents coming and going with their freshmen, pushing them gently out into the brave new world. Sara didn't want to meet anybody yet. She wanted to just get used to that one room before she moved on to the hallway. She stood up and grabbed the sweatshirt off the bed where it had landed. As soon as her fingertips felt the soft but pilled fabric of the sweatshirt, her chest constricted and tears sprang to her eyes. She snatched her hand away. Without thinking she tried again and her pulse fired rapidly, her stomach flipped over and her knees buckled. She landed hard on the bed and drew her hand into her stomach, cradling it with the other like an injured animal.

"Oh my god," she said.

For three weeks, Sara thought the sweater was cursed, but couldn't think of any way that it was possible. Nor could she ask somebody what they thought. The last thing she needed was to be classified as a kook her first semester in college. But she had nightmares that wouldn't let up, waking up every night for those three weeks, without fail, sweating and quietly crying. The sweatshirt was under her bed. She had kicked it there on her first day in her room, too afraid to touch it again with her hands, and she left it there. She shoved her empty suitcase under the bed, against the hoodie, pushing it back as far back as she could.

On the last night of the third week, she woke again, sweaty, breathing heavily, her pillow soaked in tears. Her roommate was shaking her, hard, and whispering her name.

"Sara, wake up, kiddo. Wake up!"

Sara opened her eyes and looked into her roommate's eyes, relieved to feel nothing like what she knew she felt only moments before. Her dreams had no action; no cast of characters. Her dreams were just shapes and colors colliding and the combination filled her with the same emotions she felt holding that awful sweatshirt. Without thinking, she said to her roommate, "The hoodie under my bed is cursed and it won't let me go."

Surprisingly, her roommate did not laugh or even raise her eyebrows. She just said, "It's under your bed?"

She then knelt down, moved the suitcases, and using a flashlight on her key chain, found the sweatshirt shoved in the corner under the bed. Sara wanted to warn her, to tell her she shouldn't touch it, but she couldn't find the words. She still couldn't believe she had told her roommate. But her roommate stood up with the sweatshirt in her hand and looked completely normal. No tears, no heaving chest, no panic in her eyes.

"Is this the shirt?"

216

Sara nodded.

"What's the curse? What does it do?"

Sara opened her mouth and closed it again. She looked at the shirt then up at her roommate. Her roommate's face held no judgment. There was no sarcasm in her tone or in her expression. She asked "What does it do?" the way someone would ask about a football that is really a lighter — as if she really wanted to know.

"It makes you cry. It makes you feel like—" She drew in a ragged breath, unsure if her panic was related to the sweatshirt, or the potential loss of a good friend and roommate. "—It makes me feel like dying."

Without speaking, her roommate sat down on her own bed with the sweatshirt in her arms. She looked like she was thinking. When she looked at Sara, she didn't look like she was considering "what should I do with this crazy girl I'm stuck with?" In fact, she looked like she was trying to help Sara solve The Mystery of the Cursed Hoodie.

"Weird question," she finally said. She wasn't whispering and her voice sounded loud in Sara's ears. She must have winced because her roommate apologized and repeated it again in a whisper. Without asking anything, she walked over to her own closet and pulled a box down from the top shelf. Sara had never seen the box before, and wondered what it was. It was a brown and black box with an Asian look to it, though her roommate was not Asian. Her red hair made that pretty apparent. There was no writing on the box or any indication that it held anything at all. Sara would probably have used the box to hold all the scrunchies she owned, or maybe her makeup.

Her roommate dug around inside the box for a minute and Sara saw her lifting up letters, photos and other things that looked like memorabilia. Finally, she stood up and walked over to Sara with something in her hand.

217

"Okay," she said, whispering now, aware that Sara was a little freaked out by the moment. "This may seem weird, but I want you to hold this and tell me if you feel anything."

Did her roommate have a cursed item? Is this a test to be sure Sara isn't some nut job she's stuck with for her own first year at college? Are her parents shrinks? But Sara trusted her roommate. She did from the first moment she met her and shook her hand and had lunch with her. Sitting beside her, she felt nothing but goodwill and her own personal worry.

She opened her hand, waiting for whatever it is her roommate wanted her to hold. Her roommate then dropped into her palm a Walt Disney World button, Mickey Mouse's faces smiling up at her.

Sara grinned. She giggled a little and felt her cheeks flush with warmth. Her body felt loosy-goosy and light, flutters of air pockets coasting over her skin like cool bubbles bursting when they landed. She felt amazing, happy, content. While she felt those feelings, however, Sara recognized, very clearly, that those were not her feelings. Because while the giggles gripped her throat, she felt something deeper inside her reaching out.

"You look happy," her roommate whispered.

Sara nodded. "I am. I feel amazing. I feel *free*."

Her roommate smiled softly. She lifted the button out of Sara's still open palm. She flipped it over in her own hands a few times, looking down on it lovingly, then met Sara's eyes with her own.

"And now?"

Sara blinked. She looked at her hands.

"Now...I just feel fine. I guess. Freaked out about my dream, but..." She looked at the button and lifted it with her fingertips. The same contentment and joy filled her body again. She dropped the button. "Is that cursed too? But with something better?"

"No. This is something else. Not this-this, the button. But you. You're something else."

Sara wanted to laugh. Usually people said something else like "I can't believe you just did that; you're something else!" but her roommate said it as if she were about to say "you're actually an alien from another planet and I'm here to take you home" – only with sincerity. But she couldn't bring herself to laugh.

"What do you mean?"

Her roommate took a big breath. She stood up, returned the button to the box and the box to the top shelf of her closet before sitting back down on her own bed, opposite Sara.

"This is going to freak you out. It freaked me out too. But before you let yourself get freaked out, just hear me out and answer my questions and work through it with me. And if you still feel freaked out, or don't believe me, then you can file for a new roommate tomorrow and I'll understand. Sound good?"

Sara nodded.

And that's when her roommate told her she was a witch, and when it came to Brookwick, she wasn't the only one.

Two weeks later, she went to her first meeting where she met Deidre, Elva, and Michael Fernlee. And she and Jocelyn became good friends, sharing dorms until they both graduated. Later, her parents told her of their witchy family history, and Sara learned she had been to meetings when she was a little girl.

"Sara? Are you with me?"

Sara blinked. Melinda was waving her hand in front of her eyes.

"Oh my goodness! I'm so sorry, Melinda! I drifted away, I think!"

"I'll say! What were you thinking about? I said your name so many times I was beginning to worry!" Melinda giggled a little uncomfortably and sat back in the chair. She leaned forward again for her water and took a sip.

"Oh, I was thinking of college. When you told me about Addison just hopping into her car and taking off, I thought about what I was like when I was her age."

"Did you do something similar?"

"Don't look so surprised!" Sara laughed. "But no. I mean, my parents – Bostonians their entire lives – were a bit surprised I didn't want to stick so close to home, but in some respects coming to Brookwick was like running away. For them, it was anyway. I was just wondering what could have made her come to Brookwick, and I got carried away with memories."

Melinda nodded. "I understand. It's exciting to have someone new. Especially someone so intriguing."

"In what way?"

"Hm?"

"In what way is she intriguing?"

"She hopped in her car shortly after graduating *high school* and drove thousands of miles over two years, using her back seat as a bed! I'd call that intriguing!"

"Right! Right!" Sara shook her head and laughed. "So did she mention why she did it?"

Melinda shook her head as she swallowed another gulp of water. "No. She just said she hopped in the car, didn't look back, and explored the world in her Toyota. She seemed happy about it though, so I don't think it was anything sinister."

Sara wondered if Addison knew she was a witch and if something happened in her old town.

"Did she mention the name of her town?"

Melinda raised her eyebrows. "Sara Giles, are you gossiping with me?"

"No! No, of course not!"

Melinda threw her head back and laughed.

"Melinda." Sara joined in her laugh. "Okay, yes. I am. I'm sorry. I can't help it! She was such a nice girl, I suddenly feel worried about her realizing she spent two years sleeping in a car!"

Her visitor shook her head as the laughter died down and smiled at Sara. "Really I understand. I felt the same way when she told me. I'm only sorry I couldn't talk to her longer, but she works at the shop, you know, so we can stop in anytime. And we can try to extract the dirty details." Her wink made Sara feel mildly ashamed and amused at the same time.

"Very funny."

"Anyway, I do think she likes Nick though. Wanda's son."

"Oh really?"

"Yes. Who wouldn't though, right? If you were her age?"

"How's that sweater coming?"

Henry was about to pull into the parking lot at the college when a small car nearly hit them head on coming around the corner and screeching off down the road. He came so fast, Henry called out and Elva could hear the fear in his cry, echoing her own. She reached her arm out to grab Henry's and folded her body in on itself.

Henry cursed, spit flying from his mouth as he twisted his body to get a look at the car, now completely gone. He was so angry, and so *scared*, he couldn't speak. He just looked at Elva, their car not yet in the parking lot, his foot still pressed hard on the brake pedal. Elva could see the entire whites of his eyes, his pupil swimming in the middle, nearly bulging.

Elva slowly let out the breath she had been holding and waved her hand in front of her toward the parking lot. "Park." When Henry didn't move, she said, "Before we get killed."

Henry eased his foot off the pedal, and driving more slowly than she thinks was really necessary, he parked in the first space he found despite that it was farthest away from the path leading to Broom Lake.

"I think I'm going to need a minute here," he said.

"Yes. I think I'll get out and breathe in some nice, fresh air."

"Be thankful you can, my dear. Be thankful. That man was crazy."

Once they made their way to the lake, they sat on an empty bench facing the treeline behind which the turret of the campus's administration spiraled in the air. It was still early in the day and the sun shone high above them. It wasn't officially summer yet, but they could feel it coming, having already enjoyed several weeks of excellent weather. They were just waiting for their spirits to catch up, which still expected rain every now and then.

"Do you remember when Deidre took us here for our anniversary?" Elva leaned her head on her husband's shoulder and admired how comfortable it still felt, even when they were filled with tension from the careening car in the parking lot.

"Oh, yes," he replied. "How could I forget?"

"Remember the fire lights she cast in the sky, how bright they were?"

"Mmm," he said. She felt his shoulder rock as his head nodded. "I do."

"It was so beautiful, how each spark swooped and curled in the air, like sparrows." Elva smiled at the memory and closed her eyes. She suddenly wished it were early evening so she could better capture the feeling of that night so many years ago. "She was so happy for us."

"She still is," Henry said.

After a moment, Henry added, "It's too bad things didn't work out for her and Michael. He could be a real ass sometimes, but he seemed good for her. Not many men can take a woman like Deidre – being bossy and all that."

Elva giggled. "Actually!" She told Henry about Michael and Deidre coming to the shop together. She didn't mention Addison, only saying Deidre had called on Michael while doing some research for the group. "Deidre was glowing! I swear to it! Her cheeks were red and if I didn't know better – and maybe I don't – I would even say that maybe they had... you know. Done an *all-nighter.*"

"Well, well!" His chuckle rumbled in his chest and his shoulders shook up and down. Elva raised her head and wrapped her arm through his. They watched a jogger run by them, her rhythmic pants regular and steady even as she lifted her hand in a wave and smiled quickly at them before all her facial muscles relaxed again into concentration and determination. Both Elva and Henry watched her go down the trail and said nothing for a while.

As they sat and Henry began to tell her about the maps he was studying earlier that morning, a young man walked by, his hands stuffed deep in his pockets and ear phones in his ears. The music was loud enough that Elva could hear the tinny noise of the music being played. She recognized the young man as Brian Grosse. He manages the coffee shop across the square from A Stitch is Cast. Elva watched his face, ready to catch his eye and say hello. She liked the boy, and felt sorry for all the problems he encountered in high school. She didn't know him well, but she knew a bullied kid when she saw one, and wanted to always extend kindness. As he hurried along and got closer, Elva winged it and shot out a small spell that lifted a stick and let it fall again. The action worked, and Brian's eye, caught by the movement, lifted. Elva smiled brightly. He pulled the earphones from his ears and met them at the bench.

"Oh! Hello, Mrs. Doring! How are you doing? Mr. Doring! Good to see you!" Brian's smile was warm and wide. He accepted Henry's hand and after stuffing the earphones in his pocket, he leaned in to give Elva a hug.

"Brian, please. I have told you repeatedly not to call me that. Please, call me Elva. If it makes you uncomfortable, you can call me Aunt Elva."

"Sorry, Mrs. Doring. The sheriff tried that with me once too, but it just isn't my style. And I'd teach my kids the same. But I appreciate the reminder."

"Makes me feel old!" she kidded with him.

"Nice try, Mrs. Doring, but I'm not falling for it." He chuckled and looked behind him at the lake. "Great day, isn't it? Still a little cool, but really nice. Are you sad about the warmer weather, Mrs. Doring? Can't really knit scarves when it gets hot, right?"

"Actually, you can knit many things in the summers! Maybe if you came to a class, you could find out. Many men knit, you know."

"Oh, no. I wouldn't be able to afford it anyway."

Elva blushed. She didn't mean to sound like she was just trying to promote her business, and she knew Brian had a hard time, living on his own and paying his own way. "I hope your managers over at the coffee shop are treating you well."

"Of course. I like it there. It's not a great job, and sometimes I wonder if maybe I should try to leave

Brookwick and find something better, but I do like the job. I get to meet a lot of people, and talk, and I make good drinks, right?"

Elva smiled. "Yes, you do. Though I haven't been in there in a while. Too much caffeine is not good for an old bird like me. I take my tea at the shop and hope for the best."

"That, or she takes a nap on the yarn," Henry joked.

Brian laughed.

"I met your new sales girl," he said. "She seems really nice. She drinks hot chocolate. Even when it's hot outside."

"I like her very much."

"I was supposed to meet her yesterday, you know. We're sort of friends. I think." His toe started digging in the dirt. *Just like a little kid,* Elva thought. *Bless his heart.* "But something must have happened because she never showed up, and I didn't think to get her phone number and I didn't want to knock on her door at the apartment because I didn't want to freak her out because she didn't really tell me where she lived, even though I know where all the new girls live who start working for you and stuff, and... Well. I'm blabbing."

"You like her, huh?" She couldn't wipe the smile off her face.

Brian shrugged. "Nah. Not really. I mean, she seems nice and stuff but I hardly know her. And I don't want to be that guy who likes every first girl he sees, you know? Besides, like I'd tell you! You're her boss!" Brian laughed. At first, the laugh sounded light and careful, but it escalated into something a little panicky. Abruptly, he cleared his throat, and let the laugh die there.

There was a moment of uncomfortable quiet as the last of the laugh rolled away with the lapping waves of the lake.

"How's your car doing, Brian? Some jerk almost killed me coming in here and I know you probably drive better than that fool. Think I saw you with something sporty once, yeah?"

Brian looked surprised by the question. "Um. My car is good. Good. Doing fine. Just a car, really. What happened?"

Henry shrugged. "No big deal, really. Just some college nut probably fleeing the scene of a crime. Who knows what kids are doing these days, really."

Elva ducked her chin to her chest. The chance meeting was beginning to feel strange and she no longer felt the romance she did only ten minutes earlier. She looked at her watch.

"Oh, Henry. We really do have to get running. I'm sorry. It's so lovely, but I did promise Deidre I would meet her at the shop to go over the class schedules coming up, and we have to make some changes to the website and now that Katrina isn't here, I have to figure out how to do it all."

"I know how to do some web page things, Mrs. Doring. I could help you out."

"What a lovely offer, Brian, thank you! I will make the attempt on my own first – with Deidre, of course – but if it doesn't work out, hopefully you can fix whatever I mess up and still do what needs doing. That would be great. I'll let you know, yeah?" She stood up and met his gaze, smiling again, trying to forget the strange laugh and ignore the tickle that now crept into her brain, right in the back, where a memory was trying to come into focus.

"Sure thing. No problem." He was still standing where he had stopped when he first spotted Elva, but now that Elva was standing, she felt very crowded. She could swear it was Brian's warm breath on her eyes and not a breeze from the lake – that's how close they were. Elva took a deep breath and tried to look like she wasn't uncomfortable. At the same time, she swung her leg to the side and tried to face Henry. But when she did, she twisted her knee and cried out in pain.

Henry jumped from his seat and gave Brian a push. Elva reached out for the edge of the bench as she fell sideways, her elbow landing hard on the wood and her hip crunching the dirt.

"You okay? What is it? What happened? Tell me where it hurts? Is it your chest? Your jaw? What happened?"

Elva chuckled through the pain and tried to ignore the sting of fresh tears at her eyes.

"My knee. I'm an old fool, and I twisted my knee. And then I landed on my elbow. And then I landed on my hip. And I'm realizing very suddenly and with little grace, my dear man, that I am old."

Henry stared at her, fear still etched on his face.

"Yes," she said, smiling, and lifting her hand and placing it gently on his cheek. "'Tis true. I'm afraid you have the same affliction."

She tried to laugh and ease his fear, but it made her hip rotate slightly and she realized she had yet to draw her knee in. She rolled onto her backside so her knee was more straight.

"I'll need help getting up."

Henry reached under her, one arm around her back and the other grasping her hand. He blew out the air in his lungs as he tried to lift, but he couldn't raise his wife.

"Brian, honey. Could you be a dear and please help my husband lift his poor sac of a wife?"

Brian was still standing where Henry had pushed him, watching.

He stepped forward, got on the other side of Elva, and wrapping both hands around her upper arm, just beneath her arm pit, he lifted when Henry said to. Elva was easily placed on the bench. She thanked them both. Henry wanted to immediately look at her knee but Elva shooed his hands away.

"So sorry to have interrupted your walk, Brian. Thank you for stopping to chat with us." She made her smile bright and as cheerful as possible. "It was lovely seeing you again."

"You too, Mrs. Doring." He looked at Henry and raised his eyebrows. Elva squeezed Henry's hand, hoping Brian wouldn't notice. She wanted him to leave. When Henry nodded, Brian said his last good byes, and as he started walking the trail again, he pulled the earphones from his pocket and put them back in his ears.

It wasn't until a full minute later, when the last of his jacket was seen through the trees and he was out of sight, that Elva let out the breath she had been holding since he wrapped his fingers around her arm.

"Henry." She turned to her husband whose face was full of worry for his wife. "Get the car. We have to see Sara."

CHAPTER THIRTY

Addison was watching the coffee shop when Nick came around the corner and met her at the front steps of the diner. It was a cute diner, with a curved curb for stairs on the corner that led into the entrance. It reminded her of diners in old movies, with the bright Broadway Diner neon signs and caboose-style windows, lined with couples paired together behind the glass, most likely eating pie or sharing a milkshake.

She thought that asking to meet him at the diner would feel normal, like meeting any old friend at a diner (not that she's done that before but she thought she could do it easily with somebody. Maybe Melinda? The girl she met at the last knitting class?), but as soon as she spotted him and her stomach did a flip-flop, she knew she was just kidding again. She wondered briefly if that's how it would have felt if she had met Brian at the coffee shop when she was supposed to. She probably will never know, because what guy would agree to see her again after her complete and total brain-wipe? *How embarrassing that must have been for him*, she thought with some shame. She didn't know what to do about it, though.

"Hey!"

Addison smiled. Nick leaned in and gave her a friendly hug (she tried to think nothing of it) and he walked up the steps and held open the door. "Ladies first," he said, waving his arm before him and through the door, just like an usher would do, she thought.

The inside was just as charming as the outside and they did have pie stands with cherry pie, banana cream pie, pecan pie and apple pie.

"Remind me not to eat much because I might want to try some pie."

"Noted," said Nick. He led them to a corner booth that put them almost directly across from the record store. Nobody seemed to be shopping just then and she wondered why it was so quiet.

"Why is it so quiet today?"

"What do you mean?"

She looked around the diner and immediately felt silly. Nick didn't lead them to the corner booth because it was cool and charming. He led them there because it was the only seat available. And it wasn't quiet. There was an old-fashioned jukebox at the opposite end of their "aisle" playing "Oops, I Did It Again" by Britney Spears. Addison shook her head. "Just when you think a town can't get any more cute."

Nick looked over at her. "You like it, right? It's great. Reminds me of old burger joints, like the one in *Back to the Future*."

Nick and Addison looked over the menu. Addison really did want pie so she decided to order a Caesar salad and some coleslaw while Nick got the burger, probably inspired by his own movie reference and nostalgia. When the burger came it was the most picture-perfect burger she had ever seen, with crisp green lettuce, a juicy red tomato, and even layers each of mayonnaise, ketchup and mustard, perfectly placed beneath a shiny white onion slice.

"Wow!"

"Right?" He bit into the burger, and she dove into her equally delicious looking salad, savoring the creamy taste of parmesan cheese. Now that she had a job, a guaranteed paycheck was in her future. The luxury of meeting a friend at a diner was a fantastic way to end her first week at Brookwick.

"One week," she said between bites. "I've been here for one whole week."

"Really? It seems longer. Are you sure?"

Addison nodded without thinking about it, quite sure she knew how long it's been since she even stepped foot in her car.

"Oh no!" Addison jumped up from the booth and ran outside. She ran as fast as she could around the corner and down another block. When she saw her car was still parked where she had left it a week ago, she whispered a "Thank you, car gods, thank you!" and walked over to it. Pasted to the windshield were three bright yellow tickets. She grabbed them and walked around her car, her heart hammering, confident she'd find a boot on her wheel. But there was no boot. Satisfied with just the tickets, grateful she still had her car, she pulled the keychain that now had three keys on it (her car, the shop and her apartment) and climbed inside. She tried to push away the sad thought that her first paycheck was spoken for, but the three bright envelopes did little to help.

She inhaled. The smell of her car reminded her of her old life which felt just as Nick said: longer. Was it really only a week ago? That's it? A week ago when she ended a two-year car ride, sleeping in the back seat and eating tacos from the center console? The discman lay on the passenger seat floor with the tape adapter. They looked so lonely. She bent to pick them up and nearly jumped out of her skin when Nick rapped on the window. She rolled down the window.

"I am so sorry! I completely forgot about my car!"

Nick shrugged and laughed. "I figured it was that, or maybe... Actually, I don't know. Something else. I know the salad isn't that bad though."

Addison smiled. "Want a ride?"

After Nick ran back into the diner and paid for their meal, which he brought back to the car in styrofoam containers, Addison started driving. She took the main drag about the square and then turned down the same street she was parked on only moments earlier. Nick liked her plan to drive around – no maps, no cell phones, no plan. Addison was keenly aware that now that she had a home, getting lost could be a problem, but Nick grew up in Brookwick assured her he could get them home. Just in case, he had a cell phone. So Addison did what she always did. She just let the road lead her, and took off.

Definitely not a date, she thought. *This is too fun to be a date.*

Addison and Nick drove for over two hours, through winding country roads and small suburban neighborhoods. Addison was sure to turn off main routes whenever she could, sticking to small roads she didn't think could be found on maps. Once on a main road too long, she found it was too easy to end up somewhere *typical*. She had no other way to describe it. Each town along a major route looked the same as the last town. The grocery stores were owned by huge chains, the shopping plazas were filled with fast food restaurants that ran ads everywhere, and there was nothing that said "You are somewhere *new*, somewhere with personality, where people still say hi when they pass each other on the road, and where the mailman will chase you down if you get an important letter, and maybe even recognize the handwriting of the person who sent it." She wanted more of those towns. Brookwick felt like one.

There wasn't one fast food chain in the square. Everyone seemed to know everyone else, and even though it had been only one week, she felt comfortable. She felt real. She felt like a member of a community. She hoped it would never change.

Nick seemed excited by the change, stunned with Addison's ability to lead them down roads he had never noticed before. "It's uncanny!" he said. "I've lived in this town my whole life, gone on plenty of joy rides with friends, cruised down roads after getting my license just because I *could*, and thought I discovered every place there was to discover in a fifty-mile radius. You've been here one week and you've taken me down more streets that I've never even *noticed* in one hour than I managed in all that time. Unreal!"

Addison laughed. "Maybe it's because I *don't* know Brookwick that I see it so *well*, huh? Ever think of that?"

"I can see that," he said, bobbing his head up and down.

"So did you have a lot of friends in your high school?"

"I had enough."

"Were you ever friends with Brian?"

"Brian?"

"The guy who works at the coffee shop. Dark hair?"

"Oh!" Nick laughed. It wasn't the same laugh he had before. It was the laugh the teenagers had when they harrassed Brian. "You mean Brian Gross-man. Yeah, I know him, but we weren't friends. Different circles."

Nick snorted. The sound turned Addison off, but she ignored it. "Gross-man?"

"Everybody called him that. Dude was filthy sometimes."

"Don't you think it's maybe a little..." Addison wanted to tread carefully. She liked Nick, but she didn't like picking on people. Especially Brian, who she really sort of liked – even though he may hate her himself right now.

"Juvenile?" he finished for her.

Addison breathed a sigh of relief. It was so much easier to be disappointed and then relieved when he filled in the bad adjective for her. "Yes. Exactly. High school is over, right?"

"Of course, yeah. Of course. No, listen. I'm not trying to be mean. It was high school. We're a small town. And Brian was just... you know. Honestly, he was just dirty. Seriously."

He looked over at Addison as if feeling her out. She looked at him in expectation, letting him know she wanted him to finish.

"Literally," he added emphatically. "Dirty face, arms, hands, jeans looking like he was working on a farm."

"Well did he have a farm?"

"No. His mom and he lived on Cedar Street, only a few blocks from my place. Nice place to live, big back yard. With *grass,* not a chicken coop. It was kind of weird, because nobody knew how he got so darned dirty in the first place."

Addison didn't know what to say. "Does it matter?"

Nick was quiet for a minute. "You like him, huh?"

"What? No! Not like *that.* Just other than you, and maybe two minutes with Melinda, he's the only other person I've ever had a conversation with."

"And Elva."

Addison rolled her eyes. "Yes. Ms. Popularity, that's me, with the gray-haired old ladies for friends, dishing out the gossip and giggling over fashion magazines. Sure."

Nick laughed. "Well, as far as I know, Brian has never had a girlfriend and—"

"I do not like him like that!"

He guffawed, as if hanging out with buddies and one just snorted soda pop out of his nose. He threw his knee up in sync with his hand and his covered his mouth. A small snort came from his throat.

"Did you just snort?" she asked, eyes wide, her teeth bared, ready to laugh again.

"Yeah. Sorry. Sorry!" Nick wiped his hands on his jeans and rolled the window down a little. He was wiping tears from his eyes. "Whew! Sorry. That's so embarrassing. It happens sometimes." With shoulders lifted by his ears, he held his hands out. "Still be my friend?"

"Nope. Done-so, Gonzo."

Unfortunately, Nick's episode resulted in a casualty. Her discman got the brunt of his stomping foot and the cover ripped off the top. To add insult to injury, the tape adapter was split in two. Nick apologized up, down and sideways, and Addison tried her best to assure him it was nothing, but the tears told him something else. She felt stupid for crying about a discman. She wasn't even sure if people could still buy them in stores and she hated the thing, fighting with it on every drive, risking death just for the sake of a different song. But something about it still crushed her.

"I think you should pull over. It's not safe to drive when you can't see that well." His voice was soft while still managing to be stern. And she had to admit that it was reasonable. Turning on her hazards, she pulled onto the shoulder of the road. There were no houses to be seen. It was really dark, because there were not street lights either. She left the car running, put it in neutral and pulled up on the emergency brake. Nick handed her the discman and tape adapter pieces. Addison held them. Her hands were trembling.

"I'm really sorry, Addison. I can replace it for you."

Addison shook her head. She sniffled and without thinking, she reached under her seat for a tissue from the thin bag she kept there. Dumb place to leave tissues – talk about an accident risk – but it always worked best for her. She wiped her nose, trying not to think too much about the fact that the most handsome boy she had met in all her life was right there witnessing her snot, and shoved it in a bag behind his seat meant for trash.

"*I'm* sorry," she insisted. "I'm so dumb. I barely know you and I'm crying over a relic." She choked on the last word and was horrified to feel more tears coming. She pressed her lips tightly together and closed her eyes, willing the tears back in.

"Hey. It's okay. I hardly think you're sad about just the discman, since you can always get another one." He paused. "I think."

Addison laughed once, the laugh forcing its way through wet lips, but happy to be out there nonetheless.

"If it's any consolation at all, I know being on the road that long must have had its ups and downs, and Brookwick will too, but I am really glad you're here. You're *very* cool, and I hope you stick around a while."

Addison tried not to look up at him even though she desperately wanted to see his face, but she really didn't want him to see hers. His hand reached out and grabbed her chin. Rather than fight it, she let him turn her face so she had to look at him. He grinned. She smiled as best she could, hoping she wouldn't burst into tears again, wondering if he planned on kissing her with snot all over face, but she didn't have to worry.

He snorted like a pig, and she burst out laughing.

After several minutes of polite protest, Elva finally laid down the law and threatened to drive the car – magically, if need be – before Henry finally agreed to not take her to the hospital.

The ride was excruciating. Yes, her knee was aching. She was sure, however, that one of the other witches could fix it. Both Jocelyn and Rebecca were healers; Jocelyn was faster with more long-lasting results, but Rebecca needed the practice and though the pain sometimes came back, what she could accomplish helped the injury heal. Henry, however, created a new pain by following all posted road signs and ignoring her faster directions.

"I understand you have some big emergency here, Elva, but I will not risk our fool lives on this errand. What will we accomplish if we get a flat tire or hit a tree?"

Elva kept her mouth shut. This was the same conversation she's had with Henry for every wedding, funeral, shopping trip or outing, period. He wouldn't convince her and she wouldn't convince him. In some ways, she liked their predictable pattern. So much, in fact, she wondered – in the midst of her fury – why she was so angry with his *impertinence*.

It didn't matter. After the long and winding drive up Sara and Tom's driveway, Elva was sad to see that both their truck and Sara's small car were missing. Just in case, she walked up to the side door and rapped hard, shooing Henry back in the car when he saw her limping.

A note would have to do.

Deidre and Michael were thigh-high in historical texts and mythological anthologies in his office on the Brookwick College campus. It had taken them all morning to find, stack and move the books from the library to his office several buildings away, on the other side of the campus from the library. But they felt they could discuss their theories, failures and frustration better if they had some privacy. Both struggled to stay focused. Deidre kept remembering the way his arms felt around her only two nights before, how much softer his skin had become, yet how strong he still remained despite their long time apart. Michael remembered too, remembering how delicate she was, and how more tender she seemed to be in her approach. He remembered how frequently she met his gaze and held it, no expression on her face, her eyes simply opening up before him, allowing him entry into whatever he could gather. But now all signs of vulnerability were gone. His memory would have to do.

"Do you need anything to drink?"

Deidre licked her finger as she flipped a thin page of *Obscure Magickal Peoples and Relevant Histories*. "No, thank you," she said quietly.

"Anything in there?"

"Not yet," she said.

"Okay. I'll be right back. Just going to the office for some tea."

Deidre lifted her head. "Could you get me some tea?"

"Absolutely. Earl Grey?"

Deidre nodded. She bent her head again over the book and using her finger to read the page – finding that it helped her stay focused – she hoped for a miracle.

The books offered very little by way of craft witches. Just as she expected. But it did offer insight into some spells she didn't know about. Finding information on "striking" was proving tedious. Striking was an old spell used mostly by darker witches; that is, witches with ill intentions, such as thieves, vandals and even murderers. To be struck meant that one had been manipulated. A witch had cast a spell on a person, compelling them to commit a crime (usually) at a very specific time in the future. It was a complicated spell and required immense skill. It was no wonder that the witches who knew how to strike a person were typically well-off, their pockets heavy with stolen treasure.

It didn't sit well with Deidre or Michael that the witches he met in Erfurt used this sort of magic on him. Though a person could not remember any details of being struck, what they were forced to do, if they had done it, or usually who had done it to them (or that it was ever done at all), they can often remember how they felt before, during and after the spell was cast. Literally, whether or not they were scared, happy, comfortable, or otherwise. Michael very clearly remembers feeling *willing*. He knows, without a doubt, that he wanted to be struck, agreed to it, and was feeling charitable.

"They needed something desperately and I could provide it. That's the feeling I have. I feel like I was doing something that would make me feel honorable, valued, proud. There is no doubt in my mind that I wanted them to do this."

Deidre believed him. They were soul mates, and she would not waste another moment doubting *that*, and as such she could feel his conviction. Just as he believed what he said, she believed it too, as if she were there herself to remember.

When Michael returned with the tea, he set them on coasters on his mahogany desk by the window and walked back to the low, round table in the middle of the room.

Michael had an opulent office. For a history professor he did quite well, but he was very thrifty and barely spent any money at all. Besides, the college provided well for their best history professor. Deidre was embarrassed to admit she knew very little about what made him so valued by the college, but each year they awarded him something and asked him to speak at several events. Michael always agreed, and seemed to enjoy it. She could only suspect that it had something to do with his vast knowledge of obscure history, thanks in no small part to his secret life as a witch. He traveled extensively, visiting other witch communities, seeking them out, and speaking to so many different kinds of witches. Many of them were old, and he recorded their conversations, covering topics such as local village lore, histories of the lands, the royalty and the families, as well as covering wars, plagues, politics and economic fall outs. He recorded them all.

What Deidre found most interesting was how he seemed to avoid the topic of witch craft, yet sought out only witches in studying history.

"I am not interested in studying the history of witches," he said, when she asked him ealrier in their relationship. "I am interested in studying the history of the world."

"But surely your research must be labeled as history of witches?"

"Why?"

"Because all your accounts of history are from the perspectives and memory of witches! For centuries, witches have lived vastly different lives than normal people."

"They have experienced the same world events, have they not?"

Deidre grew frustrated. "Perhaps, but from the perspective of witches. When the economy collapsed, they could trick people at market into seeing more money than they really had; when the crops failed, they could help it along with magic; when a woman was pregnant and the child was being strangled by the cord, they could move it out of the way without ever seeing it. These are well- and oft-used spells by witches, and that's just in my own family.

So surely their experience of world events cannot be compared to those of regular people?"

Michael smiled. "I understand what you're saying, and I don't know how to comfort you—"

"Comfort me?"

"Well, yes. You're upset that you don't understand—"

"Don't understand?"

"Dee, honey, listen—"

This is when Deidre usually left the room and decided she'd leave the conversation hanging. She never did understand how it was supposed to work, and she was chagrined to find that it did work, because the accolades continued to come in, the awards still piled up around his office walls, and there was no sign that he would ever be accused of treachery, trickery or tomfoolery. If he was fooling everyone, or making it all up, he was doing such a good job that decades of students, colleges, professors and administrators have not noticed.

Deidre stood up and walked to his desk. She lifted her mug and looked out the window.

"Be careful, Dee. It's very hot."

Deidre nodded as she contemplated what step they should take next. She blew her tea lightly. There was a knock on the door, which Michael forgot to close.

Michael looked up and greeted what must have been a student. A young man with shaggy, dirty-blonde hair stood at the door, a red long-sleeved t-shirt with a hole at the hem under a ratty looking brown back pack.

"Professor Fernlee. David. David Brown from your Vienna class."

"Yes, David, I know who you are. What can I do for you? It will be have to be quick, I'm afraid. This is not my office hours."

Deidre used the opportunity to put her tea down and go to the ladies room. When she returned, the student had gone and Michael was hunched over a new book with a bright green emerald cover.

"Is that embossed with *gold*?" she asked him.

He glanced at the cover and grinned. "It would appear so." He rubbed his finger over the metal gently and blew a thin stream of air on the metal he had touched. The shimmer that resulted was like fairy dust after a horse had stamped its hooves in protest. It rose beneath his finger and settled back down on the binding. "Yes. Real gold. Imagine that!"

"I wonder if the library is aware of that little treasure."

"No idea. Maybe it will offer us something we can actually use though."

Deidre returned to the desk and got her tea. She brought Michael's over as well.

"Are you absolutely positive that in all the interviews you've done over the years, in Europe and South America and everywhere else, that no witch had ever mentioned knit witches?"

CHAPTER THIRTY-ONE

She had long brown hair lying in waves across her back. It was thick, beautiful and so shiny it almost looked unnatural, greasy, or wet. But it was obvious it was not. Her dark brown eyes were odd but striking – save for the dark black pupil, they had no other contrast or shimmer. Simply brown, matte, alone in their steadfastness to remain so. Her high cheekbones were carved with dimples and her pointy chin was softened by age. A long neck and broad shoulders made her look taller than her five-foot and seven-inches tall, which to Addison still looked tall enough.

Addison knew she was looking at her mother. And her mother was looking at her.

Addison was wearing jeans while her mother wore a light blue dress, cinched high at the waist with a polka-dot belt, cream-colored peep-toe sandals on her feet. Her ankles were crossed delicately and for a moment, Addison wondered if her grandmother taught her mother to sit that way. On the floor was a toy train, very much like the one Addison was playing with as a child, in her first dream about her mother. This train was a slightly different color; it looked older, the color more faded.

"Did I get it right?"

Her mother's voice was tired, but even Addison, who had never heard her mother's voice before, could tell she was excited and nervous.

"It looks only a little different."

"Yes. It's hard to make something come back that was never there to begin with."

243

Addison wondered if that was supposed to mean more than the words, but she didn't want to ask. She felt funny speaking. Her hands were curled tightly in her lap and she knew she could move them, but she was afraid one movement in her dream would wake her. Any sane person having this sort of dream would want to stay asleep, so she refused to move.

"You can move. You won't wake up."

Addison looked at her mother and smiled shyly. "Can we not talk about it? I don't want to..." she let the words drift and linger, disappear, hoping the thoughts about waking would disappear with the breath she left behind the words. A breeze came through the window beside them and Addison could see the street outside, the lamp post at the end of the walk way, the purple and yellow Johnny Jump Ups that lined the concrete blocks of the path to the sidewalk. The grass that bordered the path and spread before her was well-manicured, each blade of grass exactly as tall as the one beside, before and behind it. "It looks nice here," she said to her mother.

"It isn't real."

"None of this is real." Addison bit her lip.

"You are wrong, sweet love."

"Let's not..." Addison tried again to move on, out of threatening territory, convinced she was tossing and turning in her bed at just that moment.

"Addy. love. You cannot wake up right now. I have made sure of it. I need you here now, and so here is where you will be."

Addison was afraid to look back at her mother. She noticed that the yard and everything outside the window ended at the sidewalk with the lamp posts. She saw no neighbors, no street, nothing beyond the edges of the grass. Literally nothing. Just a wide expanse of neutrality. She couldn't even define the color or the *nothingness* of the space. It simply *wasn't*.

"Like I said, it's not real." Her mother looked out the window and she uncrossed her hands, which had been lying over her knees. She placed one hand on the round end table that sat between them, directly center of the window, and used the table to lean and look out the window.

"Look," she whispered, and pointed a long finger. "That's our first car. It barely worked."

Addison looked out the window and saw an old car. It looked French. She wasn't sure she could ever identify it. The yellow paint was almost gray and the tires had wide white stripes that were scuffed with black from too many run-ins with curbs. The car wasn't there a moment before.

"And that there is our first apartment." She pointed again, a little behind the car, and Addison leaned in to look. "My mother was so angry." Her laugh was small and delicate; it made Addison's hair stand up in a pleasing way, as if warm breath were kissing her everywhere.

Behind the car was a tall red building. All the windows were dark except those of the french doors on the balcony two floors up. It was a small balcony with two pots on either edge; the pots were overflowing with Johnny Jump Ups.

"I love those flowers."

"They're the only flower I can recognize and name," Addison told her. "I've read about plenty of others, but I couldn't tell you what they look like. But I know about those ones. One of my foster mothers used to—"

Addison bit her tongue. She closed her eyes to avoid tears and felt she was doing that too much lately. But this was her mother. How could she say something so thoughtless?

245

"Oh, my sweetheart." Addison felt her mother's warm hand cup her cheek and her thin thumb wipe under her eyes even though no tears had yet fallen. "You have done so well, Addy. So well."

Not knowing what else to do, Addison nodded. She did not want to cry. She wouldn't.

"We left him something for you. We didn't know when you should have it. It will come when you've started, but until then... we don't know. I'm sorry. This is confusing."

A breeze came through the window and Addison heard a windchime. It was small, delicate. She opened her eyes and found that she was on a bench, looking at a lake. Her mother sat beside her. She was wearing pale yellow capri pants and black peep-toe sandals. Her light blue shirt had cream-colored polka dots. It was sleeveless, small buttons down the middle, and it was tucked in. Her mother was very thin. Her dark hair was pulled up and sat in a low ponytail. A matching blue and cream polka dot head sash wrapped around her head. Addison liked her mother's style.

"You look really nice," she said. Her mother smiled softly. Addison could see her mother's eyes get wetter. Then her lips pressed together and Addison watched as spit gathered around the corners of her mouth. She turned her head to look at the water, unsure how to react to seeing her mother cry, a woman she had never met. But the lake was gone. They were on a porch swing in the woods, gliding back and forth. There was a line of tall pine trees standing before them and a short distance down from the trees was a small creek, just big enough to be seen and heard. The noise was like a loud gurgle from a pipe after turning off an old faucet. It practically groaned. Her mother was wearing the dress again. This time she had no shoes on, but thick wool socks.

"Did you knit those?" asked Addison.

"Your grandmother knit these for me," her mother replied. Her voice sounded steady and even and Addison was relieved to hear it; she immediately felt guilty for feeling relieved.

"They're nice."

"They're meant to comfort me."

"They look cozy enough," said Addison.

"I don't know where to start with you."

Addison turned her head. Start? What does she mean? Addison didn't want to ask. Was her mother going to try to give her the history of their "family"? Was she going to say why Addison does not even know her name?

Start?

Addison was surprised to feel how angry she had become. What caused this? She didn't want to feel angry. In her dreams with her mother, she wanted to feel how she always thought she should feel with her mother: safe, warm, comfortable, happy, joyous. Not angry. Angry is what she wasted years feeling in high school when she thought she deserved her parents, or at least that her parents provide her with answers to the questions that were continually pelted at her by guidance counselors, principals and teachers who thought their positions of authority meant they had full access passes to her life. Angry was over, done. She wanted to feel her mother, and to know that her mother felt for her the way all mothers felt for their children: loved.

"I have never loved anything more than I have loved you, Addy-baby. Never."

The words made Addison's heart thump and beat fast. She could hear it beating beneath her breast plate and she felt it dip into her stomach when it reverberated, it hit so hard. The lump that formed in her throat choked any reply she may have tried to say, though she had nothing in mind. Her hands gripped the bench beneath her legs and the swinging continued. How odd that the swing should keep swinging at the same pace when so much has happened. *So much has happened.*

"You are more than you know. Your father and I are different people and so are you. Someone has the binder and the binder will tell you."

Addison looked at her mother's socks. As her mother's voice filled her ears, the soft words repeating "you are more than you know" — the socks looked as if they were pulsing, in and out, softly squeezing the feet like a massage.

She heard a splash and looked up. She was back at the lake and the bench where her mother wore the yellow capri pants. A boy was standing at the edge of the lake. Addison was alone on the bench. She wrapped her arms around her shoulders and leaned on her elbows, watching the boy throw rocks. He wasn't even trying to skip them. He looked about fifteen-years=old. He didn't seem to notice Addison as she watched. He bent over and picked up each rock. She wondered why he didn't just pick up a few at a time, save himself the extra effort. But with each reach for a new rock and each toss into the lake, he seemed to look more relaxed, his shoulders not quite as high or bound together, and his legs looking as if they grew and fell sideways, relaxing in a stance much like a cowboy waiting on his horse. Addison didn't want to make a sound; the splashing and the crunch of his heels as he bent and stood sounded nice in her ears.

After a few more rocks, he began to whistle. Addison didn't recognize the tune, but like the rocks, it felt pleasing to hear. His whistling paused briefly as the rock met the water and made the small splash and soon it sounded orchestrated, as if he were whistling and the splash was like the triangle at the recital. She closed her eyes and listened, suddenly feeling exhausted. Whistle, splash, crunch. Whistle, splash, crunch. Addison leaned back into the bench and crossed one leg over the other. All she needed was a ball cap to pull over her eyes and she was sure she could fall asleep.

"Except you're already asleep."

Addison opened her eyes. She was back at the window with the yard that didn't exist. The car was still there. Her mother was not in the seat opposite her but the train was now on the table. Along with the train was a note. It said, "It was made for us, to make us feel like we were at home. To make us feel safe. I never forgot. They could not give me what I missed most about my home." The words disappeared and the paper disappeared and the train rolled forward until it fell off the table and landed softly on the carpet at her feet, a thick and plush blue carpet. Addison reached out to grab the train. With her hand around it, she sat back in the chair, but instead of a train, it was a fistful of Johnny Jump Ups. She was on a bench in the square at Brookwick. The flowers had come from the cauldron beside her. She let them fall to the ground and leaned back, disappointed. Tired and confused, she wanted to cry and let her eyelids cover any tears that might pour out. "Too much. Don't want to," she said to herself in a whisper, not at all happy with the croaky voice that came out.

A person sat next to her. Addison did not want to open her eyes and so she sat still. Deciding she was going to take control of the dream herself, she thought about who she would most like to see sitting beside her. She still felt badly about standing up Brian on Sunday night and a dream would be a perfect place to apologize, make up for it, and craft a conversation that went her way.

"No," said a man's voice. Addison was startled by the voice but she did not open her eyes. "But," it said slowly, "I have something for you."

That made Addison jump up. She started running for the gazebo and heard footsteps behind her. Deciding to change course, she darted to the right and headed for the yarn shop. The 'open' sign was in the window and she knew she just had to make it to the door, turn the handle and she would be safe. She ran faster, her chest beginning to hurt. Something was hurting her feet and she didn't want to look, but the pain was coming faster and faster. Still hearing his footsteps, Addison decided to try to trip him up, so she darted left as if she were heading back toward the gazebo. As she did, she caught her reflection in a car window and nearly fell over on her face – or her mother's face. The footsteps behind her had stopped but she kept running, and once in the gazebo she ran straight through it to the other side and circled back around. Nobody was following her anymore though. She was sure of it. She didn't know why, other than the quiet, but she knew she was alone. Slowing at the record store, she crossed the street to the shop windows and looked in the window.

Only her own face peered back at her. But behind her, in the square, she saw two figures running. She spun quickly but could see nobody in the square. Turning back to the window, she saw the same two people. A woman was being chased by a man. She was running for her life. Addison leaned forward to get a closer look and that was when she heard the woman's cries. The woman was screaming! The two figures were getting closer to each other, and running closer to Addison. As they came barreling down on her, the woman's voice got louder; and as it got louder, Addison could recognize both it and the face of the woman fearful for her life: it was her mother.

Addison turned on her heels and ran as far and as fast as possible from the window and the reflection of her mother and an attacker. Going with her original plan, Addison ran to the yarn shop. She threw the door open and once inside, turned all the locks. She ran to the light switches and turned off all the lights and then slid down on the ground behind the counter where the register was. Hugging her knees, she wiped tears from her face and buried her cheeks between her legs. She was wearing her jeans again, she noticed. And the same flats she wore her sophomore year of high school on the track and field team.

"Addison, is that you?"

Elva peered her head over the counter. "Oh, Elva. This has been a horrible dream."

"Then just wake up, dear. That's what I do."

Addison wiped at her face and leaned back, feeling how puffy her eyes were. They felt just as if they had been scratched, over and over, and she wanted nothing more than an ice pack to lay across them.

"I'm actually exhausted, Elva. Honestly." She stood up and opened the register. She took out three twenties and four quarters and put them in her pocket. "For my lunch later," she said.

Elva shrugged and walked over to the coffee table and chairs in the center of the store. Addison followed. They sat opposite each other. Addison started knitting with a pink yarn.

"What are you working on?" Elva asked.

"A baby sweater."

"Oh really? For whom?"

Addison held it up. "For me," she said.

Elva giggled. "It will look great on you," she said.

Addison pushed her needle through the front leg of the next stitch. She waited for the yarn to wrap around the needle so she could draw it through, but nothing was happening.

"Nothing's happening."

251

Elva leaned forward in her chair and reached across to Addison. As she did so, the tea that was on the coffee table knocked over and spread across the table, threatening to soak several balls of yarn and a few knitting magazines.

"Oh, drat!" Elva stood, her knitting fell off her lap and hit the floor, the needles clattering on the edge of the table.

"I'll get towels."

"No need, dear! Or did you forget we have other means?" And with dancing fingers, Addison watched as Elva made the tea water bead up and rise into the air. Like a bubble suspended, the now-huge ball of tea water moved sideways and Elva laid it gently in the tea cup.

Addison stared.

"Come knit, you. And remember: '*Stitch in one makes it two, blessed be this spell's for you.*'"

Elva was not happy to hear that Deidre and Michael had no ideas for figuring out the spell put on Michael. Their limited knowledge of craft witchery didn't help, so they focused on what they knew. They admitted they just better start with the most obvious thing. Michael said it first.

"This is going to have to come second," he said, looking at the women closely. "I know this is hard. I like her too, but she has three of us. We are all good witches. We are all good *people* and we care about her." Elva felt like crying.

"I'm scared for her," she admitted, her voice high.

"Oh, honey," said Deidre, standing to go sit beside her friend and wrap her arm around her. "We are all scared for her. This needs to be done. She is more likely to be hurt if we don't do this." Elva nodded.

"I think we should do it the old-fashioned way. Like a band-aid." Elva was still sniffling into a linen handkerchief Deidre had given her. Elva admired that Deidre had such things. "So let's go." Michael lifted his tweed suit jacket from the back of the chair he was sitting in, and stood up.

"You don't mean we are going to go do it now?" exclaimed Elva, all tears dry on her face.

"Of course I do. Why not?" He stepped toward Elva. "Do you foresee some better time to crush her with the news that she is a witch? Would it be better to wait until after she's had dinner? Or a good night's sleep? Or perhaps watched more movies?"

Elva opened her mouth, her eyes wide. She stammered. With reddening cheeks, she slammed her mouth closed, thin white strips replacing her lips.

"Michael," Deidre whispered. She looked into his eyes and felt his love there. With a quiet shake of her head, she drew Elva in close. Michael let out a slow breath.

"I guess I'm just nervous," he said. He sat down heavily. "I apologize, Elva. I do. And of course we can't tell her. Once she knows, it will be impossible for her to keep the magic out of her knitting, or who else knows however else she can use it. We have to tread lightly."

Deidre watched Michael. He seemed very stressed. The pressure to have the answers was weighing heavily on his shoulders.

"The only one of us to have met knitwitches and I have nothing to offer."

"I have an idea," said Deidre to Elva.

"It won't work," Michael said.

"I have the feeling you two have already discussed this." Elva shot glares between the two of them. "So let's have it. I'll be the judge." She turned to Deidre, pointedly leaving Michael out of her line of slight.

Deidre sat back down and looked at Michael. "I know you don't agree, but I really think there's something there."

"I've told you, Dee, it's just—"

"Dut, dut, dut!" Elva stuck her hand out between the two with one finger raised, her piercing "dut-dutting" breaking the tiff between the reunited couple. "We are going to get through this conversation. This is too important to bicker. And Michael, surely you know that all things need to be tried, no matter what."

"We don't have *time*, Elva."

"We don't have anything, Michael. Not a thing. Well, we have one thing. A wayward witch who doesn't know she's a witch. And she apparently has a death sentence over her head that is due any day now, and she's knitting. So I'd like to find solutions fast because we don't know much. What if she dies because she knits when she's angry and this entire block bursts into flames?"

Nobody laughed. The threat was a very real possibility. History has proved that enough.

"Again, Elva, you are correct." Michael leaned back in his chair and crossed his arms over his chest.

Deidre took a big breath. "Michael has done most of his studies in Europe. Yes, he studied at various universities over there, but he also has done hundreds — *hundreds* — of interviews. Every single one, off the record and not for the universities, was with a witch."

Elva nodded. She didn't know where it was leading, and she didn't want to make assumptions, so she simply nodded. Too many questions in the pot would make the whole thing explode, so she chose to keep her mind simple. He was a historian, and as far as she knew he didn't teach anything about witches. Her curiosity was peaked, but she was going to wait.

It was hard for Elva. She had to bite her lip and focus on Deidre.

"I believe that it is quite possible he had met these witches in his interviews and doesn't remember it or relate the two moments."

"Europe is an awfully big place, Deidre," said Elva.

"Yes, I know that. But hear me out. Michael was drawn to Erfurt where he first met the couple. Maybe they helped him get there because they had met him and knew he was good for whatever job they had in store."

Michael interjected. "I don't think so, Dee. I didn't really start interviewing witches until after Erfurt."

"Not true," said Deidre. "You had traveled across Europe for a year before you stopped in Erfurt, and though you hadn't met any witches – *that you know of* – you did stay with several families and couples while you sought them out."

"Yes, but I believe I would have known they were witches."

"But how? You said yourself you were very new to witchcraft and understanding what magic was or felt like. How could you know? You didn't even recognize Erfurt for what it really was, practicing magic just so you could get a tour!"

"But, Dee. I would have *known*. Knitwitches are powerful! It would have hit me like a train."

"No, Michael. I disagree." Deidre and Michael both looked at Elva. She was surprised by the strength in her voice.

"I think you're looking at it the wrong," she continued. "Knitwitches are very powerful witches, which is precisely why you could have not detected their magic." She watched as Michael realized that what she said was true. They could have very well struck him as early as first meeting him outside of the city walls. She continued, "They could have struck you as early as your first day in Europe, or the day before you saw them in Erfurt. There is no telling."

"But!" Deidre sounded very excited. "He kept a journal!"

Elva's eyes widened.

"How did you know that?" Michael asked.

"You have always kept a journal. Since the first day I met you."

"Which was after I went to Germany. Both the first *and* the second time."

"Yes, but you have always kept one. Always. Since you were a young boy. I have seen them. You showed them to me."

Michael stared at her in silence. Elva watched him think, and Deidre began to smile. When her smile was full on her face, Michael joined in. "You're absolutely right."

He jumped to his feet and grabbed his sports jacket from the back of the chair. "You are absolutely right!" He bounded around the table, grabbed Deidre's face between his hands and kissed her full on the mouth. "You are wonderful!"

As he ran from the store, he called out to the two women, "Meet me at Dee's in an hour!" The bell above the door tinkled and the door slammed shut behind him.

Elva beamed at Deidre. "Well," she said slowly. "This seems to be going well." With a raised eyebrow, she sipped her cold tea.

CHAPTER THIRTY-TWO

"I'm sorry to call you so early, but Elva insisted. She isn't coming in until later and she wanted to know if you could come to the shop and help me out?"

Addison could hear Nick stretching and yawning on the other end of the line. She was mortified she had to call him. She had such a good time with him last night. Now she had to ruin the time she was looking forward to daydreaming about him by actually having him next to her. She felt like a nutcase. Most people would want to spend the next day with a person, but not Addison. She didn't want to push it. Her own feelings embarrassed her; she felt like she wasn't really allowed to have crushes, as if she was only passing through – again – and didn't have time to see real possibility in relationships.

"I told her that it would probably be fine, but she insisted. She doesn't want me here alone. She even sent Professor Fernlee over until you got here, and—" Addison looked around to make sure the professor wouldn't be able to hear her; she lowered her voice to a whisper, "I don't think he knows a thing about yarn."

"Like you do?" Nick was waking up.

"Ha. Ha. Ha. You coming or not?"

The barb had made Addison relax a little and she reminded herself, for the hundredth time, to just chill out and not think about how much she liked him. *Just a friend. Let it be.*

"Yeah, I'm coming. Try not to burn anything in the next half hour."

Addison hung up the phone. Michael was in the back drinking coffee and reading a magazine. He was still doing that when Nick came through the door exactly twenty-three minutes later looking just as good as he did the night before. How could he look this good twenty-three minutes after waking up? Addison swallowed hard.

"Rise and shine!" She saluted to Nick. Nick nodded to her and looked around the shop. He had his backpack slung over his shoulder.

"What do you carry in that thing? You seem to bring it everywhere."

"It's my man-purse." He winked at her. "All the Europeans are doing it. Hush."

He threw the bag over the counter so it landed in the corner by the random balls of leftover yarns left by students. Elva used them to demonstrate techniques to patrons who needed help with something.

"Ah! Nick! Good morning!" Professor Fernlee emerged from the break room with a yellow coffee mug still in his hand. He had a knitting magazine tucked into the back pocket of his jeans. "Very good man, getting up this early to help out in a *yarn shop*." He smacked his lips together at the end of the word "shop" as if he were about to launch into a speech made entirely of alliteration using the letter 'p' — like "shopping for paper paws in perfect happenstances." He seemed a little whimsical to Addison, but then again, she was the one making up sentences — and paper paws.

"Well, to be honest, my mother is sort of hoping it means I'll be able to get her something." He pulled a list out of his back pocket and handed it to Addison.

"What is she making? A car cover?"

Nick laughed. "Matching sweaters for me, my dad and my grandfather. She does it every few years. It's a thing." He shrugged his shoulders.

"That seems really nice," said Addison. "A lot of work."

Nick nodded.

"I would have loved something like that growing up," Professor Fernlee added. "Is it a long-standing tradition in your family, Nick?"

"Tradition? Well, I don't know. I got my first one when I was about five. It was a sweater vest. Matched the one she made my dad. His actually fits me now, but it's got a hole or two in it. And then I got another one when I was about nine. For a while, I got one every year. Then they stopped. But in the last few years I got another vest and a hoodie." He nodded, satisfied he had given an accurate report.

"Traditions are great things. They are missed eventually and sometimes, it's only after you've started missing them that you realize it was ever a tradition! So yes. To answer your questions, Nick, which you sort of asked, I would say that that is a tradition. I hope you wear those sweaters often. I bet it makes your mother very happy to see it."

Nick smiled and shook the professor's outstretched hand. The professor then turned to Addison.

"Addison, I wonder if you wouldn't mind taking care of this mug for me? I wasn't sure where I should put it and I didn't want to leave a mess or anything, so... would you mind?"

Addison washed the mug in the sink in the back room. When she went back into the shop, Nick was sitting behind the counter with a book and pencil. The professor had gone.

"That guy is kind of awesome," Addison said. "When I first met him, I thought he was kind of creepy."

"He is kind of creepy, are you kidding? Who is that jolly at eight o'clock in the morning?"

"Can't you see him as a leprechaun?"

"Yes! He'd be a perfect leprechaun!"

They both laughed, imagining the professor dressed in green parachute pants, wearing suspenders and growing sideburns out that covered half his cheek. "He'd have to look a little older though," said Addison. "His hair is too dark."

"Yes, and he needs brighter blue eyes. He has the red cheeks though."

"Yes, but no Santa is he. Not rotund enough. Needs to drink more beer."

"Seriously, if teaching or history or the combination makes you that jolly and pleasant, maybe I'll consider it when I go to college."

"You think? Aside from the fact that I think people may want to consider a limit on their jolly, but you think you'll go to college? And maybe teach?"

Nick looked up from his book, which was actually some Sudoku puzzles. Addison tried them out a few times when she wanted to hang out at diners or rest areas, but she grew bored with them pretty quickly. She also tried crossword puzzles, but only got frustrated and felt no momentum. She refused to cheat, but found herself doing it at least fifteen times for every puzzle – even in the "easy" books. She would never admit it to Nick or even Derwin, but she preferred the word finds. Too bad she'd never do one again, not when there was the risk someone else would find them. Not living on the road every day has its disadvantages.

"Well I know I'm going to college. I'm undecided about what to study, but I keep thinking maybe English, maybe History. I don't know yet. Something along those lines though."

For some reason, this news took Addison by surprise. She supposed it was because Nick was her age, and not in school, and so maybe that's the way it was going to stay. It occurred to her that she really didn't know much about what he did do during his days.

"So, how will you pay for it?"

"I've been working every summer since I was thirteen and then when I was sixteen, I started working full time in the summers and part time during the school year at the high school. At first I started by helping the janitor out in the summers, and then the administration offices needed someone to help them out in the offices. I started doing that during study hall hours. After school, though, I went back to helping the janitor out, mopping hallways and stuff. My mother hates it. Thinks I should go to the grocery store off Route 24 and be a cashier or something."

"And that's enough? To pay for college?"

Nick snorted. Not a pig snort; just a laugh snort. The almost-pig snort made Addison smile, remembering how he had cheered her up last night.

"Absolutely not. My parents will help, of course, and then there is financial aid and maybe some scholarships. To be honest, I haven't applied yet."

"But you know you're going?"

"Yeah, of course."

Addison watched as Nick started working on his puzzle again. Or he at least appeared to be working on it.

"It would take a few years for me," she said.

"What's that?"

Addison ignored the question, feeling Nick asked in a half-hearted way, hoping he was really concentrating more on the game than he seemed. She grabbed his mother's list and walked out from behind the counter to find the yarn. She started looking at all the shelves, trying to find the right colors and then matching lot numbers. Nick's voice carried across the room.

"You could go too, you know."

Addison swallowed hard. "I don't really see how that's gonna work," she said. She tried to make her voice sound normal. She didn't need to have another emotional breakdown in front of Nick right now.

"There are a ton of programs out there that help students find a way to go to school. You should look into them."

"Maybe," she said.

Realizing that she was about to cry – again – she used the last of her strength to swallow hard and said to Nick, "For a thrill, I'm getting a hot chocolate. Want one?"

"No, thanks."

Addison practically ran out the door and drew in deep breaths of the cool air. It was warming up fast, but she liked feeling the coolness for a little while, especially after feeling like she just escaped emotional fallout. She dug her hands in her pockets, assuring herself she remembered to bring a ten dollar bill, and walked rapidly across the square to the coffee shop. It wasn't until she walked over the threshold and heard Brian's voice that she remembered she hadn't seen him since before she stood him up.

Shit.

Too late now, she thought. Hoping Brian hadn't seen her, Addison considered moving back outside, but she knew that would only draw more attention to herself and then he would know she was actually avoiding him. There was no way to fix that mistake, though she had no idea how she was going to fix her last one. She got in line behind a small black woman wearing big sunglasses, like the ones worn by Jackie O. She carried several shopping bags on one arm and stood perfectly still in high wedge heels. Addison had no idea where in the world this woman was shopping a little before nine in the morning, and how she got so much done already, but she was mighty impressed.

Addison tried not to look ahead too far and risk catching Brian's eye, but she also wasn't sure if he had seen her yet. If she hadn't stood him up, she knew she'd be looking for him, give a wave and a smile. That's what friends did when they saw each other. Not that she's had much practice, but it seemed a decent thing to do. Risking complete failure or being rejected immediately, Addison raised her head to see if Brian had seen her there yet. But Brian wasn't behind the counter. Instead it was a young girl who looked like she was new to the job. She was bending over a lot, looking for supplies, and the man she was helping had to point to a cupboard behind her, telling her where the coffee filters were.

Addison breathed a sigh of relief. She thought Brian worked every day. Finally excited to actually taste the hot chocolate, Addison closed her eyes and leaned her head back. She heard the woman ahead move her bags and shuffle forward, so opening her eyes only slightly, Addison made sure she didn't bump into the woman when she moved ahead as well. The woman wanted only hot water with slices of lemon.

Just as Addison was about to start paying attention to the world again, she heard Nick call her name. "Addison! Man! I'm glad I caught you here."

She turned to look at Nick, who was out of breath. The door still hadn't closed by the time he made it to her side. "Sorry. But I forgot that Professor Fernlee said I wasn't to leave you alone, not for one second, no matter what. He was pretty fierce about it. And then Elva called while you were out and I told her you came over here for a drink and she nearly cut my ear off with her yelling!"

Addison's mouth dropped. "What? Why?"

Nick shrugged. "You got me, but I high-tailed it over here. No way will I face the wrath of Elva and risk getting no cookies this Christmas. Sorry." He shrugged his shoulders.

Addison was confused and a little angry. Why in the world would Elva not let her be alone? Did she not trust her or something?

"Aw hey, Brian. How have you been doing?"

Brian was standing behind the counter, watching the exchange between the two. And he didn't like it. Addison could see he was angry, his lips were thin white lines and it looked like every muscle in his face was tight. Addison's heart hammered in her chest. The last thing she wanted was to see Brian, but the absolute last thing she wanted was to apologize to him for missing their date *and doing it in front of Nick*. She tried to think of a way to make Nick go away, but it would be so awkward. Wouldn't it?

"I'm doing okay, Nick. And yourself?"

"Can't complain."

Addison took a deep breath.

"You the manager here or something?"

Someone came in the door and took up a spot behind Addison and Nick. Addison stepped to the side to let the person go ahead. Nick didn't move. He seemed oblivious to the new customer in the store.

"Or something."

"I hear you do the hiring and stuff here?

"Yes, I do. A new girl started just today, in fact." Brian tilted his head to the side, as if pointing to the girl, who was nowhere to be seen. "She's washing some dishes in the back right now. First day."

Nick smirked. "Get to do the fun stuff on the first day, huh?"

"You know how bullying works, Nick, you tell me."

Addison gasped. Nick stood up and took his knuckles off the counter top. It occurred to Addison then how arrogant he looked, leaning that way, talking sideways to Brian.

"Hey, sorry, man. I was just trying to make conversation."

Addison felt sick. What was going on here?

"Did you or your girlfriend want a drink?"

Her jaw dropped. He tried to let the word out comfortably, as if it were just what he thought, but she heard it stressed between his teeth. She laughed. "Oh no. Sorry, Brian. Nick is *not* my boyfriend."

She was horrified to see Nick's smile fall.

She was spiraling. This day barely started and already she wanted to crawl under her covers and die. She put her hands up to her face, unable to control herself. "Nick," she pleaded through her fingers, "could you please wait outside for me?"

"Elva and Professor Fern—"

"Will be just fine knowing you can see me through the very transparent glass, and to be perfectly frank, I don't care. They are not my parents. And look," she pointed out the window. "There are customers waiting to get in the shop. You did bring the keys, yes?"

Addison was sick to hear her own voice, obviously annoyed, irritated and uncomfortable. First she thinks about college and how she probably will never be able to go; then she remembers she has to apologize to a boy she likes for acting like she really didn't like him at all – a boy who seems to have been through the wringer when it comes to friends; then she gets relieved; then she learns that some creepy guy who teaches history and her boss want her to be watched at all times; quickly followed up by seeing the guy she stood up is actually there; and bonus! Thinks that she has a new boyfriend, who he obviously doesn't like and this is just great. *Freaking fantastic! Welcome to Brookwick, Addison!*

Nick pouted as he left the coffee shop and Addison was a little embarrassed to see him stomp. Really?

"Hey, Brian," she said, finally facing him and looking him in the eyes. Brian smiled at her though it wasn't as great a smile as she remembered. It was more a "you're the customer and I'm here to help you" smile.

"Hot chocolate?"

Addison nodded. The man standing behind her in line shuffled his feet. Addison followed Brian down the counter a little so she was opposite him as he poured milk and pumped chocolate.

"Brian, I am really, truly, honestly sorry about the other night. I have no idea what happened."

Brian looked like he was about to say something, but then decided not to.

"One minute I was eating some food really fast, made sure I looked okay—" she felt her cheeks burn admitting that part, "—and then I knit for a little while and all of a sudden, it was so late! I couldn't believe it! I ran over here and of course you weren't here because it had been *hours* and I felt so horrible. I didn't have your phone number so I couldn't call you, and I didn't tell you how to get in touch with me. And I usually am not quite so flaky. Honest. I'm not."

He had his head down as he listened, slowly stirring her cold milk and the chocolate syrup together. He put the cup up to the steamer and turned the machine on. He still hadn't looked at her.

Addison sighed. If this is how it was going to be, then fine. It's not like she had invested much into the friendship anyway. But she did like him, and she didn't want him to think she was some thoughtless jerk. She turned her head to look out the window. Nick peering in only ignited her irritation and she growled.

The espresso machine turned off, and Brian moved down the counter a little further to the whipped cream, lids and cup sleeves. After he put them on, he held the cup out to her at the very end of the counter. He held it in his hand. When she reached across for it, he kept holding on.

"You checked to make sure you looked okay?"

Addison blushed. She shouldn't have said that, but she really only remembered those few moments, and she wanted him to know she had no idea what happened.

"Well—I was going out in public," she said.

Brian smiled. "No worries. Don't worry about it. Just a fluke, right?"

Addison smiled. "Really? You aren't totally and completely pissed with me? I'm so sorry!"

Brian laughed. "No problem. We'll try again. When would be a good time?"

"Let's go tonight! When do you get off?"

He looked at his watch again, like the first time, as if it would tell him when his shift was over. When he looked back up, his face was much more relaxed than it was before. "How does six-thirty sound?"

Addison nodded. "Awesome. Sounds great." She took her hot chocolate from him and smiled. "I promise I will be there on time. I swear."

Brian nodded. "I know."

Addison wanted to get through the day with no more drama. Seriously – she had been awake only two hours and already she felt like a soap opera. Taking up Nick's mother's list one more time, she scoured the shelves for the requested yarns and when she didn't find some of them, she searched high and low in the back room. She wanted to avoid Nick. She was disappointed to see a side of him that wasn't as awesome as what she had seen already. What was it about him and Brian? Why didn't they get along? Why did Nick seem like such a jerk to him? Not that Brian was any better to Nick; but if Nick was a bully, does Addison really want to be friends with him?

Addison liked Nick. He was a good friend, and she's already cried in front of him. They have a good laugh and like a lot of the same things, and he's been nothing but generous with her. Maybe she at least owed him the chance to explain things to her before she continued to be so completely and utterly irritated by him.

She went back into the main shop area. Nick had traded in Sudoku for knitting. *See, Addison? See that? He's freaking knitting! Find something to be irritated with* now.

"So I got most of what your mom wanted, but this one, in the chartreuse – no go. Can't find it anywhere."

Nick leaned over and looked at the list. "Personally, I'm glad you can't find chartreuse. Any man's sweater that requires 600 yards of chartreuse is a sweater *not* for a man."

Addison laughed. She pulled together all the various hanks and skeins and put them in a bag. "Does she need these wound?"

"Nah. She has her own stuff for that. Thanks for getting this all together. Here's the check."

Addison started ringing up the order and was wondering how to ask Nick about his relationship with Brian when the door to the shop opened. It was Sara, who Addison had seen in the park the other day. She ran away pretty suddenly though, and told Addison to be careful. What an odd town.

"Hi, Sara! How are you?"

"Addison! Good morning! It's so good to see you! I was wondering if Elva was in this morning? I need to see her."

"No, she's not in. She said she wasn't going to be here until maybe this afternoon, but she wasn't really sure about that either."

Sara contemplated that and looked around the shop. "How about Deidre? You know her friend Deidre Wylie? Is she in?"

Addison shook her head. "Sorry. Haven't seen her in a few days, actually."

Sara nodded. She turned to look out the door and across the square. When she turned back to Addison, she saw the coffee cup on the counter.

"Did you get that at the diner?" she asked.

"No, I ran over to the coffee shop. It's hot chocolate. Do you want some coffee? There's some made in the back."

"The coffee shop?"

Addison nodded.

"Who is there today?"

"Brian."

Sara nodded. "If Elva comes in or calls, can you please let her know I stopped by?" She looked around the room again. "Oh! Hello, Nick. How are you? How is your mother?"

Nick looked up from his knitting. "Hi, Sara! We're doing great. Doing great."

"Good." Sara watched Nick's hands. "Beautiful work, Nick." She looked at Addison. "On second thought, Addison, I'll probably just go to Elva's house. So if she calls before I get there, would you let her know?"

Before Addison could confirm that she would, Sara was out the door.

"She likes to leave in a hurry," she said to Nick.

Nick humphed in response. "I think all old ladies like to do that."

"She's not old!"

"She's not young," he said.

"Man. You're something else."

Addison turned back to ring up his mother's things.

"So," said Nick. "You and Brian friends or something?"

Addison almost forgot she wanted to talk to him about Brian, and now that he was bringing it up, she wanted to back out of her own idea. Figures. The day wouldn't be matchy-matchy without some flip-flopping and confusion.

"Is that bad?"

"No. I don't think so."

"You guys don't seem to get along."

Nick sighed. He pulled his project onto the cables so he wouldn't risk losing any stitches when he put the project down on the table. He bent over to fetch the ball of yarn he had on the floor at his feet and he wrapped the excess around the ball before putting it on top of the project. Addison watched the ritual patiently. She wanted him to have his chance to tell his side of things, and maybe, depending on how things were going later with Brian, he would get his chance too.

"Brian has had a hard time. His mom died not too long ago, and he was still in high school, and his dad – well, nobody really knew who his dad was. So I think Brian had to go through this big process to be able to live in his mom's house, but not until after he lived with someone else. I'm not sure... anyway." Nick took a big breath. "All that is to say that the kid got depressed and moody. Before that, he was just sort of quiet. You didn't really notice him. When we were kids, he played kickball and stuff during recess, but you hardly noticed him. He was just weird like that."

He looked at Addison, as if asking for help.

"It's not like he was weird because he wore only one color clothes or because he listened to strange music or maybe he wrapped his legs in duct tape or something. He was weird because he just seemed to completely *plain*. It was *weird*. I don't know how else to describe it."

"So that meant he had no friends?"

"Not for lack of us trying! Any time someone tried to talk to him, he just said what he needed to say to get by and that was it. He just stood there. He didn't engage. You'd be like 'Hey, Bri. What's up?' and he'd answer that he was good and then that was it. He didn't even ask back. For high school, it was pretty hard. We were psychologists. His problems weren't our problems, you know?"

"Yeah, but why does it seem kids in this town are so mean to him? Even younger ones?"

"Because by the end of his junior year – I think that's the year his mother died – he changed. He *turned* into that other kind of weird. He started wearing the same clothes every day, and he wasn't showering. You could tell that from a million miles away. He stopped carrying books and didn't take notes and he just stared at the teachers. It unnerved them."

"That does sound weird." Addison hated admitting it. It also sounded incredibly creepy.

"Listen." Nick rested his hands in his lap. "I'm sorry I sound like a huge jerk for calling Brian 'gross' and talking about how dirty he was in high school. And I'm sorry if I seemed a bit put off at the shop earlier. But the guy just skeeves me out."

"Skeeves?"

Nick rolled his eyes. "It's a putz thing to feel around a guy I barely know. I admit I picked on him in high school, but I don't even know why I did it." He looked in Addison's eyes.

Addison shifted her feet and looked over at the shelves and then the magazines, and then she looked at Nick to find he was still looking at her so she took to twirling her hair and inspecting the ends. "I don't know what you want me to say to you."

"I really just..." Nick let out a big sigh. "I really just want you to like me, Addison."

Sheriff Emory sat both deputies down and closed his doors.

"Tell me what you found out."

Deputy Desmond Lafayette looked over at Lynley as if seeking support. She nodded her head slightly. The sheriff ignored the moment; he knew Desmond was quite capable of speaking for himself, but Deputy Lynley could be intimidating. It had to have something to do with their age differences; she had four kids and often acted motherly, even around the sheriff. Two days out in the field together probably wasn't easy on either of them; and it may just be they formed a bond. There was nothing wrong with that. The sheriff liked to think his team could be like die-hard partners seen on television, a romantic notion of hard-nosed detective work and home cooked community. Worked for him.

He leaned back in his chair and looked at the deputies, waiting for Desmond to start speaking.

"We went to every shop on the square. We learned some interesting things."

The sheriff nodded. He didn't always love his job. The nodding and the prodding and needing to rely on other people to do the investigative work when he'd really like to be out there himself – it got frustrating. There was something to be said for being a deputy and not being a sheriff. Less paperwork, for one, and he didn't think he'd ever say that. He was glad he didn't have to answer much to anybody else. The heavies above him were off the radar. Brookwick was a safe town and not much happened. They didn't have to worry about a budget too much, the crime level never seemed to rise, and the townspeople were generally happy. Car accidents stayed low and speeding tickets were the biggest joy a deputy could ask for in a night, if they weren't swayed too much by the sob story of the driver. But it weighed on him. And this girl, missing from his aunt's apartment, it made him feel *stress*. He didn't like feeling stress. He was a laid back man who liked things to remain simple. Cut and dry.

He was going to have to talk to Elva soon and he wasn't looking forward to it. She had called no less than four times in the last two days and he's managed to avoid her questions though he's not entirely sure how. She was insistent he speak about Katrina and it took all his might not to say "You were right, Elva. I'm scared for her too." He has beaten himself up enough about it, really. How many times can he berate himself for not taking Elva more seriously? Not many more. The guilt has him trapped enough as it is; he feels like his head is being squeezed like a tube of toothpaste.

"We don't have a picture of her, but one guy at the record store remembered her because she always asked about bands he had never heard of."

"How do we know it was her?"

Deputy Lynley spoke. "Desmond realized that in the bags of things your aunt brought over there were a lot of band t-shirts. Apparently, they are very specific to a certain genre of music. It occurred to Desmond that her taste in music would stand her apart enough from everybody else

273

that we may be able to get some good identification from folks."

"So the record store was a good place to get that. I see. Nice thinking, Deputy," Jim nodded at Desmond. Desmond smiled uncomfortably and shifted in his chair.

He cleared his throat. "Thanks, sheriff."

The sheriff waited. When Desmond didn't begin speaking again, he said, "You can go on, Deputy."

"Right." He cleared his throat again and looked down at his notes. The sheriff had a feeling he didn't really need them. "So this kid at the record store, he remembers her because she always came in looking for these bands he had never heard of."

The sheriff tried not to mention that he already heard this part. He was impatient to get to some real meat and find this girl, but he needed to let his deputies work the way they worked. If he rushed them, or let them see how stressful this had become for him, they could lose their own focus. He didn't want to risk them missing anything that might help. God knows they needed all the help they could get saving a girl nobody knew.

"He saw her a few weeks ago. Says he got an order in for her. She walked in with the guy from the coffee shop down the way. The kid wasn't sure of the coffee shop guy's name, but he said he's there all the time. From his description, Deputy Lynley and I think he means the Grosse boy – Sheila's son."

Sheriff nodded and turned his chair to look out the window. He remembered Sheila. She had a tough fight with breast cancer a few years ago. She insisted people keep quiet about it, but that didn't stop folks from gossiping and leaving pies on her porch. If he remembered correctly, her death hit her young son pretty hard. Always a quiet kid who stayed out of trouble and seemed to like reading and drawing, the school reported him for angry outbursts in class shortly after his mother died, even throwing a chair at a window in one incident. The sheriff had let it go; the boy had, after all, just lost his only parent. As far as he knew, there were no relatives. He did know there was a lot of legal work that took place after so that Brian could stay in his mother's house. The thought of that young boy – what, seventeen at the time? - living there alone, in the house where he cared for his mother and where she died... Jim couldn't imagine it and he really didn't want to.

Deputy Lynley spoke. "Apparently, this boy's mother – Sheila – passed away and he became a bit of a loner."

The sheriff turned back toward the deputies. "Actually, he was always a loner, from what I understand."

"Right. Well, it seems to me it might make sense. Maybe they had a music connection or something, or just that she was from out of town, because according this boy at the record store, the kid from the coffee shop—"

"Brian. His name is Brian. But we should get a confirmation that's who the record store clerk is talking about." He nodded toward Desmond as he said it, and Desmond wrote the task down in his notebook.

Deputy Lynley muttered agreement before finishing. "He says this kid—Brian—he says Brian ended up being a bit of an outcast. Real dirty, seemed to stop taking care of himself, said he became really odd, talking to himself in hallways, looking like he was angry all the time. He said Brian had no friends at all that he could remember."

"So we were thinking," Desmond said, looking at Deputy Lynley for any protest that he was about to take over. Not getting any, he turned back to the sheriff. "We were thinking that maybe because she didn't really know anything about him, except his work at the coffee shop, that they became friends."

"That seems likely. Is that it?"

Desmond and Lynley looked at each other.

"If that's it, it isn't much. What do we have that we can use? I'm assuming you haven't spoken with Brian? If that is who the record store clerk is talking about?"

"No, sir."

"Well – let's go do that, shall we?"

The deputies stood up. The sheriff stood with them. He was reaching for his hat off the hat rack standing by his office door when the deputies turned to look at him. With wide eyes, he stared them down. "Yes. I am going with you. Now let's quit gawking and get a move on."

CHAPTER THIRTY-THREE

"So why didn't you two stop in to see Brian yet?"

Desmond cleared his throat. He did that a lot around the sheriff. Jim knew it was a nervous habit but Desmond had been part of the sheriff's office for over five years now. You would think he would have shed his nervous habits around his boss by now. "Well, sir, we did stop at the store yesterday but it wasn't open even though the sign said it would be. So we just canvassed what we could."

They were driving the three blocks that it took them to get to the square, where the coffee shop was. The sheriff toyed with the idea of walking instead of taking the car, but if they had to take the boy in for questioning they would need a vehicle. And the slower pace of walking would only drive him crazy. He was desperate to find something out and remaining calm was difficult. If it weren't for the fact that Aunt Elva was going to call him again at any moment, he probably would have felt better and could actually focus on just doing his job, getting things done, figuring it out. But the memory of Elva's tears in his office two weeks ago made him think again about how stupid he had been to ignore her. And now he had to tell her. Meanwhile, separate from Elva, was a girl who sounded like she was maybe taken prisoner by some lunatic, and he had to get her.

"Anything else fruitful show up?"

In order to speak more clearly to the sheriff, Desmond turned around in the front seat so he could see the sheriff through the black cage between them. Jim liked to sit in the back when he was traveling with his deputies. It gave him a sense of his deputies, how they looked at the streets when they drove, how they handled the radio, how they handled *him*.

"Not really, sir. It was frustrating. I really wish we had a picture or something."

"Well, I'll tell you what. If this Brian kid turns out to be just another friend who is wondering where she is, we can ask him to make us a sketch. Heck, he could do it himself. From what I remember, he was actually a great artist."

Jim knew better than that. Brian Grosse was an excellent artist. When he brought Brian home in his unmarked vehicle after an incident in eighth grade, when he gave a teacher the finger and threatened to throw a book at her, he accompanied both Brian and his mother to his room. Sheila insisted the sheriff look for drugs in the boy's room. The sheriff refused, asking to speak with her privately, but not before he glanced around enough to see several portraits on the wall. Sheila later confirmed that her son drew them. She believed it was an escape for him. She had said his father used to be abusive before he left and as a way to cope, she often gave Brian paper and crayons. Brian's talent just grew and grew until he could do life-like portraits of anything: animals, fruit and people. The words she were saying sounded proud to Sheriff Emory, but by her tone, he never believed them. She seemed almost bored.

When he learned she had been diagnosed with advanced stages of breast cancer, he thought that maybe that day was just a bad day. He liked that more than thinking she just didn't care about her son, who was obviously in need of some attention.

"That would certainly be helpful," Deputy Lynley muttered. They pulled up in front of the coffee shop and put the car in the park. The shop was open, so all three climbed out and went in.

Elva had started crying anew into the now soggy handkerchief. "No, no. You are absolutely right, Michael. You are. I know you are." She stepped away from Deidre and looked around the living room as if it were her own shop. "So many women have learned to knit in that shop," she whispered, her voice raw. "And many have lived upstairs. I have chosen to surround myself in yarn." She looked at them both, as if pleading with them. "Why? Why, in all this time, have I loved every girl who enters the shop and works with me... why do they always seem to leave me? Why do they leave this shop in pain?" She started sobbing.

Deidre went to her friend. "She won't leave, Elva. She won't."

"I want to help her."

Michael and Deidre knew Elva cared about the girls who came to Brookwick, but it was unlike her to take to someone so strongly after only a few days. Michael sat down at the table again. "Elva," he said gently, "has something happened today or yesterday to make you feel this strongly?"

She shook her head and wiped at her nose. Deidre went to her bag at the kitchen table and walked back into the living room with a new handkerchief. "No," Elva said, and thanked Deidre for the hankie. "Just that Addison destroyed the shop and Ed's store those few days ago. I went to check on her, and she was sleeping, so I didn't disturb her—" Michael let her take a few breaths. Talking was forcing her to calm down enough to get the words out.

"What else did you do today?"

"Nothing."

"Yesterday?"

279

"Nothing."

Michael sighed. Her reaction was too strong. Something wasn't right. "Elva," he said slowly, with as much reassurance in his voice as he could, "take me through your day. Step by step. From waking up Saturday to now."

Deidre rubbed Elva's back and sat beside her, handing her a fresh handkerchief and tucking the old one in her pocket. They had had a long night and even longer morning. Michael had a lot of journals that spanned decades. They wanted to start from the beginning, believing that it was early in Michael's discovery of being a witch when the knitwitches would have spotted him and wanted him to help them with something. But the task was tedious. Michael's journals were very disorderly and worst of all — they weren't dated. It infuriated Deidre, and she repeated it over and over how ridiculous it was for a man of Michael's intelligence to fail to date his journals. Deidre's fit got so bad at one point that Michael actually went outside and walked for fifteen minutes. In that time, Deidre drank some tea and complained bitterly about Michael's lack of foresight while Elva just tried to read the handwriting. It was beautiful penmanship, but she was unaccustomed to reading such flowery script.

The journals were boring to Elva, chronicling roads and buildings, describing them in such detail that she wanted to chuck the whole thing into Deidre's fireplace. She didn't, of course. She was desperate to help Addison. When Michael returned, he put new tea water on for everybody and sat down with them to look through the journals. Deidre whispered, "Really, not even a year?" Michael had had enough. With a sharp twist to his arm, he forced the books from Deidre's hands. Elva watched in amazement as all the books around Deidre flew in the air and followed the first to a pile at Michael's side. When Deidre tried to speak, no words came out. Michael was still staring hard at her, his arm outstretched.

"Michael!" gasped Elva. "Stop that right this instant!"

Michael looked at Elva. "If she cannot help with what we have..."

"She is. And she will. This is too important. Now stop it right this second!"

Michael dropped his arm.

Elva stood up and looked at both of them. "Sit, Deidre. Right now. Sit!" She pointed her finger fiercely at the empty spot on the couch next to Michael. After Deidre sat she said, "Stop this childishness. Right now! Just stop!"

They both nodded. Deidre had a smile on her lips. Michael began to smile as well. Elva threw up her hands and turned back to her spot on the floor with the books. She ended up sleeping on the couch while Michael and Deidre, after an excruciating and awkward hour of hemming and hawing, went off to Deidre's bedroom. They started again on the books as soon as the sun was up.

It wasn't until her third cup of coffee, and Michael's mention of maybe having someone else make the coffee for them instead of wasting time doing it themselves, that Elva remembered her odd meeting with Brian the day before.

She shared the story with them both, trying to explain as carefully as she could what made her feel so uncomfortable around the boy. She reminded Deidre of Sara's account at their last meeting – how she had felt from Brian that he had a frantic emotional attachment to somebody and that it was laced with hate and anger.

"When he said he was supposed to meet her and take her to the campus, and when he did that odd laugh and, well... he *is* a rather strange boy."

281

Michael and Deidre were silent for quite some time. "But he's so young," Deidre finally said. "Could someone so young possibly be an issue right now? Aren't teenagers just teenagers?"

"Well, yes," Elva nodded. "But you should have seen him."

Michael interjected. "I see why you're concerned, Elva. But it is really going to have to wait. Addison can knit now. And she has powers even without knitting, we just don't know how strong it is and if or when it will get stronger. And at some point, she might knit this entire town out of existence. Her love problems will have to wait another day."

Elva wanted to insist they talk about it more, but she knew Michael was right. She called the shop after that to see how things were, and despite Deidre and Michael's dismissal of her fears, she nearly lost her mind when Nick told her Addison had left – alone – to the coffee shop. It was after the call that Elva gradually came to be so emotional, finally crying in fits at the thought of something dangerous happening to Addison. Her complaints lasted about two hours before Michael had had enough.

"Elva," Michael repeated, "take me through your day. Step by step. From waking up Saturday to now."

Slowly, Elva started to tell them about her weekend and yesterday. At each point, Michael asked her questions. When she said hello to a customer on the sidewalk, had she seen this customer recently? Did anything seem different about her? Did she look at Elva in any significant way? To which Elva had her own questions: What do you mean by significant? Why is any of this important? And so on. Elva had just reiterated her visit to Kate, when she said, "And then I came back to the shop."

Michael sat back in his chair. "No!" she yelled, surprising them all. "And then I went to the apartment, and couldn't go up because Jane was there and she *had a package for Addison.*"

The sheriff was disappointed they had missed Brian. Apparently, he had a date later that night and left early to get ready, leaving some new girl who looked completely lost to take care of things on her own. The sheriff and deputies got back in the car and drove to Brian's house, which was actually a few miles on the outer part of town. When they arrived, they saw that Brian was home. The deputies made to exit the vehicle when the sheriff made them wait.

Deputy Lynley looked back at him. "Sir?"

Deputy Lafayette smiled. "We should wait, right, sir?"

The sheriff looked at him. "Yes, deputy. I think I would rather wait right now."

The sheriff had been thinking more and more about Brian Grosse, his mother, his absent father, and the personality change in Brian. He wondered if it was really a personality change at all? He had known who Brian was for a long time, longer than the two years or so since his mother had died. In eighth grade he was already threatening teachers with violence and it wasn't the first time. A life like that had to be hard, but Brian was different. He was moody, surly, a loner, and now he worked at a place with a lot of traffic, opening opportunity to meet everybody in town, especially newcomers like Katrina. Who didn't want coffee or hot chocolate or a muffin? A small coffee shop in the main square of town was a perfect and quaint place to rest a while and enjoy Brookwick.

He also considered Katrina. A new girl in a new town with no past to speak of; who would get to know her most and first? Would it be the gray-haired, slightly rotund shop owner who offered her a house and grandmotherly affection, or the loner boy with the dark and brooding good looks at the coffee shop, drawing and reading books? Sheriff Emory was placing his bets on the latter.

It was another forty minutes before Brian emerged from his house. The sheriff was glad they had taken the unmarked car, though almost everybody in town could identify it. He was hoping Brian was too excited about his date to notice it himself.

Brian was dressed in dark gray slacks and a black sweater. He carried a duffel bag. Nobody in the vehicle approved of the duffel bag. As he put the bag in the trunk, then opened all four doors of his vehicle, Deputy Lynley noted that the boy seemed to be talking to himself.

Desmond said, "What if she's right in there?"

The sheriff replied, "What if she's where he's going?"

They all remained quiet as they watched Brian clean out his car, shoving papers, coffee cups and water bottles into a huge black trash bag. When it seemed about to burst, Brian seemed satisfied. He walked over to the edge of his yard and heaved the bag up on his shoulder. Then he shot the bag forward into the woods where the deputies and sheriff could see several more bags, rotting away.

"What a punk!" Desmond whispered roughly.

Brian got in his car and drove.

"Be careful, deputy," the sheriff muttered.

Deputy Lynley, rather than upset by the obvious warning, nodded gravely, and started up the car.

CHAPTER THIRTY-FOUR

Elva entered the break room holding a medium-sized box. "I completely forgot I had it. It's addressed to Addison and I think I was going to give it to her this morning, but we were – well, you know. I'm glad she didn't find it herself."

She laid it on the table.

"Yes, I'm glad as well," Deidre said.

They all leaned forward to get a closer look at the package. At the same time, Deidre and Elva gasped.

"Well, I'll be," said Elva.

Michael whispered. "I can't believe it."

And Deidre, too shocked to believe what was right in front of her, turned to Michael and asked, "Isn't that your handwriting?"

He felt he had everything in place. The key was securely around his neck with a spare key tucked into his wallet. He thought about leaving his wallet at home, but did not want to appear suspicious in case he got pulled over for anything he can't account for, and he needed gas.

From the basement of his house, he heard soft moans.

He smiled as he went over everything again.

Black hoodie, freshly washed. Black jeans. Black t-shirt and sweatshirt. Black socks. Black sneakers with reflector strips blacked out using a permanent black marker. Three rolls of duct tape. One long length of rope. Three black lawn and leaf bags. A duffel bag. A small, metal mallet. The letter he wrote to the old woman that he would leave behind so she knew the girl did not leave. He took her. He took the others. He wants her to know.

A moan came from below.

"Shut up!" he screamed. He ran to the door and threw it open. "Shut up!"

The moaning stopped.

He went back to the table and looked at the pile of supplies.

"You can do it," he told himself. With a sneer, he held up the hunting knife. It glinted under the sun shining through his window. It will be dark soon. "Almost time."

Addison stood in her room looking at her crap wardrobe. "It's not a date!" she yelled. In the less-than-two-weeks she has been in Brookwick, she didn't spend one day getting new clothes. Elva assured her that comfortable clothes and a nice attitude was all she needed to work at the shop. There was still the skirt she had worn that she found in the closet, but a skirt felt too much like "This is a date, right?" than "I just look this good every day, so don't make a big deal out of it." She had been going at it for over forty minutes and more than once, for one of the first times in her life, she wished she had a girlfriend her own age who would sit on her bed, watch her make herself crazy and remind her, "It's not a date! Ooh, that's cute."

Her closest friends in Brookwick, besides the guy she was trying *not* to impress, were a couple of old ladies who knit sweaters and baked cookies. Addison briefly thought about Melinda, but it would seem too much like she was using Melinda rather than trying to be friends with her. That was the last thing she needed: friend drama. She returned to the thought of her old lady knitting friends who baked cookies. They were reliable. With a smile, Addison couldn't help liking that small truth that they were her friends. *Good cookies, good knitting, and they won't play games,* she thought. Those friends sounded none too shabby to her.

Derwin sat on the end of the bed, his head lying on his front paws. He looked at her as if to say, "Really? You're that desperate?"

"What?" said Addison aloud. "You don't want to help me act like an idiot?"

Derwin yawned. Addison had to remind herself that Derwin was a cat because she felt an incredible urge to throw a pillow at him. Just as she thought she might try the skirt on with some new shirt-sneaker combinations, she heard a loud knock on her door.

Addison stood in front of the stove, tapping the side of it nervously. They looked tense. Professor Fernlee – Michael, she corrected herself – was sitting tall in a chair, absently petting Derwin. Deidre sat beside him at the end of the couch, looking at Michael's face. Sometimes she looked happy, almost as if she were in love with the professor, but then her face would become serious and she'd glance at Elva nervously. Elva definitely seemed nervous. She wrung her hands in her lap and cleared her throat often, a white handkerchief sticking out of the back of one of her hands. What were they here for? Addison was terrified it was to kick her out of the apartment. Perhaps Elva was afraid Addison would pitch a fit and so she brought reinforcements to help carry her and her things off the premises.

She remembered then that Michael had been at the shop this morning and Nick had been told to watch her all day. Oh God! Addison wondered in horror if they thought she was a thief. Of course! It made perfect sense, but... Chills crawled up Addison's spine at the thought of being accused. Especially by these two women. She loved Elva already, as if she's known her her entire life, and Deidre made her feel so comfortable. She also envied the woman, though she didn't understand why. But she liked the way she walked, how she spoke, and that she taught her to knit. She did it with so much authority, her voice stern as if to say "This is the most important thing you will ever learn in your life." She *liked* these women, and more than that, she *loved* Brookwick. She had a home for the first time in her entire life and she was terrified they were going to ask her to leave it.

When she first opened the door, Addison immediately saw that they were not here just to see what she had done with the place. Before they could barely say hello, Addison asked them to take a seat and offered to make tea, not waiting for an answer before rushing to fill the tea kettle with a loud burst of water from her pipes. She chose to stay by the stove so she could think and prepare herself for disaster. If she did have to leave Brookwick, the two weeks she worked at the shop would give her enough to stay on the road maybe five days, and then she'd be in trouble. She had used what little money she had to buy groceries and a few drinks at the coffeehouse. Biting her lip, she stared at the kettle. When it started to whistle, she did not move it right away, but just continued to look at it, not wanting to see what would happen next.

"Addison, honey?" Elva said, looking at her from the couch she shared with Deidre. "Are you alright? Would you like some help?"

Addison snatched the kettle from the stove and waved Elva off. "I hope chamomile is okay with you guys! It's all I have right now." One by one, she poured mugs full of hot water and a tea bag and carried each carefully into the room, setting it before each person. She finally grabbed her mug, and turned to face the room. Stalling time was over.

She sat in the remaining chair. Derwin immediately left Michael's side and hopped onto the arm of the chair to sit beside her.

"He likes you," Michael offered, nodding his head.

"Yes," said Addison possessively. "He's my buddy." She wrapped her arm around the black cat and pushed him into her lap. His warmth and his purr offered some comfort to her. She would miss him.

Michael looked at Elva. "Elva?" he said.

Elva shook her head fiercely.

This is bad. This is really bad. Addison was going to cry, and she didn't want to cry. She firmly pressed her lips together and could feel spit forming in the corners of her mouth. Crying for two days in a row was never a good sign. Maybe the town wasn't good for her. Maybe she's better off leaving a place that makes her cry so much.

The thought wasn't helping; it physically hurt her heart to imagine it. She wished they would go away so she could get all the cry out of her before they pelted her with bad news.

She took a sip of her tea and called out. "Oh, God!"

"What is it?" yelled Elva, standing up faster than Addison thought possible. Addison covered her lip with her hand.

"The tea," she said, holding back tears. At least now they could be blamed on the tea. "It's hot."

Elva sat down. She reached over and patted Addison's arm. "Are you okay?" Addison nodded. "Blow on it, dear," said Elva. Addison laughed at Elva's advice. She was going to miss the shop owner.

289

Addison saw Deidre reach her arm out to Michael and gently touch his arm. Deidre liked him; Addison could tell.

"Addison," Michael began. "Elva received this package for you at the shop." He tilted his head to the coffee table. Though Addison had placed the mugs of tea on the table, she did not notice the package, which now seemed to stick out like a sore thumb. It was an average sized box wrapped in brown paper. Addison leaned forward and reached for it.

Michael's hand pulled the box back before Addison could grab it. She looked at him. "What is it?" she asked.

"We don't know," Michael said. Addison wanted to smile but her huge relief was slowly turning into heebie jeebies. Her body wasn't going to be able to handle the emotional roller coaster much longer. Her arms started to feel cold, and she could feel this bubbly feeling come up under her skin, the kind that would make her talk really fast and maybe laugh inappropriately for no reason..

"Why would you know when the package is for me, right? Do you think it's dangerous or something?" She looked at the box, at how innocuous it looked. "You don't think it's like, a bomb or something, do you?"

"Well," he said. He looked nervous.

"Why in the world would someone send me something dangerous?" She shoved her body back in her seat, far from the box. "We should call someone!" Cold, panicky, bubbly nerves shimmered on her skin. How much more stress could she handle?

Michael raised his hands and pumped them up and down in a 'calm down' gesture. "Relax, dear. I'm hoping it is nothing like that. The thing is, and this may seem a little odd," he paused at the word, as if taking stock, finally, that this entire meeting was odd, "but it would seem that I am the sender of this box."

Addison looked at Deidre and Elva. What was going on here?

Deidre took a big breath. "We believe that things," she stressed the word 'things' as if she were really saying 'packages.' Addison waited patiently, but her nerves were giving way. "We believe that things can possess--" she stopped and looked carefully at Addison.

Michael took over again. "Addison. We think this box may possess something that will hold great power. We ask that you be careful opening it, which is why we are here. I just want to warn you: no matter what it is in that package, we are here to support you and to answer any questions you have."

Addison's eyes widened. *What was going on here?* Elva had her head bowed over her hands, still gripping the handkerchief. When Addison leaned forward to say, "What do you think, Elva?" she noticed that her friend looked tired and as if she'd been crying.

Michael moved the box across the table toward Addison. All three of her visitors moved forward in their seats. Elva rolled up the sleeves of her cotton cardigan. Deidre placed her hands palm down on her knees. Michael clasped his hands in front of him, between his knees, which now reached almost to his chest because of how long his legs were and how low Addison's chair was. He seemed like he wanted to look relaxed but she noticed how ram-rod straight his back was, and though his hands were folded in on each other, they looked ready to pounce.

Addison lifted Derwin from her lap and placed him on the arm of the chair. He leapt from the chair to the table and rubbed his teeth against the brown wrapped package.

Addison didn't know what she expected. Their reactions made her feel something would blow up, or something would jump out, but nothing did. After painstakingly lifting the tape off the package — an attempt to simply rip it proving unsuccessful (how tough could paper get?) - she found that beneath the brown wrapping was a regular cardboard box. She lifted the flap, left unsealed.

Michael leaned forward and looked inside, as did Deidre and Elva. Together, all three let out loud sighs. Addison had hung back, waiting for their reactions, afraid of what she'd see, believing what was in the package was more for them than it was for her. She knows nobody, so nobody knew she was in Brookwick. The entire idea that someone sent her a package was insane, but what was more insane is that apparently, the person who sent it was in the room acting like he'd never seen it before!

Michael smiled. "Wow," he whispered.

Sheriff Emory watched Deputy Lynley's back. Deputy Lafayette looked at him anxiously. "What did the police say, sir?"

He spoke to Deputy Lynley, "Same procedure, every time. Keep at him.

Looking at Deputy Lafayette, he couldn't stop thinking about his aunt. He felt like an ass. How many times had he told Elva, "They probably just got sick of this little town and went somewhere else"? And now he was getting the same response from the police department.

"Maybe their patrols will pick up something," said Deputy Lynley. Sheriff Emory nodded.

"Maybe. But I think we're doing good right now, without them."

He had few options. Katrina was out there, of that he was sure. She was in danger, of that he felt certain. Would he find her? He had doubts. He had no idea where she was. The cell phone companies could offer little help. He felt like a fool asking them about triangulation and winced when they told him that television rarely offered the truth. They even asked him if he was a real cop.

"What am I going to tell my aunt?" he said, looking at the young deputy who found his wife because of Elva. He had worked with Jim for five years; he had worked with Deputy Lynley for ten. He knew it was okay to show her his doubt. They were friends.

"She knows you're going to try your best to make this right," she replied. "And I'm going to help you. You know that."

Sheriff Emory nodded. The blonde woman with the four kids pointed up ahead. "Looks like he's going back toward the square," she said. She looked in the rear view at Jim. "Are you ready?" she asked.

I don't get it, Addison thought. Elva, Deidre and Michael seemed impressed by the simple three-ring binder inside the box. Plain vinyl and three inches wide, it sat by itself among newspapers holding it in place. Attached to the front of the binder were two post-it notes, one on top of the other. In the same handwriting as on the packaging, the top note (a pink post-it note) were the words, "I was told to send this when you were ready." She lifted the pink note and read the blue one, "I have something for you."

Michael murmured the words as he read them over her shoulder, his head one of the three dark shadows covering the table. When Addison heard him say the words, she felt chills all down her spine and her stomach started a new series of knots.

"Um," mumbled Addison, "could you sit down? I'm feeling a little claustrophobic." All three of her guests surrounded her as she sat in the armchair with the box on her lap. They reluctantly shuffled away. Michael sat on the couch with Deidre, and Elva took her seat at the other end. They all scooted down toward Addison after a moment of squirming.

Addison looked at Michael. "I've heard that before. I've heard you say that. Only you weren't around me when I heard it." Addison's eyes were wide. She could feel them burning, like when she's stayed up driving too late and knew she was tired, and had to consider pulling onto the shoulder. She was afraid.

Michael looked back at her. "I never meant to frighten you," he said. "I didn't say it though." He nodded at the package she hadn't yet touched. "I think that did."

"Open it," whispered Deidre. Addison looked at her face. She looked sad, but hopeful. Michael looked expectant.

"What is this, Professor Fernlee?" Was she angry? No. But she was confused. She heard this voice, those words, and with them she saw her mother's face swim before her. How much more could she take in this town? Was this really what home was supposed to feel like?

The professor looked her in the eyes, as if trying to learn something in her gaze. A warm rush filled her chest and she felt a heavy hand press on her back as if holding her, protecting her from fear.

"Open it," he whispered.

Addison lifted the binder from the box and laid it in front of her on the coffee table. Catching the corner of the cover with her thumb, she slowly lifted it. From the binder spilled pages covered in plastic sheeting. She tried to catch them, but could not. Elva leapt forward to grab them, but Michael quickly grabbed her and pulled her back to the couch. He shook his head in warning. Addison laid the binder on the table, careful to push what papers were sliding, and began picking up what had dropped. As she did, she looked at the pages. Schematics and patterns. Knitting patterns. Every single page in one of the slippery covers was a knitting pattern. Tiny notes were scribbled in the margins with different color pens in writing too small to read. When she looked closer, she saw that each page was worn, as if handled hundreds of times, some with brown smudges on the edge, folded corners, and creases marking where they had been folded. Of course! This is how women's patterns looked when they came into the shop, unfolding them hastily, begging for help with an instruction they couldn't understand, or a pattern they couldn't figure out, nearly begging, "Where is Elva? I can't figure this out!" Addison recognized them all for the heart and soul of a knitter's prized project: a knitting pattern.

She went back to the binder and lifted the cover. Carefully, she flipped through the pages. There were hundreds. Some sheet protectors were filled with ten page patterns, some only single pages, lined pages. All were handwritten. Every single one had notes written in the margins — sides and bottoms, backs and fronts. Some had diagrams and exclamation points. Some had writing she had never seen, another language she didn't think she could recognize.

"Knitting patterns," she whispered. "Hundreds of them." She looked up at Elva. Elva looked back, her face revealing nothing, not even surprise. Michael and Deidre were holding hands. Addison noted the embrace between them, but couldn't remark on it, not even with a smile or a joke or a realization. She didn't have the energy to speculate. She looked down again. "What are these? Who are they from?"

She continued to turn the pages. Sweaters, cardigans, shawls and cowls, hats, mittens, socks… a lot of socks. She didn't recognize any of the patterns from what she had seen in the shop or in magazines, which she had often flipped through out of curiosity. They looked, at first, like simply patterns, the foundation of what everybody used when knitting. One sock looked like a plain old sock, but then Addison saw that really there were intricate textures on the legs and soles. The same was true for sweaters, with combinations of stitches she didn't yet understand. She only knew they all looked complicated.

Addison almost missed it. There was a baby cardigan pattern. The cardigan had a hood, flowers along the bottom hem with matching flowers on the hem of the hood. It was adorable. As she passed the page over, ready to see the next one pattern, she noticed it. The words. "Stitch in one makes it two. Blessed be, this spell's for you."

Addison gasped.

"What is it?" Michael and Elva asked together. Addison didn't know what to say. They may think she's crazy. Maybe she has seen the words before, just like the words on the post-it note. Maybe it wasn't Michael's voice at all. Maybe her dreams just used his voice. That seemed believable, even to her. She would even say that out loud. But this? Those words were only in her dream. She had never heard them before. Not ever. She tried to think of something that would make sense. Maybe she could convince herself. Did she hear them in the shop? Did she read them in a magazine? Dreams can hold details that pass people by, so surely this is just a coincidence. The handwriting was the same as all the others, small and feminine, in blue ink. She looked at the sweater. Something about the sweater looked familiar too. She reached into the sheet protector to pull the pattern out so she could look at it without the glare of the lamps.

"No!"

Her three guests looked terrified, all of them with their arms outstretched. The book skidded off the table and crashed onto the floor.

"You can't touch those," Michael said hurriedly. "I'm sorry." He turned to Elva who was clutching her chest. "We're going to have to explain."

Elva sat back on the couch. Addison was sliding off her couch and onto the floor to retrieve the binder and patterns when Deidre said evenly, "Those will have to wait, Addison. I'm sorry. This will all make sense in a minute. Please sit. Don't worry about those."

Addison's heart began to race and she sat back up on the chair. She looked down at the binder now surrounded by loose pages slipping over each other.

"Addison, honey."

She turned her head to look at Elva. Her boss and landlady was terrified, and sad. Addison no longer thought their unexpected visit had anything to do with her job or the apartment; something else was going on. Elva's tired eyes were half closed. The crease in her brow, pinching above her nose, made her worry apparent. She looked as if she were pleading with Addison for help. The young girl who stopped in Brookwick for gas and a toilet tilted her head.

"What is going on, Elva?" Elva's eyes wandered over Addison's shoulder. She leaned her head forward, pushing it forward like Derwin does when he wants Addison's attention. From her waist, two of Elva's fingers were lifting and slowly twirling. Addison turned her head, following Elva's gaze.

The binder was floating off the carpet, raising itself into the air, hovering above the table and gliding over it before finally resting on top of it, exactly where it was before it somehow flew off. With wide eyes, she watched as the sheet-protected patterns began to float above the carpet as well, and the binder's front cover opened. The three rings separated softly – without the loud click that always annoyed her when she used binders in libraries and study halls – and the patterns spun until they were right side up, the punched holes aligning with the rings of the binder, finally lying gently one on top of the other. As the last page floated by her and settled on top of the others, and the rings closed, and the cover rested on top as it was when she first held it in her lap, Addison realized she was not breathing. She couldn't bring herself to take in a breath or even to blink, but when she opened her mouth, the air rushed in, and suddenly she was gasping. Wild eyed, she looked at them all. They sat as if they noticed nothing, their postures calm, Elva with sad eyes, Deidre with anxious eyes, and Michael... he seemed to just be waiting. All were turned on Addison.

Addison tried to swallow, but her mouth was too dry. She looked at the floor and the binder. Were they really all on the floor only moments before? Did she imagine it? Was she going crazy? Was this another dream? And Deidre, Michael, Elva! Addison didn't know if she should be angry with them. Why are they here? She reached for her tea with both hands, shaking she realized. She grasped it firmly and brought it to her lips to wet her mouth and found she could only take the tiniest amount. It barely wet her lips.

"You did not imagine it," Deidre whispered. She separated herself from Michael and walked around the table, coming to Addison, kneeling in front of her. She took the mug from Addison's hands and then held them gently between her own. Her soft skin comforted Addison. They were cool in Addison's sweaty palms. "Shhh," Deidre soothed. "This will all be hard at first, but we are here to explain and to help you. Please just listen and *feel me*. Can you do that? Can you *feel me*?" And Addison did. From her hands, she felt a rush of warm air blow over her skin, from the tops of her hands to her wrists, elbows and shoulders. The sides of her torso were cooled by a breeze beneath her shirt and her neck felt loose. The roots of her hair lifted slightly, resetting and falling back, awake. Her mouth filled with saliva and she found she could swallow again.

Addison nodded. "I feel you," she whispered. She felt strange saying the words.

Deidre smiled. "Addison, honey. We--" she nodded to Michael and Elva, and tilted her head softly to acknowledge herself, "We are witches." Addison couldn't help it, but a tiny giggle escaped her, more out of nervousness and confusion than actually finding it funny.

"And so are you."

CHAPTER THIRTY-FIVE

Addison stared at Deidre so long she started seeing spots, and black started moving in, blocking out the sides of the room. This was all too much. She was expecting to wake up, to find that she was in another dream.

"Is this another dream?"

"Have you been having dreams?"

Addison looked at Michael, who leaned forward expectantly. She tilted sideways a little before catching herself. "Yes. Ever since I came to Brookwick. They're all weird, and they all have that in it," she tilted her head toward the binder.

"You've seen this book before?" he asked.

"No. The words. I've heard those words before." She looked at Michael, expecting him to repeat them, to say them again, to verify that it was him in her dreams. But he said nothing. "In your voice. Like... as if it were you saying them to me. Over and over."

"What words?" Michael asked.

Addison tilted her head toward the book again. "Those ones."

"'I have something for you?'" Chills ran up and down Addison's spine. It crept inside like a cool gel. She nodded slowly and tried to calm her breathing.

"What else happened in these dreams?" he asked.

Addison didn't want to tell him about her mother. It seemed...too personal. How funny was that?

"There were other words that came up. Everyone in the square. Elva. They're knitting and they're all saying the words. It was like a huge whisper, just everybody doing it at once, like a microphone and they sometimes felt like drones..." She was out of breath, but she wasn't moving.

Carefully, Michael asked, "What words? But, wait." He held out his hand with his index finger pointed out, and he turned to Deidre and Elva. "It is very possible her dreams have magic in them. She saw the words on the box in her dreams--"

"No. You said them to me."

"Are you sure it was me?"

Addison hesitated. Yes, she was. But...she never saw him. Only heard him. She told him that.

He nodded and turned back to Elva and Deidre. "Those words were real. We have to be sure that if I ask her to tell us the dreams in full, we are all ready."

"Ready for what?" asked Elva, her eyes wide.

Deidre answered for him, her eyes on Addison, worry creasing her brow. "For anything."

Michael sat back. "Tell us the dreams, Addison."

Addison wanted to. She could tell it was important, and she knew now that the dreams weren't just some strange way of her psyche transitioning to her new life. It had to do with this stuff; this *witch* stuff. But her mother. She wasn't ready to share her mother yet.

"I don't know if I'm comfortable sharing it all with you. I'm sorry." She felt like she was going to cry.

"We understand, honey," said Deidre. She leaned forward to assure Addison and a small smile sat on her lips. "We understand. Just tell us the parts you feel okay sharing. Dreams are very personal spaces. They aren't meant to be aired out. Will you be okay with just telling us some parts? We'll sort things out best we can."

Michael interjected, "Yes, Dee is right of course. But I urge you to try your best to share as much as possible."

Elva shot him a look that Addison noted. Good ol' Elva. Michael ignored it, however. "Like Dee also said, dreams are very personal spaces, and we haven't told you yet, but you are a powerful witch. So your dreams may have information in them that can help us better to help you."

Addison flinched at the word 'witch.' Really? Honestly? He said it as if it were *normal*, spoken everyday, like saying "You're twenty years old now! Hooray!" She was starting to feel sick. Derwin hopped onto the coffee table and sat beside the binder again.

"I was in a park, I think. I'm not entirely sure. It feels like it was forever ago, but I was in a park--"

"Is this the dream?"

Addison sighed. He was starting to annoy her and she wasn't sure she could maintain her composure. She nodded quickly and moved on, wanting him to know she was getting tired.

"I was in a park. I think I was a little girl. And there was this man by a fence. And I don't know if it was him who said it, but I heard the words right in my ear."

"'I have something for you'?"

Again, she nodded.

"Did you recognize the man?"

She shook her head.

"When else did you hear it? Just the once?"

She shook her head. "I heard it again." She stopped. She wanted to say she heard it again, but that wasn't right. She doesn't remember *when* she heard it again. "It's kind of weird. I feel like I heard it again but I can't remember when, and if it was in a dream or not."

She turned to Elva, looking for advice.

"It's okay, dear. Just keep going. Sometimes, the empty spots in our memory tell us the most."

"Well, the shop was in there a few times." She gasped and looked at Deidre and Elva. "In one dream, you two were wearing witch hats! Oh my god! And you were *cackling*."

Deidre and Elva chuckled together. "You must have been the cackler," Elva muttered, "because you're evil."

"Nope. It was you Elva. Freaked me out."

Deidre guffawed. The sound made Addison feel a little more relaxed. Laughing was normal. She could do laughing.

"And you both said something. Or was that after? There was one point when everyone in the square was saying it. They were all knitting and I think it was before I heard them say it, when I heard you two say it, but anyway. It was 'stitch in one makes it two; blessed be, this spell's for you.'"

Michael sat up straight, his back rigid. The binder thumped once on the table and Addison jumped back. Deidre quickly snatched her hands up from their folded position in her lap and radiated a calming spell from her hands, the palms growing red as she did it.

"Dee," said Michael. "Dee…" His eyes were closed and his hands gripped his knees, bunching his pants up in the process, exposing his dark green socks, knit by Deidre twenty years before, darned over twenty-five times. Derwin jumped onto the couch and butted his head against Michael's thigh. Michael swayed slightly by the movement. Derwin bumped him again.

"You'll see her at the cauldron, shining by the sun, listening to her blood," he said, his voice soft, resonating in all their chests. "And when you do, let her know you have something for her. Send this then, with care and speed. Let her see that it comes from me – her mother, me, through you."

The pattern book thumped on the table again and once again the cover opened. The pages flipped quickly.

The binder pages opened to the baby cardigan pattern that she thought looked familiar. She looked up at Michael, who remained upright with closed eyes. His skin was pale and his spine unnaturally straight.

"Is he okay?"

"You cannot touch the pattern yet, Addison," said Deidre, ignoring her question. "You are a special sort of witch who is affected by anything related to the craft of knitting, and possibly more crafts. Knitting is likely it, though." Addison heard her speak but could not look at her directly. It was more than she could handle, and she knew she recognized that sweater from somewhere.

"I can't let it go," she said.

"What's that, honey?" Elva said, her voice barely heard above the hum Addison heard in her head.

"The sweater. I know that sweater."

"Michael," Deidre said.

Michael did not move. His eyes remained closed. Derwin bumped him again, harder. Michael swayed slightly. Finally, Derwin leapt in the air and landed on Michael's shoulder. Deidre watched with wide eyes as Derwin nipped at Michael's earlobe. Michael threw his hands up at the cat, who bounded from his shoulder. "Ow!" Michael yelled, rubbing where Derwin's claws had dug, looking for purchase. Deidre eyed the cat.

"You are good," she said with a smile. Turning to Michael, whose eyes now appeared clear, though confused. "It seems you were struck twice," she said. "Do you remember?"

"I do. I was meant to deliver this to Addison when I saw she could knit. But I do not know who sent me."

"My mother," said Addison, startling everybody. She had seemed lost in the pattern, though she was careful not to touch it.

"Your mother?" Elva asked, confused. "But wouldn't she have told you herself?"

Addison smiled. "You are really awesome, Elva, but if I knew my mother, I probably would never have come to Brookwick. I never knew her. I got here because I didn't want to be where I was."

Elva wanted to bury Addison in her arms.

"This sweater was in my dream. The same dream with the words," she bit her lip, reminding herself that she should not repeat them until she knew more, convinced those words are what made Michael act so strangely and caused the book to move on the table. "She was about to make it. I remember the yarn she was using. It was a creamy color, and very soft." This time, she let the tears come. What secrets could she possibly keep from three witches and a crazy cat?

Whispering through the tears, trying to make sense, she went on. "I was already in her belly. She was setting up her space, you know. Getting the yarn ready, and the pattern." She let her fingers hover just above the pattern page. "This pattern was on the table beside her. The flowers... I think she particularly liked the flowers."

Addison hardly thought of her birth parents. It was hard to think of people you knew nothing about, except, of course, yourself. She had wondered about the little stuff, like their color hair, eyes and if they were tall or short. She wondered if they had ever met her, or was she born and then separated immediately, and did they ever have a chance? She had entered foster homes as soon as she was born – she knew that much – and changed homes every year, that particular pattern ending in high school, staying with the Grovers for nearly two full years. Nobody could speculate with her on her real parents. Social workers insisted there was nothing in the files, and foster parents waved off her questions. And here before her is a pattern for a baby sweater that she knew her mother wanted to make for her, something she knew from a dream, and given to her by complete strangers. By witches!

Was her mother dead? She thought so because how could her mother leave her alone this long? But she didn't feel it.

Addison sniffled and wiped her nose with the back of her hand. For a split second, she thought of how gross she must look, and she wiped her hand on her jeans.

Was there another dream? Were there others before Brookwick? She thought so. She had in her head more images and memories. The woman, who she now recognized as her mother, was looking into her eyes and saying "this never happened." Addison was about two years old in that dream.

"I was playing with a train and she told me it never happened." She looked up at the three witches in her living room. "She never got to see me as a two year old."

That woman had looked so lonely, so hurt. And also so proud. She smiled on the baby Addison with adoring eyes, such loving eyes, in fact, that Addison could feel her chest swell with the love of it as Deidre kneeled beside her. Tenderly, she lifted Addison's hand and closed both of her own around it.

Addison let Deidre's hands hold hers for several seconds before she gently pulled her hand away. "I'm okay," she said to Deidre. She looked down at Deidre's hands. "You calmed me." She did not know if she was asking a question until Deidre nodded and confirmed it.

Addison was afraid to say it next, not sure how to phrase it or what they would think. "So. Is that magic? The calming me? Touching me and then making me feel better?"

Deidre nodded and smiled. "Mostly," she said. "Mostly it's magic, but I like to think that there is more to it than that." She reached up and smoothed the side of Addison's hair, her hand cupping Addison's face. Her smile had love in it. "One does not always need magic to help a person."

Addison was tired. "What can I do?" she whispered. "Is that a selfish question?"

They all looked confused.

"If I'm a-- a--" she laughed a little, unprepared for the way it would sound when she said the word "--a witch--" *Whoa*. It felt strong. She expected for it to feel stilted, broken and embarrassing. She lifted her head higher and smiled. "If I am a witch, then what can I do? Deidre can calm me. Is there more?" she asked Deidre.

"Oh, yes."

"Can I do that? The calming?"

Deidre shrugged. "Maybe not the same way I can do it, but we think you can do many things."

"You are a special witch," Michael said. "There are very few witches who can do what you do. In fact, witches used to not believe in your kind."

Addison was startled by the use of the phrase 'your kind' to describe her. They weren't talking about being a foster kid, or a girl who lived out of her car and didn't go to college. She was a witch.

"What makes it so different?"

Elva finally spoke up. She had been sitting quietly, watching Addison take in the news. It was amazing to watch. Elva was sure the girl would cry one second only to watch her sit taller. She was scared – that much was obvious. But she was also *strong*. It was almost unbelievable, if she didn't witness it with her own eyes. She leaned forward and smiled at Addison. It was a big smile, full of joy and happiness. She knew this was going to work out.

They would all make sure of it. "You are a knitwitch." Her laugh was infectious. Addison laughed, Deidre laughed, and Michael laughed.

"A knitwitch, huh?" she repeated. She looked at the pattern. "I'm a knitwitch, and I can barely read a pattern. How funny is that?"

The old woman from the store went in with two other old people just as he pulled into the parking lot. It was his habit to watch the apartment for several hours, building the anticipation. He played through what he most wanted to happen, imagining each movement and possible reaction. They have not all worked out the way he wanted, but in the end, he got what he came for. This time would be no different – he just had to take a few extra steps.

His back pack sat in the back seat, the handle of a hammer peeking from the side zipper where he couldn't zip it completely. He wasn't happy part of it was showing, but he got sick of trying. It wouldn't matter. Nobody will notice him walking up to the building. Nobody ever does. He liked it that way.

When he saw them go to the door, fighting with the lock again, he grinned. Idiots. He only had to bend the keyhole a little bit with a tool his cousin gave him to make his own key work, a trick his cousin taught him the first time they broke into a house together. His cousin got caught finally. "But not me," he thought to himself. "I'm not a moron." But then the old folks were in there a long time. He was getting irritated. Imagining the moment was no longer exciting or fun – he was just pissed. Music irritated him, cars driving by irritated him, the temperature outside – it all irritated him. But he wouldn't leave. He wouldn't let anybody control him. He wouldn't let anybody laugh at him, walk all over him, tempt him and turn away to titter with someone else. No.

Finally, after what felt like hours and hours, they came out the back door. It had grown dark. The streetlamps were on in the parking lot, but as usual, only one was working. He watched them walk up to the street and take the sidewalk toward the square. He'll wait just a few minutes more, to be sure they won't be back, and then he'll make a visit. It was time for their date.

"Get ready to say bye-bye to Brookwick, lady friend," he whispered.

Addison closed the door tightly behind them as her three unexpected guests left the apartment. It took some convincing, but Addison's assurances that she would be okay were eventually believed. Either that, or they started to feel rude milling about in her apartment when she so desperately wanted to be alone. She promised she would not try to knit anything until she was with them. When Elva told her about the state of the shop when she walked into it Sunday morning, Addison laughed hysterically, horrified by what she could do, unbelieving. As she laughed she watched herself, feeling like she was another person in the room watching herself laugh like a hyena. She was confused by the reaction. It were as if she were dreaming. She had never felt so *out of it*. The feeling led her to tell them about her dreams, in as much detail as possible, explaining that knitting was all she could think of to calm her nerves and help her get back to sleep.

"I did eventually get calm though," she admitted to them, embarrassed to know that her feelings held strong power when combined with the very thing that so effectively calmed them. *That would figure, wouldn't it?* And now she just wanted to sit, but when she sat down, she wanted to stand. Pacing felt awkward, but it was all she could think to do. The binder still lay open on the coffee table and sitting in front of it was proving to be a bad temptation.

Derwin leapt from the arm of the red armchair and walked to her feet, bumping his head gently into her legs. She looked over the living room and rubbed her face with both hands. She was tired; downright exhausted! It was as if she had never slept at all since having her dream last night. Surveying the room, she contemplated going to bed and saving her thinking for tomorrow. She was a witch? *A witch*? Who could possibly swallow that? And yet they showed her. Magic happened right before her eyes. Deidre explained one of her skills as empathy, making others feel things they may not without her help. Addison tried to remember what it was like to meet her, when Deidre said she first used it on her, but Addison's brain was too addled. She remembered feeling it tonight, right before Deidre told her she was a witch. Addison shook her head from side to side every time she remembered it. And Professor Fernlee too! Though she really should call him Michael. After all, they were all part of the same team.

She wanted to kick herself. "Part of the same *team*?" she said to Derwin. "Really?"

The three empty mugs still sat on the coffee table, and the box the book had come in remained in the middle of the table in all its disarray. She grabbed the mugs and was about to return them to the kitchen when she thought she saw something in the box. Putting the mugs down, she leaned over and looked. Yes, right there. Lifting a piece of newspaper used to pad the book, underneath she found a clear, plastic bag zipped at the top. Inside was a beautiful cream-colored cardigan, sized for a tiny baby. It was unfinished. The circular needle still hung from the bottom, secure in its stitches. Addison lifted the bag and put the box on the floor by her feet. Derwin jumped on the couch beside her.

It was the sweater in her dream that she had seen her mother prepare to knit! She was sure of it! She held the bag up to the light and finding it too dim, leaned over the arm of the couch to hold it beneath the lamp. The same creamy color. It was definitely the sweater she saw in her dream.

"It's all true," she whispered. "I can't believe it, but look! Look at this! I saw this in my dream. I *definitely* saw this in my dream…" No matter how many times her common sense tried to bat it away – that she was a witch, that witches even existed, that she could somehow perform *magic spells*, that her dreams appeared to be more like omens – she clung to the truth she was just beginning to really *see*. How can she explain this away? How can she deny that she held in her hands the very thing she did not know existed yesterday, but dreamed about last night? Addison smiled. She looked at Derwin, who was staring at her, as if he understood.

"My mom made this, you know," she whispered. He purred and rested his head on her lap. Tears stung her eyes. She sat back on the couch and pulled the top of the bag apart. She knew she probably shouldn't. Elva and Deidre and Michael were all so afraid when she went to touch the patterns in the book – but her mother touched this. Her mother *knit this*. For her! She just wanted to put her finger in the bag and touch it, just a little bit… Maybe smell it? Could her mother's smell still be on it, after all this time?

Addison's back slammed against the couch when a man burst through the door directly in front of her. Stunned, she grabbed the bag in her arms and screamed.

CHAPTER THIRTY-SIX

"I think she took it pretty well," Elva whispered. "Better than me anyway. It broke my heart watching her go through that."

They sat around the table in the back room, staring at the center of the table. "She admires you, Elva. Anybody can see that. I think it helped that you were there." Michael's voice was soothing. "I had been afraid she would bolt, to be honest. Nobody wants to hear such life-changing news from complete strangers. But she seems to like it here, and she seems to like you two particularly. Maybe I underestimated her ability to adjust so quickly."

Deidre giggled. "Did you see how scared she was when she saw us all at the door? You could feel the fear and the anxiety just pour off of her!"

Michael smiled. "Yes. It's not like we could comfort her though. 'No, no. Relax, Addison. We're not here to kick you out, we just want to tell you you're a witch.'"

They all laughed. They were all weary, but immensely relieved. Somehow, it felt over. Calm. Tomorrow was going to be an interesting day.

"Shall I make more tea?" Elva asked. She was tired, but she wasn't yet ready to go home. Her husband would be asleep, content in his slumber, and the thought of being alone after such a heart wrenching evening did not appeal to her. She gathered all the familiar items and prepared three mugs. Elva was grateful for her friends, and for the shop. Without *A Stitch is Cast*, she's not sure how she would cope. Knitting was soothing, certainly, but the shop surrounded her with the joy of others who find joy in the same thing. It was rare to find such a large group of people she could call friends simply because they all shared a hobby, and yet it was true. She had never met a knitter – a passionate knitter – that she did not like. And then there were the witches. Deidre, Michael, Sara and the other women at the monthly meetings who kept to themselves most times, but opened themselves to share what else went on in the witch world. Wait until they heard about all of this!

"It's been some day, huh?" said Elva, taking her seat at the table as the water heated in the electrical kettle. She looked at Deidre and Michael. Her smile brightened suddenly and she lifted her head from her hand. "By the way! I'm so pleased to see you two together." Her hands clapped together lightly and she leaned forward to beam at them. "I've missed seeing you both, like this." Deidre and Michael reached across the table to hold hands. As Michael was about to lean forward and place a warm kiss on the back of Deidre's hand, she pulled it away. She looked up at the ceiling.

"We have to go." Her voice was hollow, as if she only had time to gather the edges of her breath and send out the warning. Her face had gone pale and her eyes were wide with fear, the lower lids red with it. "We have to go now!" she bellowed.

Michael was the first to run to the front door, his chair clattering on the linoleum floor. Elva struggled out of her chair and Deidre took no time in helping her. They heard the bell ring out as Michael threw the door open. "Run!" she yelled to Michael. "Help her!" she screamed.

Addison thought she saw a hammer in his hand as he stood opposite her on the other side of the coffee table, his legs and arms spread wide apart. She could not see his face because he wore a face mask, but she saw enough of his eyes to tell he was grinning. She could hear it in his voice. "Are you ready?" he said in a growl, his voice hoarse and low. It was horrible. The hammer spun in his fist; it spun so fast she couldn't believe it was real. *He must have practiced that,* she thought, simultaneously stunned that the thought occurred to her. She looked at the hammer, the claw bigger than her own hands, and then at him. Her feet were curled under her, and she couldn't think how to move them. She wanted to just fly straight up and get away, but she couldn't move. What was she going to do?

"Ha!" he said, the sound muffled by the mask. "Are you gonna try to run? The other one didn't even bother." One leg popped out from beneath her, and he darted a little to one side.

Addison's heart thumped madly in her chest. "What do you—"she tried to talk but her voice caught in her throat. Isn't that what victims are supposed to do? Try to disarm their attacker with words, get him to know you so he'll feel sympathy and find it harder to put a hammer through your skull? She cleared throat. She mustered up what strength in it she could and said, "What do you want?"

It came out exactly how she wished it didn't: shaky and scared, high and horrible, cracked and bleeding. She bit her lip. She could feel her chin quivering and inside, she screamed "No! Stand up! Stand up!"

He laughed. His body looked ready to pounce on her. She tried to look around without moving her head. She saw the coffee table and the three mugs. The television was against the wall, too far away and far too heavy to help her. The chairs on either side of the coffee table barred her way.

Straight at him over the coffee table? She saw the box on the floor that had held her mother's book of knitting patterns. She felt her eyes stinging again, but she didn't dare close them.

"Crying, are you?" he said. "Good. Cry. I want to make sure you hate this. I want to make sure everyone knows that the tramp hated every minute."

Addison barely heard his words. A million thoughts were going through her head, and yet she heard nothing. It was like her head was hanging from the window of a speeding car and all she heard was the wind. Derwin snarled, and leapt at the man. It was a giant leap, from the couch, over the coffee table, and high enough that he landed on the man's chest. His claws dug into the black sweater he wore and Addison jumped off the couch, her mother's baby cardigan gripped in her hands as she ran toward the kitchen, hoping she could somehow get around him to her only exit: the door directly behind him. He screamed at the cat and tried to pull it off but Derwin held fast, his jaws crashing shut whenever the man's hands came by him. She had reached the edge of the carpet where it met the kitchen floor and tried to dart back into the living room, hoping to crash into the intruder's sides, toppling him over, but instead he grabbed her wrist and she screamed. "Let go! Let go!"

Derwin was stuck on the man's sweater, his paws scratching his way up the shirt, trying to climb. One paw came loose and flailed before it got caught in the ski mask. Addison could hear the man's scream of pain as he let go of her arm. "You son of a bitch!" the man yelled, and with his hand he surrounded the cat and squeezed. Derwin yowled as he flew across the room and slammed into the wall above the couch. Addison stepped forward, reaching for the door, but the man pushed her down. She slammed into the armchair and tumbled over it, her legs crashing into the lamp on the end table. It fell onto the couch and her foot was caught in the cord. She saw him come at her, the hammer raised in the air, the claw end of it pointing directly at her. Her arms flew to protect her head, the cardigan from her mother still in her hands. "Help me!"

When Michael reached the back door, he found Nick standing on the landing, bending over and looking at the lock on the door. "Nick! Move!"

"What's going on?" Nick asked.

Michael looked up at the door and down at the handle. He started banging on it, yelling for Addison. "Do you have a key?" he asked Nick.

"Me? No! Why would I have a key? What's going on? What's wrong? Where's Addison?"

Michael bent over and looked at the door handle.

"Her lock is all messed up. I got it open the other night with my knife. I left my bag here last night and thought we could get something to eat. I wasn't doing anything wrong, I swear. Elva needs to put a bell here or something. So, I know it looks weird, but—"

Elva and Deidre came around the corner, both of them out of breath.

"The key, Elva," Michael said, his arm outstretched.

Nick looked at all of them. "What's going on? Is something wrong? Is Addison okay?"

"No," Deidre said. "We have to get up there." Nick's face fell.

"What do you mean no? What's going on? Should we call someone? Is Jim coming?" Everybody ignored Nick's questions. He stood there, feeling helpless. "Come on! What's going on?"

Michael leaned over and tried to put the key in the door. "It won't fit!" he yelled in frustration. Nick pushed Michael aside.

"I can get us in," he said. "Just give me a second." If nobody will talk to him, he'll find out himself. He had to get in to Addison. He thought of her tears the other night, and how she laughed at his pig snorts. He hated not knowing what he was worrying about! He put his knife up to the lock and pushed it in. He wiggled it carefully, waiting, trying to keep his hands calm and stop his hands from sweating. His fingers ached from the tight grip he had on the key.

"Deidre," he heard Elva say. "Do something."

Deidre moved to Nick. "Nick, look out. I have an idea."

Nick refused to move. They didn't have time for new ideas. Something was wrong – he didn't know what, but they must. Michael was running like a bat out of hell and Elva and Deidre looked terrified when they saw that Michael was still on the front landing. "I can get it!" he yelled. "Just move! Move away!"

Deidre reached over to grab his hand, prepared to use her magic in front of Nick, no matter what happened afterward, but Nick refused to let go. He pushed her away with his body as he hunched over the door handle, protecting it from any other interference. The lock gave way and he threw the door open, taking the stairs two at a time before Michael even realized the lock had been freed.

Nick's shoulder rebounded off the walls of the narrow passageway as he raced his way to Addison's apartment. He still had no idea what was wrong, but he trusted the panic he felt at the bottom of the stairs. He smelled the air and called out Addison's name. Was that smoke? He couldn't be sure, but he smelled something. He heard Michael's feet behind him, having just reached the top of the stairs.

Michael watched Nick's back, wishing he had paid more attention and reached the stairs before the boy. Nobody knew what was behind that door, but Nick did not have magic, and Michael was afraid only magic could protect them and Addison from whatever danger Deidre sensed. He was too old and too slow to get close to Nick. Relying on the boy's youthful strength and quick reflexes, he had to trust that Nick would be okay. He raced ahead as fast as he could, just the same. He heard the women stumble up the stairs behind him.

"Stupid," Michael said. "We were stupid!"

"Move!" Deidre yelled.

"We thought we were done! We left the rest for later and we were stupid!"

"Move!" Deidre said with more force.

When Nick reached the door, he heard a bellow through the rushing of blood in his ears. "Addison!" he yelled. He tried turning the handle on the door but it wasn't turning. Banging on the chipped red door, he yelled again. "Addison!" He swore as he fished in his pockets for his knife, but he must have left it down stairs because nothing was in his hands. Michael came up behind him and reached his hand out to the door handle. "It's locked!" Nick yelled. "It's locked!" He banged his fist on the door, calling again for Addison. Both he and Michael threw themselves on the door, but it wouldn't budge. Nick slammed it again with the balls of his hands when it suddenly opened wide.

Elva reached the hallway before Deidre did. She saw Michael and Nick standing before the open door, their faces drawn and eyes bulging. "Oh no," she whispered. "Deidre!

Hurry!" She ran down the hallway, praying she wouldn't have a heart attack, and not caring as long as she saved Addison first.

Nick didn't know what he was looking at. He couldn't understand it. On the red chair beside the couch was a large sphere of *fire*. At least, that's what it looked like. The base of it was as red as the couch, and as it curved out, around and up, it turned from red to orange and then to yellow and blue. It shimmered and moved as water or fire did, but could not have been fire. He could see that nothing was burning. He smelled nothing burning, though he did smell something (more like the lingering odor of rotting eggs). More than that – he could see Addison *inside it*. With legs pulled into her chest, her arms were wrapped around the back of her head. Something white stuck out of her hands. He couldn't see her face, but he knew she was alive – she was rocking back and forth. Rocking in a chair, back and forth, inside a *bubble of fire*. Standing beside Addison, outside of the fire, was the source of the bellow he had heard through the door. A short man, dressed entirely in black, was screaming at Addison. His arm was striking the bubble, up and down, up and down, hard. When Nick could finally stop focusing on the bubble, he recognized the hammer. With a roar, he charged into the apartment and tackled the masked man. Forgetting about the ball of fire, he spread his limbs, hoping to catch the man in a bear hug and take him away and down. He tucked his head into his body, trying to stay aware of the hammer, and aimed to get the man's arm against his side. Nick flew with such force that he and the man both hit the opposite wall above the couch. Nick's head bounced off the wall and everything went black.

Michael focused on the man who was struggling to stand. Nick had landed on the couch, his face pale and eyes closed, obviously knocked unconscious. When the man noticed Michael, he raised his hammer and growled, but he had been dazed. He was unfocused and swaying. Michael's arms shot out, blue light emanating from the tips of his fingers. He crossed his index and middle fingers, sending the near-purple light from both hands to the man's knees. The man called out in pain, his knees buckling beneath him. Elva ran into Michael's back, breaking the spell. Addison's attacker gritted his teeth and rushed at them both, stumbling over the box that held the pattern book, and sliding across the coffee table. As he struggled to stand, he swung his arms wildly. The hammer caught Elva in the jaw. Her head reeled back and she stumbled into the television. As she did, the man in black jumped forward and pushed Michael to the side. Michael raised his hands again, but Deidre was now in the doorway, face to face with the masked man. Michael didn't dare risk hurting Deidre. She was looking at the fire that covered Addison, mesmerized by its flame. She didn't see the masked man standing directly before her. He stood watching her, his hammer raised.

Michael called out. "Dee!" Deidre's head turned slowly, her eyes still focused on Addison, and as the hammer came down, she whispered to the man. Before his hammer had started its descent, a flame almost identical to the one surrounding Addison climbed over Deidre's body. She held her arms out, fingers flexed and pointing to the floor. Her body swayed as her hands traced an arc around her body, and she slowly moved them up, like a yoga pose. As she did, the flame followed.

"It will protect her," Michael whispered. When the man's hammer bounced off the flame and he screamed, grabbing his wrist with his other hand and bending at the waist in pain, Michael closed his eyes briefly in thanks. And then he spun on his heels and raised his arms again. With hunched shoulders, using every ounce of magic he could feel in his body, he sent his blue light into the man's lower back. Elva crawled to Michael's feet and she grabbed hold of his ankles. When she did, Michael's light grew thicker and the man fell to his knees. Their magic pulsed inside his bones, every muscle rocking with a heavy pressure. His sobs filled the room.

When Deidre saw through the flames that Michael had stopped the madman's deadly attack, she let the flames fall. She bent over and grabbed the man's hammer, lying by his limp hands. Michael stopped the light. When it was no longer touching him, Deidre lifted her foot and shoved it into the man's shoulder. He fell onto his back, his body no longer tense, surrender called out by the flop of his arms and back as they hit the floor. Then Deidre sat on him.

"Elva." She tilted her head toward Addison. The flames had disappeared. Addison was curled into herself on the couch, her arms still raised above her head, the baby cardigan grasped tightly in her fist. She rocked back and forth, whimpering.

"Okay, okay, okay, okay, okay..." she said.

Elva raised herself on all fours and slowly crawled to Addison.

Deidre looked at Michael. "It's time to call Jim," she said.

"No need." Jim's voice was quiet. He stood at the door and looked at the mess in the living room. "We're already here."

Deputy Lynley peeked in from the hallway, her head barely fitting beside Jim's wide frame. She had a smile on her lips, and reaching her arm in by Jim's knees, the only space available, she gave a small wave. "Howdy."

CHAPTER THIRTY-SEVEN

Deputy Lynley stood by Nick with her notebook open but she had barely written a word. Her mind kept wandering and she forgot what questions she had already asked the boy. Not that it mattered; Nick could barely concentrate himself. The paramedics gave him the okay to go home but he was still refusing to let Deputy Lynley call his mother, insisting he was okay and it would only make his mother worry. She could only agree with him. Honestly, she wasn't sure how she would handle the phone conversation. She wasn't comfortable with lying; it went against her nature, but she had no idea how to tell this kid's mother the truth. Not that Nick even knew what it was.

Nick was a good kid. She liked him, and she trusted his instincts. Though she wanted Nick's mother to have the opportunity to feel and express the pride Deputy Lynley knew she'd feel had it been her son, this was going to have to do. She put her hand on his head and smiled at him. "You did good tonight, Nick." Nick had played lacrosse with her own son for four years on the high school team. They were never best friends, but she had seen enough of him at her own house to trust that he fought tooth and nail for the new girl in town. "If you need a ride home, let me know. I'll be over here for a little while." Nick nodded.

When Deputy Lynley had left him, Michael went over to see how Nick was doing.

"I didn't say a thing about that creepy fire," he said to Michael. They both watched the lights fill the parking lot. Michael didn't tell him that it probably didn't matter. He wasn't sure yet how much of it the sheriff and deputy had seen, but they would have to find out. For now, he would trust they were too stunned by what they saw to go blabbing immediately. They had a little bit of time. Thankfully, they had left Deputy Lafayette to watch the vehicle left in the parking lot, or else there would be three people they'd have to deal with. Things in Brookwick were getting just a bit too exciting.

Addison was sitting in the end of the ambulance, a blanket wrapped around her shoulders. She had barely a scratch on her; it seemed Nick took all that the attacker could give. It was honorable. Nick wanted to talk to Addison, to make sure she was okay, but as soon as he woke up in her apartment, paramedics were all over him. He only now got to look at her and see that that he didn't have to worry.

"We got there in time. Right?"

Michael nodded. "I think we did. She certainly got a scare, and I'm sure it wasn't any fun before we got there... but it could have been worse. A lot worse."

Nick sighed. "Think she'll leave?"

Michael shook his head. "I don't think there's any way she could leave now."

Nick remained quiet. He shifted his weight from one foot to the other and put his hands in his pocket.

"Anything you want to ask me, Nick?" Michael asked quietly.

Nick responded with a weak laugh. His eyes stayed fixed on Addison. "Is she..." He let it slide, then picked it up again. "Is she okay?"

"Physically, Addison is right as rain. Emotionally?" Michael sighed. "I think she'll be alright emotionally too. She's been through a lot."

"Lost my knife, I think. Elva's gotta fix those doors."

The parking lot was drawing some attention. Nick turned to the small porch that lead to Addison's apartment. "Who was the guy?"

"You might know him, actually. He works at the coffeehouse. Brian Grosse."

"Brian Grosse?" Nick spun on his heels. Michael stood up straighter.

"You know him?"

"Yeah, I know him! So does she!"

"Apparently, he's been working at the coffeehouse for at least five years. Sheriff Emory is at his house now, where he had Elva's old tenant locked up in his basement. It's disgusting." Michael let out a ragged breath. He looked down at his feet and kicked at some loose gravel. "Addison is going to need a good friend, Nick."

Their eyes met. "I know," Nick said, his jaw set.

"Addison has secrets that she'll need help keeping."

Looking at Addison, he said, "I think I know that too." Michael waited. "The fire, right? Is that a secret? That she can do that?"

Michael smiled. "That was her mother's doing. She left a gift for Addison and when Addison needed protecting, her mother provided it."

Nick was confused, but he figured it would all come out in time. He said nothing.

"Do you know much about knitting, Nick?"

Nick laughed again. "Yeah. I know knitting. I've been knitting since I was a kid. My mother taught me."

"Addison can knit magic."

Nick shook his head and watched his feet, his arms crossed over his chest. "Okay," he said. Maybe he would have had more to say if he didn't see what he saw upstairs. Maybe he would have laughed, or said 'Yeah, whatever!' or punched Michael in the shoulder to let him know he was in on the joke. But not now. He saw a sphere of fire around Addison, and there wasn't a burn on her or in the apartment. There were no fire trucks, no smoke, and yet he knew what he saw. "So she can knit magic," he whispered.

"Her mother did too, apparently. And she knit a sweater for Addison. I can only speculate, of course, but my guess is that she was knitting it to protect Addison."

Nick closed his eyes. "I'm glad it worked," he said.

"Oh, and Nick?" Nick opened his eyes. "I didn't see your back pack up there. Maybe that's it?"

Michael tilted his head and pointed his chin to a small red bag that leaned against porch, away from the porch light. Nick chuckled.

"Jealousy. Straight up jealousy, man. I was going to see Brian at the coffee shop to apologize to him for being a jerk. And he told me he had a date with Addison tonight. He was creepy, professor. I didn't like it. Or maybe I was just... jealous. Either way, I came over to just give her a little... I dunno..."

"Advice?"

"Maybe."

"You aren't the only one who got weird vibes from him, so don't worry."

"She was pretty mad at me for being a jerk to him."

"I think she'll get over it."

"I hope so. I'd like that."

Addison mumbled to the police and the paramedics a little bit more, but she was tired of answering their questions. She wanted to be away from the lights and the strangers. Elva and Deidre stood off to the side while people in uniforms asked her the same questions over and over. She assured them she wasn't hurt, and when they finally confirmed it for themselves, they asked her to wait just a little bit longer. She looked desperately at Elva and Deidre. She had so many questions! What happened? was at the top of the list. She remembered thinking she was going to die, but suddenly the room had gone quiet. She could still see him through the space in her arms, but she could not hear him. She could not feel him. She couldn't explain it. Her ears had felt plugged, as if someone put suction cups around them to block out sound, and she had become dizzy. She kept her head down and closed her eyes. And then she heard a voice. "You are okay." Addison didn't dare raise her head as long as she knew her attacker was there. She just kept her head low, and held onto the voice. "I'm here, baby. Momma's here. Nothing is going to hurt you."

Elva and Deidre came to her side.

"How are you feeling?" Elva asked. Deidre wrapped her arm around Addison's shoulder.

"Did you save me?" she asked them.

"No," Deidre whispered. "We just helped catch the man who came after you. It was your mother who saved you."

Addison nodded. She didn't quite understand how her mother did it, but she believed what Deidre said.

"After I get a good night's sleep," she said, "we have a lot to go over."

They all nodded. "Stay with me tonight," said Elva. "I have good tea."

A paramedic jogged over with a blanket in her arms.

"Oh, I'm good. This is plenty warm, trust me," said Addison.

"Oh, no!" said the young woman. "You're going to want this." She held the blanket out to Addison and folded back a portion by her elbow. Inside, Derwin looked up at her expectantly.

"Derwin!" yelled Addison. A smile spread across her face.

EPILOGUE

Addison was safe. For Deidre, Michael and Elva, that was all that mattered. Elva was recovering from the concussion she received when Addison's stalker and Katrina's kidnapper knocked her in the jaw with his hammer. Deidre was proud of her friend and the bravery she showed in the face of such violence and hatred. Deidre would be thinking twice before ever thinking something would be too much for Elva – too emotional, too violent, too dangerous… Elva was a powerful witch, and Elva knew what she could and could not handle. It was fast thinking what Elva did, holding onto Michael and sharing her power with him.

Elva was happy and no longer afraid for Katrina, who was safely recovered from Brian Grosse's basement. She had been in the basement for at least three weeks. Severely dehydrated, suffering from hypothermia, and delirious, she had gone through a lot and had a long road ahead of her. According to Sheriff Emory, it didn't look like Katrina was the first person to be kept in that basement. There were signs that at least two other people had been kept below ground and given the same treatment. Unfortunately, it looked as if Brian were one of them. What they couldn't figure out was if Brian had been kept there before his mother died, or if he kept himself there after she died. It was Sheriff Emory's theory that he locked himself down there, allowing himself only three meals a day, two trips to the bathroom, and no other provisions. He didn't understand it, but he didn't have to. The boy nearly killed

Addison and Katrina was never going to be the same. They knew that Brian would speak to her constantly at first, then seemed to forget her entirely by the end. And it was cold. She had only the clothes she was wearing when she was taken, and got no showers.

Katrina has returned to her parents in Ohio. Her wounds were severe, but with a combination of the care received at the hospital and the spell Jocelyn and Laura had cast her way to increase healing, she should feel right as rain in about a week – physically. Deidre and Michael worked together to place a salve on Katrina's memory, so she could remember what had happened to her, but the pain she felt was lessened, as if she were watching a movie.

Elva has already received one email and one postcard since Katrina left a few weeks ago. Elva didn't mind. The memory spell and the pain of her experience would mean few communications. It did not mean, however, that Elva had to do the same. She was going to spoil Katrina from afar if it was the last thing she ever did. Katrina had already received three rather large care packages chock full of fine yarns and notions, muffins, cookies and a few magazines. It was Elva's hope that knitting would help weave the broken ends of Katrina's spirit back together. But Deidre hoped Elva wouldn't get too out of hand and send a package like that every week or her shop was sure to go out of business. Elva did send an awful lot of cashmere.

"If anything can cheer a knitting woman, Deidre, it's cashmere. Don't look at me like that. You know it's true!" It made Deidre smile just the same, watching her friend Elva open her big heart to whomever needed it.

Michael had been living with Deidre for the last week, his boxes nearly unpacked save for one or two filled with books from his study. Her studio has been converted into a shared office. The warmth that came from his old office chair with the leather seat and the settee from his office made her feel fuller than she had in years. His knick knacks on the book shelves and his art on the wall were all pieces of him she didn't realize she missed; seeing them again, mingled with her own belongings, made her see how big the empty spots had been without him there.

The closet was another matter. She finally donated two large bags of horrible clothes and older shoes – all of which belonged solely to her, making room for his tweed jackets and flannel collared shirts. It has been satisfying to Deidre to make room for Michael, giving up pieces of her furniture so his could take its place, deciding what art work on the walls suited and pleased them both, happy with every decision they had made.

Sitting on the loveseat, Deidre curled her legs up under her and looked out the window. Leaves were green and vibrant on her trees, new buds opening wide exposing its essence to the sun. Everything was alive with the heat of summer. It was coming fast. Yesterday, students poured from their final exams and rushed to disappear to their summer jobs. As happened every year, they would soon grow anxious, anticipating the return to the friends they have met and didn't realize they would miss. Addison may be one of those students next year. Elva and Deidre already have her toying with the idea, though they are trying hard to conceal how much they like it. With Nick's help and possible enrollment, it felt like a done deal, as if Addison was just thinking of a major. Textile arts? suggested Deidre. History? said Michael. "Let the girl make her own choices!" scowled Elva. But everybody knew Elva wanted her to major in business. They were all nervous about how it would affect her newfound power, but Michael and Deidre think it may also teach her to focus and perhaps improve it. It really was all too soon to tell. Addison was still new to

Brookwick, and nobody could fault her for wanting to relax and simply *be a witch* for a while.

Michael came from the bedroom, an olive green shawl knit in a fine merino wool, falling from his hands. "Look what I found!" he exclaimed in excitement. He spread the shawl out before him, lying it against the back of a chair across from Deidre. "I wore this shawl nearly everyday, summer or winter, for about ten years," he said, wonder in his voice. He slid his hand along the fiber, as if remembering every day spent with it. Deidre could understand the care in his voice. It was a beautiful lace, unlike any pattern she had ever seen. She couldn't identify any one foundation. It had Finnish appeal, as well as Irish. She saw rolling hills and falling water. She could eye feathers and owls and leaves. It was hard to focus on any one part without another pulling her gaze. How many motifs were there in this one garment?

Deidre stood, placing her own knitting on her seat. She walked to the chair and bent over, looking at the scarf. Up close, it was even more magnificent. Every stitch was beautifully folded over another. She could not see any mistakes, but she also did not know *how* to look at it.

"Where in heaven did you find this?" she asked him.

"You sound impressed!" he said proudly.

Deidre looked up at him, awe in her gaze. "This is probably the most intricate and beautiful lace shawl I have ever seen! And trust me! I spend a great deal of time looking at pictures of shawls." They both grinned. While Michael read his history books and military fiction novels, Deidre was looking at knitting patterns and studying the history of some obscure knitting technique. He did not doubt her eye.

"I actually don't know," he said. He tilted his head back to think.

"Why did you stop wearing it?"

"Oh! Well because…" his voice trailed as he turned the shawl this way and that, searching for something. "Ah!" He held it out to her, showing her a section on the edge of the shawl. She leaned in and looked. Several stitches had come undone, it seemed. Worn or rubbed apart. "I didn't want it to start unraveling, so I stopped wearing it until I could find someone who could fix it."

Deidre eyed it carefully while Michael continued to hold it.

"Do you think you could fix it?"

"I'm not sure. I can't see it very well." She grabbed the shawl in order to bring it under the light. Except she found herself in Erfurt, Germany, squirreled away in the dark. Before her stood a tall woman with green eyes and wavy, brown hair. Beside her stood a man, similar in features, they could have been siblings. But they weren't. Deidre knew they weren't. These were knitwitches, a husband and a wife. The woman smiled as she placed a hand on her belly.

"It isn't that we don't trust you to keep our secret," she said to Deidre. "We do. Please understand. It's just that it is dangerous for you to know them. To know us." She turned to her husband.

"We need someone to know, though. For our daughter's sake." Deidre looked again at the woman's belly. "Are you in agreement?" he asked her.

"Agreement about what?" she asked, except it wasn't her voice that said the words. It was Michael's voice.

The knitwitches laughed. "I'm sorry," he said.

"You can't have purposeful memory," she said. "About us." Her hand shook between herself and her husband, as if Michael could confuse who she was referring to. "This shawl will protect you from the memory of us, and all that we have told you. It is a keeper of history. Our daughter will find you when it is time, and it will all fall into place."

"You'll see," said her husband, Addison's father. "It is hard to believe, we know. It's not your kind of magic. But we know what we know."

Deidre's head nodded. "Of course," said Michael's voice. "I am honored that you trust me with this."

They gazed at him with love in their eyes. They cared for him. They were indeed trusting him with something very important. Addison's mother looked sad. "It's in the package, but I want her to know I love her. I love her so much." A sob escaped her.

Deidre felt her legs move forward and watched as Michael's arm appeared before her, reaching out to Addison's mother. He held her hands in his.

"She will come to you when it's time," said Addison's father. "Our magic will not fail. You will know when you have all you need, and only then can it be used. Do you understand what power we are giving you?"

Deidre felt her love's heart thump once, madly, in her chest. Her Michael felt fear? Excitement? Pride?

Her head nodded.

"Be safe," they whispered together.

The woman with the pregnant belly stepped forward and tied the shawl around Deidre's neck, but not before Michael's voice said to them, "I pray you make it safely."

She stood looking at Michael again, in her own living room, the new summer sun shining on her walls. "It's here," she whispered.

"What is?" he asked.

"The history. The way to train Addison." She rubbed the edge with the broken yarn and looked at it with hope. "She needs only to mend this, and she will have all her answers."

Acknowledgments

Thank you to Chris Baty, the founder of NaNoWriMo. Thanks also go to all my first-draft readers: my sister Joey Fields; my mother, Ellen Patry; my father, Christopher Lunde; my cousin Nelya Patry; my friends Kristin Beno, Wendy Holler, Michelle Messier, and Amy Gainor. You know who your real friends are when they read the first draft and still offer to read the second. Thank you! And of course, my deepest appreciation goes out to both my husband, Charlie Comer, and our son, Oisin, who support and love me even when waiting until I finish all those rows.

About the Author

Christen Roberts Comer is an avid knitter and knitting instructor, living and teaching out of Central Pennsylvania. She lives with her husband and son, her biggest fans. If they get a cat, she might name it Derwin, or Derwinnie.

15685631R00207

Made in the USA
Middletown, DE
18 November 2014